Sign up for our newsletter to hear
about new and upcoming releases.

www.ylva-publishing.com

# OTHER BOOKS BY ROSLYN SINCLAIR

*The X Ingredient*
*The Lily and the Crown*

THE CARLISLE SERIES: BOOK 1

# TRUTH AND MEASURE

Roslyn Sinclair

# DEDICATION

The *Carlisle* series is dedicated to the readers who have given me so much support and joy over the years. You all mean more to me than you'll ever know.

# ACKNOWLEDGMENTS

Many thanks to Lee Winter and all of the Ylva staff who helped make this book into what it eventually became. And most of all to my wonderful wife, who held my hand through it all and often showed me the way. I couldn't have done it without her.

For above all things love means sweetness, and truth, and measure; yea, loyalty to the loved one, and to your word.

—Anonymous, *The Lay of Graelent,* 13th century CE

# CHAPTER 1

"I've never cared for yellow," Vivian Carlisle said absently, looking over the editorial spread. "It's so garish. Even in pastels."

Most people would assume her comment was a casual observation. Jules Moretti, not most people, knew it was the calm before the storm and decided this would be a great time to stare intently at the notes on her tablet.

Who was today's unlucky target? It couldn't be her. Vivian didn't make a habit of discussing aesthetic preferences with personal assistants. It must be somebody a lot higher up the ladder than Jules but still below Vivian. Like Simon, the creative director. Or Angie, head of copywriting. Or God.

But when Jules looked up, unable to take the long silence, she was skewered by Vivian's eyes looking directly at her from across the desk. Simon and Angie had left the room, and the heavens remained resolutely silent.

And when Vivian Carlisle said a thing to you and then looked at you, you had about two seconds to figure out whether or not she wanted you to say something back. Jules's two seconds were halfway up.

She thought fast. She didn't wear a lot of yellow and she wasn't wearing any today, and there *were* models wearing yellow in the spread, so Vivian wasn't critiquing Jules personally. At least not yet.

*Think. Think. Think.*

"They've done studies," Jules heard herself saying. "People think yellow's supposed to make you feel cheerful, but it doesn't. It can actually make people anxious." Something more seemed called for. "Uh, pink makes them calmer, actually."

Did that qualify as thinking? Maybe it was more like shoving her head underwater and shaking it around rapidly. Vivian had no patience for fools. That remark probably qualified as foolish.

Vivian raised an eyebrow.

Jules suppressed the urge to inform her that sometimes prison cells were painted pink to keep the prisoners happy. It might be taken the wrong way.

Instead of calling her foolish, Vivian looked back down at the spread on her desk.

Jules braced herself.

"Mallory," Vivian said.

Jules already had her message app pulled up, and she fired off a summons. This wouldn't be pleasant. Mallory had worked at *Du Jour* for two years now as a photography director. She'd come up with cool, innovative spreads that had put her first on Simon's radar, then Vivian's. Her last project had lacked that flair, though—Vivian had called it "vapid." This was strike two, and Vivian would make sure Mallory felt the whiff of the baseball as it barely missed her face.

Mallory seemed to sense this as she hurried in, glancing around at the sleek, midcentury furniture and the huge windows that offered amazing views of Manhattan. Mallory fit right in with it, as tall and slim as a skyscraper, clad head to toe in the latest designer fashions.

She was elegant and gorgeous, and she tried so hard. She wanted it so much. Too much. Radiating that kind of attitude in front of Vivian Carlisle was like throwing chum to a shark.

"You wanted me?" she asked breathlessly with that mixture of adoration and terror that Vivian seemed to inspire in everyone.

"Hmm." Vivian didn't look up from the spread on her desk. Her eyes traveled over the A3 paper with its photos, captions, and copy. "There's a lot of yellow in this spread, Mallory."

She went pale. "Er. Well, yes."

*Have to do better than that.*

Vivian continued as if she hadn't heard. "Studies have shown that yellow is a color that causes anxiety. Isn't that right, Julia?"

Jules's stomach dropped. She'd never liked Mallory much, but she hadn't meant to trip her up. "Uh," she said feebly, "that's what I…I mean, somewhere, I read…"

"*I've* never read that," Mallory snapped.

That made Vivian look up at last, in time to see Mallory toss her chestnut hair back over her shoulder.

"My job is to care about style, not pop psychology." Mallory finally deigned to glance at Jules. "Are you researching a paper for school or something?"

The hell? Mallory had been at *Du Jour* for less time than Jules! "I graduated three years ago from—"

"Okay." Mallory turned back to Vivian. "The truth is, I'm trying to provoke a reaction in readers. I, um, want to make them anxious."

Bullshit. Jules pressed her lips together to silence a scoff.

"You do?" Vivian asked neutrally.

Mallory should have known better than to take this as encouragement. Vivian didn't do encouragement. "Well, sure. Fashion's about pushing the boundaries, right?"

"I assume that question is rhetorical."

Mallory gulped. "And you know anxiety can be a part of that, right? So…that's what I was doing. It was on purpose. Kind of edgy."

"Edgy." Vivian picked up the spread proof and held it at arm's length. She was probably trying to get the whole picture, but it looked more as if she were holding out a piece of particularly smelly garbage. "Let's see this copy. 'Romantic Winter: Get cozy in style with the latest trends to help you look your best as you snuggle in front of a fireplace.'"

Jules repressed a snort.

Mallory squirmed as Vivian glanced at her again.

"Edgy," Vivian repeated.

"Um, I guess I can see how it'd look—"

"This is pathetic."

Mallory snapped her mouth shut.

"It's one thing to make a bad choice. I would *think* you'd know not to associate the color yellow with snow, but I would obviously be wrong."

"I—"

"But that isn't your problem, Mallory. Your problem is that you don't listen, that you refuse to admit your mistakes, and that you're convinced of your own genius for reasons that completely escape me."

Oof. This was painful. Next up: Vivian would put Mallory on notice.

Mallory threw her shoulders back. "When Simon hired me—"

"When Simon hired you, he made a mistake. But unlike you, he'll own up to it."

Mallory went even paler.

"Pack up your desk and be gone by lunch," Vivian said.

*Yikes.* So much for strike three—Mallory was already off the team. Jules looked at the wall and kept her best poker face. *Didn't see that coming.*

Nobody argued with that tone of voice. Mallory swallowed thickly, turned, and walked out of the office.

Jules slowly released a breath. She didn't like Mallory, but that hadn't been any fun to watch.

"Julia," Vivian said.

Jules pressed her lips together and looked back at her boss.

Vivian Carlisle was a striking woman. With her famous platinum blonde hair, shattered pixie haircut, eyes that bordered on electric blue, and bone structure that belonged in a makeup ad, she grabbed unwary mortals' attention right away. Her Greek nose would have earned her a place of honor in ancient statuary. She was rail thin and pretty tall—a few inches taller than Jules, who was five foot six. She still wore four-inch heels every day as if she wanted to take up all the space she could. Vivian wasn't Hollywood gorgeous, but models and celebrities paled in her shadow.

Arresting. That's what she was.

"Tell Simon to replace Mallory," Vivian said.

Jules clutched her tablet to her chest and nodded.

"And remind him of the budget when advertising the salary," Vivian added, sounding annoyed about it.

She nodded harder and turned to go.

"Did I dismiss you?"

As a kid, Jules had played a game called Freeze, where you put your body in awkward poses until the designated person called, "Freeze!" then held still in whatever position you were in for as long as you could, and the first to fall over lost.

It was like she was playing it all over again, as she stopped in place, half-turned away from Vivian with one foot in the air. "No?" she ventured.

"No. This needs fixing as soon as possible, and I need you to take notes." She placed her hands to either side of the spread and looked it over with a frown.

Jules pivoted and came to stand across the desk from Vivian, tablet and stylus at the ready. *Hands steady, girl. Keep it cool.*

For long moments, Vivian remained silent as she looked over the spread. Jules couldn't help thinking of an orchestra conductor examining the musicians before raising the baton.

"We need a complete do-over," Vivian said eventually. "Simon convinced me to greenlight it, but if this is the best we can do, then Romantic Winter is the wrong concept."

"You want a do-over?" Jules squeaked. "As in…"

"As in a new concept. New sketches. New photo shoot. And we have to do it fast."

"Won't that be expensive?"

She didn't even dignify that with a response, just picked up the large sheet of paper and ripped it in two, right down the middle.

"Mallory *was* on to something with 'edgy,'" she continued. "That's a meaningless concept, but we'll define it. I'm thinking…" She trailed off and stuck her tongue in her cheek as she looked into the distance.

"We'll combine 'edgy' with intimate," she finally said.

*Those don't seem to go together.* She couldn't help picturing two people cuddling while holding knives. Why did Vivian want something like that?

As if Jules had spoken aloud, Vivian said, "I want the spread to hold two ideas that seem contradictory but work in harmony. Not compromise"—she said that like it was the dirtiest word she'd ever heard—"but completion."

"I can message the creative team to brainstorm and—"

"Nothing as clichéd as a snowfall or a ski lodge," Vivian mused as if Jules hadn't spoken. "Definitely not a cozy cabin. We need a contrast. Something startling, something unexpected."

Jules tried to think of somewhere cold that wouldn't be a total cliché. "Maybe something like a snowy field under a gray sky?"

Vivian held up her hand. "I said unexpected. Although a snowy field's an improvement on the cabin."

*Not much of one*, she didn't add, but she didn't have to.

"Right," Jules mumbled, face burning hotter than ever as she took notes. *Unexpected. Contrast. Intimate/Edgy.*

"Not romance," Vivian continued. "Loneliness. Winter's not just a time or place but a state of mind. Everybody's locked up at home, trying to keep warm. We're not going to depress readers," she added just as Jules was starting to feel really depressed. "We're going to surprise them. The spread's going to be about connection instead of isolation. We can show the harshness of winter while *also* showing that it doesn't defeat us. Stylishly, of course."

Jules's mind began running like a hamster on a wheel. Where would you shoot something like this? A lonely city block? Behind an abandoned warehouse? You could easily find those locations in New York, and the cost didn't have to be…

"A desert," Vivian said.

Jules's hand paused over her notes.

"What do people think of when they think of deserts?" Vivian continued. "It's the opposite of a snuggling before a hearth. It's primal. No water, no sustenance. You against the elements."

"And we think of heat, but it's really cold at night," Jules said eagerly. "So that's the unexpected part. I camped in the Sonoran once, and—"

"We'll shoot it at sunrise. Have the models start out in layers. That lets us feature sweaters and jackets. They'll huddle together for warmth—fighting that sense of loneliness that winter can bring. We should also see their breath in the air. Then, as the photo spread goes on, they lose the layers and you see the outfits underneath. Their body language becomes more open as they adapt to the environment, to the contradiction."

Jules scribbled frantically. Good grief. Mallory had probably worked on her concept for weeks, and Vivian had pulled this one out of thin air in moments? It was enough to make you dizzy. "Adapt. Contradiction. Okay."

"The Mojave will do." Vivian frowned. "It's a shame there's no time to go international. Snow in the Sahara is incredibly striking."

"It snows in the Sahara?"

"Every once in a while. They had a snowfall a few years ago. That was in January, though." Vivian's frown deepened as if in disapproval of the irregular schedule.

Jules couldn't help imagining Vivian standing atop a Saharan dune, ordering the skies to dump a bunch of snow onto the sand in October. And the skies obeying her.

"We'll dial up the cool tones in editing," Vivian said. "Take this to Simon and tell him to get it right this time. I don't want to have to deal with this again."

*Now* she had been dismissed. Feeling as if she'd just staggered out of a whirlwind, she nodded and turned to go.

"University of Pennsylvania, wasn't it?"

Jules played Freeze again. Then she slowly pivoted back to face Vivian.

"You did a double major in communication and English," Vivian added. "Or something like that."

It was the effort of a lifetime for Jules to keep the shock off her face. Vivian remembered where Jules had gone to college? Vivian remembered what she'd *majored* in?

"English and communication at Penn, yeah," she said, trying to keep it cool. "I'm from around there. Outside of Philly."

Vivian frowned.

"Philadelphia," Jules mumbled.

"Simon," Vivian repeated.

And with that, Jules fled the office. It felt like the luckiest escape of her life.

# CHAPTER 2

When Jules arrived at his glass-walled office, Simon looked up and sighed. "What did she do?"

"Fired Mallory."

"Ah." He removed his reading glasses and rubbed the bridge of his nose.

She didn't blame him for getting a headache. She'd served as his assistant before Vivian poached her, and there wasn't a harder working creative director in the business than Simon Carvalho. Many times, he and Jules had burned the midnight oil as he tried to make creativity and capitalism play nice together: reaching out to advertisers, wrangling hot-tempered artists who didn't want to sully their hands with business concerns. It was exhausting.

Vivian's frequent power plays didn't make it any easier. Jules had spent many hours at Simon's side wondering why Vivian couldn't just relent a bit. Working with Vivian directly hadn't enlightened her as she'd hoped.

"I thought Mallory would get one more shot," she said. "She's done good work in the past."

"Welcome to fashion, where the past will only be relevant in twenty years. Maybe we'll see Mallory then. In the meantime, don't question Vivian's decisions. At least not to her face."

*Like I don't know that.* "She says to remember the salary budget in the next job ad."

Simon sighed. "I wonder if Mark's finally getting to her."

She had to agree. Mark Tavio, chairman of the Koening publishing group, was nobody's favorite human. Top executives weren't usually known for being warm and fuzzy types, but Mr. Tavio was a special kind of sour.

Sometimes it seemed he had it in for Vivian personally. If Vivian hadn't rescued *Du Jour* from folding five years ago, Jules had a hunch he'd have tried to get rid of her.

True, Vivian wasn't the easiest personality in the world. Jules still smelled misogyny in the room. Hard to avoid when a man resented a woman who was better at her job than he was at his. Among Mr. Tavio's petty tactics: summoning Vivian to his office for updates that only wasted her time, constantly implying that she was on thin ice, and neglecting to include her in company-wide decisions. Somehow, though, she always managed to influence those decisions, whether she was invited to the meetings or not.

Simon rolled his shoulders with a grunt. His pink dress shirt looked crisp, and the navy blazer draped over the back of his chair complemented it perfectly. He had what most people would call above-average looks—tall, broad-shouldered, hazel-eyed. But when you spent every day surrounded by models and actors, above average turned into *meh*.

Jules often felt it herself. She was cute, not dazzling. This job could be a real blow to the old self-esteem, if you let it.

"You okay?" she asked.

"About Mallory? Eh. Easy come, easy go. I'll have a hundred applicants for her position." He gave Jules a hopeful look. "Would you like to go through a hundred job applications for me?"

"Sure thing," she said. "I'll just swap places with you, and you can do my job all day."

"At my current salary?"

"Totally."

"Not enough. We both deserve to make a million bucks a year. Just wait for it. The day will come." Simon tapped his mouth with one long finger. "Speaking of a million bucks, you look like that today."

Sweet! Jules had hoped *someone* would notice the RIXO floral print skirt. She couldn't resist swaying her hips so the silk crepe swirled around her calves. "Fifty percent off."

"Don't be gauche. I do like that line."

So did she. The RIXO fall collection had been exactly to her tastes: free-flowing and exuberant. Her days might be strictly regimented, but her clothes didn't have to be.

"Was there anything else from our glorious empress?" Simon asked.

Shoot. Jules had hoped not to mention this part. "She said we have to get it right this time."

"'We' meaning *moi*. My fault—I sold Mallory's idea too hard. That'll be fun to recover from. Do I have new marching orders?"

"You know you do." She handed him her tablet with the notes.

He skimmed over them. "So much for keeping to the budget. Of course she wants to re-do the whole spread."

"Fast, too."

"Naturally." He read the notes again, looking more attentive. "But…"

"But you like it better than Mallory's thing, don't you?" she asked.

"Oh, shut up." He returned the tablet. "Send this to me ASAP. I'll make it happen."

"You always do." Jules smiled and turned to go.

Simon cleared his throat. "Before you scoot, has Vivian mentioned anything—is there any more news about…"

She waited.

He huffed out an impatient-sounding breath. "You know, her divorce."

"I doubt I've heard anything you haven't." Simon was Vivian's second-in-command. If she trusted anyone implicitly, it was him. Surely, he wouldn't be less well-informed than Jules. "He dropped the bomb on her, he's out, and I've already scheduled a meeting with her lawyer."

"I can't decide which is worse: Vivian's strategy of having three husbands or mine of not having any." He looked morose. "This industry is hell on relationships."

"Oh, great." Jules rolled her eyes while she opened the door. "Now he tells me."

Simon's wry chuckle followed her.

―――

That night, as Jules flopped onto her sofa with her phone, she found her mother had more to say about Vivian's divorce than Simon had. Specifically, she had a lot to say about how it should serve as a warning to Jules: "Remember what happened with Aaron. Make sure you don't end up like your boss."

That wasn't fair. Aaron had dumped Jules last year after being unreasonable and insisting she work an eight-hour day and be off every weekend, which, *come on*!

She had tried to laugh around the cold pit that opened up in her stomach. "Mom! I'm nothing like Vivian. I have a life outside of work."

"Really?" her mom said tartly. "Then maybe sometime you'll talk to us about something other than your job."

Ouch.

When she disconnected, Jules looked down at her phone's screen until it went dark. Then she sighed, got off the sofa, and headed for the kitchen to get water.

She loved her Lower East Side apartment. Jules was luckier than lucky—her maternal grandparents had purchased the one-bedroom when they were young and when the area was less than savory. It had stayed in the family, and now Jules had six hundred square feet all to herself on the condition that she paid her parents for the utilities and half the property taxes.

Her parents had upgraded the place about ten years ago. The worn carpet had been pulled up and the original hardwood floors refinished. Nothing fancy, but it was perfect for a generation of renters who'd been here before Jules had moved in.

Since Aaron had left and taken his dirty laundry and band posters with him, Jules had been able to redecorate. She'd watched YouTube tutorials on painting and spent hours priming and taping and cursing. Now she had an accent wall covered by squares and triangles in alternating colors of aqua, salmon, and yellow. It looked pretty cool. Vivian never had to know about the yellow part.

An assistant's salary didn't stretch far, especially when she had to prioritize clothes, so most of Jules's furniture was family hand-me-downs. Nevertheless, she'd splurged on a contemporary coffee table and a Moroccan-style rug. She'd made her own curtains. She was satisfied with the place for now.

Jules sat at the kitchen table and looked moodily at her water glass. In spite of herself, her thoughts wandered back to her conversation with her mom. Okay, maybe Jules wasn't a relationship expert. She still had to be better than Vivian, who had nobody to blame but herself.

It was easy to see that Vivian had known her marriage was in trouble for a while. Jules had given ever-more elaborate excuses when she called the soon-to-be-ex, financier Robert Kirk, to cancel dinner or a date on Vivian's behalf and had seen her texting him with an increasingly furrowed brow. She had even on one occasion overheard her voice crack when talking to him.

So why hadn't Vivian been able to compromise with Robert, to try and be more available to him?

In the months she'd been working here, Jules had seen that Robert was clear about what he wanted: for his wife to spend time with him. It was hardly unreasonable. No, this divorce hadn't been sprung on Vivian out of nowhere. So why hadn't she acted to prevent it?

Not Jules's problem, except when it came to canceling the dinners and scheduling the lawyer. It was time to put it out of her mind. She sighed and reached for her computer.

Now for her second job.

She opened the laptop and glowered at the Google doc that had been waiting patiently for her return. Another article she was slaving away at in the hopes that this time it would go somewhere. Last time *The Cut* had sent her a personalized rejection email, which was more than she'd gotten before. Now that she was on their radar, this effort had a chance to land.

It had to land quickly, though. This time she was writing an article about Jimmy Choo's collaboration with Timberland to create an haute couture hiking boot. It'd be old news by the end of the week, even though the boot was selling out in Bergdorf.

*Why?* Jules's article asked. It was the same as a regular Timberland boot, except it had crystal trim and cost $1,300. Why was such an unnecessary, extravagant item flying off the shelves?

She knew the answer: the boot was a status symbol. People would still click on the headline, eager to read about the excesses of the wealthy.

It wasn't an article about climate change in *The Atlantic*. It could be a step on the way to a real career, though. If Jules could elevate the topic beyond clickbait, argue that this stuff mattered and get her name in a national publication…

It was all about the baby steps. Jules had to start somewhere, and successful writers grabbed opportunities as they came. Everyone said so.

She had to grab this opportunity fast. That meant another sleepless night.

Maybe Aaron had a point after all. Maybe both he and Robert did.

No, dammit. It wasn't the same thing, and Vivian's messed-up priorities weren't Jules's. Sure, Jules had ambition, but she had humanity too. They didn't have to be at odds.

And she'd show Vivian Carlisle it was possible, even if it killed her.

Not that she wanted to tempt fate or anything.

# CHAPTER 3

As the week went on, the idea of proving anything to Vivian began to seem laughable. Something was going on with her, and Jules didn't like it.

She wasn't looking well. Her pixie never had a hair out of place and her lipstick was always perfect, but there was a tired look in her eyes Jules had never seen before. An outsider might not be able to tell, but it seemed obvious to someone who was at Vivian's beck and call 24/7.

Meanwhile, Jules wasn't on top of the world either. *The Cut* had rejected her Jimmy Choo article, and she was too busy to think about her next effort. Back in college, she'd thought breaking through would be easier. She'd written a lot of local pieces and even landed a guest column in *The Philadelphia Inquirer* about the rise of student housing costs. Turned out investigative journalism wasn't her forte, but she'd developed an unslakable thirst for writing nonfiction, gravitating toward pieces on fashion and its cultural significance.

Too bad nobody else seemed thirsty for what she had to offer. *Next time*, she told herself.

As crappy as she felt, Jules still wouldn't trade her place for Vivian's. In the middle of a long Thursday, she walked into Vivian's office just in time to see her rub her hands over her eyes. Her shoulders slumped. She looked utterly miserable, in a Vivian-ish way.

Jules cleared her throat. Vivian started and looked up.

"Um," Jules said, wondering why she'd even opened her mouth, "you're good to go for the meeting with Mr. Tavio tomorrow."

A sour twist of the lips let Jules know how Vivian felt about that. No wonder. It was obviously a half hour set aside for Mr. Tavio to posture, complain, and waste her time with another power move.

"Wonderful," she said dryly.

"Uh, yes. Do…you want me to get you some coffee?"

Great. No, stupid. If Vivian wanted something, she'd ask for it. You never offered to do things. She didn't want to hear your voice when she was trying to—

"Water," Vivian said and looked back down at the photos on her desk as if Jules hadn't spoken at all.

Jules made it to the mini-fridge by her desk in record time. When she arrived with the Perrier, Vivian didn't look at her but reached up and took the bottle directly from her hand. Her fingers brushed against Jules's.

They had never touched before. Jules fought not to snatch her hand back because she felt the shock all the way through her body, which must mean she hadn't liked it, right? When you touched someone and felt it reverberate from head to toe, that didn't mean you *liked* it.

That'd just be idiotic.

Instead of jumping backward, she managed to drop her hand to her side in a way that hopefully looked natural. "Is there anything else?"

Vivian looked up as she brought the bottle to her lips. A thoughtful crease appeared between her eyebrows as she regarded Jules. After a sip, she said, "Are you growing your hair out?"

Jules touched the ends of her dark wavy hair. It was nearly past her shoulders now. "I guess so. Just haven't made it to the salon lately."

"Get the ends trimmed," Vivian ordered, "but it suits you longer. You seem to be using adequate products."

It took Jules two stunned seconds to say, "Thank you."

Vivian wasn't finished. "Use the assets you have, Julia. Play them up. You haven't made a bad beginning"—the gaze she swept up and down Jules's body was entirely clinical, but it felt like lightning—"but you'd benefit from taking more risks. Try high-waisted pants."

Jules looked down. She'd never had enough confidence in her hips to try those. Mainly because she had hips. That was a tough sell around *Du Jour*. "Really?"

"Mm. There's a Katharine Hepburn biopic in the works. It'll have award buzz next year. Get ahead of the trend and grab her look. You can pull it off."

Jules was five foot six with curves and a tiny waist, and she was a big fan of flowy fabric. She'd never exactly thought of herself as a Hepburn type. "Well, I'll…"

"Am I going to get a call from Christian Siriano before I die?" Vivian glared at her. "I'm starting to wonder."

Jules opened her mouth to say, *I'll get right on it*, but Vivian had already returned to work and was back to ignoring her.

Yeah. Something was definitely going on here.

---

The next five days at *Du Jour* were frenetically busy. The Mojave shoot had to be done right away, which meant spending exorbitant sums. Meanwhile, two of the models for the LA shoot had backed out and one had been fired. Agencies were offering dozens of potential replacements that had to be screened before the glossy eight-by-tens finally made it to Vivian's desk. Insurance might or might not come through. Mark Tavio was making even more growling sounds about costs. Jules suspected Vivian might be forced to listen to him.

She was forced to do a lot of things, most of them involving moving around a lot. Meetings, lunches, attorneys, and late nights all meant that Vivian didn't have a single quiet moment, and therefore, neither did Jules. Vivian practically kept her in her back pocket. They often didn't leave the Koening Building until one in the morning, only to stagger back inside at eight. And Vivian, who usually operated as well on two hours of sleep as she would on ten, looked to be on the verge of collapse.

Everyone was worried. Jules caught herself exchanging nervous looks with Simon more than once as they watched Vivian struggle to remember a name or an appointment. Jules tried to be more vigilant than ever, doing her best to anticipate Vivian's every need. This wasn't any easier than usual, and she was afraid she was going to give herself an ulcer.

By the end of the week, it was obvious—to Jules, at least—that Vivian wasn't just stressed out or unhappy. Something was really, really wrong.

It was half-past midnight on Sunday, and she'd canceled her brief appearance at Marc Jacobs's party that evening in favor of working. So of course Jules was working on a Sunday night as well, sitting at her desk within sight of Vivian so she could leap into action at a second's notice.

Vivian seemed even less happy than her. More than once, Jules caught her staring off into space and appearing unaware of her own surroundings. Was she losing it? No wonder, with the way her life was falling down, and she wasn't giving herself a moment of peace and quiet.

*I'm not like you.* She watched Vivian glance out the windows for what seemed like the thousandth time. *Nope, not me. Definitely not.*

Even Simon wasn't here at this hour. Jules and Vivian were the only ones in the office, and Jules had nothing to do. She couldn't call anyone, and Vivian was fully updated on everything. To be fair, she wasn't just killing time—she was inundated with emails, with copy, with decisions she had to make. The LA shoot was in a week, and everyone was panicking. But Vivian didn't actually need Jules for anything except, apparently, silent company.

Jules had a copy of *This is Not Fashion* hidden in her desk drawer, though, and with a little luck, she could hide it in her lap and read it without Vivian noticing. King Adz's history of streetwear was something she'd been meaning to get to for a while. The pictures of cityscapes grabbed her imagination, especially those in Europe and Asia. There was something about the way towers and skyscrapers coexisted with older, even ancient, buildings. Might that not be reflected in style as well? Clothes and accessories that seemed to clash at first but combined to tell a unique story about the wearer?

It wasn't too different from what Vivian had said about fashion being completion, not compromise. There might be an article in there somewhere. Jules had just started making notes when Vivian called out, her voice hoarse (though she hadn't been talking to anyone), "Water!"

She sighed silently, tucked the book back inside the drawer, and hurried to fetch a bottle of Perrier from the mini-fridge. When she headed into Vivian's office, she froze inside the doorway.

Vivian was staring off into space, as white as chalk. She was biting the knuckle of her right index finger, her eyes wide. She looked petrified. Jules's stomach twisted at the sight of it.

She cleared her throat.

Vivian jumped at the sound and stared as if she'd forgotten Jules was in the office.

Jules set the glass on Vivian's desk, trying not to let her hand shake. Vivian looked at the glass as if she'd never seen anything like it before.

"Here you go," Jules said brightly.

Vivian looked up at her with even less comprehension than she had at the glass.

It took every ounce of self-control not to ask, *Are you okay?* You never asked Vivian Carlisle stupid questions that had obvious answers. Clearly, all was not okay.

Then Vivian spoke. "I…" she said and dragged one shaking hand across her forehead. "Thank you."

*Thank you?* She never thanked people for doing the basics of their jobs. Jules's hands started to get cold from nerves. What the hell was going on here?

Vivian took a careful sip. Then she set the glass back down, swallowed hard, and hid her face in her hands, breathing deeply.

"Vivian!" Jules gasped, but Vivian held up one hand for silence. Jules realized that she was trying not to be sick.

How long had this been going on? For that matter, had Vivian even eaten dinner tonight? Jules realized that she hadn't been dispatched to get any food that evening and that Vivian had canceled her lunch, which meant she hadn't eaten since breakfast. If she'd had breakfast.

Vivian lowered her hands, taking another deep breath. "Well," she said.

"Do you want me to call a doctor?"

"No, not yet."

The "not yet" made Jules's heart start racing in panic.

Vivian rubbed her hands over her face. "God. I haven't even had a moment to myself in…I haven't been able to…"

Jules waited. When nothing else seemed forthcoming, she blurted out, "Is there something I can do?"

Vivian glanced at her.

"I mean, get you something to eat, or…?"

Tapping her fingers on her desk, Vivian stared off into space again. The haunted look was back in her eyes.

Jules's insides started to squirm like snakes.

"I need you to go to the store for me," Vivian said quietly after a moment.

Jules was trying to work out whether she meant Hermès, Blahnik, or Tiffany's—and how to tell Vivian that all three were closed for the night—when she realized Vivian had paused.

"Okay," Jules prompted after Vivian hadn't spoken in nearly thirty seconds.

Vivian drummed her fingers against the desk again and appeared to finally come to a decision. "Bring me back a pregnancy test."

The room seemed to dip and sway for a second.

Vivian darted her a quick, sharp look.

Operating purely on instinct, Jules nodded and said, "All right. Be right back." Her voice contained only its usual helpful inflection. Then she was walking past her own desk, grabbing her purse as if in a dream, and standing in one of the gleaming elevators that would take her down to the lobby, from which she would walk to the streets, which would look the same as they always did, and…

*Holy. Shit.*

It made sense, even if Vivian was kind of…old for this at forty-two. The exhaustion, the nausea, the—whatever else. Jules didn't know much about being pregnant, all things considered.

But she'd had a pregnancy scare herself in her senior year of high school. It had been the worst forty-eight hours of her life before her period had finally shown up. Was Vivian feeling anything like that? Surely not. She was a grown woman worth millions, not a scared kid afraid of missing college.

Who was the father? Was it Robert's? It had to be Robert's. Because wouldn't Jules have noticed by now if Vivian was sneaking around? Vivian couldn't possibly be very far along, and Robert had bolted so recently. Apparently he'd loved her and left her. Asshole.

The closest Duane Reade drugstore was half a block away. Jules frantically scanned the "family planning" aisle. There were several tests available, each one claiming to be the best on the market. Jules had a feeling that Vivian would be even less patient about this than she was about everything else, which meant Jules had to decide fast. So she grabbed two boxes: one promising *99.9% accuracy!* and another proclaiming *Doctor Recommended!*

Christ. If Vivian was pregnant, if the kid was Robert's, what would that mean for the divorce? Surely they'd halt it or at least delay it or—

It wasn't her problem, she tried to tell herself, waving her pass at the night security guard when she passed back through Koening's revolving door. Vivian's private life wasn't her problem, and she wasn't going to concern herself with anything about it.

She kept telling herself this until she arrived back at *Du Jour* and saw Vivian whirl around from the window to face her. Trembling, Jules set the plastic bag down on the desk.

Vivian glanced at it, sat down, and began working on her laptop again without another word. Jules gulped and headed back to her desk. She'd never be able to concentrate on her book now, and she hoped Vivian would send her home soon. Surely she would because of course she'd want to go home herself and…

All of a sudden, there was a flurry of movement. She watched in speechless horror as Vivian stormed past Jules's desk and into the private restroom, the pharmacy bag clutched in one white-knuckled hand.

Here? She was going to do it here? *Now?* With Jules right outside her office? Fuck. Oh fuck. Jules did not want to be here when Vivian came out of that restroom. Vivian probably wouldn't want her to be either. Should Jules leave? Would that be the best thing to do, and tomorrow they could pretend like nothing had ever happened?

Even as she thought about it, Jules knew she wasn't going anywhere. And so the minutes crawled by. She finally looked at her watch and realized Vivian had been in the restroom for twenty minutes.

What the hell was going on in there? Had she fallen and hit her head? Was she trying to drown herself in the sink?

Just as Jules was wondering if it would be a bad idea to check on her, the door opened and Vivian emerged. One look at her face told Jules everything, but before Vivian could meet her eyes, Jules bent down and pretended to study the surface of her desk.

Vivian returned to her own desk.

Jules didn't look up.

"Julia." Her voice was thick.

Jules headed on unsteady legs to the door of her office. "Yes?" she whispered.

"Tomorrow," Vivian said, staring vacantly into the distance, "schedule an immediate appointment with my doctor. And contact my attorney as soon as his office opens. Eight o'clock. Sharp."

"O-of course."

"Call my driver." Vivian rubbed her forehead again. "Let's go home."

Right. It was past time to call it a day. Jules helped Vivian put on her coat and walked her to the elevator, where she stood stock-still in the car, not speaking.

What the hell did you even say to someone at a time like this? Congratulations? Condolences? She didn't even dare look at Vivian.

"I don't believe this," Vivian said.

Jules froze.

"I don't," Vivian repeated.

Jules finally turned to look at her, just in time to see Vivian close her eyes. "I'm sorry," she whispered. Then Jules heard herself blurt out, like a total idiot, "You know, whatever I can do—of course I'll..."

Vivian ignored her completely. "Wait until Mark Tavio finds out," she muttered, then laughed bitterly. "Well. If our chairman thinks he can use this to get rid of me, he'll get to know my lawyers on a personal level."

Jules bit her lip.

"What?" Vivian demanded.

"Nothing." Jules shook her head.

"Say it."

Okay, then. Okay. "So...you're going to keep it?"

Vivian was silent for so long that Jules wondered if she'd heard. Then, just before the elevator doors opened at main floor, she spoke, sounding bewildered. "I don't know."

They stepped into the lobby. Vivian headed for the exit, apparently without noticing that she'd just become irrevocably human to Jules at last.

Once they'd reached the car, Jules held the door open. "I'll make all those calls as soon as I get here tomorrow," she promised.

"Get in," Vivian said without looking at her and slid in herself.

Jules stood, stunned, for a moment. Even as she walked around the car, she considered sprinting down the sidewalk. Vivian had decided that she must be silenced; she was going to have her driver take them down to the docks, kill Jules, and then dump her body in the river. Or worse, Vivian was going to think of something else for her to do before going to bed and trying to process the day.

But all Vivian did as Jules buckled her seat belt was lean back against the headrest, close her eyes, and say, "Take me home, and then drop Julia off at her apartment."

"Yes, ma'am," Ben said as he smoothly pulled into the street.

Jules was getting personal chauffeur service after the working day was done? That had never happened before.

She wasn't about to question it. Just ride in silence; just let Vivian rest. She needed a break. She needed a lot of things, most of which Jules couldn't give her, but Jules could manage a peaceful car ride.

When they'd gone four blocks, she dared to look at Vivian out of the corner of her eye. Then she blinked in astonishment. Vivian had slumped against the window. Her eyes were closed, and she was breathing deeply. She'd fallen asleep.

Jules met Ben's eyes in the rearview mirror. She blushed without knowing why. But Ben's own eyes were wide, and she realized he was as astonished as she was. Almost five years of driving Vivian around and apparently he'd never seen her sleep in the car before.

When they got to Vivian's Upper West Side home, she was still sound asleep, and Jules realized she had to wake her. She didn't have the courage to touch her. You didn't just touch Vivian.

She cleared her throat loudly and watched Vivian twitch into wakefulness, inhaling through her nose. Then Jules looked out her window so Vivian could pretend no one noticed her sleeping.

At the sound of Vivian unbuckling her seat belt, Jules turned her head and managed a weak smile. "Thanks for the ride."

Vivian's brow furrowed. Her hand fumbled a little as she finished unbuckling, and she blinked sleepily. It would have been cute if it had been anybody else; as it was, it was a little scary. Without a word, Jules undid her own seat belt, got out, and hurried around to open the door for her.

By the time Vivian was on her feet and on the sidewalk, she appeared a little revived, perhaps because of the cool air. She gave Jules a quick glance as if waiting for something. Jules had no idea what, but she blurted out before she could stop herself, "The tests could be wrong."

Vivian narrowed her eyes.

Jules winced and hunched her shoulders. Yeah. Okay. Shut up.

Vivian turned and mounted the steps to her house without a word.

Still cringing, Jules got back into the car, but Ben didn't drive away until they'd both seen Vivian get safely through the door.

"What's going on?" he asked as he pulled away.

"She had a long day."

"She's had lots of them lately," Ben said. "I've practically taken to sleeping in my uniform just so I can be ready to go whenever you call me."

"At least you get to sleep," Jules said snidely

Ben only chuckled. "True enough. Try and get some sleep tonight, okay? You look like you're dead on your feet lately too."

"What else is new?"

He chuckled again.

Jules had a hard time following Ben's instructions. She should have been exhausted, but instead she shivered with nervous energy. She paced her apartment, looked restlessly out the window, and opened her laptop to see that *The Cut* was still open in her browser.

Maybe the third time would be the charm. There was a column called "I Think About This a Lot" that wasn't for news or think pieces but open submissions from readers. The subjects ranged from movie scenes that had deeply affected them to confessions about their marriages.

"I think about my pregnant boss's disaster of a life a lot," Jules said to herself, trying out the title. Then she laughed, the sound a bit sharp and hysterical. That was catchy. She'd probably get published. Then murdered. Put six feet under by Vivian Carlisle.

The thought wasn't helping her get to sleep, but it made her laugh again. She'd take what she could get.

# CHAPTER 4

She stumbled into the office the next morning at seven forty-five. Hopefully, Vivian wouldn't show up today. If there was ever a time to take a break and regroup…

But she called Jules at eight thirty and said, "I'll be there in an hour. Have you scheduled those appointments?"

"I got your doctor to fit you in at four this afternoon, and your attorney will see you tomorrow at ten."

"Fine." Vivian ended the call.

Jules exhaled a heavy breath. It was going to be a long day.

At nine, she hurried to the Koening cafeteria in search of Vivian's breakfast. Normally Vivian got her breakfast from fancy local cafes with overpriced scrambled egg whites and turkey bacon, but she'd been calling for that less and less. Now Jules would lay odds it was morning sickness. Other options had to be sought.

She looked over the breakfast options. Vivian was anti-simple-carbs, so no toast. Fruit ought to go down pretty easily, so Jules bought a banana, a couple of nice-looking plums, and a pear.

What else was okay? A quick search on her phone taught Jules that pregnant women weren't supposed to drink more than two cups of coffee a day. There was no way she was going to tell Vivian that. She sighed and filled a to-go cup.

She rushed back to the office and placed the whole lot on Vivian's desk just as the woman herself was walking through the door. She was already talking a mile a minute on her cell phone.

"No, I've told him I'm not going to budge. Well, you'll just have to arrange it. It's your job to—" She stopped when she saw the plate of fruit.

Jules held her breath.

Vivian continued, almost without missing a beat. "Call me when you've resolved this. Which will hopefully be before ten o'clock tomorrow morning."

Oh. The attorney. Jules didn't envy him having Vivian as a client.

"Goodbye." She ended the call and in the same breath said, "Julia."

Jules straightened her back. *Oh boy, now what?*

Vivian raised her coffee cup. "Is this a regular coffee?" she demanded.

Jules blinked. "Yes," she said. "I mean, it's your usual—"

"Decaf," Vivian snapped, scowling at Jules and giving her the worst ever how-could-you-be-so-stupid look.

Jules's jaw dropped. So Vivian had done some reading too. That was fast. She looked around to make sure they were alone, lowered her voice, and said, "I looked it up, and you can have two cups of regular a day, if you want."

Vivian looked at her.

Jules swallowed. "Is the fruit okay, or do you want something else?"

Vivian glanced at the plate again. "It'll do." At that moment, her stomach growled. Her cheeks reddened.

Jules quickly turned before Vivian could see her smirk and raced back to the cafeteria. When she returned with a decaf coffee, the banana, one of the plums, and half the pear were gone.

At three o'clock, Vivian announced to the nearest underling, "I'll be out for the rest of the afternoon. Julia, come with me."

Jules couldn't stop herself and shared a surprised look with the underling, who she was pretty sure came from editorial. Then she shook herself, called for Ben, and packed up.

Once inside the car, Jules expected Vivian to give her some kind of errand—like, go to Alaïa after Ben dropped Vivian off or something. But she only said, "To Dr. Latchley's office. Julia, I hope you brought something to take notes."

Jules stared before she managed, "Yes. Sure." Then she fumbled in her bag for her tablet.

"You won't need that until we get there," Vivian pointed out acidly and turned to gaze out the window.

"Right." Jules snapped her bag shut, blushing. Vivian wanted her to sit in on her doctor's visit and take notes. She could do that. No matter how incredibly weird it seemed.

"So," Vivian said without turning to look at her, "you 'looked it up.'"

"Um. Yes. Just stuff about, uh, diet. Maybe I should get a book?"

"Maybe you should."

Jules gulped.

---

Especially for a GP, Sandra Latchley had a very nice office—the kind that bespoke rich patients. As Jules had thought, Vivian was there chiefly to have her suspicions confirmed and get a referral.

Jules was not actually expected to follow Vivian into an examination room, so she lingered in the waiting room. Thank goodness. The thought of Vivian Carlisle in one of those open-backed gowns was actually embarrassing. In the meantime, she fidgeted.

About half an hour later, a nurse came down the hall. "Julia?" she called. "This way, please."

A fully dressed Vivian was sitting in her doctor's office in a chair across the desk.

Dr. Latchley had various papers and charts in front of her. She smiled in welcome. Her brown eyes were warm and kind, and Jules hoped against hope that she'd had a soothing effect on Vivian.

"Have a seat," she said.

Jules managed a smile of her own as she lowered herself into a hard leather chair. She'd had her tablet at the ready ever since they'd arrived at the clinic just so she could be available at a moment's notice.

"All right," Dr. Latchley said. "Vivian told me she doesn't mind you hearing whatever I have to say, so now that you're here, shall we begin?"

"Please," Vivian said. "I'm on a tight schedule."

"Well, so am I," Dr. Latchley said calmly. "So let's get down to it. Vivian, you are indeed pregnant. Your test showed the presence of a hormone that only appears when—"

"Yes, yes." Vivian's face remained neutral at Dr. Latchley's confirmation.

Dr. Latchley seemed unwilling to be rushed. "The pregnancy is quite recent. When was your last period?"

"It was supposed to be almost a week ago."

"And you got a pregnancy test already? That timespan isn't normally enough to be a cause for alarm."

"It is for me," Vivian said flatly.

Jules held back a smile. Of course Vivian would be as regular as clockwork. Her hormones probably lived in as much terror of her as the *Du Jour* staff.

"Besides," Vivian said, "just a couple of weeks before, Robert and I—well."

That answered that question. Vivian and Robert had had sex while they were in the divorce process. Jules's head spun. Was it a last-ditch effort to save their marriage, one last hurrah, what? Either way, it sure had come with enormous consequences.

"Have you been undergoing fertility treatments?" Dr. Latchley asked.

"No!" Vivian snapped, losing her cool for a fraction of a second. "This was an acci—unintentional."

"The odds of a woman your age getting pregnant without assistance are extremely low."

"I thought so too," Vivian muttered. "I didn't have any 'assistance.' What's next?"

"Next, I refer you to an obstetrician. I recommend Dr. Viswanathan. She's well-regarded. I can get you in the door, but you'll need to make all your appointments well in advance"—she gave Vivian a knowing look—"and keep them."

Vivian glared.

"What's her first name, please?" Jules asked, ready to write it down.

Dr. Latchley smiled again and gave her a business card, which Jules carefully filed in her bag.

"And how's that going to work?" Jules continued. "You'll make the initial call, or—"

"I'll tell her to expect you. She knows me. Call her office tomorrow morning, and you should be able to set something up."

"Thanks." Jules scribbled away. "Any receptionist in particular I should talk to?"

"They're all very nice, but if you get ahold of Mary, tell her I want to know how her dogs are doing these days."

"Dogs…are…doing. Mary. Okay." She looked up from her notes to see Dr. Latchley grinning at her and Vivian looking at her like she was from another planet. Jules winced.

"In the meantime"—Dr. Latchley turned back to Vivian—"if you plan on continuing this pregnancy, I've got a basic care sheet." She pulled a pale pink sheet of paper from a folder. "This lists dietary and exercise recommendations as well as typical symptoms you should expect. Let me just take this time to ask—what questions or concerns do you have?"

Vivian looked at Jules.

Jules immediately readied to stand up. Vivian probably didn't want to talk about her pregnancy-related fears in front of Jules, if she wanted to talk about them at all. Especially the possibility that Vivian might not want to continue her pregnancy.

"Julia, what concerns do I have?" Vivian asked.

Or maybe that was not, in fact, an issue. "Diet stuff?" Jules ventured. She looked down at the sheet Dr. Latchley had given her. It was the same information she'd found online.

"Yes," Vivian said to Dr. Latchley. "Diet."

"Oh-kay." Dr. Latchley elongated the word as if making room for incredulity. No wonder; most pregnant people didn't delegate their worries to their personal assistants. "You'll want to pay careful attention to that. Geriatric pregnancies are much more likely to result in gestational diabetes, along with other complications."

*Geriatric pregnancies?* Jules bit her bottom lip and did her best to look at Vivian from the corner of her eye without turning her head. From what she could see, her face remained composed, but the grip on her handbag was white-knuckled.

"How have you been eating?" Dr. Latchley asked.

"Quite normally," said Vivian, the great big fibber.

Before she could stop herself, Jules gave Vivian a look of outrage, which Dr. Latchley saw before Jules could hide it.

Fortunately, Vivian did not appear to notice.

"And what's 'normal'? What did you have for lunch today?" Dr. Latchley asked.

"Beef tartare," Vivian replied. "From BABS."

Dr. Latchley clearly didn't care where the beef tartare came from. "No. Protein's good but red meat isn't the greatest, and you definitely shouldn't eat anything undercooked. What about breakfast?"

Vivian shot Jules a quick look. "Fruit."

"Bananas and pears and stuff," Jules added. "And plums."

"All right," Dr. Latchley said. "But you need more variety. I suggest melons too. Eggs are great—"

"No eggs." Vivian's cheeks went a little green.

"—and dairy," Dr. Latchley finished. "Plenty of calcium. Caloric requirements are on the sheet, although Dr. Viswanathan will be able to go into more detail with you. You can also consult a nutritionist or a personal trainer, if you have concerns about exercise."

Vivian already had a nutritionist and a trainer. Jules made a note to call them and set up appointments as soon as possible.

"And above all else," Dr. Latchley added, sounding stern for the first time, "get adequate rest. I know you're a busy woman, but you have to be prepared to take it easier than you normally would." She tilted her head at Jules. "She's young and chipper. Put her to use. Get her to do things for you."

Jules's eyes widened.

All Vivian said was "I'll consider it." Her lips twitched.

"Do you have any other questions?" Dr. Latchley asked.

"Can she have regular coffee?" Jules blurted out before she could stop herself. "I read two cups a day were okay." She probably shouldn't try to prove Vivian wrong in front of her doctor, but *I'll consider it*? Seriously? After Jules had been throwing her back out for a year in this job?

Vivian snapped a death glare at her. She found herself looking right back.

"Two cups are okay," Dr. Latchley said absently, looking down at her paperwork.

"Oh good." Jules never broke eye contact with Vivian, whose own eyes narrowed farther. "I thought so."

"But try to limit your caffeine intake, Vivian," Dr. Latchley added.

"Thank you," Vivian said sweetly and stood up. "We really must be getting back."

"Of course." Dr. Latchley stood up too and extended her hand to Vivian, who took it gingerly before letting go again. "Please call me if there are any problems or if you have further questions. Oh—and congratulations."

Vivian didn't even manage a thin smile this time. Instead, she gave a curt nod and left without another word.

Jules turned to the doctor. "So," she said urgently, "this sheet is all the stuff I should know? Should I look out for anything else?"

Dr. Latchley chuckled. "Your first child too, I take it?"

Before Jules had time to sputter a response, an impatient "*Julia*" sounded from the hallway.

"Good luck," Dr. Latchley mouthed as Jules hurried out the door.

*I'll need more than that*, she reflected gloomily as she caught up with a frowning Vivian.

"I don't recall the doctor asking you for your input, Julia." Her tone had gone cold.

Jules pressed her lips together. She better not get fired over two cups of coffee. "I was asking about something I'll need to know to do my job."

"I've had a lot of people doing your job. None of them have dared…"

Vivian trailed off as if she couldn't remember what previous assistants hadn't dared to do. Breathe without permission, probably.

But they hadn't taken notes on Vivian's pregnancy either, and if this was now Jules's job, then she shouldn't be berated for doing it right. She looked straight into Vivian's eyes, silently telling her so.

Without another word, Vivian turned on her heel and headed outside to the car.

Jules could have sworn she growled.

They approached the car, where Ben held open a rear door. Just out of his hearing, Vivian muttered, "You'll make the obstetrician appointment."

"Of course."

Vivian slid inside the car, and Jules hurried around to her own door, knowing that Vivian hated even the five-second delay between bullet-rapid instructions.

"Ben, take me home and then return Julia to *Du Jour*. Julia, confirm that we have Praeger, Lawson & Day tomorrow at ten," Vivian said as soon as Jules slid into the seat next to her.

"I've called them. You should be good to go."

"*I* should be?"

Jules blinked and then made the connection. Well, asking about coffee hadn't been enough to boot her out of this job after all.

"We should be," she said, strangely breathless.

"Arrive at their offices at nine thirty," Vivian said. "Don't bother stopping by *Du Jour* first. And don't be late."

"Right." She was already anticipating sleeping in.

"Then get in touch with my personal trainer and arrange for her to come to my home this weekend. Early Saturday morning, and I mean early. And tomorrow afternoon, go to Givenchy with Lucia. Bring me back a full report. Hers aren't up to scratch these days."

"Got it." Jules's thumbs flew over her phone screen.

"Good." Vivian looked out the window, her hands folded in her lap. She didn't look appreciably calmer after her doctor's visit—maybe she'd been hoping she was wrong, that she wasn't pregnant.

Jules looked out her own window, remembered her own scare, and decided for the fiftieth time that she wouldn't trade places with Vivian for all the Fendi bags in the world.

When they arrived at Vivian's home, Jules made to get out of the car as she had the last time. Vivian waved her off and unbuckled her seat belt. Before she got out, she gave Jules an intent, penetrating look.

Against her will, Jules shivered.

"Be discreet," was all Vivian said. Then she was gone.

"What's going on?" Ben asked in the car as he pulled away from the curb.

Telling him everything wouldn't be a good start to discretion. "Things," she said weakly. In the rearview mirror, she caught him rolling his eyes. "Look, you heard what she said. It's my job if I don't keep my mouth shut." And any job Jules might contemplate in the future.

"Right," he sighed. "Guess I'll find out eventually."

Everybody would soon enough. Unless Vivian decided to end the pregnancy. Jules supposed Vivian would talk to Robert about that first, though. After talking to her attorney. God, telling her attorney about her pregnancy before telling the baby's father? What a wild world to live in. Jules groaned in exasperation.

"You okay back there?" Ben asked, sounding alarmed.

"Fine," she mumbled. "It's just Vivian."

"I hear you."

Their gazes met in the mirror again, and against her will, Jules laughed with him.

# CHAPTER 5

Playing it safe, Jules arrived at Praeger, Lawson & Day the next morning at nine fifteen. Good thing too, because Vivian swept through the door not five minutes later.

She jumped up from the uncomfortable couch in the reception area and hurried to the desk. The receptionist, who looked far too harassed this early in the morning, looked balefully up at her.

"Hi. Vivian Carlisle's arrived for her meeting with Preston Praeger." She tried a winning smile.

The receptionist was not won. "That meeting isn't until ten o'clock, ma'am," she said, giving Jules the barest glance before returning her attention to her computer. She clicked her mouse, and the printer behind her began spewing out paper.

"Well, yes, but she's here now."

"That's fine." The woman remained laser focused on her computer as if gold might fall out of it. "Please help yourselves to bottled water or coffee. There's a cafeteria on the third floor if—"

"No, no," Jules said quickly. "I mean she's here, and she wants to start the meeting. Right now. I'm her assistant," she added, like that was supposed to make a difference.

The receptionist gave her a look that said she hated her job and Jules too. "Mr. Praeger is not available." Then she turned her back on her and began gathering the printouts.

Already cringing, Jules headed over to Vivian, who was tapping her foot impatiently. She looked pretty good this morning, all things considered. Actually, she looked great: beneath her cashmere swing coat, she was dressed to kill in an eggplant-shade pencil dress and leopard-print Christian Louboutin pumps.

She hoped Vivian would notice her own fashion choice as well. She'd had to go to a little extra effort to make it happen, and it wasn't her usual thing.

Vivian, however, did not seem inclined to notice. "Well?" she asked.

Jules drooped. Maybe it hadn't been as dramatic a choice as she'd thought. Well, on today of all days, she couldn't blame Vivian for not noticing. "Um, the receptionist said we can't go in yet."

Vivian's eyes darkened.

"But there's a cafeteria," Jules added. "Have you had breakfast?"

"Yes." She stalked over to the reception desk.

Jules followed her and arrived in time to see the receptionist give Vivian a look of pure hatred. She also looked frightened, though, and picked up her phone.

"Mr. Praeger," she said, "Vivian Carlisle has arrived, but I know your meeting with her isn't until—" She stopped and scowled. "Yes, sir. I'll tell her." She glared at Vivian. "You can go on up. Ninth floor."

Vivian kept looking at her.

"Ma'am," the receptionist mumbled.

Apparently satisfied, Vivian turned on her heel and strode toward the elevator. Getting knocked up hadn't robbed her of the ability to scare the crap out of random strangers.

Jules hurried after her, trying not to slip on the marble floors in her four-inch heels. By the time she caught up with Vivian, the elevator doors were sliding open. Jules followed her inside.

Vivian mashed the button for the ninth floor. "You let her say no to you."

"Um—"

"I'm disappointed in you."

Jules gaped at her. "Wh-what?"

"When you're dealing with somebody, you do what it takes to get what you want. You don't decide to curl up and die."

"But I did ask her, more than once, and she just—"

"You never 'ask.' And you never say anything more than once. We dictate the terms, not them. I hope I never have to remind you again."

"No, Vivian," Jules mumbled, wishing she could sink through the elevator's polished floor. "Sorry."

Thankfully, at that moment the elevator stopped. The door opened to reveal a slim suited man waiting in the corridor, smiling at them. He was of middle age with salt-and-pepper hair and was obviously accomplished, wealthy, and distinguished. This did not stop him from looking at Vivian with something like fear in his eyes.

"Vivian," he said as they exited the elevator. He bent forward to kiss the air at either side of Vivian's cheeks.

"Preston," she said without preamble, "your receptionist is appalling. She was deliberately rude to my assistant. Isn't that right, Julia?"

Even if the woman had been rude, it still seemed wrong to throw her under the bus. "Well, I just think she—"

"I see." The man extended his hand to Jules. "I'm Preston Praeger. And you?"

"Jules Moretti."

"A pleasure. Vivian, I'm so sorry about Betsy. I'll speak to her later today. This way, ladies."

He led them down the hallway. Jules couldn't help but notice the stark contrast between this place and *Du Jour*, where the office walls were either made of glass or painted in cream, the floors either pale hardwoods or beige carpet. Everything there had the feeling of being transparent, like gossamer, as if you were floating on air.

That, and also of being a surveillance state where Vivian could see everyone in their glass-walled offices and make sure they weren't wasting her time.

This place was like something out of a Victorian novel, with red carpets and heavy wooden doors and black marble walls. Jules half-expected a butler with a British accent to step out of nowhere.

"I've spoken to Robert's lawyer," Preston was saying as he led them down a side corridor to an open doorway at the end. Shiny leather chairs were placed on each side of the door. "Looks like everything is in place. And so far Robert's been willing to compromise—"

"Oh yes," Vivian said bitterly.

"—and to be punctual." Preston looked over at Vivian with an attempt at a smile. "I'm willing to bet that two hours from now we'll be fairly close to a resolution of terms."

"I'm not so sure about that," Vivian said. "I'll need to speak to Robert alone."

It took some effort for Jules not to stop dead in the hallway. Robert was going to be here today? This wasn't just Vivian and her lawyer? Which meant…

Oh shit. It meant Vivian was going to tell Robert she was pregnant today with Jules in the same building, which would be about a million times worse than waiting for Vivian to finish taking a pregnancy test in the bathroom.

Jules's parents had wanted her to major in one of the sciences and go to med school. She should have done that. Then she'd be doing something more relaxing right now, like cutting open a cadaver.

Preston was frowning. "Are you sure that's a good idea?" he asked carefully, leading them into a conference room with an enormous oaken table surrounded by plush chairs. "So far he's been, um, resistant to…"

"I know what he's been." Vivian slipped out of her coat and seated herself in a chair precisely at the middle of one side of the table. "This is important, Preston."

"If you're sure." He hung the coat on a rack by the door.

"Where would you like me to sit?" Jules asked.

She'd addressed the question to Preston, but Vivian tapped the table with her right hand. "Here."

Preston said to Jules, "I see my position has been usurped." Then he smiled to show there were no hard feelings. "Vivian, I've got a few matters to take care of in my office before our meeting starts. Did you have any particular questions for me before I go?"

Vivian gave him a half shrug. "No, thank you, Preston."

With the air of a man who had received a brief reprieve, he left.

She hefted her bag onto her lap. It was a python drawstring from Michael Kors. Jules wasn't sure that today was a good day for Vivian to appear snakelike, all things considered.

Rummaging inside, she came up with a bottle of Tylenol. She shook it, and it gave a hollow rattle. "Almost out," she muttered. "Get me some more when we're done."

"Okay. There's also some in your car, in the box below the driver's seat. Just for future reference."

The box had been Jules's idea. She privately called it the Vivian care kit. It also had travel-sized hairspray, hand lotion, and sample sizes of Vivian's favorite makeup products, all nicked from the beauty department with Simon's permission. There were also Band-Aids, a tiny bottle of hand sanitizer, and a couple of little foam pads you could stick into your shoes. Whenever they were out, Jules had all these things at hand since Vivian invariably needed at least one of them.

Vivian never appeared to question where they came from, but at least Jules could pride herself on being the first assistant to think of it. She made a mental note to add some anti-nausea medication.

"Hmm." Vivian glanced at the sideboard where a pitcher of ice water and glasses sat. Jules took the hint, hurried over, and poured her some before sitting down. Maybe she could get away with slipping off her shoes under the table. She'd give it a few minutes.

Vivian took two tablets, chased them down with the water, and rubbed her forehead.

"I'm not looking forward to this," she muttered.

Neither was Jules, so she tried to appear sympathetic. Then it occurred to her that she ought to know something, and she cleared her throat.

"Uh," Jules said, "does Preston know? I mean, have you told him about, you know, on the phone…" She waved her hand vaguely.

Vivian raised her eyebrows as if she had no idea what Jules was talking about when she totally did.

Fine. "You know, the baby."

"It's not a baby," Vivian said dangerously. "It's an embryo. A thing. And unless I decide otherwise, that's all it is."

Chagrined, Jules nodded.

"And, no, Preston doesn't know. Yet." Vivian drummed her fingers on the table and looked away again. "No one does."

Except the doctor, of course, who didn't really count, and…Jules.

She felt the knowledge like a blow to the stomach. Jesus. The idea that Jules was in on this before Vivian's husband or, hell, even her lawyer… That was weird. And wrong. And weird.

Time to distract herself. She looked at a clock on the wall: nine thirty-five. She had time to make a few calls.

Before she could, Vivian said, "I see you tried the high-waisted pants."

Jules managed to keep the smile off her face. Unfortunately, she couldn't do anything about the blush. So Vivian *had* noticed.

"Yeah," she said. "I stopped by The Row after work." Shopping had been much easier when she wasn't hanging around *Du Jour* until midnight.

"Mm." Vivian continued to regard her with the same intent, contemplative gaze that made Jules squirm. Then she turned to look back at the wall. "They're reasonably flattering, but choose a less frivolous top next time."

Jules frowned and looked at her blouse. She loved this blouse, billowy with a pattern of roses and vines. Vivian had never criticized it before. "Doesn't it complement the structure of the pants?"

"It does," Vivian acknowledged, "but the clash of styles is distracting—boho and contemporary often don't mix."

"Isn't fashion about getting people's attention?" Jules dared to challenge. She might be risking her life, but she hadn't slogged through four years at *Du Jour* as intern and assistant to turn down the chance to talk fashion with Vivian Carlisle. That'd be like making it to the top of a Himalayan mountain, meeting the Dalai Lama there, and saying, "No, thanks, I've got a pretty good meditation app."

Vivian regarded her, seeming thoughtful. After a moment, she said, "I've always said fashion is about two things: expression and context. As my assistant, is it your job to be flamboyant and attention seeking?"

"Um. Not exactly." *Expression and context.* Jules filed that away to think about.

"Express your taste and style within the appropriate context. As you gain seniority, your scope broadens. When you're at Simon's level, feel free to wear feather boas. As my assistant, your job is to be chic."

Coming from the world's foremost fashion authority, *chic* suddenly seemed like a low bar. Apparently Jules couldn't even manage that. Her shoulders slumped.

"But you're correct," Vivian added, "about the structure."

Jules straightened up again. A flash of inspiration struck. "Dries van Noten! He's doing geometric prints. The silhouettes…"

Vivian considered for a moment. Then she nodded decisively. "Broad shoulders. Small waist. Then the flare of the pants. A bold, structured pattern on the blouse that complements the trousers' angles." She looked at Jules's blouse again. "Yes. It'd change the whole look."

"Not super Katharine Hepburn-y, though," Jules felt obliged to point out.

"Neither are you, as far as I can tell." For a moment, Vivian seemed amused.

Hopefully that was a compliment. Perhaps she didn't like Katharine Hepburn very much. All Jules could say was "maybe not" as she tried to figure out how to get her hands on a Dries van Noten blouse without destroying her credit limit. Time to touch base with the consignment stores again and see if any of her contacts could do her a favor.

"I wouldn't have thought of van Noten with that piece." Vivian sounded absent as she looked inside her handbag. "That's an innovative idea."

Was Jules going to fall out of her chair in shock? Probably not the chic thing to do. "Th-thanks. I—"

Vivian closed her handbag with a thump. She sounded as if she were confessing to murder when she said, "I need something to eat. Bring me a yogurt from the cafeteria. Nonfat and plain."

All the yogurt in the cafeteria was nonfat. None of it was plain. Vivian glared when Jules placed vanilla before her.

"There's a Whole Foods—" Jules began.

"There's no time." Vivian took the yogurt and devoured it, seeming resentful, while Jules stared off into space and pretended not to be there.

"I *had* breakfast," Vivian said when she was done and tossed the empty plastic cup into a nearby trash can with unerring aim.

"Well, the doctor said that dairy is good," Jules said. "Calcium and stuff."

"I hate this," Vivian said. "Don't get pregnant, Julia."

"N-not planning on it anytime soon."

"Planning doesn't always enter into it," Vivian said darkly and sipped her water.

Jules had the sudden, horrible feeling that Vivian might actually start talking about her birth control when, mercifully, voices sounded down the hallway. Robert and his attorney had arrived early, and Preston was with them.

"—no interest in anything private," Robert was saying.

Vivian stiffened. Jules's desire to vanish into thin air redoubled.

"Well, we can talk about that," Preston said jovially as he led the way into the conference room.

"My client said no, Preston," Robert's lawyer said. He nodded at Vivian as he and Robert seated themselves across the table. "Ms. Carlisle."

Vivian pinched her lips and did not return the nod. "Robert," she said neutrally.

"Vivian," he replied in the same tone. He looked at Jules. "What's she doing here?"

Jules had never liked Robert. This was yet another reminder of why. He'd always talked about her as if she weren't right in front of him. She fought the urge to wrinkle her nose.

"I asked her to be here," Vivian said coldly.

"And she is?" Robert's lawyer asked.

"Ms. Carlisle's personal assistant," Preston interjected. "I believe it's Jules—?"

"Julia Moretti," Vivian said coldly.

*Julia.* Vivian had called her that since the beginning. She had always wondered why but had never dared to ask, since the answer was probably *because I hate your nickname and command you to stop using it.*

Robert's lawyer said, "Nice to meet you, Julia. Sam Johnson." He turned to Preston. "I see no reason not to begin."

"Robert," Vivian said, "I'm sorry, but we have to speak alone. Just for a minute."

Jules wondered if anybody else heard the nearly hidden urgency in her voice, the note that was almost pleading.

Robert didn't seem to. "Vivian," he said, sounding tired, "we've been through this before."

"Not this we haven't. We need to—"

"No. Now, Sam—"

"There has been a *new development*," Vivian growled.

Finally, something seemed to get through to Robert. He blinked and frowned at her.

"Just a few minutes," she added, and now everybody could hear her plea.

Something deep inside Jules twinged. How could he ignore that note of desperation? Coming from Vivian, it was practically a scream.

"Okay," he sighed after a moment. "Let's give it ten minutes, Sam."

"Robert," Sam said warningly.

He held up a hand. "Ten minutes, okay? And then we'll move on."

Jules was on her feet before he'd finished speaking, gathering her coat and bag with shaking hands, feeling absurdly as if she didn't want to leave a single trace of her presence behind that might intrude on Vivian's privacy.

An astonished-looking Preston held the door open for her. He and Sam followed her out of the room.

"What's going on?" Sam demanded of her as soon as the door shut behind them.

"Don't answer that," Preston said at once.

Like Jules needed the instruction. Instead, she shook her head and plopped down into one of the shiny leather chairs beside the door. She could just barely hear the low murmur of voices speaking in normal tones but couldn't make out any words.

"Come on, Sam," Preston sighed. "Ten minutes. There's coffee in my office."

"I'd prefer Scotch," Sam said, sounding rueful.

Preston chuckled. "Wouldn't we all. Julia, would you like to come along?"

Jules shook her head. She didn't trust them not to try to pry information out of her. Besides, she wasn't sure her knees would support her right now.

Preston and Sam had barely rounded the corner when the voices inside the room rose in volume, climbing toward shouts.

Her stomach squirmed even more. Okay, she should have gone with the lawyers.

Robert seemed to be doing most of the yelling. Even through the heavy door, Jules could catch tiny snatches and phrases. The one that stuck with her the most was Robert shouting, "—did it on purpose!"

Vivian's voice said something in reply that Jules couldn't catch. Probably just as well.

*On purpose.* She could understand why he'd feel that way. Vivian Carlisle was the most calculating person she had ever met. It made her great at her job and terrible at her personal life. Robert might well believe she'd done this just to trap him in a failing marriage.

But Jules remembered the look on Vivian's face when she'd come out of that bathroom. Robert was wrong. Maybe she *was* trying to use the pregnancy to save her marriage now, but there was no way she'd planned this.

The voices were still raised when Sam and Preston returned, and when the two men heard the voices through the door, they looked apprehensively at each other and at Jules.

"Little talk's not going well, huh?" Sam asked Jules.

She shook her head again.

"Not much of a conversationalist, are you?"

"That's enough," Preston said to Jules's relief, and he rapped sharply on the door.

Then, without waiting for an invitation, he opened it just in time for Robert to yell, "It doesn't make any difference! I didn't ask for this."

"Neither did I!" Vivian cried.

Jules had never heard Vivian raise her voice until today. She felt frozen to the chair.

"For God's sake," Vivian continued, "you don't honestly think I wanted—"

"All right." Sam stepped into the room and out of Jules's sight. "What's going on here?"

"Is it even mine?" Robert demanded.

"*What?*" Vivian said.

Preston's eyes widened, and he entered the room behind Sam. Jules rose, unsure if she should follow them or not.

"Robert," Jules heard Sam say urgently, "if this is what I think it is, then you and I need to consult priv—"

"No. It doesn't matter. It's over, okay? I don't care if you've got quintuplets in there, we're through. We're done. Okay?"

"Robert," Vivian said, and Jules could hear how hard she was straining for control. "I just wanted to tell you. We can't decide anything right now. We just need to take some time to think, now that—"

"There's someone else," Robert said.

"Robert, please," Sam interjected.

"No," Vivian said, her voice trembling, "There isn't. What do you want, a paternity test? I'll—"

"I meant for me," Robert said. "I have someone else."

Jules stopped breathing. The room went deadly silent.

Then Sam groaned "Robert" right before Preston shut the door, leaving Jules alone in the corridor.

She collapsed back into the chair, her heart racing.

Nobody shouted after that. Sam must have calmed Robert down, and Vivian was likely in shock. Oh Jesus. Robert had been cheating on her. There was a lot about Vivian Jules didn't understand, but she knew Vivian didn't forgive easily. Or at all.

Jules's head spun. It explained the apartment Robert had rented. He'd just spoken to his wife as though he hated her, so he hadn't just been looking for a Vivian substitute. That was what their relationship had become.

Jules shuddered. Nope. She was never getting married, she was never having kids. She was going to move to Tibet and become a nun and dedicate the rest of her life to serving the poor or something.

The door flung open. Vivian bolted through it, wearing her coat and clutching her bag. Her face was bone white, and she didn't seem to see Jules as she dashed down the hall.

Jules grabbed her own coat and bag and followed at top speed.

Footsteps followed them both. Jules looked over her shoulder, half-terrified that an enraged Robert was pursuing Vivian. But it was Preston, and he called out, "Vivian!"

Vivian whirled on her heel. The snarl on her face made her look like an animal. A wounded one, caught in a trap.

"Everything," she whispered, her voice shaking. "We take him for everything he's got. Do you understand?"

Preston pulled his handkerchief out of his breast pocket and mopped his forehead with it. "The pre-nup—"

"And fire that *fucking* secretary." She headed off without another word.

Preston opened his mouth again. Before she could stop herself, Jules pressed her hand to his elbow and said urgently, "Not now!" Then she followed Vivian, who was already at the elevators.

One look at her face told Jules that they would not be sharing an elevator for the trip down, and she focused on the marble tiles as the brass door slid shut between them.

She caught the next car and called for Ben. "Please hurry," she begged. "Oh my God, she is not going to want to wait."

"Jules, are you okay?" He sounded alarmed.

"No," she wailed and ended the call. By the time she reached the lobby, Vivian was waiting by the glass revolving door, staring through the floor-to-ceiling windows and obviously seeing nothing.

Jules took a deep breath, prayed for courage, and went to stand next to her, not daring to speak.

Vivian didn't move until her Audi pulled up at the sidewalk. Then she broke out of her reverie long enough to tell Jules: "Find a clinic. A decent one. By tomorrow."

It took Jules a second to figure out what she meant. Then she swallowed hard. "Okay."

"Not a word to anyone. Not one word."

"I won't. I haven't. To anybody."

Vivian went to the waiting car. To Jules's surprise, she waved Ben off and held the car door open for her but did not get inside herself. "Go back to *Du Jour*. I'm walking."

What? Where was she walking? Home? Well, they were already in the Upper West Side, so she could manage it if she wanted to, although Jules didn't envy her the task in those shoes. Or was she going somewhere else? Maybe she just wanted to keep moving without any destination in mind.

It wasn't Jules's business. She wasn't supposed to care.

"Okay," she said. "I-I'll be at Givenchy with Lucia, if you need…"

"I know." Vivian walked away.

Jules remained still for a few moments, then got into the car.

Ben pulled away. Jules looked back through the rear window, watching Vivian until she vanished completely into the crowd.

# CHAPTER 6

At her desk, Jules took a deep breath, turned the browser's privacy mode on, and started poking around the internet for reputable abortion clinics in Manhattan.

After ten minutes or so, she narrowed it down to an absurdly expensive clinic that offered what it called VIP treatment, where for a price you could get the whole office to yourself during your appointment. No other patients in the practice: just you, your doctor, and a nurse. Vivian would want that. Jules jotted down the number, made sure to close the browser, and hurried out of the receiving area with her cell phone. No need to be overheard.

The clinic receptionist was pleasant, soft-voiced, and helpful. Jules found herself almost wanting to burst into tears as she spoke to her, which was just ridiculous because it wasn't *her* problem, wasn't her embryo or her marriage, or anything other than her job. Her distress was so evident that Jules had to reassure the woman a few times that, no, the appointment wasn't for her but for her boss.

"Okay," the woman said, her voice still soothing and patient. "And you wanted the VIP arrangement?"

Jules's heart was going quadruple time. "Yeah. That's great. Thanks."

"We've got her in the schedule. Let me stress: please be on time."

"We will. Um, she will. Whichever." Would Vivian want Jules along for this too? Jules tried to imagine sitting next to her in the waiting room. Her brain went blank. How would she…how did you even…

"One more thing: no children are allowed in the clinic. For obvious reasons."

"Right," Jules said, shaking herself back into reality. "Not a problem."

"We'll see her at eight tomorrow morning."

"Thanks. Bye." Jules disconnected. *Tomorrow at eight.* She should cancel Vivian's pedicure with Nanette.

Pedicure? What the hell was Jules thinking? She had to cancel everything. Vivian couldn't possibly go into the office after that. She'd stay out for a couple of days, depending on what the doctor told her.

Did other personal assistants schedule their boss's abortions? She'd never heard anyone talking about it during any fashion weeks.

The pregnancy care sheets Dr. Latchley had given her were resting safely in her laptop bag. Out of nowhere, she got a lump in her throat and had to fight back tears.

*Not. Your. Problem.* She told herself that for the thousandth time.

She left *Du Jour* at one thirty to go to Givenchy with Lucia, who was in charge of acquiring next season's accessories for the website's splash page. More than once, Simon had reminisced ruefully about the days when they'd only had to worry about changing things up once a month for a paper magazine. Now content had to evolve constantly. It provided the variety readers craved, but it also meant the *Du Jour* team was always on its toes.

Lucia plainly had no idea why Jules was coming along, but she knew Vivian well enough to be wary of any change in plans or routine. So while she wasn't rude to Jules exactly, she wasn't chatty either.

That was fine. She tried as hard as she could to concentrate on the meeting with Alyson Langer because that was why Vivian had wanted her to go in the first place. She just had a hard time focusing, and it was all she could do to take the notes Vivian would need.

Jules's phone rang just before the end of the meeting. It was Vivian, and Jules gave everybody in the room an apologetic smile before hurrying out into the lobby to a quiet corner where nobody would be listening in. "Hello, Vivian?"

"How many rings does it take before you decide to pick up?"

"Sorry," Jules said, trying not to sound breathless from her little sprint. "I'm at Givenchy, and I wanted to find someplace qui—"

"Have you made the appointment?"

Jules took a deep breath. "Yes. Eight tomorrow morning."

"Where is it?" Vivian asked as if she might call the whole thing off if Jules had picked an unfashionable part of town.

"East Forty-Fourth. I found a clinic where you can reserve the whole place to yourself during your appointment, no other patients. So I did that. You should have plenty of privacy."

After a pause, Vivian said, "Thank you."

The ensuing silence left just enough room for Jules's heartbeat to chatter away in her ears. She fumbled for words and landed on "Of course. Um. The clinic's named—"

"Text me the details." Vivian suddenly sounded very, very tired. "I won't remember anything you tell me right now."

Jules managed to stop herself from asking if Vivian was okay. Of course she wasn't. Jules's job was to be useful. She just had to think of a tactful way to ask if she was going to be there.

"Will I be meeting you?" she asked, proud of the steadiness in her voice.

Another silence. This one went on even longer. Just as Jules was about to apologize for her presumption, Vivian said, "I'll see you there at seven forty-five."

Jules stopped herself from exhaling audibly. Sure, it was ridiculous to feel a rush of relief. Sure, she shouldn't want to be further involved in this. But none of that stacked up against the idea of Vivian sitting in that waiting room alone.

Would Vivian tell anyone else? Did she have friends she could call for support? Other than her ex-husbands, Jules had never heard her mention any family. Vivian Carlisle seemed *sui generis,* underived from any other material.

"I'll be there," she said.

One more pause, just long enough that Jules wondered if she was about to be thanked again. Vivian disconnected instead.

She looked at her phone, her heart aching again. Vivian would be all alone tonight.

Hopefully, she'd get some sleep. She needed it. And Jules doubted she was going to get much herself.

---

As it happened, Jules got to bed by midnight for once. Vivian hadn't returned to the office, and by the time Jules got through her tasks by eight p.m., she was actually free to…leave. The liberty would have been intoxicating, if she hadn't spent most of it worrying about her impossible boss's impossible situation. Nevertheless, by the time midnight rolled around, Jules collapsed into bed and realized she was exhausted enough to sleep the whole night through.

So of course it made sense that her phone would go off in the middle of the night. And of course it would be Vivian.

Struggling into wakefulness, she peered at the display, wondering in a panic if she'd missed her alarm and was late for work or something, when she realized it was three thirty in the morning. Was there an emergency?

It was a FaceTime request.

The hell? Vivian had never wanted to FaceTime before. And she wanted to do it *now?* Jules patted down her unruly hair as she sat up, took a second to gather her thoughts, and accepted the request.

Maybe it was an accident. Vivian could have meant to call her the normal way instead. Or maybe she'd meant to send the request to someone else.

When Vivian's face looked back at her, though, Jules knew it wasn't a mistake. She looked composed, not surprised. Her cheeks were pale, even in the dim light coming from somewhere off-screen. Was Vivian in her bedroom too? A framed black-and-white photo of trees hung on the wall behind her. It could go in any room. Vivian could be anywhere right now in her house.

Normally, Vivian Carlisle's presence filled up any room she was in. Now she looked small and diminished, even on a phone screen.

"Vivian," Jules rasped.

"Cancel the clinic appointment."

"Huh?" Jules pushed a lock of hair out of her eyes. Lack of sleep made her imprudent enough to say, "What's wrong?"

"A lot of things," Vivian said, "obviously. But I want you to cancel the appointment, at least for now."

"Oh," Jules said, her head spinning, her eyelids still heavy. She meant to say *Of course.* Instead it came out, "If you're sure?"

*Fuck. Wrong.* Even this sleep-deprived, Jules should have known better than to ask that question. She was about to get her head bitten off.

"Turn on the light," Vivian said quietly.

"What? Oh." Here she was, sitting in the dark with only the phone's screen to light up her face, making her look awful. She lunged for the bedside lamp and turned it on.

Seeing herself in the tiny screen in the upper right corner, she looked a wreck with unruly hair and squinting eyes that hadn't adjusted yet to the light.

"There," Vivian said. "Now you look less like you're telling a ghost story in front of a campfire."

"Um, yeah." Her voice was still hoarse. She reached for the water glass on her nightstand and took a sip while Vivian watched.

Then she watched Vivian back, awaiting a reprimand or instructions or something other than the silence she got as they stared at each other.

Amazingly, Vivian blinked first. Then she closed her eyes and exhaled through her nose. "I said to cancel it *for now*. I won't make that decision tonight."

"Good idea," Jules said because she was still a sleepy idiot.

Vivian's eyes widened, only slightly but still enough that it was a declaration of pure shock from her. She said, "Oh, is it, Julia?"

"I-I mean," Jules stammered. Shit, shit, shit. "I just mean it's a big decision. There's nothing wrong with giving it a little more time. Whatever you decide is totally fine. I wasn't implying otherwise."

Vivian relaxed her mouth from its pucker. "Just as long as you're not about to throw Bible verses at me."

"Oh God, no. That's not my thing."

"Glad to hear it. I…well." Vivian adjusted her hair, smoothing her hand over the back of her head. She never did stuff like that. Her hair, clothes, and makeup stayed obediently in place at all times in a way that seemed supernatural.

"I guess that's it." As she lowered her hand, Vivian looked tired again, even more so than before.

Jules's heart ached more than before too. She'd never wanted to comfort anyone as much as she wanted to comfort Vivian. It was almost physically painful not to be able simply to take her hand and say, *It'll be okay.*

The thought made her fingertips tingle, just like when she'd handed Vivian the water glass. But that was just dumb. This was a…solidarity thing. Women supporting women and all that.

"Yeah, well," Jules said, "if you need me, you know where to find me."

Vivian blinked. "Yes. I do." She ended the call.

Jules flopped back down on her bed with a thump and a groan. She was certainly awake now. Her heart had started pounding again, which was normal when you got yanked out of deep sleep and thought something was badly wrong but it turned out someone just wanted to confuse you.

Or connect with you. Or something like that.

She looked up at the ceiling. So Vivian had put a hold on the abortion for now. Fine, great, whatever, but of course she hadn't been able to wait until, say, seven a.m. to tell Jules. Good grief.

Everyone, even Simon, had warned Jules that working for Vivian would be a trial by fire. She had thought she was ready for that. Not even close. She hadn't foreseen this particular situation. Not one where she'd throw her back out to help someone known for tossing employees to the curb.

Vivian couldn't be trusted, no matter how compelling she was — in a way Jules couldn't pin down at all. She thought it was something about the intensity of her eyes. Or the way amusement sometimes lurked at the corner of her proud mouth. Or the way she strode through the world as if it belonged to her and everyone else had one second to get out of her path.

Or maybe it was the way she was slogging through one of the shittiest situations ever, keeping her head up by day and lying awake thinking about it by night.

*It's not a big deal,* Jules told herself. *You're just helping her out. You're her assistant. That's your job.*

The job description *had* included the phrase "other duties as assigned."

Jules clapped a hand over her mouth, too late to stop a semihysterical laugh that sounded too loud in the apartment. How had she gotten herself into this?

She hadn't. Vivian Carlisle had happened to her, like an avalanche or tsunami, as sudden and unforgiving as any natural disaster.

That was the thing about nature, though. It was frightening, dangerous, unpredictable—yes, all that. It was also exciting. Inspiring. Even beautiful.

Jules shook her head as she pulled the blankets back over herself. She squeezed her eyes shut, determined to recoup what she could of the night's sleep. She doubted it would work, but she might as well try.

Eventually, it did. Her sleep wasn't restful, though. In her dreams, Vivian stood above her atop a storm cloud. Bolts of electricity crackled all around her before driving themselves into the ground. Jules dodged and weaved through them, her hair standing on end.

Something must be wrong with her. Because she kept wondering if maybe, just maybe, it wouldn't be so bad to be struck by lightning.

# CHAPTER 7

The abortion clinic opened at six. Jules made the second phone call of the morning from her bed, wiping sleep out of her eyes as she canceled the appointment. Good thing too because Vivian called her at six forty-five, just as Jules was putting the finishing touches on her makeup.

She looked at her phone resting on the lip of the sink as Vivian's name appeared and her heart jumped into her throat. Was it going to be weird today? Would anything have changed after last night's conversation?

Best to play it safe. She swiped the screen to answer the phone and took on her perkiest morning voice. "Vivian! Hi. I canceled—"

"Meet me at Preston's office in half an hour. Bring coffee. Decaf."

"Oh." Jules blinked at her reflection. It was weird to feel disappointed. "I mean, sure."

"You have the Givenchy notes?"

"Yes, on my tablet," Jules said, as if Vivian needed to know exactly where the notes were at any given moment.

"Good. I'll see you in thirty minutes."

"Right. Wait! Do you want breakfast too?"

"Did I ask for breakfast?" Vivian disconnected.

So much for things being different. Jules stuck her tongue out at her phone.

She didn't make it to the law office on time. The subway was crammed full. She had to wait to get in and out and switch cars. Then, on top of everything else, she waited in line at a crowded La Colombe Coffee Roasters.

For once, she didn't care. She was in a foul mood, and Vivian could wait.

As she'd reflected the night before, this job was getting more difficult than she'd thought possible. Well, Jules could walk away if she wanted to. She could. That was important. She controlled her own destiny. Sure, Vivian could fire her. Jules would get along somehow. She wasn't like Vivian, no matter what her mom said, and Vivian could go to—

"There you are," Vivian said as Jules hurried through the revolving door, jumping in spite of herself. Vivian was not in Preston's office, but had been waiting by the door, evidently in a fever of impatience. She all but snatched the coffee from Jules's hands. "Come along."

Jules checked out the reception desk. The rude receptionist wasn't there today.

Her newfound feeling of independence shriveled up a little bit as she followed Vivian into the elevator. To her surprise, Vivian pressed the button for the third floor instead of the ninth, and they exited into the cafeteria.

Vivian seated herself at a table and rubbed her forehead with her fingertips before sipping at her coffee.

Jules squirmed. "Yogurt?"

Vivian nodded. "Get yourself something and put it on our expense account."

Jules blinked. Vivian had never invited Jules to eat in front of her before. She preferred to think that nobody who worked for her ate anything at all—you weren't even allowed to have food on your desk at *Du Jour*.

As she bought yogurt for Vivian and coffee and a fruit cup for herself, Jules realized that this was Vivian's way of saying—what? Sorry? Thank you? Something, anyway.

Vivian took the yogurt without a word and pretended not to pay attention while Jules pretended not to eat.

When she was done, Jules dabbed at her mouth with a napkin, sipped her coffee, and said, "When are we supposed to see Preston?"

Vivian looked at her watch. "In twenty minutes."

It was seven forty. Jules tried to cover a yawn.

Vivian was regarding her through hooded eyes. Something about her gaze unnerved Jules. More than usual, anyway. She cleared her throat. "So," she said, "you look, er, well today."

Vivian raised one eyebrow, and Jules realized she'd just made an uninvited personal comment. Crap, time to redirect. "Oh! I need to reschedule your pedicurist. Tomorrow morning should still be—"

"I look 'well'?" Vivian asked.

Her tone had been absolutely neutral, not cold or angry. Jules still broke out in a sweat. "Sorry."

"Why are you apologizing?"

"Because—" Was this a trap? "I didn't mean to presume."

Vivian raised the other eyebrow as if trying to make sure they both got an equal workout. "Only apologize when you know you've done something wrong. And only to the right people."

*We dictate the rules, not them.* Vivian had said that to her only yesterday in the lobby of this same building. Another lesson. Jules had never heard her dispense advice to underlings before. She probably didn't call them at 3:30 a.m. either, though.

Probably.

Nothing ventured, nothing gained. "How do I know who the right people are?"

"Trial and error," Vivian said. "You've got a limited number of errors at your disposal."

Well, that wasn't news. "Right." Jules managed a smile.

Vivian did not return it—of course—but instead considered her again with a stare. "Let's go," she said and headed back out of the cafeteria.

Jules quickly gathered up their garbage and tossed it in the trash can on the way out.

This meeting was in Preston's private office. He held the door open for them. "Good morning, ladies," he said, and added more seriously, "How are you doing today, Vivian?"

"Robert's admitted to infidelity," Vivian said. "Tell me what that means for the process."

Right to the point, then. Jules had expected no less.

Without batting an eyelid, he sat down behind an impressive mahogany desk. "Under the circumstances, I recommend we continue with the original filing of irretrievable breakdown, meaning that your relationship with your spouse has been beyond repair for the last six months. We can finalize it after determining the allocation of assets and responsibilities."

Jules had to give him points for not adding *as you probably remember from last time.*

"I got pregnant less than six months ago," Vivian said quietly. "I'd think that might complicate the situation."

A hot ball of anger formed in Jules's stomach. Robert had probably had sex with Vivian knowing full well he would file for divorce soon. While he was cheating on her with someone else too. *Gross.*

But Preston shook his head. "Sexual relations do not necessarily imply that the relationship is salvageable. It just means the people in the relationship had sex." He darted a sudden, wide-eyed look at Jules.

Fair enough. Jules was fighting not to cringe. She was listening in on talk about Vivian Carlisle's sex life with her ex. What sin had she committed in a former life to be here?

It was Vivian's turn not to bat an eye. "We're all adults here, and you can rely on Julia's discretion."

Stupidly, Jules's urge to cringe vanished, replaced with the urge to smile. She suppressed it. Talk about inappropriate—this was serious business.

"So it means nothing? Adultery changes nothing?" An edge of agitation finally appeared in Vivian's tone.

Preston sounded reluctant. "In New York state, adultery constitutes separate grounds for divorce. But the court will grant you a divorce, Vivian. There's no question of that. I don't think we should make it any messier or costlier than it has to be."

"Oh, it's going to be messy," Vivian said. "Costly too. For him."

He took a deep breath. "I understand you're upset. Especially taking… everything…into consideration."

Jules had to give him further points for not looking directly at Vivian's abdomen.

"But may I ask what you are hoping to achieve beyond simple revenge?"

"There has to be something beyond that?" Vivian asked.

*Yikes,* Jules thought.

"Look, Vivian." Preston sounded firm and no-nonsense for the first time.

Jules bit her lip. He should know that wasn't going to fly.

"I know you want to do this in the heat of the moment," he continued, "but I am telling you that this can get long and ugly, and you have other things you probably want to be worrying about instead. You don't need Robert's money. You've got more than he does."

"No," Vivian said, "I don't want his money."

Jules looked at Vivian in surprise. So did Preston. Hadn't Vivian said yesterday that she wanted to take Robert for everything?

"All right," Preston said cautiously. "His property, then?"

"Oh, no, Preston." Vivian smiled. "I've thought about this all night, and I decided there are only two things I want from Robert."

Preston looked more apprehensive than ever. "And they are?"

Vivian held up one finger. "First: he'll pay child support."

"Yes, of course." Preston frowned.

"Second," Vivian said held up another finger, "he will have nothing to do with the child. He's not to be a part of its life. He gives up all his legal rights."

Preston took a deep breath. "That will entail considerably more complications."

"Will it?"

The brand-new note in her voice was not agitation or irritation. It was anger, edging toward the fury she'd displayed yesterday.

*Oh shit.*

"Yes, of course," he said, sounding surprised.

"Robert said he wanted nothing to do with it, Yesterday. Very loudly. I'm sure you remember."

"He was angry too, He probably didn't mean everything he said. And even if he did, he might change his mind later. Does he have children?"

"A son by his first marriage who's seventeen and lives with his mother. I know Robert. He's done with that part of his life. He's obviously ready for his second childhood with that infant he said he's been seeing behind my back." Her voice cracked with bitterness.

"Be that as it may," Preston said, obviously trying to be patient, "we can set those terms for you. If he agrees, well, then we'll talk more about how to make it happen. If he doesn't, then we could have a long fight ahead of us." He took another, even deeper breath. "And I'd urge you to consider the child. Wouldn't it have the right to know its father?"

Out of the corner of her eye, Jules saw Vivian swell up with rage. But she didn't explode. "Preston, those are my terms. You're my lawyer. Make them work." She stood up, clutching her handbag.

Jules quickly stood up too.

He sighed. "I'll do my best, Vivian. But please understand this is very unusual."

"I understand everything just fine. Good morning." She turned and left.

Preston and Jules shared looks of commiseration before Jules followed her.

Vivian's silence was welcome as they walked down the hallway. It gave her time to consider Preston's point. Wouldn't it be good for the child to have their father in their life? Of course, single parents raised kids every day. And based on his reaction, it seemed likely Robert wouldn't want any part of raising it.

There were going to be questions someday. *How come I don't have a dad? Didn't he want me? Why did you keep him away from me?*

What a fucking mess. Maybe Vivian would change her mind if Robert did. Nothing to do but wait and see.

When they were back in the car, Vivian said, "How did Lucia handle the meeting with Givenchy?"

Jules tried hard to remember. She'd been more than a little distracted by worrying about the woman now standing next to her, who would accept no such excuse. "Fine, I guess. I've never sat in on a meeting like that before, so I don't really know how it's supposed to go."

Vivian sounded remarkably patient when she said, "Who did most of the talking?"

"Alyson. Uh, she was mainly talking about the transitional spring stuff. You know, pieces she'd like to see featured on the splash page."

"I see. How did Lucia respond?"

"She said most of them were okay, I think. Alyson gave her some photos and a couple of sample pieces. She said she'd show them to you."

"How many photos?"

"Er…" Now that Jules thought about it, there hadn't been that many. "Maybe seven? Ten, tops."

"So," Vivian said, "my associate accessories editor meets not with Clare Waight Keller but with one of her lieutenants, lets this lieutenant run the meeting, allows photos and sample pieces to be selected for her based on what the lieutenant—possibly not even Clare herself—would 'like to see' featured in *Du Jour*."

"Um—"

"You have an interesting definition of 'fine,' Julia."

"I thought she already knew what you wanted," she faltered. "I mean, she's been doing this for—"

"Too long." Vivian held out a brisk, impatient hand. "Give me your notes on the meeting."

Jules wasted no time in handing over her tablet.

She immediately became absorbed, which gave Jules an opportunity to take care of one important detail. She fished around in her bag, pulled out the card Dr. Latchley had given her a couple of days before, and dialed the number.

"Dr. Sita Viswanathan's office," a pleasant female voice said.

"Hi," Jules said. "My name is Jules Moretti. I work for Vivian Carlisle. I believe your office was told to expect our call?"

"Oh, that's right," the woman said, her voice warming at once. "Sandra Latchley's office said you'd be calling soon. I'm Mary."

Jules grinned. "And I'm supposed to ask how your dogs are doing."

At this, Vivian raised her head and looked over sharply.

Jules swallowed. "So, do you have any openings available?"

"My dogs are great," Mary said, "and we can clear a space for you tomorrow evening after our office normally closes—say, seven?"

"Let me check." She covered the phone's mic. "Seven tomorrow night?" she asked.

Vivian, who had nothing on her schedule between five and nine, when she was going to a party, frowned, obviously running through her own mental checklist, and nodded.

"That's fine," Jules told Mary with relief. "How long will it take?"

"No more than one hour. I've got her in the system. We'll see you then!" she chirped, sounding so downright perky that Jules was thankful Vivian wasn't dealing with her directly. Perky people never came off well in encounters with Vivian. It was like watching a hawk swoop down on an adorable field mouse.

Jules ended the call. "Shouldn't take longer than an hour, so there's plenty of time to get you to the party afterward."

Vivian picked up where she had left off earlier. "Nobody dictates what goes in *Du Jour*, Julia. Nobody but me."

Jules could almost hear the screech as her brain applied the brakes and then tried to take off in a different direction. "Oh," she said. "Of course."

"Not Alyson, not Clare Waight Keller, not even God himself." It was as if Jules hadn't spoken. "I asked Lucia to bring me a *representative* sample of what's on offer at Givenchy. A lot is on offer at Givenchy. But when I return, there'll be five photographs laid out on my desk, all of which are what Alyson would 'like to see' on our website and social media."

*I sure screwed up this one.* She had to do better next time, if there was a next time. "I'm sorry. I didn't know. But are my notes helpful at all? Like—if you sent me out again, what's the sort of thing you'd want me to write about?"

Vivian flipped through the notes again. "They're not awful," she said after a moment, and Jules trembled with relief. "Anyway, now you know."

What? Know what? Was that supposed to have been helpful advice? But Jules didn't dare ask. If Vivian did send her out again to spy on people, she'd just try to…read Vivian's mind and do what she secretly wanted. Like always.

They arrived at the office. "Finally," Vivian said, looking up at Koening like a traveler might regard home after a long absence. "I can actually get some real work done today. Julia, I want you to sit in on the editorial meeting at two."

"And take notes?" Jules asked.

Vivian gave her the *what-do-you-think-you-idiot* look and got out of the car.

Fair enough. Jules had earned that one. But it seemed like somehow, some way, she'd earned Vivian's trust too.

*Don't rely on it,* she warned herself. *She's your boss, not your friend. Vivian doesn't have friends. You're an—an asset. That's it.*

Unbidden, she remembered Vivian's hand touching hers over a water bottle, Vivian's weary face on the phone.

*That's it,* Jules reminded herself. *That's it.*

# CHAPTER 8

Jules left the editorial meeting feeling almost confident in the notes she'd taken: not skimpy, not voluminous, and she'd definitely attached names to decisions. She sort of felt like she should be in the *Du Jour* version of the CIA—except that everybody else at the meeting obviously knew she was there to be Vivian's eyes and ears, so she didn't have a cover. Too bad.

She trotted into Vivian's office, her stomach clenching when she saw her poised over the glass table in the corner, looking over large glossy photographs from Givenchy. She'd been right: there were only six photos. Did Alyson think she could slip anything by Vivian? Why would she even want to try?

Jules put her notes on Vivian's desk and turned, hoping to sneak out without being noticed.

Without even looking around, Vivian said, "Julia, come here."

Rats. Jules bit her lip and approached the table.

Vivian didn't look at her. "Did they really believe I wouldn't notice this pitiful little selection?"

Jules didn't pray, but it seemed someone should—for Lucia, Alyson, and perhaps Givenchy itself. "Looks like it."

"I'll deal with Lucia," Vivian said. She picked up a photograph, sneered at it, and dropped it back down onto the table. Then she rubbed her fingertips together as if they had something gross on them. "You'll return to Givenchy."

Jules could just bet how Lucia was going to be dealt with. At least she didn't have to see it in person this time. "Okay. Who am I going with?"

"Nobody," Vivian said.

Jules stared at her in shock.

Vivian stared right back. "Don't let me down, Julia. That would be a shame."

---

Alyson had not been pleased by being summoned at a moment's notice. But since the summons was from Vivian Carlisle, she greeted Jules graciously enough. "Fancy seeing you here again," she said. "But where's Lucia?"

"Lucia won't be coming today. It's just me. Vivian wanted kind of a do-over of the last meeting."

"A do-over? What's that supposed to mean?"

"She wants to see a wider selection. She wants to see more of your accessories line. You have so many beautiful things," she added with what she hoped was a charming smile.

Alyson wasn't going for it. "I sent her the best of our new line. They'll really grab a reader's attention. Didn't she like them?"

"Well, like I said, she wants to see more." Hopefully, Alyson wasn't going to make this harder than it had to be. "So, if you could just give me more photos or samples. A wider range of—"

Alyson narrowed her eyes. "Aren't you just her assistant?"

*Just?* What an asshole. She squared her shoulders. "Yeah. I'm her assistant."

"Well," a mean little smile lingered on her mouth, "hold on a second while I help you out."

She turned and sashayed out of the room.

Jules got a bad feeling in the pit of her stomach. It couldn't be this easy.

Sure enough, when she returned, she had only two glossies in her hand. The accessories in the photos—a ring and a bracelet—looked almost exactly like the ones in the photos Vivian already had.

"Here you go," Alyson said sweetly as she thrust the photos at Jules. "You can show yourself out."

"No, I can't," Jules snapped. She didn't move to take the photos.

Alyson looked disdainfully at her. Like that was going to work after a year of being scorned by the best.

A *lieutenant,* Vivian had called Alyson. Why was she being so stubborn, especially given that it was *Vivian Carlisle's* ire she was risking? Why not just fork over a few more photos of some stuff that didn't look just like—

Oh.

"So," Jules said casually, gesturing at the two photos Alyson still held, "that's the new line? Going to be top sellers?"

"Yes." Alyson narrowed her eyes. "And this is all the time I have for you right now."

"You designed these, didn't you?" Jules asked.

Alyson started.

Jules tried not to smirk. "That's why you only want these to go in *Du Jour.* Does Ms. Waight Keller even know you're doing this? Or were you going to tell her that we just happened to pick your designs?"

Alyson recovered quickly and gave Jules a nasty glare. "I have no idea what you're talking about, but you're wasting my time. And I don't—"

"Okay," Jules said. "So I can just tell Vivian that you don't have anything else to show us, and *Du Jour* can feature absolutely nothing by Givenchy, and when Ms. Waight Keller calls us to ask why, we can direct her your way."

"Wow. You're pretty impressed with yourself, aren't you?" Alyson said. "Especially for being the next person Vivian Carlisle's going to chew up and spit out. And when that happens and you're looking for your next job, I'll still be here and—"

"Are you sure? Lucia won't be," Jules said. "She got fired this afternoon."

Probably. No, certainly. Jules was absolutely certain that when she got back to the office, Lucia's cubicle would be empty. Nobody tried to make Vivian look like a sucker.

Alyson stopped with her mouth still open and went pale.

"Vivian is about one second away from calling Ms. Waight Keller herself and demanding the same for you," Jules added, bluffing like hell. "Look, I'm trying to help you save your skin here. Why not let me look at the other photos? I'll bring Vivian what she wants, and we can put the rest down to Lucia's bad judgment." She smiled at Alyson, heart racing, wondering if this was actually going to work.

"She fired Luce?" Alyson asked faintly.

Jules tried to look appropriately sympathetic. "It was kind of scary."

"Fuck." Alyson ran one hand through her perfectly styled hair. "I told her it was a bad idea."

It had been Lucia's idea? Jules tried not to shake her head in disgust. Lucia had worked at *Du Jour* for four years. Didn't she know better than to pull this stuff?

"Well, nobody says you have to go down with her," Jules said. "Just give me what Vivian's asking for."

"Which is what?" Alyson sounded frantic now. "We have tons of things. Does she want something specific? I mean, Jesus, if I send her the wrong thing now…" She gave Jules a scared look. "What should I send back with you?"

Jules looked at Alyson.

Alyson looked back at Jules.

---

She heard Simon before she saw him.

"It'll be interesting to see how she handles herself," he was saying. "Vivian seems to think she's all capable."

"So everyone says," a dry voice replied. It belonged to Jon from PR. "Including you."

"I was sorry to lose her, believe me. But better her than me when it comes to dealing with Alyson."

Jules stopped dead in her tracks at the corner into Reception. Oh. It was about her. And…*all capable*, huh? Like she was a Range Rover or something. That was kind of cool to hear.

"I've certainly never heard anything good about her," Jon replied, "except from Lucia, and—well, look how that went."

"I'm *super* excited about replacing someone else," Simon said sardonically.

"I bet you are. Anyway, I wonder how much she'll be able to squeeze out of Alyson."

She'd never get a more perfect opening. Jules took a deep breath and rounded the corner.

Jon saw her first, and his eyes grew gratifyingly huge. Simon turned and blinked behind his pince-nez.

"Can I get a hand with these?" Jules asked. She had a thick leather-bound binder full of at least two hundred photos under one arm, and her other hand carried—dragged—two huge heavy Givenchy bags full of samples.

Simon shook his head quickly, hurried forward, and took the shopping bags.

"Thanks," she said.

"What the hell is this?" he grunted.

"Everything Givenchy is doing next year," Jules said, continuing toward Vivian's office. "For accessories, I mean. Spring, summer, and sketches for fall."

"You don't say," Simon said as they lugged Jules's loot into Vivian's office past Jon's disbelieving eyes.

Vivian looked up from her laptop as they entered. Jules and Simon paused in the doorway like soldiers reporting back from a campaign awaiting their instructions.

"Leave that in the corner." Vivian turned back to her computer.

That was it? Jules tried not to sigh.

Simon put the bags on the floor, and Jules put the binder on the table.

Well, she didn't know what she'd expected. *Good job, Julia* would probably have killed Vivian. But she had looked forward to telling her about what had happened: that Vivian's instincts had been dead-on (of course), that Alyson and Lucia had been plotting together, that Vivian hadn't made a mistake in sending Jules to fix things, that maybe they could…what? Do this again sometime?

"Simon," Vivian said, not looking at either of them, "please get in touch with Human Resources." It was a remarkably civil request for her, and Simon nodded as he left.

Jules followed him and glanced at Vivian. Vivian was watching her right back. The look on her face was unreadable.

Well…nearly. Jules straightened her shoulders and hurried out of the office, realizing that, despite the lack of expression on Vivian's face, she'd been a little impressed.

Another night, another empty Google doc. This one wouldn't stay empty for long, though. Jules was going to attempt *The Cut* one more time.

She typed: *I Think About This a Lot: Sigourney Weaver Mentoring Melanie Griffith in Working Girl.*

Working title achieved, Jules kept going.

*Viewers often say Katharine Parker (Sigourney Weaver), a ruthless businesswoman who steals her secretary's ideas, is a sociopath straight from MBA hell. They always forget the scene when Katharine gives that same secretary, Tess McGill (Melanie Griffith), some real talk. Specifically, she tells Tess that you can't wait for life to come to you. You go after what you want, and you don't give up. Ever.*

It would do for a start. It wasn't her usual subject matter, but something about it was calling to her anyway.

Jules limbered her fingers, cracked her knuckles, and took a deep breath.

*Here we go again.*

# CHAPTER 9

"Have you arranged Charles Street for Christmas?" Vivian asked as she slid into the car seat next to Jules, having just finished lunch with the photographer Mario Sorrenti.

Jules was in mid text with a *Du Jour* PR intern but switched tracks instantly. "Yes. It's all ready."

One of the many tasks Jules had had to juggle today was making arrangements for Vivian's Christmas. This year, she was going to London. It wasn't clear why since she had no family there. But she always rented the same elegant townhouse on Charles Street in Mayfair for the London fashion weeks in spring and fall. She had been specific in telling Jules to reserve it for the holidays as well.

The owners had intended to stay there for Christmas. Thank God Vivian had a the-sky's-the-limit attitude when it came to getting what she wanted; the price tag had nearly made Jules faint.

"I'll forward you the reservation," she added. "They changed the security code."

"Good. The last one was too easy to guess."

Jules looked down at her phone and swiped open the email app. Where was the reservation? She got so many emails, it was almost impossible to—

"Where are you going for the holidays?" Vivian asked.

*What?*

Jules looked up at once. Maybe Vivian had gotten on the phone in the last half second and was talking to someone else. Or maybe Jules had misheard.

But no. Vivian was calmly looking right at her after asking a personal question for no apparent reason.

"Just back to Philadelphia," she replied, trying not to sound as astonished as she felt. "Going to see my family."

"Ugh. I hate Philadelphia," Vivian said. "Dirty place."

"New York's not squeaky clean," Jules snapped before she could stop herself. *Dammit.* But what did Vivian expect when she went around insulting people's hometowns? True, Jules had been ready to get out of there when she did. Still, there was a difference between criticizing Philly when you were *from* Philly and criticizing it because you lived in the oh-so-superior New York City.

To Jules's surprised relief, instead of chastising her for sass, Vivian only said, "No, it's not." She turned to look back out the window. Jules thanked her lucky stars for her narrow escape, but then Vivian abruptly spoke again.

"I grew up in Ohio," she said. "Outside of Toledo."

Jules sat silently, shocked.

"I guess that's even worse," Vivian added with a derisive little chuckle.

"Do…do you ever go back?" Jules asked.

"No." The reply came with such finality that the subject was clearly closed. Still, it was more than Jules had ever expected to get out of her. About anything.

In fact, it was more than anybody got. Vivian had a *Wikipedia* page. Jules had scoured it before applying to work at *Du Jour*. There hadn't been anything about her childhood or family, and she never gave interviews that included personal information. But she was telling Jules?

*Okay,* she told herself as her palms sweated. *It's okay, it's not weird, and you're going to keep your mouth shut. Like she knows you will.*

So Vivian Carlisle, high-and-mighty queen of New York City, had started out as an Ohio girl. The greatest tastemaker in fashion had risen from Middle America. Judging from the look of it, she was overcompensating like hell too. If you thought about it for a little bit, it was funny; if you thought about it for longer, it was sad; if you thought about it for too long, your head hurt, so Jules stopped thinking right away.

She ventured, "Well, I've never been to London." There. Conversational gambit attempted.

"You will," Vivian said, still looking out her window.

Jules managed a smile. That had been a pretty nice response, actually. "Yeah. Someday."

"I mean, you *will*," Vivian said, and Jules could imagine her rolling her eyes. "For London Fashion Week."

"Oh." Jules's cheeks flamed. "Right. Of course." *Dummy.* How could she have forgotten?

Then she did some quick mental math. London's spring fashion week was at the end of February this year. The *Du Jour* hotel accommodations were already booked, as was the Charles Street townhouse, and there wasn't much else Jules could do until they were closer to the actual trip.

The end of February. Vivian would be more than four months along. Would she be showing by then? What the heck was she going to wear? Did Alaïa even make a maternity line?

Well, that part, thank goodness, was entirely out of Jules's hands. Vivian might expect the world to take care of all her life's mundane details, but nobody—*nobody*—told her what to wear.

---

Simon left for the *Du Jour* LA shoot on December 3. He returned four days later, a duration that seemed more like four years. Jules had never been in the office when he wasn't there and Vivian was. She never wanted to do it again either. Without Simon, Vivian was even more impatient and brusque, as if the absence of her right-hand man only made it more obvious to her how incompetent everybody else was.

So when he breezed through the door at eight a.m., Jules had to restrain herself from giving him a huge welcome-back hug. She settled for her widest smile and a hot cup of his favorite coffee: the whole milk mocha that he only allowed himself as an occasional indulgence.

"It's so nice to be missed," he said as he sipped.

"You were," Jules said fervently. "Oh, my God, do you know what she's like without you?"

"I'll let you work that little logic puzzle out on your own," he said, then headed into Vivian's office with his silver laptop under his arm. "Good morning," he said as he disappeared from sight.

"Thank God," Jules heard Vivian say. She didn't bother to repress her smile.

She was smiling less by the end of the day, though, when she was still at her desk at ten p.m.

Simon seemed to pick up on it when he stopped in front of her to drawl, "Still hard at work?"

She glared at him. He of all people knew by now that Jules didn't go home until Vivian said she could, work or no work. "Very perceptive."

"That's me," Simon said, "Mr. Perceptive." Then he leaned back until he could see Vivian at her desk and called, "Vivian? Can I steal Jules from you for about half an hour? I promise to have her back before bedtime."

She expected Vivian to give her disinterested permission. Instead, she sounded remarkably suspicious when she asked, "Why? What do you need her for?"

"Things," Simon said blandly.

Jules grinned and hoped he would get away with it.

He did. "Fine," Vivian said, sounding huffy but not really irritated. Probably because at this hour of the night, they weren't likely to get many calls.

Jules, relieved at even a temporary escape, gamely followed Simon out of the receiving area. "Where are we going?"

"Federico's."

Federico's was a stylish bar across the street. Jules was pretty sure that Vivian wouldn't have let her leave if she'd known Simon was going to take her to a bar. "Why are we going there?"

"Well, when one is celebrating, one should have a drink," Simon said.

"Celebrating?"

"All in good time, my dear."

Jules kept her silence until they reached Federico's and took a table, but she had to admit she was a little uneasy. She'd gotten to know Simon pretty damn well while working for him, and he had a telling gleam in his eyes.

So when the waiter delivered the two neon-orange-colored cocktails Simon had ordered, she said, "Okay. Now: what are we celebrating?"

"Cheers," he said.

Jules sighed, dutifully raising her glass, clinking it with his. She'd just raised it to her lips and taken a sip when Simon spoke.

"Vivian's pregnancy, of course. New life is so exciting, isn't it?"

Jules's mouthful of orange cocktail went everywhere.

He dabbed at his cashmere sweater with a napkin. "I've always wondered if people actually did that spitting thing. Now I know."

"Wh-what are you talking about?" Jules croaked, fumbling for her own napkin and trying to ignore the stares she was getting from the other patrons. "Vivian's what?"

"Don't even try it." He sounded stern. "You've already shown me everything I need to know."

Jules whimpered and closed her eyes. She was dead. Worse than dead.

"True, it was a long shot," he mused. "I mean, at her age… Well, it *is* Vivian. I guess it makes sense that her ovaries would still be kicking ass after everybody else's have thrown in the towel."

"She'll kill me," she moaned. "Simon, I didn't tell you. I didn't—"

"Yes, yes," he said impatiently.

She opened her eyes to see him regarding her intently.

"And you've been holding her hand the whole way, haven't you?" he asked. "That doctor's visit was about this, wasn't it? And she took you along."

Jules nodded mutely.

"And the lawyer too. You were there for that."

Another nod.

"My God," he chuckled. "Were you even there when Robert got the big news?"

She bit her lip and nodded one more time.

Simon's eyes widened. "I was kidding. Really?"

"It was awful," she whispered. This seemed like betraying Vivian's trust. She wouldn't, she *couldn't*, give Simon any more details, but at the same time, it was so nice not to be the only one who was in on this.

"What does this mean for the divorce?" he asked. "Will he—"

"I can't talk about that. Simon, please don't ask me to talk about it. She'd kill me."

"Is she going to have an abortion?"

"No. I mean, I don't think so." Jules looked helplessly at the door. This was weird. She'd often found herself longing to flee *Du Jour* and head straight for a bar. She'd never expected it to work the other way around. "Simon, she'll tell everybody when she's ready."

He snorted. "That'll be the day. It's not how she thinks. I promise you, we'll just all watch her expand and say nothing until the kid's actually in a bassinet." He checked his watch. "We still have fifteen minutes. I'd say you've more than earned it. Finish up your drink, but take your time."

Jules took another sip, then a horrible thought occurred to her. "She's not going to tell anyone at the office? I'm going to be the only person who officially knows?"

"Quite possibly."

"Then I'm going to keep doing everything myself?" Jules hadn't expected that. She'd planned on keeping this secret until Vivian chose for it not to be a secret anymore. Then other people would step forward and help. Jules would no longer be a lone ranger but instead part of some kind of fetching-and-carrying network with other peons. She couldn't be the only peon.

"What's 'everything'?" he inquired, looking genuinely interested. "What have you been doing for her?"

"Her food," Jules whimpered. "The doctors and the lawyers, and I've been reading stuff about babies, and she sent me to Givenchy, and she told me she's from Ohio—"

Simon stared at her. "She is?"

"You didn't know?"

He grinned. "She told me she was from North Stamford."

"Oh no." Jules hid her face in her hands. "Simon—"

"Relax. It's not like I ever bought it. 'Vivian Carlisle' isn't even her real name."

"It's not?" Simon had never divulged this kind of intelligence when Jules had worked for him. "What is it?"

"How should I know? I didn't even know where she was from. But it's not Vivian Carlisle, I can tell you that." He gave her a half smile. "If anyone's in a position to find out, apparently it's you. You'll let me know if you learn anything, right?"

"Ha, ha, ha." She took another big swallow of her stupid orange drink that she didn't even like. Too sour. "Don't change the subject. What am I supposed to do? She doesn't have anyone but me."

He looked at her in silence.

"No, really," she said softly. "She doesn't. It's—"

"I guess that answers my question about Robert," he said.

This time, Jules let her head fall all the way down until it hit the table.

Simon reached across and patted her shoulder. "Don't take it so hard. I'm sure with some practice you'll develop that thing called caution."

"Why, though?" she asked, the wood table cool against her forehead. "Why isn't there anybody else?" She looked up again pleadingly. There had to be a reason she was the one Vivian had FaceTimed in the middle of the night. "Why aren't there any friends? Or are there? Maybe she's talking to friends and I just don't know about it."

Her gut told her otherwise, and the shake of Simon's head proved it correct. "Vivian doesn't do friends. Not the kind you mean, anyway. She's had too many bad experiences. She—look, I didn't tell you any of this, okay?"

Whatever Simon said, Jules would take it to the grave if it helped her make sense of this. "Of course."

"You lose a lot of friends in a divorce. Now imagine losing three times that many. Now add in that when you're powerful and famous, it's impossible to know who cares about you and who's just using you. Now add in all the people you stepped on while you made your way to the top—"

"I get the idea." There was likely even more to it than that. Vivian was strong-willed but intensely private. It was easy to see she'd put up walls within walls. She'd have a hard time keeping close friends even without the factors Simon had mentioned.

"Are you her friend?" she asked. "Are you as close as she gets?"

His silence told her everything.

And right at that moment, Jules's phone rang. *Vivian*. She tried to keep her voice steady as she said, "Hello?"

"Where are you?" Vivian asked.

"Um. With Simon. Um—"

"Come back now." Vivian disconnected.

Jules winced. "We're being summoned. Or I am, anyway."

"Ah."

"Maybe the phones started ringing again," she said glumly. Then she glared at him. "Or maybe she realized you were going to try to worm stuff out of me."

"Or maybe she panics when she realizes you're more than ten feet away."

Jules blushed, then felt embarrassed for blushing because Simon might take it the wrong way, which only made her blush harder.

"You're heading into undiscovered territory, you know," he added. "And every explorer should be cautious."

The words gave Jules a shiver. "What do you mean?"

"To be honest, I'm not sure what I mean." He waved their server down for the check. "We haven't seen anything like you yet."

She inhaled sharply.

He looked at her with an expression she couldn't decode. "Good luck."

---

When she returned to *Du Jour*, Jules found herself in Vivian's doorway wringing her hands.

"I'm back," she said.

"Obviously." She kept her eyes on the editorial spread in front of her. "Where's Simon?"

"He's gone home for the night."

"And where did you two go?"

*Might as well 'fess up.* "He took me to Federico's."

"Sit down," she said, still not looking up.

This couldn't be good. Jules tried not to shake as she sat across from Vivian's desk.

"Well?" Vivian said.

"He knows," Jules mumbled.

Vivian looked up sharply at her.

"I didn't tell him," Jules added quickly. "He already knew. He guessed."

"Hmm." She leaned back, not seeming angry at all. She looked over Jules's head at the ceiling and drummed her fingers on the desk. "I'm disappointed."

Jules's heart raced in panic. "I'm sorry. But I didn't tell him."

"I meant in Simon," Vivian's voice went almost gentle, a tone Jules had never heard her use before. "Not in you."

"Oh," she said after a moment of surprised silence.

"He asked you, not me. Why do you think that is?"

What a strange question. Was Jules expected to know the intricacies of Vivian and Simon's relationship? "I don't know."

Vivian gave her a hooded look. "No? You worked for him for some time."

Jules took a deep breath. "I guess he trusts me."

"And should he? Is that wise of him?"

A few months ago, Jules would have said "Sure." Not because she was working for Simon but because she considered herself a trustworthy person. Trustworthy and loyal. Now she understood that was a good thing—in the hands of the right person.

"I don't think he'll ask me again," she said.

Would Vivian hear what she was really saying? *You can trust me, Vivian. I'm yours now.*

Wait, that wasn't how she meant to put it, even in her own head. *I work for you now.* That was it.

Vivian gave her a long look. then followed it up with a slight nod, as if she'd heard it after all. "Call my driver. Let's go home."

Jules closed her eyes in gratitude. Excellent. She'd made it out of this conversation alive. Plus, it was ten thirty-five and they were on their way out the door. That hadn't happened in ages.

Jules called Ben, then happily followed Vivian to the elevators. Time to rush to the subway.

But when they got outside, Vivian pointed to the car. "Get in."

Jules looked at her, startled, before obeying. Yes, Vivian had given her a ride home once. She'd thought it had been a one-time thing after Vivian's shocking discovery. But tonight it was business as usual as Vivian rattled off a litany of instructions to be fulfilled tomorrow when they arrived at work. Tonight, when they pulled up to her house, Vivian told Jules, "Ben will pick you up at seven o'clock tomorrow morning. Make sure you're ready to go."

"What?"

But Vivian had already exited the car and was heading into her house. As she left, Jules heard her murmur something to Ben.

Ben closed Vivian's door. Jules met his gaze in the rearview mirror when he returned to his seat. "Where are you supposed to take me tomorrow morning?"

"*Du Jour*," he said patiently. "Where else? Well, after we pick her up, of course."

She looked at the back of his head, unable to speak for a full thirty seconds. Then she managed, "Huh?"

"Looks like you're the first stop on my route now. She just told me so."

Her jaw slowly sagged open. "Holy shit," she said, then, "oh no, you have to get up even earlier? I'm sorry, Ben."

"Well, it's not up to us, is it?" he said, but she detected annoyance in his voice anyway.

She closed her eyes. Great. She liked Ben: he'd always been friendly and helpful, and they'd shared a good laugh together once or twice about Vivian's eccentricities. Hopefully, he wouldn't resent her for this.

Besides, while the subway was a pain in the ass, it gave Jules time to wake up and get herself together before she had to face Vivian and *Du Jour*. Now she'd be at *Du Jour* from the moment she stepped out of the door in the morning to the moment she returned at night.

*Maybe she panics when she realizes you're more than ten feet away.*

Jules watched the insides of her eyelids and decided that what she wanted was to go to sleep and wake up to find that nothing was weird anymore. That'd be great.

"She was talking about you yesterday morning," Ben said.

Jules opened her eyes again.

"About your trip to Givenchy. The second one."

Her mouth parted.

"Said the way you handled yourself was quite impressive."

Jules's mouth snapped shut.

This time Ben's voice was good-natured when he said, "Keep it up and you'll be some kind of executive vice president this time next month."

"Yeah," she said softly. "I'll be something all right."

# CHAPTER 10

At first, Jules couldn't help being a little grumpy about the addition to her commute. The subway was faster by thirty minutes, give or take. Now Jules and Ben had a forty-minute drive from Jules's place on Clinton Street to Vivian's carriage house on West Seventy-Third. From there, it was another twenty minutes to Koening. She lost a precious half hour of sleep.

After a week, though, she had started to enjoy her job's latest…perk? Responsibility? New York in December wasn't a fun place to frolic. It was nice to sit in a warm car with heated leather seats and watch the world go by during the quiet moments.

Before, being quiet with Vivian had meant Jules was always on her toes, awaiting the next instruction, holding her tongue, or trying not to be noticed. Now it just meant…being quiet with Vivian.

Until one afternoon.

"Are the Christmas gifts arranged?" Vivian asked.

"Yes." Jules had created an email subfolder just to handle the order receipts from various merchants. Seeing the massive cash Vivian dropped on gifts for people she didn't even like was enough to make Jules advocate for the abolition of money. "I had to get on Simonelli about that espresso machine you're sending to Mordechai Rubinstein, but other than that, we're all ready."

"Good. Don't forget to—"

Vivian's stomach growled. Loudly. She went red and pinched her lips.

Jules kept her face as straight as possible. This happened from time to time, and besides, it was about two in the afternoon. Vivian had eaten lunch at eleven thirty. They were on their way back to the office, so Jules thought fast. A walnut salad? The bistro down the street did those, and Vivian liked them.

"Pizza," Vivian mumbled.

Jules glanced over, not sure she'd heard right. Then her brow cleared. Oh, of course. "I'll call La Borghese."

La Borghese was a tiny, ridiculously expensive pizzeria that had opened four months ago. They only made pies with fresh, organic stuff from local farmers markets, and they put weird toppings on them, which meant it was okay for rich people to eat there and act as if they weren't at a pizzeria.

"Not La Borghese." Vivian's voice was so low that Jules could barely hear her. Her face was even redder.

"Oh." Jules tried frantically to think of Italian restaurants Vivian liked that served pizza. It was a short list. "I'll try Vitali, then."

"I don't want Vitali. I don't want La Borghese." Vivian's face was going even redder.

Was she going to have a stroke? "Okay," she said helplessly. "So, um, what—"

Then she figured it out. Oh. Wow. Her fingers flew over her phone's display. The nearest pizza joint was two blocks down. "Uh, Ben, there's a place called Frankie's at—"

"I know the one." He flicked on his turn signal.

Jules glanced at Vivian, who refused to make eye contact even as she nodded. Then Jules dialed the number for the restaurant.

"Hi," she said when they picked up on the third ring. "I need to put in an order for pickup." She avoided looking at Ben. He was probably having as hard a time not laughing as she was.

Twenty minutes later, Vivian had her revenge. Of course she wasn't going to eat some greasy commercial pizza in front of anybody else, so Ben and Jules had to stand on the sidewalk, stamping their feet and watching their breath turn into ice crystals while Vivian wolfed down a pineapple-and-olive pizza in the comfort of the car. The toppings were disgusting. The cold was worse.

"London can't come soon enough," Ben muttered. He looked around nervously. The only parking space had been a loading zone, and it was a miracle nobody had yelled at them yet.

"God, yes," Jules agreed fervently. "Roll on, Christmas. It's not going to be any warmer in Philadelphia, but—"

"But it's not here," he said. "Lucky you. I'm stuck in town. How long will you be with your family?"

"I'm coming back to New York on the twenty-seventh."

"Any big plans for New Year's?"

"Not a one." Jules didn't pretend to sound disappointed. After the year-round whirl, she couldn't think of anything more heavenly than sitting on her sofa in sweatpants, watching the ball drop down in Times Square on TV. "What about you? You and Shelley having a night out?"

"Actually, Shelley and I broke up last week."

"Oh no!" Breaking up was shitty. Breaking up before the holidays seemed even worse. "I'm sorry, Ben."

"Yeah, well, it was the same old thing. Long hours, she never saw me. You know."

"Do I ever." Jules could just imagine Aaron's smirk right now.

"Yeah," he said, then added casually, "so I've been thinking, maybe if you're not doing anything—"

At that moment, Vivian rapped sharply on the window of her car door. The two of them jumped. Ben hopped immediately back into the driver's seat while Jules opened the door, took the pizza box from Vivian's hands (she'd eaten half the slices), and tossed it in the nearest trash can.

"We're late." Vivian glowered at the back of Ben's head like it was his fault. Her face was a little flushed, though, and her eyes actually seemed to glow with satisfaction.

Jules had seen herself looking like that a couple of times in the mirror. Usually after she'd just had good sex.

She looked out the window before Vivian could catch her staring. Well, heck, if Vivian could get some postcoital bliss from eating a pizza once in a while, good for her. It'd be good for everybody else around her too.

But the memory of Vivian's glow and the huskiness of her voice bothered Jules all day. For some damn reason.

---

Jules had the sinking feeling that Ben had been leading up to asking her out before Vivian interrupted him. That didn't have to be a bad thing.

He was nice and not much older than she was. Thirty or thereabouts. He'd never be able to complain about her long hours. And she had a feeling he'd actually be a lot of fun to hang out with outside of work.

But dipping into company ink was a bad idea. Honestly, he ought to know that, and she was kind of pissed he'd put her into the position of having to turn him down—if he had asked her.

Which he hadn't. And might not. So she ought to get over herself, all things considered.

Besides, after her breakup with Aaron, she wasn't really feeling men. It might not hurt to explore the other side of the fence again. It had been a while since she had enjoyed what a woman had to offer. Why not now?

Because she was too busy to breathe, that's why not.

Luckily, Jules and Ben were *both* so busy for the next few days that they didn't get a chance to talk, even when they were alone—they were still sleepy when Ben picked Jules up in the mornings and half-dead when he dropped her off at night. It probably wasn't good to have that much in common with somebody you dated.

---

Vivian left for London on the twenty-second. Jules accompanied her to the airport to take care of last-minute details and instructions before she vanished through the security checkpoint.

Now at said checkpoint, Vivian was glaring at the metal detectors, the long lines, and the miserable TSA agents. "Look at this. For God's sake, a handful of terrorists got lucky over two decades ago, and we're still making things as inconvenient as possible."

Jules looked deep within herself and failed to detect even trace amounts of sympathy. Vivian had Global Entry, which sped her through the security process. Plus she was traveling first class, which meant shorter lines for everything.

Meanwhile, Jules was taking the train to Philadelphia tonight, which wasn't exactly glamorous. But all she said was "yes, it's awful."

Vivian barreled on. "And when I spoke to Michelle this morning, I could barely understand what she was saying. Terrible phone reception."

Michelle was the temporary personal assistant Vivian had retained in London. Michelle's recruitment firm had pushed her forward as their best and brightest choice, and Vivian had accepted their recommendation with apparent disinterest.

Which was fine. Jules was not jealous. At all. It was temporary, and it would be nice for some other sucker to be at Vivian's beck and call for a few days.

Besides, Michelle wouldn't be as good at working for Vivian as Jules was. No way. This wasn't arrogance or anything, she told herself. Vivian was the arrogant one. It was just a fact.

"And the weather's dismal," Vivian continued. "They haven't seen the sun for days."

"I'm sorry," Jules said through her teeth. *Gosh, going to London for Christmas and you've got some fog. How terrible.* Vivian should have rented in Tahiti instead.

"And of course I'm going to have to check in with Preston almost every day," she spat, "now that Robert—"

Vivian suddenly seemed to realize where they were and how angry she sounded because she cut herself off.

Jules stayed quiet this time. Robert had been remarkably amenable so far to Vivian's request that he sign himself right out of his own kid's life. Preston was still drawing up the paperwork, ensuring there were no loopholes.

It was pissing Vivian off like nothing else. She probably hadn't expected Robert to put up *no* resistance. She'd been anticipating battle and victory. Instant surrender wasn't as satisfying.

Vivian looked at the security lines and sighed as if she were about to be led off to a firing squad. "Well, here we go."

Jules cleared her throat.

Vivian glanced over at her.

She hoped her smile didn't look too timid or weird. "Have a good trip," she said. "Oh, and, um, Merry Christmas. Or happy holidays. Whichever."

Vivian's lips quirked up in something very smile-like, but it disappeared almost immediately. Then to Jules's shock, she said, "You as well," before heading for the Global Entry line.

Jules left right away, already thinking about whether she'd packed everything yet and what time she'd have to leave her apartment for Penn Station. Before she turned the corner, she looked over her shoulder just in time to see Vivian dropping her Marni bag on the conveyer belt with an expression of profound irritation.

Jules laughed and hurried for the exit. To her surprise, Ben was still waiting at the curb. Jules dithered for a second, then got in the back seat. Getting in the front would have given him the wrong idea.

"You didn't have to wait," she said. "I was going to take the subway home."

"Yeah, well, my afternoon's kind of open now." He sounded downright perky.

Jules couldn't blame him. She closed her eyes, luxuriating in the realization of her own freedom for the next week.

"What time's your train?" he asked.

"At 6:05 p.m." Jules checked her watch. It was 2:45 now. She wanted to be at the station about twenty minutes before departure. The subway was going to be nuts, so she should leave by—

"Want a lift there?" Ben said.

Jules managed a weak little smile. *Crap.* "Oh, no, Ben. I'll be fine. Thanks, though."

"I mean, I wouldn't mind, you know?"

"I know." She tilted her head toward the window, toward the crush of traffic outside. "But I'm not going to make you get out in this again when you don't have to. I'll be fine. Thanks," she added, hoping her tone was final enough without sounding mean.

"Well, if you're sure." To her relief, he didn't press.

Looking for an excuse not to talk for the next half hour, Jules said, "You mind if I catch some shut-eye? I hardly slept at all last night, and getting back together with my family's going to be chaos."

"I guess I can hold off on playing deadmau5," he said.

Jules couldn't stop a smile. He really was nice. But…no. Bad, bad idea.

"You get some rest," he added.

Jules hadn't planned on actually falling asleep, but she did. It was a nice surprise.

# CHAPTER 11

Being back in her parents' house was like being on a different planet. Her dad had given her a bear hug at the train station, her mom had kissed both her cheeks when she'd walked through the door, and her older sister, Robin, had squeezed her tightly. Jules hadn't realized how much she'd missed affectionate physical contact since Aaron had left.

She remembered Vivian touching her hand over a cup of La Colombe.

Oh no. This wasn't happening. Vivian Carlisle was not going to cross her mind again until Jules had to return to New York.

Easier said than done. Everyone wanted to know about her exciting job working for a fashion publication in Manhattan. When she went out for a few drinks with college buddies, when she helped her sister set the table, even when she was hanging out with extended family at a party, Jules found herself trotting out the same old stories about busy days, late nights, designers, and celebrities.

And influencers. Her two younger cousins were excited about Jules getting to meet people with popular Instagram accounts and YouTube channels, and they wanted to know if Jules had any tips for growing their own audiences.

"I don't do a lot with social media," she tried telling them. "I've got a Twitter account, but I don't have time to update it much." She also hated Twitter. As a hustling writer, that was a cardinal sin, but she couldn't help it. Her life was already full of frenetic activity—no need to add constant online chatter to the mix. "Mainly I'm a writer."

"Where?" her fourteen-year-old cousin Madison asked. "Do you write for *Du Jour*?"

She'd be laughed out of town if she tried. "Maybe I will someday, but right now I'm just trying to break in. It's tough. In fact, I've submitted to—"

Her twelve-year-old cousin Daniel looked at Madison. "Do you have the Switch? I want to play Mario Kart."

"Let me get it," Madison said with a clear expression of relief. "That's, uh, really cool, Jules. Bye!"

Jules could take a hint. So much for the youth. In the meantime, *The Cut* still hadn't gotten back to her, so Sigourney Weaver hadn't been a good bet either.

Onward, then. Vox should be her next stop. At least she could try more serious fare.

Something had to land eventually.

---

On the morning before Christmas, Jules and her mother were drinking coffee at the kitchen table. "So," her mother said, "any boys in the picture? Men," she amended quickly.

Jules sighed. Surprising that her mom had waited two whole days. "Not unless you count Vivian's driver," she said gloomily. "I think he wants to ask me out."

"Is he nice?"

Jules glared at her. "You're the one who told me never to get involved with anybody I work with. You always said it was bad news."

"Well, yes," her mother said, "but is he nice?"

Jules groaned and took another sip of coffee. "Can we please change the subject?"

There was a pause. Then her mom said, a bit hesitantly, "Any…girls?"

Jules almost choked on her coffee.

"I'm just asking. I remember in college, you and—what's her name?"

"Chelsea," Jules said, her hands tightening on her mug. Chelsea had been a brief relationship in her junior year at Penn. They'd spent four months together before deciding they were incompatible, and Jules had met Aaron shortly after that. It was the only relationship with a woman she'd ever had, and sometimes she thought it had been a mistake to tell her parents. It let them ask awkward questions about more than one gender while clearly hoping she'd pick one over the other.

"Yes, Chelsea! So, you know, any girls?" Her mom's voice was too bright, too full of hope that Jules would say no.

"No," Jules said, trying not to sound depressed about it.

She gave her mom credit for keeping the relief off her face. "Well, just as long as you're happy, honey."

"Oh yeah." Jules rose to her feet and took her coffee cup to the sink, even though it was still a quarter full. "I'm happy, Mom. Trust me."

---

The morning of Christmas Eve dawned. Jules woke up already excited, as if she were a kid again.

The Morettis' Christmas Eve followed a well-ordered tradition. It was filled with delicious food and last-minute gift wrapping. Jules's grandparents arrived for dinner, armed with hugs for Jules, Robin, and Robin's fiancé, Rick. Post-midnight mass, the family stayed up late drinking eggnog and singing Christmas carols, the quality of which decreased correspondingly with the eggnog intake.

By two o'clock in the morning, they'd be laughing more than they were singing and would applaud themselves before staggering off to bed. The older she got, the more Jules grew to appreciate it; time with her family felt more precious than any gift she'd receive the next morning.

Thinking of this and looking forward to the evening, Jules was ensconced in the recliner in the den. Might be time for a nap. She was just contemplating the climb upstairs to her bedroom when she heard her phone ringing in the kitchen. Groaning, she lumbered to her feet.

She idly checked the screen. Then she gasped. Vivian was calling. *Vivian* was calling. And even after all the surprises of the past few months, it seemed highly unlikely she just wanted to wish Jules a merry Christmas Eve.

Her father, who was sitting at the kitchen table, looked up from his newspaper. "What's wrong?" he asked.

"Nothing," Jules lied as she answered the phone. "Hello, Vivian?"

Her father sat up ramrod straight. "You're kidding. Isn't she in Lon—"

She held up a hand for silence as Vivian barked, "Michelle has *pneumonia*."

"Uh…" Still stuffed and sleepy, Jules couldn't think of anything to say but "I'm sorry." She grimaced; she had to do better than that. "I mean, is she—"

"I dismissed her immediately, of course. I can't have an assistant who coughs her lungs up all over my schedule."

Jules shook her head as if that would help to clear it. "I'm, uh, sorry. Are you asking me to find a replacement or…"

"Be here by tomorrow," Vivian said.

Jules's voice died in her throat, and she stood stock-still at her parents' kitchen counter, looking out the familiar window and watching traffic go by on the street where she'd grown up.

"Julia?" Vivian snapped, and Jules jumped.

Her father had risen to his feet and was looking at her with concern.

"Tomorrow?" Jules was short of air. "Vivian, I can't. I'm home with my family—"

"Philadelphia has direct flights to London. I checked."

"You did?" Jules blurted out. Then she recovered. "I mean, I guess so. But my passport is in New York."

"*What?*" her dad said. "She can't possibly want you to—"

She flapped her hand frantically at him. "Listen," she said, inspired, "I know the London agency has other PAs. I'll get them to send one over right now, and you won't have the hassle of waiting for me."

"Is there some part of 'be here by tomorrow' that you didn't understand?" Vivian's voice was a dangerous murmur.

Jules dug her free hand into her hair. "No, but—"

"Let me repeat myself, just in case: I. Want. You. Here."

Jules closed her eyes. The words rolled through her, electric and irresistible. And that's all there was to it. She was going to London, like it or not.

She didn't like it. She couldn't *possibly* like it.

"Use the company expense account," Vivian continued. "Fly first class. There should be some available seats. You know how to make it happen."

Of course she did. Vivian Carlisle's name opened doors in a way that had to be seen to be believed. That didn't make this okay. "I do, but—"

"Stopping by New York first will slow you down." Vivian's voice dripped with scorn for Jules's thoughtlessness in not bringing her passport to Philadelphia. "Get the first flight out that you can."

"Vivian—"

"I'll see you tomorrow." She ended the call.

Jules stared at the phone in her hand, her head whirling, wondering if she was about to pass out. Or if she could just go upstairs, take that nap she wanted, and pretend she'd never gotten a phone call at all. No, that was no good. Her heart was pounding so hard, she'd never get to sleep.

"Jules?" her dad asked, looking at her with wide eyes.

She met his eyes with a flinch. "Um," she said miserably, "can you drive me to the train station?"

# CHAPTER 12

Her family put up a fuss, but in the end, there wasn't much they could do. It wasn't until a tearful Jules was on the verge of calling an Uber that her father consented to give her a lift to the station.

During the car ride, Jules realized she hadn't told anybody in her family about Vivian's pregnancy. It wouldn't exactly be a violation of her unwritten confidentiality agreement if she told her dad. It wasn't like the Morettis would tell all of Twitter.

So she spilled the beans, concluding with "And her husband doesn't even want anything to do with it. He's been cheating on her for months!"

Her father wasn't entirely unsympathetic. "That's a lousy thing to go through, no matter how rich and famous you are. And I'm sorry it's happening to her. But, sweetie, it's ludicrous that she's calling you and threatening you and…" His voice dropped into a growl. "People aren't things, Jules."

"I know," she pleaded. "But…I don't know. I mean…" She looked down at the hands in her lap, then back at him. "She needs me."

Her father rolled his eyes.

"No." Suddenly, Jules had to make him understand. It'd be tough since she didn't understand it herself. "I know it's weird, but it's true. I'm practically the only person she talks to now. I'm the only one in the office she's even told officially."

Her father slammed his hands against the steering wheel and scowled. "You shouldn't be in that position."

It wasn't anything Jules hadn't thought before, but she heard herself say, "It's not Vivian's fault this happened to her."

Her father sighed. "I don't know what to tell you that I haven't already said. You're grown up, and you're on your own. You make your own decisions."

The words suddenly made Jules feel very young indeed, and she fumed in silence the rest of the way to the station.

---

An exhausted Jules exited Heathrow Airport to find Jimmy, Vivian's London driver, waiting for her in a Jaguar XF. She'd called him the moment she'd landed and the flight attendants said it was okay.

"Glad you made it all right," he said. "There's bottled water, if you're thirsty."

"No, I'm okay."

"Happy Christmas, then."

Jules fought the urge to glare at him. He was just trying to be nice. He probably didn't want to be working on Christmas either. "Thanks. You too."

"Plans got spoiled, I expect. London's a good town, though. Been here before?"

"No. I've always wanted to."

"Well, there you are," he said heartily.

"Um…yeah." Jules sat back and looked at her phone. She'd flown out of New York at 10:30 p.m. on Christmas Eve and had staggered into Heathrow at 10:30 a.m. on Christmas Day, local time. Jet lag was going to suck, and worse, she'd be the only one suffering through it. Vivian would have adjusted to the time change and would be as fresh as a daisy.

Coffee would help. Jules leaned toward the pod-style coffeemaker nestled between the front seats and picked up a pod. Sumatra blend, nice.

"Looking forward to the luncheon?" he asked.

She looked up with a frown. "The what?"

"The luncheon. Didn't you know?" He glanced at her in the rearview mirror. "When I told Ms. Carlisle what time you were getting in, she told me to make sure you got there in time to attend."

*Fantastic.* Jules dropped the coffee pod back into its holder with a moan. "No, I didn't know. Where is it? What's this luncheon for?"

Hold it. She knew this. Vivian's itinerary was already etched into her brain and had been for weeks. Today was Christmas, which meant, oh God, it was—

"The Christmas Day luncheon at the Ritz," he said. "In the Music Room. Loads of publishing supremos. Very posh."

Jules looked down with horror at her wrinkled pants and shirt. "We're going straight there?"

"Yes," Jimmy said patiently.

No. No way could she show up like this. "We have to make a quick stop somewhere. It won't take me more than a few minutes to change. Please!"

He quickly held up a placating hand. "Don't worry, we'll set it right. Let's see… My friends John and Nora have a flat not too far out of the way. I'll ring them, see if they're home."

Twenty-five minutes later, Jules was practically sobbing with gratitude in front of a bemused-looking British woman. Christmas music played merrily in the background.

"Well, Jimmy's told us stories about Vivian Carlisle," Nora said, looking over at him with wide eyes. She had a sprig of holly pinned to her sweater. "I suppose they must be true. Here, you can change in our bedroom, love. Down the hall."

Jules hauled her suitcase to the bedroom and threw it open. There must be something that would work. "Very posh," Jimmy had said, but how posh was posh? It was lunch, so no evening gowns, which was good because Jules hadn't thought to pack one, though obviously she should have. *Shit!* Well maybe this gray skirt would do. And this green blouse. And these black heels.

Dammit, she looked like a secretary. Well, she kind of was a secretary, but still… She rummaged around her jewelry and found a pair of pearl drop earrings to lend the ensemble a little more elegance. She could fix her makeup and hair in the car.

"Thank you so much," she said as she hurried back out into the living room.

Jimmy stepped forward to take her bag.

"Oh, don't you look nice," Nora said.

"Really?" Jules looked down at herself anxiously.

"Oh yes," Nora said. "Very sophisticated. I especially like those pearl earrings." Her voice was a little too placating, but Jules decided to take what she could get and thanked her yet again.

"I'll tell John about this," Nora said. "He won't half laugh." She took Jules's hand and squeezed it. "Enjoy your party."

"I'll do my best," Jules muttered, and she and Jimmy hurried back down to the car.

"We'll be cutting it a bit close," Jimmy said as Jules slapped on lip gloss in the back seat. "But we ought to get you there in time. It's just that Ms. Carlisle is—"

"—particular about this kind of thing," Jules finished for him. "Believe me, I know." She put away her lip gloss and spent a risky couple of minutes with her mascara wand before deciding she looked good enough—well, except for the dark circles beneath her eyes—and then she went to work on her hair.

Thick, wavy locks were a nightmare to arrange at the last minute. There was only so much she could do with a brush and a few bobby pins, but by the time Jimmy pulled up to the Ritz, she'd managed an acceptable—if slightly sloppy—bun. Hopefully, it would pass for shabby-chic sloppy instead of I-practically-got-dressed-in-the-car sloppy. Either way, it was too late to do anything about it now.

Time to enter the fray.

# CHAPTER 13

The Music Room was...pink.

Seriously so. Pink chairs, pink tablecloths, wide stripes of pink on every wall. It was like stumbling into the world's fanciest gender-reveal party. At least the elaborate holiday décor provided some relief: holly, ivy, ornaments, and gold ribbons were everywhere. Two splendid Christmas trees didn't hurt either.

The room was also filled with flower-festooned round tables. A string quartet played unobtrusively in a corner. The food hadn't been served yet, so everyone was still standing in little groups, chatting and laughing through their teeth as they sipped from glasses of wine or the occasional cup of tea. All very civilized.

But make no mistake, blood was in the water. It always was. When you got this rich and this powerful, you lost any sense of proportion. Or so Jules had observed over the past few years. The more these people had, the more they wanted. At this level, it was rarely about material possessions. It was about dominance. Being the best.

Right at that moment, she saw Vivian in the corner of the room talking to a couple of people. She looked transformed. Gone was the weariness. Today Vivian's head was held up high, her pixie hair as precise as if she'd been to the salon two minutes ago. Her emerald sheath dress could have come right off the Proenza Schouler runway. Unlike Jules, she didn't look like someone who'd stumbled off a plane before being thrown into the maw of high society.

She looked incredible.

Then Vivian looked up and saw Jules staring at her from the doorway. Her eyes widened, and a spasm of panic hit Jules. *Shit!* Her outfit was gauche. Her hair looked awful. Her makeup was clownish. She'd flown all the way out here only to disgrace Vivian and embarrass herself in front of some of the most powerful people in the industry. She should just bolt.

Before she could, Vivian gestured imperiously for Jules to join her. Her face had already reverted back to its cool mask. Jules headed toward her on shaking knees. Maybe after mumbling a hello, she could lurk in the corner until this was over. Or until Vivian ordered her out of the room in disgust.

But as she approached the group—Vivian, two men, and another woman—Vivian turned to look at her again. Her gaze was neither hard nor disapproving. It was almost…amiable.

Jules blinked. Vivian never shied away from expressing her displeasure, even in front of other people, since she could do it so well without speaking a word. Maybe she didn't look as bad as she feared. Clinging to a newfound shred of confidence, Jules managed a smile for everyone and said, "Hello." It only came out a little bit squeaky.

Vivian came forward and said, "Hello, Julia," then—what the ever-loving bejesused fucking *fuck?*—leaned in and kissed the air to either side of her cheeks. Vivian's skin was soft and warm as she brushed against Jules's face.

When Vivian pulled away, Jules fumbled for an expression that wasn't shocked. A smile would do. Hopefully, it didn't look too ghastly.

Her face was tingling. It was not unpleasant.

"This is my assistant, Julia Moretti," Vivian said to the three others. "She's just arrived from Philadelphia this morning." Her voice was pleasant without being cooing or false, just as if she were introducing a friend or something.

"How nice to meet you," one of the men, a portly, balding guy in his midfifties, said. He held out his hand. "Geoffrey Barnhardt."

Jules shook it while Vivian said, "Geoffrey is the managing director of Koening's operations in the UK. And these are the Goldsteins…"

During the next ten minutes, Jules found herself being introduced to several ritzy-looking people who drifted toward and then away from Vivian as she held court, letting people come to her. This shindig wasn't her doing, but somehow she still managed to be the center of attention.

Everyone here knew her. Few liked her. Most of them feared her. That was obvious right away.

Then it was time to be seated for the actual food. Jules scanned the tables and saw tiny nameplates at each place. Rats—she hadn't been able to look around before Vivian had pulled her aside. Everybody else had already had time to find out where they were sitting.

Jules didn't want to be the only one wandering around like an idiot, so she dared to ask Vivian, "Sorry, but do you know where I'm supposed to sit? I haven't had a chance to—"

"We're at the center table." Vivian gestured, then proceeded like a queen to the center table with Jules trailing in her wake.

It wasn't until catching other people watching her with raised eyebrows that Jules realized how unusual this had to look. The center table was prime real estate at any function and usually occupied only by the people in charge and their most important guests. People like Jules, if they were lucky enough to get invited at all, always sat at the tables on the outermost periphery. But there it was, a tiny card made of embossed cream paper with Jules's name in beautiful calligraphy, right next to Vivian's.

She lowered herself into her seat, feeling as if everybody in the room were watching her. Which they weren't. Of course they weren't.

Vivian was already chatting with the man seated at her left, and the woman on Jules's right was talking to the person on *her* other side, so Jules was left to sit mutely and try not to fidget. Fortunately, at that moment, waiters emerged carrying trays of salad with scallops and prawns. Jules had eaten a decent breakfast a few hours ago on the flight—first class food was a world apart from coach—but her mouth still watered, and she had to force herself to eat sparingly. It would look bad for Vivian Carlisle's assistant to gobble her food like a starving animal.

She glanced at Vivian, who appeared to have the same problem. Hunger pangs again, and not a pizza in sight. Jules bit her lip and looked back down at her salad; if Vivian caught her smirking, she'd be more likely to slap Jules's cheek than air-kiss it.

Jules blushed again. That had been so weird. So unexpected. Nobody at *Du Jour* would ever believe it. Why were her fingertips tingling again?

The woman on Jules's right turned to her. They had already been introduced, but, to her horror, Jules realized that she couldn't remember anything about her. She looked to be in her late forties, possibly early fifties, with blonde hair a few shades more natural than Vivian's.

"Did I hear that you have just come today from Philadelphia?" the woman asked with a German accent.

"Yes, ma'am," Jules said. "I was visiting my family for the holidays." *Was* being the operative word.

"I've never been to Philadelphia. Is it far from New York?"

"Er, no. A little over an hour by train."

The woman pursed her lips. "One of your famous figures lived there, I think. What was his name…Franklin?"

Jules straightened with pride that absolutely would have labeled her a nerd back in school. "Ben Franklin, yes! He did a lot for the city. It's a pretty cool place, actually, though people tend to ignore it in favor of New York. Lots of history."

Oh no. She was rambling. The German woman was already starting to look bored. Jules fumbled for something more interesting. "Where are you from?"

"Berlin."

"Oh, there's a lot of history there too," she said as her brain scrambled to catch up with her mouth. "Uh, the war, and Soviet occupation, and…so much." *Shut up, shut up!*

Vivian cleared her throat. "Helga, how's your son doing?"

Oh, thank God. Jules was saved. Helga Schumann was her name. And her husband Georg sat to Helga's right. He was a big shot executive who owned tons of shares in Delton Wright, Koening's main rival publishing house. Corporate scuttlebutt was that they'd tried to lure Vivian away from Koening several times over the years.

"Karl is wonderful," Mrs. Schumann gushed, looking away from Jules as if she'd already forgotten all about her. "He turned sixteen last Wednesday. He's at the top of his class. We are so proud."

"How wonderful." Vivian's voice was bland.

"And you, my dear." Mrs. Schumann returned her attention to Jules with a gleam of interest in her eyes. "You look so young! How old are you?"

"Twenty-five." Was Mrs. Schumann about to take revenge for Jules's conversational idiocy?

"A baby," cooed Mrs. Schumann. "Isn't she, Vivian?"

Vivian's expression remained inscrutable as she sipped her water. "I wouldn't say that."

"Hmm, I suppose not. But doesn't it seem that as we get older, twenty-five seems younger and younger? I thought I was so wise at that age." Mrs. Schumann shook her head. "But it does seem like that. Perhaps they are just taking longer to mature than we did."

Jules didn't love being talked about as if she weren't there. "I don't know, Mrs. Schumann. I think in some ways we're having to grow up faster than our parents did."

Mrs. Schumann's eyes widened.

Vivian inhaled audibly through her nose.

"Although you're both younger than my parents!" Jules added instantly. "I wasn't implying—um, ha-ha."

Helga Schumann pursed her lips, then opened her mouth to reply.

"You aren't completely wrong, Julia," Vivian said mildly.

Jules actually grabbed the arm of her chair to make sure she wasn't about to fall out of it.

"The amount of time your age group spends on social media is both a blessing and a curse," Vivian continued. "It's made you socially aware and tragically misinformed."

"Social media!" said Mrs. Schumann. "Do not get me started!"

"I wouldn't dream of it, Helga," Vivian said.

Jules tried to shrink down into her seat as the two women stared at each other, Mrs. Schumann trying to decide if she'd been insulted, Vivian cool as a cucumber.

Thankfully, at that moment, Georg Schumann said something to the man on his right, and Mrs. Schumann turned from Jules to participate in the conversation.

Jules gave Vivian an apologetic look. Vivian returned a look that seemed sort of…amused. Which had to be impossible.

Suddenly, Jules desperately wanted to know how she was—if she was less fatigued, if she was eating enough, sleeping well. But of course she couldn't ask any of that here, so she just said, "Have you heard from Simon since you arrived?"

There. Conversation that wasn't small talk. Vivian had limited tolerance for small talk.

Vivian sniffed. "The LA pictures didn't come out as well as either of us had hoped. But they could be worse, I suppose. We'll make do."

*We'll make do?* That one sentence told Jules volumes about how Vivian felt. She never "made do." Was she tired, or was she bending to Mark Tavio's pressure to keep costs down? Or both?

She wondered yet again what Mr. Tavio would say when he learned that Vivian was pregnant and the circumstances surrounding it. Robert dumping her, an extremely acrimonious divorce, Vivian being a single mom… It'd be all over the papers, on the lips of all of New York society. Of course, it would reflect on *Du Jour*, on Koening, whether that was fair or not.

Jules had heard that any publicity was good publicity. She just hoped Mr. Tavio felt the same way. Vivian had threatened legal action if he didn't, if she faced any discrimination related to her pregnancy, but she was fighting so many battles right now—would she have energy for one more?

"What?" Vivian's eyes narrowed, and Jules realized she'd been staring with what was probably a blank, stupid-looking expression.

"Oh!" she said. "Sorry. I was just, um…"

Vivian tilted her head away as if already bored by whatever excuse Jules was about to offer and turned to speak to the man on her left again.

Feeling oddly dejected, Jules spent the next ten minutes poking at her food. She should just stay quiet and pray she wasn't noticed for the rest of the meal. That'd be a dumb move, though. She was wasting an opportunity to meet important people. How many assistants got a chance like this?

So she made a deliberate effort to make eye contact with and smile at those important people over the roast fillet of halibut. By the time dessert was served, she was chatting shyly with none other than Vincent Wright: the CEO of Delton Wright, the host of the luncheon and clearly the most important person in the room.

Vivian appeared pleased that Jules was managing to fumble her way through a conversation about Broadway musicals, which was something, anyway. She also looked relieved not to be speaking. Was that why she'd wanted Jules at the luncheon, to take up some of the slack?

If so, that was pretty easy. Once Jules had engaged the CEO's attention, naturally everybody else wanted to get in on the conversation, and she didn't have to say much after the initial observation on how much she'd liked *Hadestown*. The conversation ran from there. It turned out some of the most important people in publishing were dying to talk about show tunes, so long as Mr. Wright was too.

Vivian said little but sipped from her water glass and looked idly around the table, moving her gaze from face to face. Even the quickest of glances told Jules that she was tired.

*Well, that makes two of us.* Her former irritation returned just the tiniest bit. This might be a great opportunity, but she was starting to fade again, now that the initial rush of adrenaline was wearing off.

Then she was saved yet again. Jules hadn't even taken one bite of her cardamom cream with basil jelly when Vivian announced, "This has been wonderful, Vincent, but I've got to run."

Mr. Wright didn't look surprised, but he put up a token protest anyway, along with the other people at the table. "So soon, Vivian? Surely you can have dessert."

Vivian shook her head, wearing a fake gracious smile. "Thank you, but jet lag strikes again. Let's go, Julia."

Jules quickly put her spoon down, dabbed at her mouth with her napkin, and rose to her feet while a nearby waiter pulled out Vivian's chair for her. All the men at the table stood.

Jules smiled at everyone and said, "It was so nice to meet all of you. Thank you very much," she added to Mr. Wright. "I had a lovely time."

He shook her hand. "A pleasure to meet you, Julia. Happy Christmas. Enjoy London."

Best not to say that she probably wouldn't see much of it. Instead, Jules thanked him again, then quickly followed Vivian, who was already hightailing it out of the room, pausing only to wave at certain acquaintances on her way out.

Once they'd left the room, Jules pulled out her phone to call Jimmy and tell him they were ready to go.

"Get my mink." She handed Jules her coat check ticket.

Jules hurried to fetch their things and returned wearing her own coat and carrying Vivian's mink stole.

Jules slid the garment around Vivian's shoulders. Lately she'd been allowed to help with stuff like that. Jules had no idea why, what it meant, or if it meant anything. Vivian could just be tired. Or distracted.

Either way, it wasn't the worst feeling to watch Vivian Carlisle's slender shoulders disappear beneath the luxurious fur.

They reached the curb as Jimmy pulled up. "Home, Ms. Carlisle?" he asked as they settled in.

"Yes." She closed her eyes briefly, then gazed out the window. They'd just pulled into traffic when she murmured, "Thank God that's over."

"The food was nice," Jules offered.

"The fish was bland and poorly cooked."

"Except for the fish," Jules mumbled.

Vivian sighed. She rested a hand on the black Hermès clutch in her lap, tapping her fingernails on the pebble-grained goatskin. "You're too easily impressed. A little longer at this and you'll acquire—"

*Snobbery.*

"—enough taste to tell the mediocre from the good. Don't be overwhelmed by a famous venue and a pretty room."

Hey, that wasn't fair. Since she'd started at *Du Jour,* Jules had seen plenty of famous venues, and it wasn't like Penn hadn't had its own fair share of opportunities. She'd studied abroad in Italy for a semester and seen some of the world's most beautiful buildings, fashion, and artwork. She hadn't been invited to sit down with the Pope, but being in his general vicinity had to count for something.

She meant to say so, but what came out of her mouth was, "That 'pretty room' was too pink."

A poorly muffled laugh emanated from the driver's seat.

Vivian frowned at the back of Jimmy's head. "I didn't know your standards were so high, Julia. I didn't mean to bring you to a hole in the wall for lunch."

"Wait, no," Jules said in horror. "I—"

"And to make you slum it with such unimportant people."

"I didn't mean that!" Jules dug her fingers into her skirt.

"What *did* you mean?"

"I just meant I wasn't... I knew how sophisticated the venue was, Vivian. And I *really* appreciate that I got to meet all those people. Thank you. But I don't just walk around with stars in my eyes instead of paying attention."

Vivian regarded her for a long moment. "You do pay attention to things," she said eventually. "I've noticed that."

Jules's job was about paying attention, noting the minutiae of what each day needed. But that was every PA's job. Vivian meant it in a different way. It wasn't totally clear how, but Jules dared to glow anyway.

"You handled yourself well," Vivian said absently.

That wasn't how Jules remembered it. "I did?"

"Once you got past your history lesson, yes." As Jules cringed, Vivian waved her hand. "Talking to Helga Schumann is an Olympic trial in patience. Nobody likes her. You did better with the people who mattered."

Jules's shoulders relaxed. "I'm glad."

She didn't seem to care whether Jules was glad or not. She turned to look out her window.

Jules should do the same. She was on her first trip to London and hadn't once taken the time to look at her surroundings. It was a city she'd always wanted to visit.

But for some reason, when she tried to focus on the scenery, she couldn't take any of it in. She remembered the air kiss Vivian had given her. Her cheeks burned again, and she wondered if she'd fallen into some alternate dimension.

"Now," Vivian said out of nowhere, "we need to discuss tomorrow."

Oh. Right. Jules was here to work. She pulled out her phone. "Do you want me to schedule a meeting with someone?"

"Why would I want that?"

She blinked at Vivian, who frowned right back.

"Then…um, what do you want?"

"It's dinner at the Chislehursts'," she replied slowly, as if speaking to an idiot. "Don't you remember? That's what's on the schedule for tomorrow. The only thing. I had to give up my Christmas Day to a bunch of sharks. Is it asking too much that I get the day after—one single day—for myself? What are you staring at?"

"Nothing. I don't know. What?" Jules pushed a stray curl out of her face, knowing she'd narrowed her eyes in disbelief. "You don't have anything for me to do tomorrow?"

Vivian had called her way the hell out here, and there wasn't even anything for Jules to *do*? Was she out of her mind?

"Did I say that?" Vivian examined Jules's outfit. "That skirt's all right, but you'll want a different top for the evening. Lady Chislehurst is obsessed with formalities, but you'll never meet a better canapé in your life. I repeat, what are you *staring* at?"

"I'm going with you to the..." There was no point in finishing the question. She was going to meet the Chislehursts, whoever they were. And that was it? That couldn't be right. Vivian wouldn't have flown her all the way out here just to be her fucking dinner companion. She couldn't be in that desperate need of a, of a—

She closed her eyes, took a deep breath, and collected herself. *Don't think. Just do. Don't think. Just do.* "What time are we leaving?"

"Seven." Vivian still didn't look her way.

"Fine."

The slightest blush was creeping up Vivian's throat, though whether it was from anger or embarrassment, Jules couldn't be sure. The woman must know how ridiculous this was.

She must really feel like shit to pull this kind of stunt for company.

"So, what are we doing tonight?" Jules heard herself ask.

Vivian turned quickly to look back at her. "Do you have short-term amnesia or something? The schedule—"

"I know what's on it." Jules dropped her phone in her lap. "The schedule says *Christmas Day*, just like the calendar. What are we doing for Christmas?"

Vivian sneered. "I didn't think you were the sentimental type. Maybe we should go home and watch *It's a Wonderful Life*?"

"Maybe we should. Or some dumb Christmas movie on Lifetime. Do they have Lifetime here?"

"Are you kidding?"

Jules crossed her arms.

"I don't like Christmas," Vivian said.

Jules fought back the urge to laugh. Of course Vivian didn't like Christmas. She was the most fashionable Grinch ever. She probably also disliked kittens, rainbows, and sunsets. "Well, I love Christmas. I was going to celebrate it with my family, but now I'm here."

Vivian crossed her own arms, far more elegantly than Jules had. With the tilt of her head, she could have been a queen glaring at an impertinent subject. "Celebrating it with me?"

"Celebrating it with you," Jules confirmed.

"Don't be ridiculous."

"I'm not being ridiculous. It's not like I expect a present or anything."

What would a present from Vivian Carlisle be? A book titled *An Underling's Guide to Debasing Yourself More Efficiently*?

"You don't?" Vivian asked. "Then you must not have noticed the one you just got."

"Huh?"

Vivian gave her a level look. "Didn't you just say you appreciated meeting some of the most powerful people in publishing?"

Jules returned her look, dumbfounded.

"Do you think that disease-riddled PA was going to sit at my table? Or that she was attending at all?"

Her head was spinning again. The luncheon had been her Christmas present? It was supposed to make up for snatching Jules out of the bosom of her own family?

Yes, it was. In Vivian's world, it was adequate compensation and then some. She had fled from Toledo, Ohio, to more glamorous things as soon as she could. She couldn't imagine that everybody else wouldn't have done the same. She'd given Jules the kind of present she would have wanted for herself.

It was weirdly sweet. And also pretty messed up.

All she could think to say was, "I…guess she wasn't."

"You guess correctly." Vivian snapped open her black clutch and peered inside. "Anyway, that's enough sentiment. If you're insisting on Christmas, then have at it, although I have no idea what it's supposed to look like."

Jules just bet she didn't. "I know what it looks like. Let me take care of it." *It's what I do best, and you know it.*

"Well, Julia, I'm intrigued now." Vivian raised an eyebrow. "Fine. Impress me. For Christmas."

"I will."

They rode in silence then. Jules took another deep breath and looked out the window once more. Now was as good a moment as any to get that passing glimpse of London.

Although, who knew? Vivian might just decide to take her on a personal tour of St. Paul's Cathedral and the Tower of London. Jules's parents had gone to London on vacation last year, and they'd raved about both places.

Oh dammit! She'd forgotten to text her parents when she arrived. She'd call them at Vivian's place instead. They must be worried. They'd also want to know what the deal was here.

Too bad Jules would have no idea what to tell them.

# CHAPTER 14

Jimmy set Jules's luggage in an out-of-the-way corner of Vivian's townhouse where it could remain until Jules knew where she'd be staying that night. Normally she'd have found that out before leaving New York, but her usual acumen was out of whack. It hadn't occurred to her to ask, and Vivian hadn't bothered to tell.

Jimmy discreetly left. Jules put her coat and Vivian's stole in a nearby hall closet and turned around to see Vivian standing there in the hallway, looking lost.

Maybe that was because this wasn't really her house. It didn't look like anyone's house. There were no Christmas decorations, no merry holiday music like at John and Nora's flat. It felt so empty.

Without Jimmy's eyes on her, Vivian took a step backward that almost looked like a stagger.

Jules's eyes widened in alarm.

Vivian righted herself and rubbed a hand over her forehead. "Whatever you're plotting for tonight, give it a rest first. We can both use one."

Wow. Jules hadn't expected that, and some rest before she enacted her plan sounded like heaven. Then she wondered where exactly she was supposed to get said rest, since she didn't even know where she was supposed to stay. Perhaps Vivian had a hotel in mind already—if not, Jules was on her own to figure something out while half-dead with fatigue.

"Okay," she said. "Er, where would you like me to go?"

"Up here." Vivian headed for a nearby staircase.

Jules rocked back on her feet, too stunned to follow her.

"You might as well get your bags," Vivian added acidly.

Jules turned around and headed mechanically back toward the front door. Here? She was staying here? In Vivian's house?

Well, she supposed that made sense on some planet that wasn't this one. It'd mean Jules was available 24/7 without Vivian needing to call or text or send a homing pigeon. She could yank her out of bed at three in the morning, if she felt the need. Say if she wanted some fish and chips or something. Great.

But Jules had been invited to stay in Vivian's home. Vivian didn't just do this sort of thing with people. What did it mean?

She grabbed her luggage and hurried back to the stairway, where Vivian was already looking impatient, then trailed behind her up the stairs.

As she climbed, she looked around. So this was how the other half rented houses. The townhouse was all done up in shades of cream, gray, and white with pale blond hardwood floors. Enormous windows let in plenty of light. Traditional fixtures like chandeliers mixed with clean lines of modern furniture, and the walls were hung with framed prints and photos designed not to offend anyone. An Ansel Adams repro featured prominently over a white painted brick fireplace.

It was all tasteful, expensive, and sucked clean of personality. No wonder Vivian seemed restless in it.

The second floor, which featured plush cream carpet to match gray walls with white crown molding. Were these owners allergic to color?

Vivian stopped and pointed down the hallway to the left. "You'll be sleeping in Robert's r—"

She made a sudden choking sound.

Jules immediately started looking around as if she hadn't heard.

"In the room at the far end of the hall." Vivian cleared her throat. "My room's at the other end. You should have absolutely no reason to disturb me."

"Of course, right. I-I should call my parents. Let them know I got here safely."

"Do whatever you want. Just keep it down." She suddenly seemed so exhausted, it was a miracle that she was still standing. She headed for her bedroom without another word.

Jules hauled her suitcases to the designated doorway.

There was a huge four-poster bed in the middle of the room that sat on plush cream carpet next to a deep bay window with a cushioned perch. It was surrounded by mahogany furniture. A giant TV hung on the wall opposite the bed. Everything was spotless, of course.

*Robert's room.* Vivian hadn't meant to say that. But Robert had tagged along on a couple of London Fashion Weeks, always staying with his wife. Apparently their cohabitation had limits.

It wasn't surprising that Robert and Vivian hadn't shared a bedroom by the end of their marriage. Or had it been like that since the beginning? Vivian did like her space. Maybe she and Robert had only shared a bed when…

Then Jules looked at the bed. Oh God. It was entirely possible that she was going to sleep somewhere Vivian Carlisle had had sex.

It should have been the most horrifying thought of all time. Instead, Jules suddenly pictured Vivian lying on the bed before her, wearing a negligee and a come-hither look. Reaching out to her partner. Beckoning.

*Come here*, imaginary Vivian murmured. *I want you here. Right now.*

Jules's face got so hot that she put her hands to her cheeks, like that was going to help. She must be more tired than she'd thought. So, so, so much more tired.

She took a second to get herself under control, then flopped down on the bed, pulled out her phone, and called her parents. Her mom picked up after the first ring.

"What took you so long?" she asked without preamble. "I checked online and your flight got in hours ago!"

"I'm sorry, Mom. As soon as I got in the car, the driver told me he was taking me straight to some luncheon. This is the first free minute I've even had. I swear."

"A luncheon. I was ten seconds away from calling you in case you were dead in a ditch somewhere, and she wouldn't even care if you were missing!"

"Oh, she would have noticed I was missing," Jules said. "Trust me."

"Is she there? You know what I'd like to do? I'd like to talk to her."

Jules's mom was usually very pleasant unless she got riled up…and it looked like she hadn't calmed down much since Jules left. "Okay, that's not happening."

"What if someone treated her new baby this way? How would she feel about that? Your father told me. I think this is ridiculous—"

"On that we agree," Jules said. "Sure. But—"

"She's got no right to treat you like this. You graduated summa cum laude from Penn. I mean, my God!"

"Is Dad there?" Jules asked desperately.

Thankfully, at that moment she heard her father's voice saying, "Okay, calm down, Laura," then the sound of the phone changing hands.

"Glad you got in okay, sweetheart." Her father's voice, calm and reassuring, relaxed Jules at once.

"Yeah, me too. The flight was fine, everything was fine. Is fine."

"Did your mom say something about a luncheon?"

"Yeah. At the Ritz. It was okay." She hesitated. "But the fish was, um, bad."

Her dad snorted. "I'm sorry to hear that. And your boss? How's she treating you?"

*How, indeed? Let me tell you about my Christmas present. I talked about musicals to a CEO.* "Not too bad. She looks kind of sick."

"She's already got you running errands and making calls, I guess."

"Not...not really," Jules said. "I don't have much to do, other than the lunch. Well, and she's bringing me to some dinner tomorrow night."

"Some dinner?" His voice rose in apparent disbelief. "What do you mean? I thought she dragged you across the ocean on Christmas Day because she needed an assistant right away."

This wasn't going well. "Uh, I'm sure she'll have something for me to do. She's just tired right now."

"Fine." There was a growl of impatience there. "Where are you staying? I hope, at least, it's some fancy hotel she's paying for with the company card."

"Uh, no," Jules said. "I'm actually at her place. I guess she didn't want to pay for—"

"Her place," he said. Jules heard her mother say "what?" in the background.

"I-I think it's kind of nice, actually," Jules said. "I'm sure she'll keep me busy"—*eventually*—"but I don't think she usually puts people up in her house."

"She calls you over there not to get to work but to go out to lunch and dinner with her, she's in the middle of a divorce, and you're staying at her house," her dad said.

"What?" Then Jules realized what he meant. She sat bolt upright as her heart started hammering. "No, Dad. Come on, that's" —What word was strong enough?— "Outrageous!"

"No, this is outrageous. Quit your job," he said. "Quit and come home. I don't like whatever this woman is up to."

"Oh, my God, Dad!" Jules dug her hand into her hair just as she had when talking to Vivian on the phone in her parents' kitchen. It was like she'd fallen down Alice's rabbit hole. "No! It isn't like that. She wouldn't—"

"Look, after what I've seen and heard, I'm starting to think there's nothing she wouldn't do."

Thank God her parents would never know that Jules had imagined Vivian in lingerie only a few minutes ago. The memory lit her up like a match, which was just *so stupid,* and now was definitely not the time for it.

"It's not like that," she repeated, hoping she sounded firm instead of hysterical. Then she remembered where she was and lowered her voice, just in case. "If you could see what she looks like now, then you'd know."

"Honey, I know you like to think the best of people—"

"I don't think the best of her, but this is something she wouldn't do. I mean, she likes men," she added, turning red. She couldn't believe she was here in Vivian's ex-husband's bed talking about her boss's sexual orientation to her parents. This was hell.

"She likes power," he said quietly.

"Can we please stop talking about this," she moaned. "You said I could make my own decisions."

"Okay," her dad growled again. "Okay. I guess you know what you're doing," he added in a voice that suggested precisely the opposite. "But, honey—and I mean this—you give us a call and we will put you on the first flight out of there. Day or night, no questions asked. Just call us."

"I will. I promise. But everything's okay. It's weird, but it's okay. I mean, with Vivian, weird's normal," she added, with a horrible-sounding little laugh.

"Jules…"

"Dad, please. I'll call you if anything happens. I swear."

"We love you, sweetheart," he said. "We only want the best for you."

"I love you too." She hunched her shoulders. "I'll be in touch. Um, I don't think I'd better talk anymore to Mom yet."

"Probably for the best," he agreed. "Bye, honey. *Call us.*"

Jules heard her mother's voice saying "Let me talk to—" before her dad disconnected.

Taking a deep breath, Jules prayed that he could keep her mother from calling her back. She headed for the bathroom and washed her makeup off before returning to the bedroom, already longing to collapse again.

She undressed and slipped under the immaculate bedcovers, letting the phone drop from her hand to the mattress. It was a nice mattress. It was a nice room.

Her father's suggestion had been ludicrous. Even if Vivian hadn't been married twice—no, wait, three times now—to *men*, it was still true that the only thing that excited her these days was pizza. Vivian looked so wretched that even the idea of sex was probably enough to give her morning sickness in the afternoon, especially since sex had gotten her into this mess in the first place.

No, Vivian hadn't brought Jules here to…do what her father had implied. Even if Jules still wasn't sure why Vivian had brought her here.

She wondered if Vivian knew.

In the meantime, Jules had plans for later—plans to impress Vivian as she'd said she would—but no energy to implement them now. She set her alarm for an hour. A nap was required.

Sleep was a long time coming, though. And when Jules did sleep, she dreamed about weird, improbable things involving Vivian and the lost, lonely look on her face. That look was awful, and Jules wanted to make it go away, to make it better.

So she reached out and touched Vivian's cheek and watched her close her eyes and turn her face into Jules's palm as if she wanted to hide there. Jules's heart squeezed in a way that was both painful and good.

Vivian said nothing but kept her eyes closed. Jules rubbed her cheekbone with her thumb.

"It'll be okay," she whispered. "I promise."

# CHAPTER 15

Thank God something was open in London on Christmas.

Jules had worried, but a quick Google search showed her that the Ritz wasn't the only fancy place serving meals today—not by a long shot. She'd skimmed over the options and now found herself waiting for her takeaway order at the Ham Yard Hotel near Piccadilly Circus.

"That's right," she told the clerk. "One order of roast duck and one of turkey."

The clerk looked at his notes. "Plus carrot terrine?"

"Plus that," she confirmed.

"And one order of our Christmas pudding."

"Yup. I've never had Christmas pudding." Jules handed over the company credit card. Let Vivian explain this one to the expense department.

"You're in for a treat, then. Be right back." The clerk headed behind the stone-patterned bar to the cash register.

Jules took a moment to look around at the decorations and the festively dressed patrons, who seemed to be having a much more normal Christmas than she was. Well, if nothing else, she was going to have a traditional Christmas dinner, even if it was the British variation. No cardamom cream or whatever: she was talking turkey.

If anyone had asked her a month ago whether she'd dream of stuffing her face in front of Vivian Carlisle, much less asking Vivian to join her, she'd have laughed in that person's face. But if Jules couldn't be with her family today, she was at least going to have this.

So would Vivian. She might not like Christmas, but she'd have a taste of it. Something to make Christmas be…*okay*, as Jules had promised in her dream.

"You dumbass," she growled to herself, but her spirits still rose when the clerk handed her two paper bags full of Christmas fare. The food smelled wonderful, and Jules's stomach growled. Time to get home and eat.

Her Uber arrived after seven minutes, and they drove back toward Mayfair. Feeling happier than she had all day, Jules looked at the snow that had just started falling. It was starting to gather on the ledges and eaves of the great stone buildings. On the northern side of Piccadilly Circus, a large video display on a building corner advertised performances of *The Nutcracker* at the London Coliseum. The bags of food felt warm in her lap, and her stomach growled as she smelled the turkey and duck. The sweet, spicy scent must be the pudding.

No, it wasn't the Christmas Day she'd imagined—not by a long shot—but this wasn't half bad.

She bounced up the townhouse stairs, mindful not to slip. The snow was lovely, but she was glad not to have anywhere else to go tonight.

Vivian was nowhere to be seen as she hustled into the kitchen with the food. Still asleep? She hadn't emerged from her room since Jules had woken up, and that was hours ago now. It was nearly seven and fully dark outside.

"Time to get up," Jules muttered as she dumped the bags onto the kitchen island. She reached for her phone and texted Vivian:

*I'm back with dinner.*

There. Vivian would either come down or she wouldn't, but Jules's stomach had started to growl again. She'd hardly touched her lunch and was ravenous. Time to throw some food onto a plate and scarf it down as soon as possible.

Then she paused with a frown. No. That wasn't right.

She looked at her phone again, then at the Echo unit on a countertop. A few minutes later, she'd linked the two devices, and "Deck the Halls" played in the kitchen while she looked for the flatware.

By the time Vivian arrived, Jules had finished an impressive table setting for two. The linen napkins were even in rings. She hummed "Silver

Bells" along with Dean Martin as she lit two white tapered candles she'd found in the buffet.

Vivian stopped dead at the entrance to the kitchen. She looked genuinely taken aback.

In spite of Jules's determination to enjoy her Christmas evening, she felt a pang of anxiety. "Well?"

"Well, what?" Vivian shook her head. She'd changed out of her green dress into a cream-colored blouse and pair of loose black pants with a pair of black flats to match. She was hardly dressed to the nines, but at least she hadn't wandered down to Christmas dinner in a T-shirt and yoga pants. (Did Vivian even own T-shirts?)

Meanwhile, Jules wore a red sweater and her own pair of black slacks that hugged her hips and ass beautifully—the closest she could come to Christmas garb. She hadn't bothered with hair or makeup, but this was festive enough for a quiet night in. And for once, she looked better than Vivian Carlisle.

Not that it was a competition.

Vivian rubbed her hand over her eyes as if trying to push the sleep out. She seemed dazed, what Jules's sister called "nap-slapped."

"I went to the Ham Yard Hotel," Jules said, hoping the place wasn't on Vivian's shit list.

If it was, Vivian seemed too tired to put up a fuss. "Fine. Just turn off that god-awful music."

Jules looked at her, stricken. She should have expected it, but still.

"Oh, come on," Vivian said. "Stop looking like a kicked puppy."

"You don't even have any Christmas decorations," Jules protested.

"What is this, a shopping mall in October? I had to look at enough holly back home."

"Hold on," Jules said, suddenly inspired. She peered at her phone and began sorting through Spotify playlists. Soon she found one that focused on classical guitar covers of Christmas songs. "Away In a Manger" was the first track, and when she selected it, the tender chords and familiar melody filled her with a warm glow.

She looked hopefully at Vivian, who listened to the music for a moment, and then said, "Not bad."

Whew. Jules busied herself with opening the cardboard boxes and setting them before the plates.

Then she felt a light touch on her arm. She glanced over to see Vivian plucking a white piece of fluff from her sweater sleeve. For a moment, her fingers lingered on the wool, and she looked at them as if they were confusing her.

Jules's heart began jumping on a trampoline. What—how—

Then Vivian pulled her hand away quickly. "Don't gather lint like a dryer," she muttered, not looking at her. "How did you pay for the food?"

Oh shit. Jules winced as the question brought her back down to earth. "Um…"

Vivian sighed. "I guess I can argue that feeding my assistant should be a company expense."

Jules managed to contain her own sigh of relief. "Yeah, that was, uh, my thinking too. Turkey or duck?"

"Some of both." Her brow furrowed as she caught sight of the Christmas pudding. "Dessert?"

"We didn't have ours at lunch."

Vivian looked her up and down, no doubt noting she wasn't a rail-thin model, and shrugged again. "They're your hips."

Jules couldn't restrain a *humph* as she carefully placed food on Vivian's plate: a slice of duck, another of turkey, and two slices of the terrine. But when Vivian's stomach rumbled, it was a full commitment to dinner.

Vivian waited for Jules to seat herself with her own plate. Then they tucked in without speaking.

Jules just managed not to moan when the first bite of savory duck seemed to melt on her tongue.

After a few minutes, though, the silence began to feel awkward. Even "Jingle Bells" couldn't fill it. Jules had so many things she wanted to say, but none of them could be said…or asked. *Why do you hate Christmas? Why did you come to London for it?*

*Why did you want me here too?*

"You called your parents?"

Jules hunched her shoulders. She'd wanted to talk but not about this. "Er, yes. Just to say—"

"What do they do?" Vivian asked.

Really? Vivian caring about Jules's family seemed as likely as her shopping in Old Navy. And yet here they were.

"My dad's a lawyer. Property law. My mom works for an insurance agency." She decided not to add, *And they think you're sexually harassing me.*

"What do they think of your career ambitions?"

*What do* you *think about my ambitions?* Jules wanted to ask. *Do you know anything about them?*

"They've always been supportive," she said instead. "Fashion journalism wasn't their first choice for me, but they understand this is a great opportunity. And…they want me to be happy."

Vivian smiled bitterly. "How nice." She speared another piece of turkey with a little more force than strictly necessary.

With anyone else, this would have been the time to return like for like, to ask Vivian about her own family. Jules, however, was not suicidal, so she searched for a neutral response. She opened her mouth to say *Did you see it's snowing?*

Instead she heard herself ask, "Why'd you come to London for Christmas?"

Vivian gave her a sharp look. "How is that any of your business?"

Jules couldn't help the incredulous look she gave in return. How was it Jules's business? Vivian had yanked her from her family's lap to join her all the way out here, that was how.

Vivian seemed to come to the same revelation, judging by the way she pursed her lips. With no follow-up, she returned to her food with less enthusiasm than before.

Okay. Fine. Jules should have expected as much. Grouchily, she reached for the brown dome of the Christmas pudding and cut herself a nice big slice.

"Mark invited me to his house in the Hamptons for Christmas," Vivian said.

The slice of pudding fell off Jules's fork on the way back to her plate. She caught it in her palm just in time. Mark Tavio had wanted to spend the holidays with Vivian? That sounded strangely ominous. "He did?"

"Yes. To join his family. Since I'm now all alone, you see. He called it an 'olive branch' after some of our less-than-pleasant discussions over the last year."

She and Jules looked silently at each other for a moment.

"What's he up to?" Jules asked, dropping the pudding onto her plate.

Vivian's mouth twitched. "Maybe it was just a nice gesture."

*Yeah, right.* If Vivian believed that, Jules would sell every pair of shoes she owned. "Okay."

"What do you *think* he's up to? He wants to keep an eye on me. I lied and said I'd been planning to come here for months. If there's anything worse than spending the holidays by yourself, it's spending them with people who hate you."

Her tone had been indifferent, but she'd just answered one of Jules's burning questions nevertheless. Vivian thought that being alone during the holidays blew. And here Jules was, not running herself into the ground with work but joining Vivian at meals and sleeping in her spare room.

It should have seemed pathetic. Who didn't have enough friends that they had to make a PA hang out with them on Christmas night? This was even worse than Simon had led Jules to believe.

She couldn't point fingers. Yes, she had a loving family, but Vivian clearly didn't, and Jules didn't have many friends of her own. Not anymore. She didn't have time to get close to many people at work, and during the last couple of years, chats with college friends had become rarer and rarer. As for high school buddies, forget it. Everyone was a different person now.

In Vivian's place, Jules would have been, well, in Vivian's place. That was a sucky place to be.

"I'm glad you didn't go with him," she said. "Sounds like it would have been awful."

"Oh, thank you for approving, Julia." She looked at the Christmas pudding on Jules's plate. "You know, you're supposed to warm that up first and then set it on fire."

Jules's fork hovered over the pudding. "What?"

"With brandy," Vivian clarified. "It's traditional."

Jules looked at one of the burning candles.

"Don't be *ridiculous*," Vivian said.

"I like traditional. And they stocked the liquor cabinet."

Vivian sat back and crossed her arms. "Now, this I have to see."

Jules looked back defiantly. "I bet it'll be delicious."

At least the smoke alarm hadn't gone off.

Jules looked dolefully at the charred husk of her dessert. Her heart still raced from how fast the pudding had gone up in flames. Maybe she'd been too heavy-handed with the brandy.

Luckily, Vivian had quick reflexes and her water glass had been nearly full. Now Jules was left with pudding that was both soggy and scorched.

"It's not too bad this way," Vivian said, and popped in another mouthful of her own unburned, unsoaked pudding.

"At least I tried," Jules muttered.

"Mm-hmm." Vivian swallowed and pushed her plate toward Jules. Over half of her own serving remained. "Here."

Jules looked at her in shock.

Vivian returned the look tranquilly, amusement unmistakable in her eyes. Maybe it was her way of thanking Jules for the entertainment.

Well…as far as Christmas dinners went, this one could have been worse. Jules ate Vivian's leftover pudding while "Silent Night" played in the background.

Vivian didn't look at her. Instead, she kept her gaze trained on the nearest window. She rested her chin on her folded hands, the glow of the candlelight touching her face gently as she watched the snow falling outside.

# CHAPTER 16

Jules's alarm went off at seven the next morning. Vivian hadn't given her a particular hour to rise and shine, but this seemed reasonable.

It probably wasn't good form just to roll out of bed and wander out into the house. Jules ignored the grumbling of her stomach and showered in the spacious bathroom. Then she made her hair presentable, dressed, and decided not even Vivian could care that Jules wasn't wearing makeup at seven thirty in the morning at home.

She sighed and headed downstairs to make breakfast. The farmhouse-style kitchen worked nicely for the cook she'd hired months ago on Vivian's behalf but was way too overqualified to work for the two of them.

The enormous refrigerator's capacity was more suited to a restaurant. The hood over the gas stove alone could house a family of four. Jules almost wanted to apologize to the place as she turned on the Keurig.

Vivian was nowhere to be seen, but about twenty minutes later, Jules heard the sounds of movement upstairs. Just in time—she'd finished her coffee and was starting to get hungry. She raided the pantry and popped two bread slices into the cavernous toaster oven before cutting up a piece of melon and dropping a decaf K-Cup into the Keurig to brew.

A few minutes later, she heard footsteps descending the stairs and glanced up to see Vivian entering the kitchen. She was fully dressed and made-up, appearing totally composed.

Looking closely, Jules could see that her skin looked too pale beneath the makeup, but otherwise she seemed pretty steady on her feet.

"I made you some breakfast, if you want it," she said. At that moment, the toaster oven clicked off, and Jules whisked out the slices.

Vivian just stared at them.

She suddenly felt self-conscious. "It's just toast and melon. Do you want something else?"

"This is fine," Vivian said. "You're making coffee?" She sat down at the table.

Jules set a plate with toast in front of her. "Decaf." This was going okay so far. "Water too?"

Vivian nodded.

As Jules went to fetch it, she added over her shoulder, "Your facialist is opening her practice for you in an hour, so I'll call to confirm she's ready."

When she turned back with a glass of water, Vivian was looking at her in obvious surprise. "You already have the number?"

Jules looked back at her, surprised as well. Since when did Vivian expect her or anyone else to be anything less than perfect?

"Well, yeah," she said. "It's on my London contact list." Along with Vivian's physician, her housekeeping service, her hairdresser, her favorite florist, and, of course, the main office of *Du Jour UK*, plus a few others. When it came to Vivian, you could never, ever be too prepared. You could never be fully prepared at all, in fact.

"Oh. That's…good," Vivian said.

They blinked at each other. Jules felt herself turning red from both pleasure and embarrassment, and she could have sworn that, beneath her makeup, Vivian's cheeks had gone faintly pink.

Just yesterday, Jules had imagined her wearing a skimpy—

At that moment, the Keurig beeped. Jules immediately poured the decaf, ordered herself to stop blushing, and brewed some regular for herself.

"Tonight is dinner at the Chislehursts. Before then, you're going to the London *Du Jour* office to get your outfit for New Year's," Vivian said, her tone far more businesslike.

"I remember." She sat down and took the second piece of toast, careful not to get crumbs everywhere.

"Try to wear something interesting. Something more challenging than your usual boho-whatever-it-is."

Jules almost choked on her toast, unable to believe what she was hearing. *Boho-whatever*? That was ridiculous! She pushed the fashion boundaries plenty. She'd even tried those high-waisted Hepburn pants, and both her outfits yesterday had been almost conservative. She wasn't stuck in a rut. Was she?

"You don't like my clothes?" she asked.

"That's not what I said." Vivian gave her a level glare. "I said to be challenging."

Jules glared right back. It was too early in the morning, and she hadn't finished enough of her coffee to take this shit. "I think I can handle that just fine, Vivian."

Dammit. Vivian looked pleased.

---

Everyone at *Du Jour UK* was remarkably accommodating. Jules didn't try to speak to any bigwigs but rather reached out to her fellow assistants, all of whom were sympathetic to the demands of people like Vivian—and surprised that Jules got to go to the New Year's ball.

"I'd kill for an invitation," said a tall, skinny young woman named Georgie.

"Imagine all the people you'll hobnob with," added another tall, skinny young woman named Janys.

"She wants me to be more challenging." Jules brushed down her corduroy Tach pants, which until this morning she'd thought were fine. But apparently *fine* was a dirty word to Vivian. This could be just a mood swing. Hormones or something. "She thinks my clothes are too predictable."

Georgie and Janys nodded, and within twenty minutes, Jules found herself in front of a mirror wearing a scarlet silk plunge jumpsuit with fluttering kimono sleeves. The low neckline made her blush: her breasts were large enough that she didn't usually wear tops that opened nearly to her stomach. Thankfully, Georgie and Janys also provided her with boob tape and a silicone lift bra that offered support while staying out of sight.

The outfit was out of her comfort zone, but Jules had to admit she looked fierce in it, especially when she added gold Jacquemus sandals with jewelry accents on the stiletto heels. The sandals were edgy and unusual, and she'd been coveting them ever since they'd first appeared on the runway. Now she actually got to wear them. As for accessories…

"I'm thinking a lariat necklace," she said.

"With that Michael Kors gold stud cuff," added Georgie.

"High *five*," Jules said in delight, and they slapped palms.

When the ensemble was complete, Georgie clapped. "Perfect!"

"I wish I had tits like yours," Janys sighed. "So many old men will buy you drinks."

"Pass," Jules said, although her boobs did look fantastic. She headed back for the dressing room to disrobe.

Then it was time to leave. Georgie and Jules carefully folded the jumpsuit into a garment bag while Janys bagged up the shoes and accessories. They bid each other cheerful farewells, and Jules left the office feeling much more optimistic than when she'd arrived.

Vivian called Jules just as she was heading out the door. "Are you on your way back?"

"Yes," Jules said, and practically ran for the waiting Jaguar. At least the garment bag wasn't too heavy to lug. "We should be back in twenty minutes." It wasn't even nine o'clock yet. Vivian had plenty of time to make it to her appointment. Jimmy helpfully opened the door so Jules could toss the bag into the back seat.

"I've just arranged lunch with some associates," Vivian said, "so I won't be home to eat."

"Okay." At least Vivian had found some other "associates," even if for just a few hours. "Uh, where will you be?" she added as she slid inside the car and buckled up.

"RŌKA," Vivian said absently. She was probably multitasking as always. "Some sushi place, apparently."

Jules sat bolt upright. "You can't have sushi!"

"What?"

"Because…" Jules suddenly remembered Jimmy in the front seat and said, "I mean, I heard that restaurant wasn't good."

"Julia." On a scale of one to ten, Vivian sounded about level eight impatient.

"Raw fish is bad," Jules muttered, staring out the window. "You, uh, you can't have it. Or undercooked anything." Dr. Latchley had said so on the very first day.

"I know that," Vivian said. "They serve more than sushi. Now, come home."

"We're on our way," Jules said. "Oh, and they loaned me a jump—"

But Vivian had disconnected.

Whoops. Jules winced. Vivian had been acting so…differently for the past couple of days that Jules had forgotten her intolerance for idle chatter. Vivian had not asked about the outfit; Vivian did not want to know about the outfit.

Jules looked at the garment bag lying on the seat next to her. The jumpsuit was stunning on her. In a few days, London high society would get a look at her in it. She'd be at Vivian's side in scarlet silk with a scandalously low-cut top.

*Brace yourself, Vivian Carlisle. I'll challenge the hell out of you.*

# CHAPTER 17

By six thirty p.m., Jules had given up poking at her hair. Vivian had told her it would look better down anyway.

As usual, she was right: it looked better, although it wasn't distinctive. Jules wished she had the guts just to do what Vivian did, go for one iconic hairstyle and never change it. It would make things so much simpler. The problem was you had to be an actual icon first.

She hissed at herself, fluffed her hair with her fingers, grabbed her clutch, and hurried downstairs. Not a moment too soon. When she hit the bottom step, she heard Vivian's bedroom door open and close, followed by her footsteps heading down the hardwoods of the hallway.

"Julia?" she called.

"I'm down here," Jules said.

"Are you ready for dinner?"

Dinner with the Chislehursts. Even more surprising than all the rest of this Christmas was the fact that people named Chislehurst actually existed. "Yes. And Jimmy's outside with the car."

Vivian came down the stairs. She wore a basic black sheath, but over it she wore a laser-cut black leather jacket that Jules recognized from the most recent Akris collection. She'd also put on bold red lipstick and towering red stilettos to match.

*Damn.* Someday Jules hoped to pull off that effortless confidence.

For now, she aimed for presentable in the black slacks she'd worn yesterday, dressed up with a purple crepe blouse and a chunky necklace. She straightened as Vivian gave her the once-over.

After a moment, Vivian nodded briskly and headed for the coat closet. She withdrew a wool swing coat that somehow managed to pull her ensemble together even better. Meanwhile, Jules was just glad her green peacoat didn't have any stains on it from traveling.

She took in a deep breath and followed Vivian down the front steps. The day had been fair and warmer than yesterday, so at least there wasn't any ice to navigate in high heels.

"Who's going to be at this dinner?" she asked as they drove off. "Uh, the Schumanns won't be there, will they?"

Vivian's lips quirked in a half smile. "No. Herr Schumann and his heinous hausfrau will not be in attendance tonight."

Jules longed to laugh but didn't dare.

"It's a much smaller gathering, and you won't be seated next to me. Try not to disgrace either of us. Or *Du Jour*."

Jules nodded, still biting her lip to keep from grinning. Vivian seemed to have regained her spunk in the last hour. She had more color in her cheeks, though Jules couldn't be sure how much of that was credited to the best makeup in the world.

"What?" Vivian asked, not looking at Jules.

Jules twitched. "Nothing," she said quickly. "You look nice."

"As opposed to death warmed over. Yes, I do."

Jules smiled again and bit her lip *again*. She did more lip biting around Vivian than she'd done in her whole life before *Du Jour*, she was pretty sure.

"Is something wrong?" Vivian asked.

"No," Jules said, but a giggle escaped her.

"I never noticed before that you snickered this much." Vivian did not sound pleased about it.

"Sorry," Jules said, giggled again, and swallowed to get herself under control. "You know, you said funny things, so I laughed." She shrugged helplessly.

"I'm well-known for my sense of humor." Vivian rolled her eyes.

"Well, no," Jules admitted, "but—"

"Why don't you save your voice for the party?" Vivian suggested.

Jules took the not-so-subtle hint and sulked until Jimmy pulled up in front of a fancy London house that was bigger than Vivian's.

She'd never understand why Vivian had to be unpleasant even when there was no need for it. She'd deliberately said something funny; Jules had laughed; Vivian had made Jules feel stupid for laughing at something funny she'd deliberately said. And she'd flown Jules all the way over here on Christmas with no explanation, talked to her like she was an idiot, and hadn't even eaten more than a few bites of the melon Jules had meticulously sliced for her this afternoon, even though she needed the calories.

By the time a real live honest-to-God butler held the door open for them both, Jules had worked herself into an impressive snit and was very glad she wasn't sitting next to Vivian at dinner. But she still had to stand by Vivian's side during the premeal mingling. Lady Chislehurst had kissed Vivian's cheeks, thanked her effusively for coming, then turned the two of them loose on the ten other people hanging around in the parlor.

Vivian did most of the introductions. At least these people seemed a little friendlier and more laid-back. They weren't all out to cut each other's throats, for one thing.

Jules got her fair share of strange looks, though. This wasn't a meeting of publishing heavies after all. It was a purely social gathering, and there was no excuse for Vivian to have an assistant at her side.

Vivian made no effort to explain, saying simply, "This is my assistant, Julia," leaving it at that while she went on to further pleasantries.

Still irritated, Jules tried to not even look at Vivian. She focused instead on the new people she was meeting, most of whom seemed a lot nicer than Vivian. It would probably be much more fun to work for them.

So she shook hands, smiled and made small talk, and did her best to pretend that Vivian wasn't there, except as a voice to her right that introduced her to people out of thin air.

The dinner gong (the Chislehursts had a *dinner gong*?) rang at eight sharp. The party drifted toward the dining room. To Jules's astonishment, Vivian took hold of her arm.

"Stop sulking," she muttered.

Jules couldn't deny it, but she could protest. "I was being nice, wasn't I?"

"Oh yes," Vivian said and stuck her nose into the air as she headed for the dining room, letting go of Jules's arm. "You just might nice us all to death."

"What?" Jules touched her arm as she followed Vivian. Was her elbow tingling?

"For God's sake, laugh if you have to and spare me the cold shoulder. Now, do your job."

Jules's head spun as she took her seat between two sweet old matrons, one of whom had already shown dangerous signs of talking about her three small dogs.

*Do your job?* But Jules had been doing her job. She'd been sweet as pie to everybody but Vivian, who didn't count because Jules was here to schmooze with other people, not with her. They weren't even sitting together. And Jules doubted anybody else would have noticed she'd been pissed off. So the "cold shoulder" remark must have meant…

Had it bothered Vivian *personally?*

The question gnawed at Jules all through dinner, and she was grateful that she didn't have to do much more than make sympathetic noises about the stock exchange and exclaim over toy poodles with the old woman sitting across the table.

"Oh yes," she said. "Breed standards. So important."

The old woman tilted her head. "It's lovely to meet a young person who understands. Especially an American!"

Best not to mention Jules's knowledge of dog breeding was limited to watching *Best In Show*. "It's a lost art, ma'am."

The old woman beamed.

Jules and Vivian stayed for the whole meal this time. Jules was glad because the food was delicious, although Vivian had made clear she wasn't the best judge of such things. And she needed time to get her bearings. By the time the butler helped Vivian into her coat, Jules, bolstered by good food and coffee, felt marginally more in control of herself.

Vivian didn't even wait for the door to close behind them before she said, "I despise passive-aggressiveness."

"Um…"

Vivian headed down the steps toward the car, where Jimmy waited to open the door for her. Jules hurried after her. "That sort of attitude is precisely what I don't need. How many times do I have to tell you? If a problem arises, you don't wait for someone to fix it for you. You deal with it."

"Deal with it? Wait." Jules stopped dead on the last step and stared at her in utter disbelief. "Are you saying you want me to tell you when I'm upset with you?"

Because that couldn't be right. No way. Vivian didn't want to know when Jules was upset about the weather, much less anything important.

"I want never to have this discussion again." Vivian looked impatiently at her. "That's what I want. There's no time for childishness." Then she slid into the car.

Jules got in at the other door, welcoming the warmth and softness of the seats. It almost made up for her utter confusion. She'd just lost all the equanimity she'd managed to build up during dinner.

But she should have expected as much. *Childishness?* Easy for Vivian to say when everyone worked on the assumption that she'd fire them for expressing discontentment.

Jules glanced at Vivian, who was making a great show of looking in her handbag. Jimmy pulled away from the curb.

"Uh, sorry," Jules said.

"Mm," Vivian said without looking up.

"I'll try and be more…direct."

"Mm-hmm."

"And you won't get mad at me?" Jules pressed because it seemed important to clear that up.

Vivian whisked a small mirror from her bag and peered into it. She prodded the skin beneath her eye. "The facialist wasn't too bad."

"*Vivian—*"

She snapped the mirror shut. "What did I just say?"

It was clearly a rhetorical question. Jules was too stunned to answer anyway, and they were silent for the rest of the ride home.

Well, mostly silent. As Jimmy pulled up to the curb, Vivian asked, "So how much of that Christmas pudding ended up on your hips?" She gave Jules an arch look.

Oh. A test as to how she could handle Vivian being a jerk? Jules lifted her chin and remembered how the red jumpsuit clung to her curves. "My hips, uh, look so good I can pretend I didn't even hear you say that."

Vivian lowered her eyes to half-mast and seemed bored.

"Oh, come on," Jules protested. "That was okay, right? I've never tried to clap back at you before!" As if she had witty comebacks lined up to prove she could give as good as she got.

"Well," Vivian sighed, "I guess you can't be good at everything."

# CHAPTER 18

When Jules woke up at one thirty in the morning, she was tempted to blame it on the time change. But she also woke up thinking about Vivian giving her permission to complain, so it couldn't be that easy.

After tossing and turning for a good thirty minutes, she sighed in exasperation and looked up at the ceiling. Okay, might as well do something with all this awake time. Brainstorm another article? No. She didn't have the brain cells for it.

She gave up and slid out of bed with a grunt and reached for her tablet. Time to go downstairs and read in that comfy-looking red armchair in the den.

Ten minutes later, she was ensconced in the chair with a fluffy throw covering her knees reading *What to Expect When You're Expecting* on her e-reader app. Every once in a while, she paused to highlight something.

Vivian was around ten weeks along now. She might start showing soon, although the book said it was different for every woman; some had baby bumps at three months while others were only visibly pregnant at six.

She snorted. She imagined Vivian ordering her kid not to show, to keep herself slender for as long as possible.

It was about time for the first nuchal translucency ultrasound. It came along with some other prenatal tests. The book said that these tests were especially important for older mothers. Then it started saying things about increased chances of complications, long-term health risks to mothers, and lots of other stuff that made Jules's heart fall.

Okay, she wasn't highlighting any of that.

Jules should focus on things she could actually do something about. She picked up a notepad on the table next to the chair and took notes for a list of dos and don'ts that she could conveniently leave lying somewhere where Vivian would see it. No sushi, for starters, or aspirin. Lots of green leafy vegetables, and take the damn vitamins, and massages were good… and—

She opened her eyes. The tablet was on the ottoman, the notepad was lying on her lap, she'd dropped her pen, and Vivian was standing over her in a silk bathrobe.

She had a weird, un-Vivian look on her face. Her eyes were wide and her mouth was slightly parted. On anyone else, it would have been bug-eyed shock.

That didn't make any sense, though. There was nothing to be shocked about, unless it was at Jules's audacity at sitting in a chair, which would be a lot even for Vivian.

The expression vanished, and Jules scrambled to wake up more fully. It wasn't easy. "Sorry. Time is it? I'm awake. Breakfast, I can fix. Um, I think I dropped a pen."

Vivian sat on the ottoman, placing Jules's tablet neatly on the floor. "Calm down. It's four thirty in the morning."

She sounded cool, but there was still something strange in her eyes that Jules was too tired to figure out. Her eyeballs felt dry. She glanced toward the window and saw that it was still dark outside. Her jaw almost dislocated itself in a yawn.

"I didn't mean to wake you," Vivian said.

How…weirdly thoughtful. Jules yawned again. "You didn't. Mostly. I couldn't sleep at first. Jet lag or something."

Vivian nodded. She had bags under her eyes and did not look well.

Jules squinted and, like when Vivian had FaceTimed her at three in the morning, let fatigue cloud her judgment. "Are you okay? Why are you awake too?"

"I wake up all the time. I got up for the bathroom, and then I saw a light on downstairs."

"Can I get you something?"

Vivian ignored the question. Instead, her gaze dropped to Jules's tablet, which hadn't gone to sleep when Jules had. *What to Expect When You're Expecting* was still clearly visible on the screen. Jules blushed.

Vivian didn't comment on her choice of midnight reading material. Instead, she picked at the sleeve of her bathrobe, her lips pursed in thought.

"What do your parents think about you being here?" she asked.

That was the second time Vivian had asked about Jules's parents in as many days. Too surprised to lie, she replied, "They don't like it."

Vivian thinned her lips.

*Fuck.* "But that's just because it's Christmas." Oh, that wasn't any better. "Anyway, it doesn't matter."

Vivian lifted her eyebrows. "No?"

"Well…I mean…I'm here, aren't I? You, um—" Jules took a deep breath. "You wouldn't have fired me if I hadn't come, would you? I mean, you didn't actually say you would or anything."

Vivian hesitated ever so slightly before looking away again and shaking her head.

Jules took another deep breath and realized she'd always known that. Vivian would have been angry, even hurt, if Jules had said no. But she would not have actually punished Jules, would not have ruined or fired her.

She just might have trusted Jules a little bit less. Leaned on her a little bit less. Felt like she couldn't count on her.

"Well," Jules said, "I'm here."

"So you are." Vivian's voice and face were absolutely neutral as she looked at Jules. She tugged her robe's collar tighter around her neck as if she were cold.

Jules offered her the blanket, but she shook her head wordlessly.

"You got an outfit for the ball?" Vivian asked.

"Oh. Yes. A couple of girls helped me pick it out." Jules cleared her throat. "Do you want me to show it to you? You can make sure it's okay."

An image flashed into her mind, one of her standing before Vivian in this darkened room wearing a low-cut red jumpsuit while Vivian looked her up and down.

A rush of heat to her face almost made her gasp aloud. What the *fuck…*

"No. I don't want to see it until New Year's. Take a risk on it. Is there something about 'challenging' you don't understand?"

"No!" Damn, that had come out sharp. "I mean, no. But what if I look bad, or…embarrass you, or—"

Vivian gave Jules a scornful look. "You might embarrass yourself. I promise you I won't be bothered one way or the other."

Wow, really? Jules glared at her.

Vivian glared right back. "Own your decisions, Julia. You don't truly care what people think. Don't try to pretend otherwise."

"I don't care about me," Jules snapped. "I care about"—she almost said *you*—"the reputation of the magazine. I work at *Du Jour*. I can't show up looking awful."

"If you look awful, I'll leave you at home," Vivian said dryly. "Does that ease your mind?"

"Yes, actually." Jules had originally wanted a nice quiet New Year's. Not one where she got dressed up and had to fake-smile at rich people she didn't know. The thought was exhausting, even if she was going to look good.

Maybe Vivian sensed this because she glared again. This time, Jules just tried to look innocent.

"I'm so sorry," Vivian said much too sweetly. "Did you have wild, exciting plans for New Year's in Pennsylvania? Did I interrupt your social whirl?"

"I was going to be back in New York by then." Another wave of fatigue washed over her. Jules yawned before she could help herself. "So," she mumbled around it, "unless you count maybe hanging out with Ben, I guess I didn't have any—"

Vivian blinked. "Ben?"

"Yeah. Ben."

Vivian looked blank.

"Your driver," Jules prompted, deciding not to clarify with *for the last five years*.

"What about Ben?" Vivian's brow drew down alarmingly and her voice got sharp.

Why did she look so pissed? "He sort of mentioned…I guess we might have gone out for a beer or something."

"My driver asked you out on a date?"

"What? No! I mean, he didn't actually say—"

"Do you have any idea how unprofessional that is?"

"Oh, my God." Jules's heart started to race again at Vivian's scowl. She tried to laugh. "No, it wasn't like that. It was just, you know, a buddy thing."

"Oh yes, Julia. I'm sure men invite you to bars all the time so they can be your 'buddy.'"

Jules's cheeks scalded.

"That kind of fraternization is completely inappropriate. Nip it in the bud, or I will." Vivian frowned. "I'm surprised at you."

"But nothing happened," Jules pleaded. "Nothing would have. Even if he was interested, I'm not." Then the words fell out of her mouth: "I was thinking I wanted to date a woman next, actually."

Vivian's head twitched back, her eyes widening slightly.

Jules gave herself the biggest mental kick ever. *What did you just say? Do you think Vivian Carlisle wants to hear about your freaking dating plans?*

Time to recover, if she could. "What I mean is—I wouldn't date Ben. Er, when you say you'd 'nip it in the bud'—"

The flash of surprise that had crossed Vivian's face had long since vanished. She rose to her feet. "I'd fire him."

Jules started in horror. "No! Vivian, he's worked for you for so long. You can't!"

Vivian gave her a very, very cold look, one that said, *I most certainly can, Julia.* Then she left without another word.

Jules slumped back in the armchair, trembling. Had she just gotten Ben fired? She hadn't meant to; she never would have wanted that. And he'd know exactly what had happened because no doubt Vivian would tell him, and he'd hate Jules for it, and it wouldn't even be fair because she'd tried to explain everything but Vivian hadn't *listened*. Or she hadn't wanted to hear.

But that just reminded Jules of the truth. Vivian was willing to throw away a man who'd loyally worked for her just because of some stupid, small thing. You could give Vivian everything you had, your entire soul, and this could still be your reward.

Jules tossed the notepad to the floor and stomped back upstairs to her bedroom. Not that she'd be able to sleep.

# CHAPTER 19

Was Vivian taking revenge or what?

It almost seemed like it. She was definitely making up for the first couple of days in London when Jules hadn't had much to do. Now, after their strange conversation, Jules was on the hop all day.

"Call Simon," Vivian said. "He should be awake by now. Tell him I want to see the applications he's screened for Lucia's replacement."

Jules fought back a sigh as she looked at her phone. It was midafternoon after a weird morning in which she hadn't quite known how to interact with Vivian, and Vivian had been curt with her. Not in a way Jules could call out, though. Just enough that Vivian could get away with saying, "Do you expect everyone to be cheerful at all times, Julia? Can't I just be tired?"

She could be. Jules said, "Sure thing. Um, how are you feeling?"

"Fine." Vivian brushed past Jules. She didn't offer any other information, didn't say what she was doing or where she was going.

Jules's shoulder tingled where Vivian had brushed against it. She shivered and opened her contacts list.

Simon didn't offer a greeting, opening instead with, "Eight thirty in the morning during the holiday. There's no way this is on your own initiative."

She sat down on a blue ottoman. "You're very wise."

"*I* never worked you over Christmas. I was the *good* boss."

Jules snorted with laughter. "There are key differences between the two of you, yes."

"Indeed. Do you regret all your life choices or just a few?"

She did, in fact, miss multiple things about working with Simon. This friendly banter was one of them. They'd started interacting when she was just an intern, and he'd been kind to her even then. She'd enjoyed having him as her supervisor. Compared to Vivian, he was just…easy.

"A few." She sighed.

"Really?" He sounded surprised, plainly having expected her to deny everything.

"Nah, not really. Some days are just…" How could she even sum up her most recent days? "You know."

"I do know. So why are you calling? Who has to jump to attention?"

"Vivian wants you to send her the applications you've approved for Lucia's former position."

"Huh. Okay. I'll email them to her in a few minutes, but why didn't she call me herself?"

"What?"

"You're in New York too," Simon said patiently. "Why did she call *you* and tell you to call *me*?"

Uh-oh. Today was the twenty-seventh, the day Jules was supposed to return to New York. "Actually, I'm…not sure."

"Too early in the morning for you? Well, I hate to be the bad boss after all, but if I have to come into the office today, I'll need you."

"What?"

"No whining. I'll buy you a nice lunch. Can you be here in an hour?"

"That'll be a problem." Her stomach squirmed at what Simon was no doubt about to say. "I'm not in New York."

"Didn't you say you were getting back in today?"

"Yeah, well, plans, uh, changed."

"Great," Simon said, clearly annoyed. "Of course you didn't inform anybody else of this. I was counting on you to be here at least by tomorrow."

"I'm sorry." Jules fidgeted. "I couldn't help it."

"You better hope Vivian doesn't find out," Simon warned. "You're not sticking to the game plan. She doesn't like that."

"She knows my plans changed," Jules said, deciding that there was no point in trying to hide anything. Simon would know soon enough that she had been with Vivian in London against all logic and common sense. Everybody would. "She changed them for me."

"She—oh. What?"

"I'm in London," Jules admitted.

There was a long silence. The explanation sounded flimsy even to her as she added, "Her London PA got sick."

"Really," Simon said slowly. "And Vivian flew you over because there were no other personal assistants in London?"

"Um…not exactly."

"Jesus Christ, Jules."

"Simon, I don't *know* why—"

"I think you do." Simon's tone brooked no bullshit. "We've talked about this."

*Maybe she panics when you're more than ten feet away.* But there was more to it than that, wasn't there? If that's all it was, Vivian wouldn't have let Jules order Christmas dinner. Wanting companionship wasn't the same thing as panicking.

Vivian Carlisle had probably never panicked in her life.

Jules couldn't explain any of this to Simon. He'd never get it. "It's been fine."

"Okay. Look, I don't have time—okay. I'll email Vivian about those candidates." He ended the call.

She pocketed her phone and gave a gusty sigh. He hadn't sounded mad, exactly. At least not at Jules. Well, why should he be? Simon of all people knew what Vivian's whims were like.

"Julia?" Vivian called from downstairs.

Jules jumped and hurried toward the stairs. "I'm here. Simon says he'll email you in a few minutes…"

# CHAPTER 20

The red jumpsuit was starting to look intimidating.

Jules had been staring at it for ten minutes while it lay on her bed. The New Year's ball was tonight, and she had to get ready to go. She'd already made a start. Her hair was in a half updo. A smoky eye and a glossy neutral lip took care of makeup.

Vivian didn't have to do anything so pedestrian. Her personal stylist had arrived, entered her bedroom, and departed two hours later. Vivian no doubt was getting dressed now. Her hair and makeup would be good enough that they could feature on the cover of *Du Jour* itself.

Meanwhile, Jules had smooshed and taped her breasts to hell and back, squeezed into shapewear for her ass, and all that was left was the jumpsuit.

*You can do it,* she pep talked herself. *It looked great before. Sexy as hell.*

Not that Jules needed to look sexy tonight. No need for that at all.

With a few wiggles and curses, Jules slid into the garment. Once she had it on, she tugged, fiddled, and adjusted until her boobs looked good but weren't popping out. No mean feat, but she had to admit the end result was worthwhile. And when she added the jewelry and the shoes, she couldn't stop a proud smile.

Hell yes. She might just be an assistant, but she was a hot one tonight. Hot in a classy, elegant way. Even Vivian couldn't look down her nose too much at this.

Beaded clutch in hand, she hurried downstairs. In spite of herself, she felt the build of enthusiasm. At least tonight would be something different. She'd adapted to the routine of making phone calls, sending messages, and venturing out on the occasional errand. She'd adapted to…well, living with Vivian.

What a weird thing to make her heart race. Jules put a hand over her chest. She was probably just nervous about tonight.

As she dithered at the foot of the stairs thinking ridiculous thoughts, there was a noise in the hallway above. Vivian.

Jules's heart started going even faster for some dumb reason, and sweat broke out on her palms as she waited to see her. She really *must* be nervous.

She heard the rustle of a skirt. A tread on the steps. Then Vivian finally descended into view.

Jules lost her breath completely and abandoned all hope of getting it back.

At formal events, Jules was used to seeing Vivian in darker colors. She looked great in them. While her dresses were never severe looking, the cut and make was always up-to-the-moment modern, not a single line or stitch wasted in unnecessary frippery or romance.

So Jules was *not* used to seeing Vivian in floor-length champagne silk with a full skirt that flowed down from an empire bodice. The color, which should have washed her out, instead matched her skin tone so perfectly that she almost appeared to be naked beneath a thin film of gold lace over the silk. The dress was low-cut, although not as much as Jules's outfit. It was not the dress of a pregnant woman in her forties. It was…

Jules didn't know what it was. Her heartbeat was painful now. Blood roared in her ears, and her whole body burned.

But she barely paid attention to that. Mostly she realized she desperately wanted to have sex with Vivian Carlisle, and it felt like every day they'd known each other had just been building up to this moment.

Jules had a horrible feeling of inevitability, of something falling into place just at the moment when she'd stopped paying attention and had let her guard down.

She heard herself say stupidly, "Oh."

Vivian glanced at her, raising her eyebrows as she gave Jules the once-over herself.

"I mean," Jules added, "uh—"

"Hmm," Vivian said, still looking Jules up and down, tapping her lips with her fingertip.

Jules wondered what it would be like to kiss her, and immediately wished she could turn off her own brain.

Then, without a word, Vivian turned and left the kitchen, heading back toward the stairs. Jules helplessly watched her go, and only when the champagne silk had vanished from sight could she breathe freely again.

Holy *God*. Did Jules have a concussion? That could explain why her ears were ringing and nothing around her seemed real.

This was no good. Jules had to pull herself together. She needed more time, but she didn't have it. So she took another deep breath, and when Vivian returned, Jules was able to look at her with her most helpful smile. Her lips managed not to tremble.

Vivian, who hadn't become one iota less stunning in the last three minutes, held out a hand to her. Shiny things dangled from her fingertips: two earrings. They were made of hammered gold and shaped like leaves. "Wear these," Vivian said. "They'll complement your hairstyle."

"Thanks, Vivian." Jules reached out with miraculously steady hands to take them. They'd look perfect with her outfit.

Vivian looked at Jules's shoes and moved upward until they were locking eyes. Jesus. Her eyes were so blue. Jules prayed not to pass out.

"Not bad," Vivian said neutrally.

Really? At least Jules had been too stunned to feel self-conscious during the inspection. "Thanks," she said again like an idiot.

Vivian hummed in response, then led the way to the hall closet while Jules concentrated on walking. Had her Jacquemus heels grown by a couple of inches? She hadn't tottered this much in them before.

Vivian pulled out a fur wrap and an embroidered shawl from the closet. "Now," she said in the tone of one giving a test, "which should I wear?"

Jules thought about it. "The shawl."

Vivian looked displeased. "I would have said the fur."

"I know."

Vivian blinked.

"Challenge everyone?" Jules dared to add. Well, once you realized you were dying to have sex with Vivian Carlisle, nothing else could scare you anymore.

Vivian rolled her eyes, but she put the fur back and donned the shawl. Then she reached into the closet, removed Jules's coat from a hanger, and tossed it at her. "Well?"

Jules snapped back into reality. Right. She could get through this. It was just one night, and there was no need to freak out about anything until she was safely in bed and had a few seconds to think.

Tonight was going to be utterly, completely, totally fine.

# CHAPTER 21

No, it was pretty much the worst night of Jules's life.

Worse than the time she'd caught her junior high boyfriend making out with her best friend at a school dance. Worse than the time her dad had discovered her sneaking back home smelling of beer at twelve thirty on a school night. Worse than the communications honors thesis competition at Penn when she'd come in second to a frat bro with questionable opinions about everything. Worse than all that.

Sitting next to Vivian in the car was awful, for starters. Jules had to pay attention, or pretend to, while Vivian talked about the candidates Simon had put forward to replace Lucia and how almost all of them were completely unsuitable and the rest were *mostly* unsuitable.

"The hair on one of them," she said with a disdainful sniff, and Jules started thinking about the way Vivian's own hair whispered and tickled at her ears and the back of her neck. Whoever her stylist was, they'd given a slight ruffle to her pixie that made it look as if she'd just gotten out of bed but in a sexy way. Like she'd just finished doing something fun while she was in there.

Vivian broke off in the middle of her tirade to ask, "What are you staring at?"

"Nothing," Jules heard herself say. "Didn't Simon like the one who works at *Elle*?"

"Oh, my God, that one," Vivian said, then she was off and running again while Jules sat there and thought about her earlobes and tried not to stare at her breasts.

By the time they arrived at the ball, Jules was pretty sure she'd used up at least a quarter of her allotted heartbeats for the coming year. And it wasn't over yet. She had to watch Vivian's shawl slide back off her shoulders and into the hands of a waiting attendant. And then she realized she was staring again, only they were in front of other people now and she had to stop.

So *then* she had to pretend she neither noticed nor cared about the appreciative looks Vivian was getting even from much younger men. That made her throat close up. Then it got difficult to breathe. And it was harder to disguise feelings of murderous jealousy than it was to disguise lust. Rage tended to gleam in the eyes.

It was easier to concentrate on the envious glances Vivian got from other women at the ball. Those Jules could handle, even take pride in, because her boss looked better than all of them.

If other women were giving Vivian looks that were more inviting than envious, Jules didn't want to know about it.

Now she and Vivian were making their way through the party. The venue was appropriately grand: the Dorchester London's ballroom. Surrounded by gilded Art Deco architecture, servers circulated in balletic patterns, and the wealthy nibbled on the hors d'oeuvres they offered. The guests were all attired in immaculately tailored formal wear. It wasn't much like the parties with celebrities filling VIP rooms and models doing lines in the back. Those venues didn't have marble floors.

Vivian seemed perfectly at home as she chatted with acquaintances. Sometimes she introduced Jules, who hardly saw their faces, let alone remembered their names. Thankfully, Vivian didn't seem to notice anything wrong.

At one point, Vivian accepted a flute of champagne from a passing waiter. Before she could stop herself, Jules gasped and had to turn it into an embarrassed cough when Vivian's current tuxedoed interlocutor glanced at her. Vivian gave her a pointed glare and didn't stop talking to him.

When he'd wandered off, Vivian's glare got a lot more pointed. "Get ahold of yourself," she muttered

"But you can't drink that," Jules protested.

"I'm not going to drink it. I'm going to hold it so that nobody else tries to give me anything and gets curious when I say no. I doubt anybody will notice that I haven't changed glasses all evening." Vivian's eyes gleamed, as they often did when she was being clever. Light from the massive crystal cage chandelier limned the edges of her hair.

"Oh," Jules said stupidly. "Right. That's a good—you know, you look really nice."

Vivian stared at her.

Jules wanted to die. She looked wildly around the room, hoping that somehow Vivian wouldn't notice she was blushing or at least would put it down to something else. "I mean, everybody does," she babbled. "This is—I wonder how many people are here?"

Vivian rolled her eyes. "You could always count them. What's wrong with you tonight?"

"Nothing!" Her voice cracked. *Shit.* That sounded unhinged. She had to come up with something plausible. "I just feel weird in this outfit," she heard herself say.

Vivian frowned. "Weird?"

Great. Now she was looking at Jules in her outfit because Jules had called her attention to it, almost as if she'd wanted Vivian to look.

She took a deep breath. Her breasts pressed against the low-cut fabric.

Vivian did not look at them.

"It's different from my usual, isn't it?"

Vivian looked away from Jules and cleared her throat. "Is it? I, ah, didn't notice."

What? Vivian had told her a thousand times to wear something outside her comfort zone! "Hey, you said I should—"

"Never mind what I said. Honestly, Julia, find something better to do than quibble over details. You're not exactly the plus-one I originally intended to bring—"

*Robert was,* she didn't say, and Jules tried not to wilt.

"—but you might as well make something of the opportunity. I hope I haven't been mistaken in your ability to—"

"Vivian!"

The two of them turned as one to see a striking woman with long dark hair in a form-fitting black gown gliding toward them. She wore a wide smile. Her carmine lipstick made it look even wider. And was that necklace made of real diamonds? It could have come out of the Cartier showroom.

"Monique." Vivian smiled, appearing genuinely pleased to see her. "Lovely to see you. I should have realized you'd be here tonight."

"Well, of course. I'd never miss it. I come to London every chance I get." Monique Whoever-She-Was looked at Jules. "Hmm. I know you."

Vivian placed her hand on Jules's elbow. She removed it a heartbeat later. That was still long enough for Jules to feel faint as Vivian asked, "You do?"

"Oh yes. Vivian's shadow." Monique held out a hand. She wore a fabulous blue sapphire cocktail ring. "Julia, isn't it?"

"Yes," she replied, doubly stunned as she remembered who this was: Monique Leung, editor in chief of *Du Jour China*. She was a rising star within Koening, known for tapping into her country's increasingly voracious appetite for luxury goods. She was also responsible for introducing many new Asian designers to Western markets.

And she was openly gay, having appeared publicly with female partners. She didn't have one with her tonight, however. Jules vaguely remembered something about a recent breakup with a society heiress. Leave it to Jules to fall for the straight *Du Jour* editor in chief by mistake.

Monique Leung remembered *Jules*?

"I saw you a lot at Paris Fashion Week last fall. You were all over the place taking care of everything." Monique laughed. "I remember wishing my own assistants were as capable. Although I suppose jet lag coming from Beijing is pretty brutal. I should be more charitable to them."

Jules was pretty sure the words *I should be more charitable* had never left Vivian Carlisle's mouth. She also should not be thinking about Vivian Carlisle's mouth.

"I'm glad I made a good impression," she managed. "I'd love to see Shanghai Fashion Week sometime."

"Would you," Vivian said at the same time Monique said, "You would?"

"Oh yes. I've never been anywhere in Asia. I've always wanted to go." Why had Vivian's mouth moved from a smile to a pinch?

"Huh." Monique put her hands on her slender hips and darted another smile Vivian's way. "I know Vivian doesn't keep assistants around if they don't have other talents."

"Other talents," Vivian said slowly.

"Of course. Well, Julia, when you get the okay to step up the ladder and if you're sick of New York, give the Beijing office a call. I mean that."

Holy shit. Even as floored as she was, Jules knew that was an incredible offer. "That sounds amazing. Thank you so much!"

"Not at all." Monique turned toward Vivian, whose face had frozen into a block of ice. "Vivian, I know it's a party, but I wonder if I might bend your ear about something Mark Tavio asked me. He said—"

"I'm sorry, but not tonight." Vivian set her full champagne flute on a nearby pedestal. "We were just about to leave."

Monique's expression reflected Jules's surprise. "Oh. You're not staying for the dinner? Alaine Ducasse is the chef."

"I know." Vivian's tone was just this side of curt. Gone was the relative friendliness she'd exhibited before. "Feel free to email me about Mark. *So nice to see you.*"

Monique's smile had faded. Her own tone became cool. "It's always a pleasure."

"Good night." Vivian whirled and stalked off without another word, presenting Jules with her perfect shoulders.

She stared at them, momentarily hypnotized, barely hearing Monique say, "It was nice to meet you, Julia. Don't forget what I said."

*Snap out of it*, she told herself. *This woman practically offered you a job in Beijing.* "I won't. Thank you so much."

Monique reached into a scarlet leather clutch that popped fabulously against her black dress. "My card."

The editor in chief of a *Du Jour* edition was giving Jules her business card. She was just doing it because Vivian had been rude (and why *had* Vivian been rude?), but that wasn't the point. Jules took it with a stammered thanks, barely remembering to give Monique her own card in return. It would probably go in the trash, but etiquette mattered.

Vivian was waiting for her by the door, her glare so sharp that everyone was giving her a wide berth.

"Uh, sorry," Jules said as she reached her. "I was just saying goodbye."

"You took your time. I'd like to get back to the house sometime this year."

She couldn't help saying, "You mean literally?"

Vivian rolled her eyes and stalked toward the coat attendant.

Jules followed the shoulders, the hair, and the graceful arms. She hoped it wasn't obvious to anybody else that she was ogling Vivian from behind, but she couldn't help herself. At least the voluminous skirt hid Vivian's ass.

They got their coats and headed for the hotel entrance. Vivian didn't pause to speak to any party guests in the foyer. She didn't even look at Jules. She was a little flushed, but she remained stone-faced as she threw the shawl around her shoulders.

Jules waited until they were in the cold night air to ask, "What's the matter?"

"Nothing." Vivian still didn't look at her. Camera flashes started going off all around them as the photographers haunting the building realized a celebrity had just exited. "Where's the car?"

Jules pointed at the Jaguar pulling up to the curb. Jimmy had spotted them, thank God. "Right th—"

"It's about time." Vivian descended the steps with Jules watching anxiously to make sure she didn't slip in her high heels.

Before they got into the car, she dared ask, "You're feeling okay, right?"

"Yes," Vivian snapped as she slid inside while Jimmy held the door for her. Jules followed suit and silently buckled her seatbelt. They pulled away.

Jules braced herself. Three…two…one…

"Well." Vivian's tone could have iced over the windows. "I've never had anyone attempt to poach an employee right in front of me before."

"I don't think that's what she was doing," Jules said in surprise. "She didn't offer me a job right now or anything." *She just said I could call her when I'm done with being your assistant. Done with you.*

What a devastating thought. Jules was supposed to contemplate leaving Vivian? Now of all times? She was supposed to think about being *done* with her? It seemed impossible.

"No, she didn't." Vivian lifted her chin.

That noble profile. Jules couldn't look away.

"Remember that. In this industry, offers and promises are more likely to be broken than not. Especially the informal kind."

True. It was likely that even if Jules did contact Monique, the editor in chief of *Du Jour China* would have forgotten she existed. Fashion wasn't superficial, but the fashion industry sure could be. Jules sighed.

"You seem upset by that," Vivian said sharply.

"Huh? No." She shook herself out of it. "It's not like I'm excited about broken promises or anything, but—"

"So she did promise something?" Vivian's eyes flashed fire.

"No!" Jules repeated, incredulous now. Vivian was determined to be mad about this? No way was Jules mentioning the business card. "You heard what she said."

"And she said nothing else after I left?"

Jules glanced at Vivian's lap. She'd folded her hands together, and her knuckles appeared a touch whitened. "No," she replied. It wasn't really a lie. Monique had just advised Jules to remember what she'd already said. That didn't count as saying something *else*.

"And on top of false promises," Vivian continued, as if this conversation had to go on come hell or high water, "in this industry, it's all too common for junior employees to be...taken advantage of."

Like Jules didn't know that. "Junior employees" were worked to the bone for pitiful wages, exploited just to get experience they could put on a résumé. It was a lousy system, and—

Then Jules realized what Vivian meant. The flush in her cheeks wasn't about assistants making low salaries.

"Um..." She had to tread carefully here. "Is Monique Leung known for, uh, taking advantage of junior employees? I've never heard that."

Surely Jules would have, if it were true. Gossip like that made the rounds. A lesbian fashion editor preying on beautiful young girls? Of course, it was salacious enough that everyone would talk, even if nobody did anything about it. Simon would have given Jules an earful for sure.

"I've never heard that either." Vivian's voice was clipped. "I would never make an allegation like that about her. I don't know where you got such an idea."

Whoa. Time to backpedal. "Sorry," Jules said quickly. "I didn't mean to imply anything untoward. Just trying to connect the dots."

"There are no dots. I'm saying it *happens*. In general." For a moment, Vivian took hold of her skirt, twisting the beautiful gold lace. Then she appeared to realize what she was doing and stopped, lifting her chin. "A pretty young thing catches the eye of someone in authority and good intentions and ethics go out the window. I've seen it happen too often."

Had it happened to Vivian herself? Was that where this was coming from? Hot outrage prickled Jules's skin at the thought. If it had happened, she'd find a way to go back in time and wring the neck of whoever it was. That's what she'd do.

Hard on the heels of her outrage came embarrassment. Like Vivian needed Jules to protect her from anything.

Vivian pursed her lips. "Anyway, never mind all that. I've always respected Monique, and I appreciate what she's done for our brand. But she mentioned something about Mark, which is the last thing I need. It would be a shame if—"

Just then, something sucked and pulled at the skin of Jules's chest. The boob tape was coming loose.

A domino effect had begun. Next thing she knew, the right side of her jumpsuit could no longer contain her. Her breast didn't pop right out, but it pressed forward enough that the translucent silicone bra was on full display, including the nipple beneath it.

"Shit!" Jules yelped before she could censor herself. She yanked the fabric back over her breast hard enough that there was an awful popping sound: snapped threads. The jumpsuit loosened over her right shoulder as it lost shape.

Vivian looked down at Jules's chest, then back up at her face, her eyes widening.

"Fuck," Jules said, her profanity filter a thing of the past.

The tape on the left side of her chest gave way too. This time, instead of pulling the fabric, Jules slapped her hand over her left breast to conceal herself. Too hard. "Ow!"

And then she sat there staring at Vivian, utterly stricken as she cupped one of her breasts and held silk fabric over the other. "Um," she said weakly, "good thing that didn't happen at the ball."

Vivian said nothing. Silence mounted in the car until Jules actively began to pray for her own death.

And then Vivian Carlisle burst out laughing.

Really and truly. Her shoulders shook, and her lips parted in incredulous glee. She clapped a hand over her mouth, too late to stifle herself.

"Vivian!" Jules spluttered.

"Oh, my God." Vivian pressed her hand to her chest as she let out another peal of laughter.

Jules growled and looked down at her chest, her cheeks flaming. It figured her abject humiliation would be what finally made Vivian crack up. Nice. "Come on, this is embarrassing!"

"Please. We're all girls here." Vivian looked at the back of Jimmy's head in the front seat as she added merrily, "Eyes on the road."

"Of course, ma'am." To his credit, Jimmy kept his voice devoid of all amusement.

"God," Vivian repeated. She wiped her eyes where tears had begun to form. Then she laughed again. "Imagine if it *had* happened at the—"

"Yeah, yeah, yeah." Jules's face was on fire. She unbuckled and struggled back into her coat. It was warm in the car, but that wasn't going to stop her from doing up the buttons. "Do you think there's a needle and thread at the house? I want to see if I can fix the shoulder. I can't afford to pay for this."

"Don't worry about it. Keep the jumpsuit and send the office my way if they chase you down." Vivian chuckled. "It's worth it for the laugh you gave me. I needed that."

Then she looked over at Jules just as they passed by a streetlight that shone into the car. Her cheeks were appealingly pink, her smile was unforced and natural, and her eyes still sparkled with mirth. She almost looked…affectionate.

Jules instantly forgave her for every absurd demand she'd ever made, every snooty thing she'd ever said. Then she looked out her own window before she could be caught staring at Vivian's mouth.

Yeah. Worst night of her life. For sure.

---

If she positioned the top just right, you couldn't tell the jumpsuit's right shoulder was messed up, and if she held her phone at the proper angle, you couldn't tell her boobs were almost falling out of it. In her bedroom, Jules took a selfie. She wanted to commemorate herself as she was after a long night.

Looking like shit.

The camera angle preserved her modesty, but it brought out her undereye circles too. Her hair looked frizzy. She'd removed Vivian's earrings and the lariat necklace, so no bling distracted from the exhaustion on her face.

That was fine. She didn't have to show it to anyone else. It'd just serve as a good reminder of the night Jules lost her mind and how she looked as messy on the outside as she felt on the inside.

She should undress and crash, but her mind buzzed too much. She should try to write something, but that wasn't going to work out either. Tired and wired, a crappy combination. Going for the compromise option, Jules opened her personal email, expecting just be a bunch of spam to delete.

There was something else.

Right there, at the top of her inbox, sat an unread message from *The Cut*. The subject line read: *Accepted: Your submission for "I Think About This a Lot."*

Jules reread the line. She was probably hallucinating. Only one way to find out.

She clicked on the email with trembling fingers. It hadn't been a hallucination. *The Cut* had accepted her article about *Working Girl*. They wanted a couple of line changes and one whole paragraph had to go, but if she got those done within a few days, she was in. Then the article would be published in two weeks.

The mattress bounced as she flopped back down on it. She looked at the ceiling and exhaled, a breath that ended in an incredulous laugh.

The article was in. It might not seem like much, but it was something, and maybe when Jules was Vivian's age and a staff writer at *The New Yorker*, she could look back on this as her first tiny step. Why not? Tonight was the night for impossible fantasies, wasn't it?

She set her phone on the nightstand and rose to her feet with a groan. Time to change, go to sleep, and hopefully dream of professional success. Better that than dreaming of Vivian.

Vivian: laughing, beautiful, incandescent. She was the one who should be photographed, not Jules. That might not be fair, though. The world couldn't handle it.

She was pretty damn sure she couldn't either. Something was clearly wrong with her. Because although she'd looked tired in her selfie, there were also—undeniably—stars in her eyes.

# CHAPTER 22

Jules had hoped that, when she woke up on January 1, she would no longer find Vivian Carlisle attractive. Like it had been the last mistake she'd made in the previous year. Something that wouldn't matter anymore when they changed the calendars, and on New Year's Day, she could start completely fresh.

She could even make a resolution of some kind: *I will not fantasize about having sex with Vivian until we are both too tired to move.*

Then again, she'd already broken that one in about half her dreams last night. So much for dreaming of professional success.

After waking from one of those dreams at six thirty, Jules staggered into the shower to start her day. Then she dressed and went downstairs, fully expecting to have the place to herself for an hour or so. She could make those changes *The Cut* wanted and forget all about Vivian dressed in champagne and gold.

This wasn't Jules's fault. Vivian had been so stunning that practically everybody at the ball had wanted her or wanted to be her. Jules couldn't be blamed for being dazzled by something so…perfect. Today would be different. Today everything would be back to normal.

But when she wandered into the living room at five till seven clinging to a hot cup of coffee, she ran smack into the sight of Vivian curled up on the love seat by the window.

She wore hunter green cotton pajamas that weren't exactly the pinnacle of bedtime glamour. No makeup, no jewelry. Her lips were thinned into a line of displeasure, and her brow was furrowed, making her look older. But her bare feet were peeping out from beneath the hems of her pajama pants, and she had a tuft of platinum blonde hair sticking up from behind one ear.

Jules's stomach plummeted right down into her feet. *Fuck. Oh…oh fuck.* Vivian looked up and scowled.

Jules immediately took a step back, her heart beating painfully hard. "I didn't think you'd be up yet."

"Surprise," Vivian said testily. She tucked the tuft of hair back behind her ear before Jules could protest that it was adorable, which would have been unbelievably stupid.

She clutched her coffee mug tighter instead. "I'll just go back to the kitchen." Maybe when she got away from Vivian she would remember how to swallow, breathe, and do other things that would help her stay alive and drink the coffee.

She'd already turned to go when Vivian said, "No. Stay here. Look at this." She held out her phone.

Jules was already extending her hand when she realized that this was Vivian's personal phone, not the one she used for *Du Jour* business. People didn't just do that. Jules hadn't let anybody look at her own phone since Aaron, and even then it had always made her nervous.

She took a deep breath and accepted the phone with a hand that shook only a bit. She hoped Vivian would put it down to fatigue. But no, Vivian was looking out the window onto the still-dark street, not paying attention to her at all.

"Preston sent that email sometime last night when we were gone," she said.

Jules sat down in the nearest chair, set her coffee aside, and studied the phone. It was the legal document about Robert's agreement to give Vivian full custody of the baby and to relinquish visitation rights. Robert had had to sign and initial it about fifty million times. He hadn't missed a single blank space. All the t's were crossed, all the i's were dotted, and all the dates were in good order.

"Oh," Jules said. This seemed like a good thing, but her chest felt heavy.

"I want this done." Vivian tapped her fingertips on the windowsill in agitation. "I want it final."

Jules couldn't blame Vivian—Robert clearly wanted out as soon as possible too. But people could change their minds once they were presented with the practical rather than the theoretical. Once the baby was born, it was entirely possible that he would want to share custody or at least be a part of his or her life.

But would that be so bad? In her head, Jules heard Preston's voice telling Vivian that the child had a right to know its father. And Vivian had seemed open to reconciling with Robert before the whole infidelity thing had come out.

What if she relented? Maybe that would be the best thing for everyone. It'd be better for the kid, who wouldn't grow up thinking that his—or her—father had never wanted anything to do with her. Or him.

But maybe…

There was one possibility that made Jules feel ice-cold inside, and she voiced it before she could stop herself. "What if he changes his mind?"

"That's what I'm worried about." Vivian gestured angrily at her phone. "Didn't you hear me say 'I want this done'?"

"Yes," Jules said and then added, "No, I mean, not about the baby, about—about your relationship or something."

She got an incredulous look.

Jules didn't see why the idea was so outlandish. Yes, the divorce would be finalized by the time the baby arrived, but it wasn't beyond the realm of possibility that Robert would change his mind. What if he wanted Vivian back? What if she took him back for the kid's sake?

"What if he does?" Vivian said coldly.

"Nothing," she mumbled, retreating in the face of Vivian's clear reluctance to discuss the issue.

But Vivian might change her mind too. And if she did, if she took Robert back and became part of a happy little nuclear family, the agony Jules had suffered last night at the ball—watching all those men watching Vivian—would be a cakewalk in comparison. Just thinking about it made her feel physically ill now that she knew…

Knew *what*?

Jules noted the time on her phone. "Um, I need to take my shoes and accessories back to *Du Jour UK*. The office opens at eight. I'll just call Jimmy, if that's okay."

And if it wasn't okay, she'd take the Underground. She'd hitchhike. She'd walk in her bare feet. She needed to get out of here for an hour or so, needed to breathe.

"Fine." Vivian gave her a long, inscrutable look. She extended her hand for the phone. "Don't forget our lunch reservation today." Yesterday morning she'd had Jules book a table for two at Core in Notting Hill, citing a desperate need to get the hell out of the townhouse. She hadn't seemed interested in meeting with any associates for this one. "Be back here by noon."

Jules rose to hand her the phone. "Do you want me to make breakfast?"

"No." Vivian's cheeks went a little paler, and a shudder ran along her frame.

Jules left without saying another word. She called Jimmy, went upstairs, and carefully packed up the accessories and shoes. She had no idea how to explain the missing jumpsuit. "Vivian said I can keep it" seemed a little thin.

She'd figure something out. In the meantime, she used the car ride to pull herself together. It didn't completely work, but she reminded herself of some salient facts.

Like the fact that Vivian was over a decade older than her. And Vivian was getting divorced. And was pregnant. And was Jules's boss. And liked men, not women, as far as Jules knew.

It had to be a defense mechanism. Jules was still stung from losing Aaron, and so she'd fixated on somebody safe, or—okay, not safe. Not safe at all. But somebody she didn't have a chance with. Somebody unattainable so that she didn't have to worry about having an actual relationship. That was all.

And this was so sudden. At least, it felt sudden. It had obviously been building up for a long time, *but that totally didn't matter* because Jules was overreacting and letting her feelings go to her head, and in a few days' time she was going to feel ridiculous about this. It wasn't a true feeling. It was an impulse, a crush on a mentor figure, the result of months of celibacy. It was anything but genuine. It'd vanish like the wind.

Jules told Jimmy not to wait for her, deciding that taking the Tube home or even just wandering around for a couple of hours would be good for her. Anything that kept her away from Vivian until lunchtime would be good for her, in fact.

The *Du Jour UK* offices were much more sparsely populated than they had been on her last visit, although they weren't completely closed for the public holiday. They felt lonely.

Georgie and Janys weren't there. Hopefully, they'd done something suitably wild for New Year's Eve. The front desk was manned by a lone receptionist, who looked sleepy.

Jules made matters easy on herself, saying only, "Vivian wants to keep the jumpsuit. You can call the *Du Jour* office in New York when she gets back to confirm." That seemed good enough for the receptionist, who surely wasn't paid enough to deal with Vivian Carlisle. She accepted the package with a friendly New Year's greeting, and Jules escaped.

The streets felt deserted when she emerged from the building. Few Londoners or tourists were out and about at eight a.m. after a night of revelry. No shops or attractions were open yet.

Jules's stomach growled, and she realized she hadn't had breakfast. At least some restaurants had lit OPEN signs in the windows. She stopped in a nearby café, glad of the warmth inside. When she'd decided to go for a walk, she'd forgotten how cold it would be, especially at this time of day. She'd been spoiled by cozy car rides.

She bought a coffee plus bacon and eggs (might as well enjoy them while Vivian wasn't around to get nauseated) and pulled out her phone as she began to eat. She'd have to edit her article later today. In the meantime, she scrolled Twitter. It had been a while since she checked her feed.

Oh wow. The first recommended tweet came from a gossip site showing pictures of the New Year's ball at the Dorchester. It was official: her phone was spying on her.

Jules tapped on the article and skimmed the photos. There was a picture of the London mayor, a couple of MPs, and socialites Jules didn't recognize.

And there was one of Jules and Vivian too. They were leaving the ball, going down the stone steps. Vivian looked elegant but also vaguely pissed off. Jules, thank goodness, was looking down at the steps so no one could really see her face.

She read the caption: *Tyrannical American fashion queen Vivian Carlisle leaves the ball with no date but a lowly assistant. Looks like soon-to-be-ex-hubby had a better time and bubblier company.*

What?

Lowly assistant? Hubby? Bubblier company? *Lowly assistant?*

Already snarling with indignation, Jules searched for *Robert Kirk New Year's*. The first result was a photo of him with a dazzling, big-chested blonde on his arm, a young British actress currently living in New York. And she was dating Vivian's husband.

Robert was looking down at her with an utterly fatuous expression on his face. His stupid, weak-chinned indecisive face that Jules had never found remotely appealing and which she now realized was downright repulsive. Asshole.

Jules fought the urge to throw her phone across the café. She'd only eaten a few bites of her breakfast, but now she couldn't stomach another mouthful. Great start to the new year.

How many websites and feeds were featuring this crap? Not that she needed to be reminded that she was just a "lowly assistant" who only got to spend time with Vivian because "the tyrannical fashion queen" couldn't find somebody better.

She left her nearly full plate on the table and stormed out of the café. This just confirmed her worst fears, didn't it? She hadn't even been able to enjoy twenty-four hours of being in…in lust or infatuated or whatever it was called before her ridiculous thoughts had been shot out of the sky.

If Robert tried to get Vivian back after this, he'd be lucky if Jules didn't kick him in the balls.

Thank God Jules was leaving tomorrow. The sooner the better. London wasn't so great.

Glad of her warm coat, scarf, and hat, Jules kept walking. She remembered how Vivian had needed to go for a walk after discovering Robert's infidelity. She must have been feeling a lot worse than Jules felt right now.

Jules walked and walked while thinking unhappy thoughts, occasionally stopping to look at things and people. When she looked at her watch, it was eleven forty. She'd wandered too far from the townhouse to get there by noon. Shit.

Well—it didn't have to be a disaster. There was no way Vivian would want to venture out of doors after a humiliation like this. Jules just needed formal permission to cancel their lunch reservation.

She texted Vivian:

*Heading back now, calling an Uber, sorry*

Then she swiped open the Uber app, not expecting a response. To her surprise, though, Vivian texted only moments later:

*If you're not here at noon, we'll be late for lunch.*

She blinked. Vivian still wanted to go? She texted back:

*Sorry, I thought you'd want me to cancel, be right there*

Before she could go back to the Uber app, her phone rang. Vivian.

"Uh, hi," Jules said, bracing herself. "I'm just about to—"

"Why would I want to cancel?"

"I, uh—never mind. I guess it'd be faster for me just to meet you at the restaurant. I'm sorry."

"Where are you?"

Jules hadn't been paying attention at all to where she was going. She looked around for a street sign. "I'm not actually sure."

"Why are you not here?"

"You said noon—never mind." Jules wrapped her free arm around herself, shivering. "Time got away from me."

"Got away from you. Well."

"I was upset," Jules said before she could think better of it. "I just kept walking. I didn't mean to. But I can get to the restaurant before you and make sure the table's all ready."

"You were upset?"

Dammit. There was no use pretending. Either Vivian knew about the pictures or she'd find out soon, and she'd be pissed that Jules had danced around the subject.

"There are some photos of New Year's on Twitter," Jules mumbled. "Of you and m—of you leaving the ball."

"Oh. How upsetting."

"No, but—" Jules bounced up and down on the balls of her feet. *Just say it.* "There are also pictures of Robert in New York. With a woman."

Silence. Jules closed her eyes. This would be ugly.

Then Vivian said, "Core Restaurant. It's in Notting Hill."

Wait. That was it? That couldn't be it. "Um, yeah. I already told Jimmy, so he should—"

"Be there by twelve fifteen." She ended the call.

The bite in her voice could have cut through steel. Jules grimaced and looked up at the gray London sky. Lunch at a swanky restaurant after the revelations of last night with Vivian in a terrible mood.

Wouldn't this be fun?

# CHAPTER 23

It was not, in fact, fun.

Lunch was a silent and awkward affair. Jules had arrived about ten minutes before Vivian. It gave her enough time to drum her fingertips on the table and force herself not to look at Twitter again.

Then Vivian arrived at twelve thirty on the dot, casually elegant in slacks and a loose red blouse. Jules exhaled slowly at the sight of her. *You dumbass. You're a goner for sure.*

Thankfully, no reporters had followed Vivian to the restaurant, but several patrons inside recognized her. A few even knew her, and as they stopped by the table to say hello, Jules saw the curiosity and sometimes even the glee in their eyes. They must have seen the photos too.

Vivian greeted all of them with a cold smile, and soon enough her acquaintances mumbled their farewells and left her alone.

Simon had told Jules that Vivian didn't do "friends." Now Jules could see why.

Core was a soothing environment, even under these circumstances. Much more chill than the pink Music Room or the golden Dorchester ballroom. The color scheme was pale mint and cream, and the furniture had pleasing contemporary lines. Jules lusted after the wooden appetizer presentation plates. It wasn't like she cooked, but they'd look great in her kitchen. It must be nice to be able to buy stuff like this whenever you wanted.

The food was excellent too, but she couldn't enjoy her roasted monkfish. Still trying to set a good example for Vivian, who looked less than enthused, she ate almost every bite. Eventually, Vivian managed to eat most of her food, which still wasn't saying much, since Core was one of those restaurants that served teeny-tiny portions for outrageous sums of money.

Total rip-off. What Vivian needed was an Olive Garden. Jules tried to imagine her in one and almost choked on her ice water.

"What is it?" Vivian asked as she set her fork down.

"Nothing." She dabbed her napkin over her mouth. "Just swallowed the wrong way."

Vivian glared. "No, you thought of something funny. I can always tell with you. What are you laughing at?"

*I can always tell with you?* Please, please let that only be when Jules was thinking funny thoughts and not lustful ones.

"Because," Vivian continued, "I don't see that there's much to laugh at today."

Oh, so she wanted to get huffy. Jules couldn't blame her—when you were in a bad mood, sometimes you just wanted to lash out. And Vivian had plenty of reasons to be in a bad mood, but she wasn't the only one who didn't want to put up with bullshit today.

"Okay, fine." Jules put down her napkin with a little more firmness than necessary. "I was imagining taking you to an Olive Garden with a ton of food instead of a fancy restaurant, and it seemed like a funny idea. That's all."

Vivian looked at her as if she weren't sure Olive Gardens existed, much less that Jules would ever go to one. "'Taking me' to an Olive Garden?"

The emphasis in her words left no doubt as to what she objected to the most. Jules's face scalded. Why had she phrased it like that, like it would be a date or something? *You idiot.* "I know it's ridiculous. That's why it made me laugh."

Vivian flagged down their server for the check. "It must be nice to be easily amused. You make your own entertainment."

"I wasn't trying to be insensitive," Jules said. "I know this publicity is bad."

There was an awkward pause. The server arrived, and Vivian said nothing until he'd departed again. Then she sighed. "You think this is bad?"

"It's not great, is it?"

"It could be worse. It will be"—Vivian gestured vaguely at her abdomen—"once this news gets out. Just wait."

"It isn't just that," Jules blurted out. "How would you like being called 'lowly'?"

A baffled expression crossed Vivian's face. "What?"

Shoot. Jules hadn't meant to mention that. Compared to Vivian, she was getting off comically easy here. The caption hadn't even mentioned her name.

"Nothing," she muttered.

"Clearly it isn't. Spit it out."

No getting out of it now. Jules sighed and crossed her arms. "The website called me your 'lowly assistant.'"

"Well, that wasn't very nice of them."

"I know it isn't a big deal," Jules said through gritted teeth. "I just—"

"You don't get anywhere by worrying about the tabloids. They'll say what they say. What matters is that you know the truth about yourself." Vivian placed her napkin on the table with a snap. "And if you think you're lowly after all this, then I don't know what to tell you."

Good thing she didn't say anything else because Jules's ears started buzzing. Had that been a compliment? It sure sounded like one.

"Uh, yeah. Th-thank you for lunch," she stammered as she took out her phone. "I'll text Jimmy to get us."

"You do that. And then confirm our flight home."

Jules blinked. "What? You know I'm not on your flight, right?"

Vivian looked at her with wide eyes. Clearly she had not known that.

Dammit. "When I bought my ticket, they copied you on my itinerary. At least they were supposed to."

"Why aren't we on the same flight?" Vivian looked like she was getting ready to throw a pretty spectacular tantrum.

"It was full! The only flight I could get was tomorrow."

"*Tomorrow?*"

This wasn't going well. *Think fast.* "Yes, but that's good, right? It means I'll get back a day earlier and I can take care of things before you arrive. Right?"

Vivian did not look one jot less outraged.

"Did you really not get my itinerary?" Jules said.

"I didn't look at it," Vivian growled. "I assumed you'd know to accompany me home."

Jules took a deep breath and prayed for patience. "Vivian, your flight was full. Completely full. I didn't think one day would make any difference."

Vivian opened her mouth.

"I've got everything lined up for you," Jules added. "There'll be porters waiting to take your bags at the airport, and you'll get priority boarding. And the VIP lounge. And Ben will be waiting to pick you up at JFK. You won't need me for anything." She tried a cajoling smile. "I even told the girl at the VIP lounge to have decaf waiting when you get there."

Vivian set her jaw mulishly but said nothing else until they got into the car and Jimmy pulled away from the curb. Then she growled, "Don't do this again."

Saying she'd had no choice would be pointless. "Of course," she sighed.

"I've decided on Lucia's replacement," Vivian said, changing the subject as if they hadn't talked about airplanes at all. "Call Simon as soon as we're home."

"Okay." When Vivian said nothing else, Jules added, "Which one did you pick?"

Vivian blinked and shook her head slightly as if she were coming out of a reverie. "The least appalling. The one from *Elle*."

Simon's pick, then. Jules was relieved.

"Judging from her application," Vivian added, glancing down and adjusting her glove, "she would be absolutely delighted to work with me."

Jules bit her lip to repress a grin. "Work *with*?" she said, trying to sound polite.

"I'm glad you understand these things, Julia." Vivian settled back against her seat with just the hint of a smile.

# CHAPTER 24

JULES KEPT HER WORD. WHEN she flew out of London at an obscenely early hour the next morning before Vivian was even out of bed, she was already running through her mental checklist of things she had to take care of when she landed. It was an exhausting list. But Jules had only staved off Vivian's wrath by promising to take care of things, so that's what she had to do.

Yesterday afternoon had been okay. Reporters were lurking across the street of the townhouse when they got back from Core, but they hadn't gotten too close. By evening Vivian had seemed her old self again, and she'd spent the rest of the afternoon giving Jules orders to be fulfilled upon her return to New York.

All in all, it had been the weirdest holiday season ever.

She called Simon once the plane touched down.

"Come to the office as soon as you've dropped off your stuff," he said.

She called her parents at the baggage claim. "Glad you're home safe, sweetheart," her dad said. "And she's still back there?"

"Yes. She's flying in tomorrow."

"And she behaved herself?" His voice was hard.

Unfortunately, grievously, tragically, "Yes, she did. I told you it's not like that." Because life sucked.

"Well," her dad said, "okay."

She splurged on an Uber and made it back to her apartment, which Jules tried not to compare to Vivian's London place. She was going to miss sleeping in Rob—in the *second bedroom,* where Vivian had definitely never had sex with Robert, as Jules had told herself every single night with different feelings on the subject each time.

She took a quick shower, telling herself that it was good to hit the ground running. Keeping busy was the best way to avoid spending all her time feverishly thinking about what it would be like to have sex with Vivian. The best part of her relationship with Chelsea had been the sex. Somehow, Jules was absolutely certain that it'd be even better with Vivian because the woman was the best at everything she did.

Jules was pretty sure that a week ago the very thought of having sex with Vivian would have horrified her. Well, okay, not horrified. If you were horrified by the thought of having sex with someone, you didn't imagine them in lingerie.

At some point, she was going to run out of ways to call herself an idiot.

Either way, Jules wouldn't have had the guts to sit around and think about Vivian's breasts and wonder if they were sensitive. Or if Vivian made noises. Or if Vivian liked having sex at all because it was entirely possible that she didn't, no matter who it was with. Or if it would even be safe for her to do it now. All the information said it was "during most normal pregnancies." But what about this was normal?

Not that it mattered. It wasn't going to happen.

Jules dosed herself liberally with coffee on the way back to *Du Jour*. She still wasn't prepared to go to her desk and be accosted by Simon within seconds.

"Well?" he said. "What kind of mood was she in yesterday?"

"Nice to see you too."

He waved negligently. "Blah, blah, blah. Where's my keychain with a little red phone booth on it?"

Jules grinned and held out the souvenir she'd bought for him in Heathrow.

Simon dangled the keychain from his fingers with a moue of distaste. "This is a teapot."

She kept a straight face. "Teapots are in right now. Phone booths are passé. Vivian told me so herself."

"Is that so?" Simon tucked the keychain into the pocket of his plaid pants. "I repeat: how is she?"

"Oh, you know," Jules hedged. "Fine. The usual."

"I saw the photos of Robert."

Jules sat at her desk with a heavy sigh. "Okay, it's shitty. She took it on the chin, though."

"She always does."

Jules fought down a silly, warm tingle of pride. "Yeah, she does."

Simon gave her a long look, but all he asked was, "So everything went okay, assistant-wise?"

She was catapulted back to the night Simon had interrogated Jules about Vivian's pregnancy. Vivian had asked Jules why Simon would do such a thing. Jules had said it was because Simon trusted her.

Simon could trust Jules to be loyal to Vivian. He should appreciate that. Weren't they both on Vivian's side, after all?

"It was fine," she said. "She kept me busy with work."

"Work and the New Year's ball at the Dorchester. Did you follow her around taking notes?"

"Mental ones, yeah."

"Jules. It is insane that she took you."

"She needed a plus-one! Robert—"

"It. Is. Insane."

They glared at each other.

"I'm an assistant," Jules said. "Don't worry. I got the message loud and clear."

Simon sighed and rubbed his forehead. "I'm not bashing you or implying—hell. It's just weird. I know Vivian has her whims and it's not up to mere mortals to question them. And I know you were just doing your job."

*Yeah. My job. That's all it was*, Jules reminded herself. *Straight from the clotheshorse's mouth. Stop being stupid.*

Luckily, she knew a welcome change of subject. "Oh, hey! Guess what? I submitted an article for *The Cut* that got accepted. You know that column 'I Think About This a Lot?'"

"I do." Simon's eyes lit up with genuine interest. "That's great. What did you write about?"

"*Working Girl*. Sigourney Weaver and Melanie Griffith's characters bonding. And don't look at me like that."

"Why would I look at you like anything? An ingenue bonding with her cold-blooded boss. Doesn't ring a bell at all."

Did Simon think Jules had written a veiled version of her own dynamic with Vivian at *Du Jour*? How ludicrous. It was totally different! For one thing, Melanie had fallen for Harrison Ford, not Sigourney. For another thing...

Jules would come up with the other thing later. "If you're implying I wrote about myself, you're wrong. You should rewatch the movie."

"With Harrison Ford in his prime? Twist my arm. When's your column coming out?"

"Two weeks. I'm about to make the edits and send it off."

"I look forward to reading it." Simon tilted his head to the side. "Congratulations. A first step. So what's your second?"

Jules groaned.

It earned her a finger wag. "You can't slow down," Simon warned. "Not yet. Chase that dream."

Against her will, Jules thought of Vivian. Talk about an unattainable dream. Simon was right—better to focus on a writing career that with a lot of effort might be possible.

She was known for making the impossible happen, but there had to be a limit somewhere.

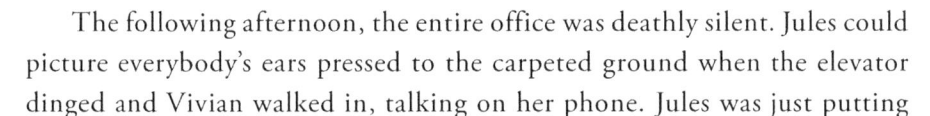

---

The following afternoon, the entire office was deathly silent. Jules could picture everybody's ears pressed to the carpeted ground when the elevator dinged and Vivian walked in, talking on her phone. Jules was just putting the silverware to either side of her salad plate for lunch.

Vivian looked like hell, though probably only Jules would be able to see it. She was dressed beautifully, impeccably made up and moving with her usual confident stride. But Jules noticed the exhaustion in her eyes and the tension in her shoulders. She'd arrived in New York just a few hours ago and had clearly made only the briefest stop at home before coming to work.

Jules made a mental note to schedule a massage for later in the week. In the meantime, Vivian walked straight by Jules's desk. She didn't look at her or stop talking. Jules hadn't really expected anything else, but it was still a little disappointing to realize that pretty much nothing was going to change after she'd spent over a week living with Vivian, making her breakfast and escorting her to meals.

Well, why should it? Nothing would change because nothing was different, except that Jules had let herself ascend to new heights of stupidity, starting with New Year's Eve.

The rest of the day progressed as most days did, with Vivian being disagreeable and Jules scrambling to obey her orders as fast as possible.

*See?* Jules told herself. *Just an assistant. Like you told Simon.*

Vivian left the office at six thirty, looking even more exhausted. Jules didn't get to go home until her own to-do list was done, so she could kiss her cushy car ride home goodbye.

That should have been that. But as Vivian strode by Jules's desk, she paused to open her Donna Karan purse. Then she took out a Ziploc bag with a round boar bristle hairbrush in it. "You forgot this."

Jules's face burned as she looked at it. She hadn't finished unpacking yet, so she hadn't noticed anything missing. "Thanks," she mumbled. "Sorry for leaving it."

"Oribe brushes are expensive. I had visions of you disgracing *Du Jour* by replacing it with something from Duane Reade. Be more careful."

Jules's face was even hotter now. On the list of embarrassing things, looking careless in front of Vivian Carlisle placed pretty high. Plus the reminder that she didn't make enough money to replace nice things.

But…Vivian had noticed, probably when doing one final sweep through the town house before leaving. Which meant she'd touched Jules's hairbrush, handled it, and then packed it up among her own things.

*That's not sexy*, Jules told herself. *It's a hairbrush. It's not sexy.*

"Thank you," she repeated quietly as she reached for the bag.

Their fingertips brushed when she took it. Jules hadn't done it on purpose, had she?

Her whole body ached with desire at just the slightest touch, and if Vivian said anything on her way out the door, Jules didn't hear it. Her blood was roaring too loudly in her ears.

Then she was alone. Jules looked blankly at the plastic bag. Well, out of all the things she'd lost in London, including her hairbrush, her common sense, and her sanity, it was nice to get at least one of them back.

# CHAPTER 25

"Have a good trip?" Ben asked in the car the next morning. "I heard you went to London."

"Don't ask," Jules said. "How was your holiday?"

"Spent it with my folks. Went out with some buddies to a bar on New Year's. Looks like you went somewhere fancier. I saw photos of you with Vivian on Twitter."

"Um, yeah. It was pretty fun."

"Must have been. That was, uh…some outfit." His voice had a hesitant edge as he clearly tried to walk the line and figure out what was allowed. He wanted to know if Jules would open the door or slam it shut.

*Time to slam.* "Yeah. Did I remember to forward you Vivian's itinerary this week?"

He gave in with good grace. "You did. It's all under control. Hey, you're from Philly, right? You follow the Eagles?"

"Do I follow the Eagles? Are you serious?" She wasn't a sports nut, but she was from Philadelphia. Of course she followed the Eagles. What sort of question was that?

Ben laughed. "Thought so. What do you think of this season so far?"

"Okay, except for when we lost to the freaking *Cowboys*. It was so embarrassing…"

Fifteen minutes passed in no time. Soon they were pulling up to the curb as Vivian descended the steps of her home. Jules, in mid-rant about a lousy referee call, hardly paid any attention to her until she opened the door the very second Ben came to a full stop.

"I swear to God they paid off the ref—oh," Jules said. "Um. Good morning, Vivian."

"Good morning, Ms. Carlisle," Ben said, clearly taken aback.

Vivian ignored Jules as she closed the door but gave Ben one of the coldest looks Jules had ever seen. Her stomach twisted. She'd forgotten all about Vivian's threat to fire him.

Ben, glancing in the rearview mirror, caught sight of Vivian's deadly glare. His eyes went wide in surprise.

"Is there some reason we're not moving?" Vivian asked.

"Sorry," Ben said quickly and pulled away.

Jules sat in silence, not even daring to look at Vivian.

"You two were awfully chatty when I got in the car," Vivian said.

Crap. Jules looked out of the window. *Please don't fire him.*

When Jules didn't reply, Ben, sounding puzzled, took it upon himself to say, "Yes, Ms. Carlisle. Just talking about football."

"Football," Vivian said. "Really."

"Yes. Uh, right, Jules?"

"Right. That's it." Jules finally dared to look at Vivian, whose face was absolutely closed. It wasn't against the law to talk about football. It wasn't even against company policy. Was it?

"Planning to see a game sometime together, Ben?" Vivian asked.

Oh no. No, no, no.

Ben glanced back in the rearview mirror. "Uh, I guess that might be… fun."

*Wrong answer, wrong answer*, Jules thought frantically.

"Fun," Vivian said lightly.

After a few seconds with his eyes on the road, Ben said, "Or not."

"Right," Vivian said. "I don't think it would be fun at all. Do you, Julia?"

"No." Jules resisted the urge to tack *ma'am* on the end of it. She couldn't believe she wanted to sleep with this woman. But she did. Even right now she did. Even right in the back seat with the privacy divider up—

"I rely absolutely," Vivian said, "on the professionalism of all my employees."

The back of Ben's neck was turning red. "Yes, Ms. Carlisle."

"I hope I never have to mention this again."

"No, Ms. Carlisle."

"Good." Vivian settled back in her seat looking almost pleased. She said nothing for the rest of the ride. But when Jules hurried to Vivian's desk with a coffee in hand, Vivian gave her a loaded glance from her chair. Locked and loaded, even.

"Well, then," Vivian said. "I didn't fire him."

Jules exhaled. "Thanks, Vivian."

"I stood to gain nothing from it." Vivian paused. "But…you're welcome."

---

Two weeks after her return from London, it was time for Vivian's ultrasound appointment. She was at the end of her first trimester. And Jules, of course, was coming along.

The hour at the obstetrician's was awful. Jules had to deal with checking Vivian in and then sitting with her in the waiting room. Vivian didn't say a word. Just once Jules would have given her eyeteeth for Vivian to bombard her with orders, look down her nose, or do anything other than sit so quietly that Jules knew she was terrified.

She couldn't deal with Vivian being terrified. It was as bad as the night Vivian had learned she was pregnant. No. Worse. And then she had to watch Vivian leave to accompany a nurse while Jules kept waiting, which was why they called it a waiting room.

When the nurse returned for her, Jules almost tripped in her haste to get to the office. Vivian looked perfectly calm as she sat in front of Dr. Viswanathan's desk, but that could mean anything.

The doctor smiled at Jules. She wasn't the type of person to smile when something was going wrong. Daring to hope, Jules lowered herself into the other chair in front of the desk.

"As I was telling Vivian, everything seems to be okay," Dr. Viswanathan said, and Jules decided that getting out of bed this morning had been worthwhile. "There isn't much we can tell at this point, but this first screening detected no serious issues. Positioning and fetal heartbeat are normal. Now, I just want to clear up a few things with you. How's your diet?"

"Fine," Vivian said.

Dr. Viswanathan looked at Jules, who nodded. Then she looked back at Vivian. "You're getting enough iron and folic acid?"

Vivian glanced at Jules. "I don't know. Am I?"

"Yes. In your food and in the prenatal vitamins I always put next to your breakfast. You're taking them, right?"

"Of course I am."

"Exercise?"

"I meet with my trainer three mornings a week." Vivian waved her hand. "She's got me doing some prenatal routine."

"Which is?"

Jules pulled a copy of the exercise routine out of her bag and passed it over the desk.

Dr. Viswanathan looked it over. "This seems good. You're sleeping?"

"Better," Vivian said, sounding evasive for the first time, earning her a very direct look. "I'm still adjusting to the time change," she added after a moment.

"You said you got back from London two weeks ago."

"I'm fine," Vivian said. "Better. I said I'm better."

"It's important that you get enough rest," Dr. Viswanathan said firmly.

"Well, she's been going home earlier," Jules said, like some kind of ob-gyn wingman. "That's good, right?"

The doctor nodded. "That's a start, but, Vivian, I want you to take maternity leave for the entire last month of your pregnancy. At your age—"

"That isn't an option," Vivian said, her tone final.

"What's more important?" Dr. Viswanathan asked. "Your job or your health? Or the child's health?"

Vivian narrowed her eyes.

Jules jumped in before the bomb could go off. "I bet all that can be decided later, right?"

"True." Dr. Viswanathan looked down at her notes while Vivian relaxed.

Twenty minutes later, as they were heading back to the car, Vivian said derisively, "'Maternity leave.' Please."

"Well, you're going to have to take some after the baby's born," Jules said. "Aren't you?"

"Yes." Vivian didn't sound remotely happy about it. She clucked her tongue. "I'm sure Mark will be ecstatic, just waiting for me to—"

She cut herself off, but Jules knew what she meant. In terms of Vivian's career, the pregnancy couldn't have happened at a worse time, when Mark Tavio was quite possibly looking for an excuse to get rid of her. Which meant that Vivian, who should be resting, would undoubtedly work harder than ever.

Jules wished she had a say in all this: that she could make Mr. Tavio leave Vivian alone, that she could make Vivian stay home and sleep in once in a while, that she could just fix everything. But wishing hadn't done her any favors so far.

It'd also be nice to have a life outside of all this. Jules doubted that was going to happen anytime soon.

# CHAPTER 26

Then, the very next day, it did.

Vivian had gone home at six thirty, her new normal. Jules was almost used to it now and told herself that she did *not* miss having Vivian's company until ten thirty, when they would go down to the car and ride together to Vivian's place without even talking to each other. It was much better for Vivian to be at home resting, as Dr. Viswanathan had said. God knew she kept busy enough during the day.

It was quieter now, though, at nearly seven p.m. Jules had finished making tomorrow's to-do list and decided to check her personal inbox before heading out the door. And there it was: an email notifying her that her column for *The Cut* had been published.

She squealed aloud and then looked around, her face heating. Thank God nobody was here to hear that. But nobody was here to share her triumph either, except…

*My column's in The Cut today!!!!*

Moments later, Simon texted back.

*Cool, looking now*

Jules looked too, taking in every word as greedily as if she'd never seen them before. She kept going back to her name at the top. *Julia Moretti.* It had seemed appropriate somehow to use her full first name. In Jules's imagination, Vivian murmured her approval.

Dammit. Jules's cheeks were heating again.

Fifteen minutes later, Simon strode into the office, phone in hand and eyebrows raised. "Nice job."

*Yes!* "You think it's good? It doesn't suck?"

"Don't fish for compliments. No, it doesn't suck. I like how you point out that Melanie Griffith ends up being just another cog in the machine." He gave Jules a wry look. "Like all the rest of us."

"Don't get cynical on me, now." She rested her elbows on her desk, propped her chin in her palms, and gave a happy sigh. "Look at me. I'm going to win a Pulitzer."

"Your delusions are adorable."

Jules laughed. She might be a little punchy. "*The New Yorker* will call me tomorrow. You'll see."

"Would you settle for *Salon* in the meantime?"

"Ha! Sure, why not?"

It took her a full five seconds to realize Simon wasn't kidding. She slowly raised her chin from her palms while he smirked down at her.

"Simon?" she asked.

He waved his phone. "This isn't substantial, but it's fun. Put it on your résumé and cook up something meatier. I'll wave it under the nose of a starving *Salon* editor, and we'll see what happens."

Simon had never offered her a favor like this before, even when she was working for him. Why now?

Her question must have shown in her eyes because he said, "Maybe I was just waiting for you to show me what you've got."

"You said it wasn't substantial," Jules pointed out. "I've written better stuff that—"

"Never got published. Do you want this or not?"

It wasn't the time to be suspicious. Simon was dropping a golden opportunity in her lap, and he was her friend.

She nodded hard. "Of course. What are they looking for right now?"

"A friend over there tells me their culture section wants new blood. Look at the website, see what they publish, and come up with something good."

"By when?"

"Do I work at *Salon*? As soon as possible, obviously. I told you to always have something on the hop."

"I will." Her head was already spinning. "I'll have it done in just a couple of days. Thank you, Simon. I owe you one."

"Yes"—he folded his arms—"you do."

It seemed an awfully serious response to abject gratitude, but Jules pushed the thought aside while she packed up to leave. She had a lot of research to do tonight.

---

She didn't go home. Instead, she headed straight to her favorite coffee shop so she could work surrounded by the comforting scents of roasting beans and baked goods. A caffeine boost could only help.

One espresso and a half hour later, though, Jules was still dry of ideas. None of the potential topics she'd been playing with were suitable for the culture section. Now she was uninspired *and* jittery.

It was just past eight and cold. Her apartment called seductively to her, but she wouldn't find anything in there. Jules recognized this itch. She needed to walk.

Good thing she was wearing low-heeled boots. Jules slung her bag over her shoulder and headed out into the night.

New York wasn't as dangerous as people liked to say, but a woman still had to be careful by herself at night. She needed somewhere with plenty of people but with enough space that she could think.

Brooklyn's Domino Park was well out of her way—a half hour by subway. It was one of her favorite places, though, and tonight it was worth the trip and the chill.

The subway ride proved similarly uninspiring, and when Jules set foot onto the park paths, she sighed. She tightened her wool scarf, tugged her beanie down farther over her ears, and stuck her gloved hands into her coat pockets. Her breath misted the air.

"Let's see how this goes," she muttered.

She walked briskly, staying to the most populated paths, checking out people as she passed. A young man rollerbladed around a fountain, heedless of the cold. A father told two kids in puffy coats that it was time to go home. Jules overheard three women planning to go for a drink. Everyone seemed to be in motion with not a second to hold still.

Except two people on a bench. As she approached, Jules saw they were middle-aged women who were holding hands. Clearly a couple.

The warmth in her cheeks was a welcome relief from the chill. She tried not to stare—rude *and* uncool—but for some reason, she couldn't help it.

One of them was a stocky woman with short hair wearing a leather bomber jacket covered with patches for different bands. Her partner wore the brightest pink lipstick Jules had ever seen. Their smiles to each other were unforced, their intimacy easy and familiar.

Jules's chest ached. What would it be like to sit next to Vivian on a park bench, holding her hand and talking about something that made them both smile?

*Not in this life.*

She couldn't help it. They were pulling her toward them, but she couldn't be that weirdo who approached strangers out of nowhere. Feeling absurd, Jules wandered closer to them, pretending to look at the East River.

"We've got to get out of town for a while," the femme woman—Jules dubbed her Pink Lipstick—was saying. "You promised."

"I know," Bomber Jacket replied, "but if you want to take your road trip, January isn't the time."

"I don't think I can wait much longer. My job's going to make me lose it."

"You said you wanted to see Montana. It'll be even colder there!"

Jules smiled. They were bickering, but there was no real anger in it. It was how you argued with someone you knew well, cared for, enjoyed having in your life.

*Must be nice.*

Unable to help it, she turned and looked at them again. What a striking picture. Enough to start wheels turning in her head.

*Leather bomber jacket...pinkest lipstick I ever saw...two women who love each other...*

"Fashion is about two things," Vivian murmured in Jules's memory. "Expression and context."

Jules's eyes widened. There it was. Her topic.

The butch woman glanced over and saw Jules looking. The lively smile on her face vanished. Her partner followed her gaze.

"See something you like?" Pink Lipstick asked.

Dammit. Caught. "Sorry," she said sheepishly. "I was just…just…" She looked at their hands, still entwined, and something in her said: "Tell them."

Okay. Why not? What did she have to lose?

"I'm a writer," she said. "I write about fashion. I didn't mean to stare. It's just that you two are such a striking picture—your styles look amazing together."

They must have heard the sincerity in her voice. Bomber Jacket inclined her head with a smile. "Well, thanks."

"So are we gonna get hired for the runway?" Pink Lipstick asked dryly, snuggling closer to her partner.

"I wish. That's…what I want to write about."

"It is?"

"Yeah." Jules pressed her lips together and took a risk: "I don't want to sound weird, but can I take your picture?"

A few minutes later, after showing them her business card and promising she wasn't a conservative in deep cover, Jules was walking away with a spring in her step and a new photo on her phone. For inspiration. For her work.

The thought wasn't fully formed. She didn't know where it would take her. But that was her topic: queer representation in fashion. Specifically, the lack of it.

The fashion industry was full of gay designers, but you could look through mainstream magazines and blogs for days and not find anything that looked like those two women and their lived experiences.

In spite of the cold, she looked at the photo as she walked back to the nearest subway station. Once they'd realized her intentions, the women had given her sunny smiles as they held hands and leaned into one another. She didn't know their names, probably never would, but the image of them would stay with her for a long time.

They just looked so…happy together.

*I wish I had someone to show this to.*

The thought was absurd—Jules had plenty of people she *could* show this to—but she was only thinking about the one person to whom she couldn't.

*What are you going to do? Show Vivian this photo, melt her icy heart, and sweep her into your arms? Time to stop dreaming and start doing.*

Jules could do that. She would do that.

Now she just needed to start writing.

# CHAPTER 27

By the next morning, she still hadn't settled on a catchy opening line, but she'd made an outline. It would do for a start. This was the best opportunity Jules had had in a long time to do something beyond her job. Something she could carve out for herself.

With Simon's help, yes, but still. It was a thrill and a half.

She'd gotten about three hours of sleep, and she looked tired—so tired that Ben asked her if she was okay when he picked her up. It didn't matter, though. She'd pulled more than a few all-nighters in college. She could power through this, and right now she was running on sheer adrenaline.

As usual, when Ben let Vivian into the car, Vivian was already talking. "Good morning, Julia. Contact Alexandra Nataf as soon as we get to the office. I want to collaborate with her on a shoot for summer and see if we can get some audience crossover with her magazine. And then I'll want coffee." She looked up just in time to see Jules beam at her, and she blinked in evident curiosity.

But Jules just said "Of course, Vivian." She began making notes of everything. There was yet another busy day ahead, and an even busier night. She had to focus her brainstorming into something coherent that might be worth reading.

It could be done. That was why Vivian had hired her, right? Because she could get stuff done against the odds.

She made it through the day. By the time she got home, it seemed impossible to push her brain any further. Then she opened her laptop, checked out her notes, and got a second wind.

*Come on, Jules,* she told herself. *You can do it. He said ASAP, so do it ASAP.*

Right. She took a deep breath and dove in.

---

She didn't make it to bed until two thirty. The next morning, all the makeup in the world couldn't hide the dark circles under her eyes.

When Vivian got into the car, she rattled off the usual instructions without missing a beat. But for a second, she seemed to look at Jules with concern.

"Julia, are you…"

Jules lifted her chin and tried to look alert. "Yes?"

After a pause, she shook her head. "Nothing. Don't forget my ten thirty meeting."

"Of course. Am I coming with you?"

Vivian considered it for a moment. "No. Not this time."

That sounded cryptic, but Jules was too tired to wonder about it for long. Vivian had her secrets, and that was that.

At midmorning, after Vivian had left for her mysterious meeting, Simon stopped by Jules's desk. "You look bushed. Success?"

She sat back in her chair with a deep exhale. "I've got a rough draft. Fifteen hundred words about how queer representation in fashion shows up mostly in street style. They're all terrible."

"I can't submit fifteen hundred terrible words to a friend, whether they're queer or not. Would you consider upgrading them to mediocre?"

She glared at him.

His smirk turned kind. "I don't mean to be harsh. There's a light in your eyes that isn't there when you're scheduling meetings or getting coffee. You're doing what you love. I like that—it becomes you."

Her heart softened. He wasn't wrong; it was satisfying to do her job well, and she loved looking after Vivian because…she just did, that was all. But this was different. She was following her passion at last.

"Which is good for you," Simon added, "because I told this friend of mine that you'd have something for her tomorrow, which is when she needs it. I'll forward you her email address. Her name is Casey Dukakis."

"*Tomorrow?*" At the delicate rise of Simon's left eyebrow, Jules pulled herself together. She'd done stuff more at the last minute than that. "I'll have it ready. But I won't have had time to show it to anybody else. I'll spellcheck it, but—"

"If you can't stand the heat," said Simon, "get out of hell."

---

She emailed Casey her article around eight thirty the next morning in between errands. She copied Simon too. She'd been up almost all night again and hadn't put the finishing touches on the article until three. And she still felt it wasn't good enough.

This was getting ridiculous. Casey Dukakis would either like the piece or she wouldn't, but at least Jules hadn't let the opportunity pass her by. Still, her hands trembled, and she was on edge all day long. Nobody would get back to her right away, but she couldn't help it. She had to get herself together.

Tonight, though, was the night Vivian didn't let her get away with it.

She'd stayed at the office later than usual. Around seven thirty, she called Jules into the office, gesturing for her to sit at the other side of the desk. Jules looked at her anxiously and hoped nothing was wrong.

Vivian looked pretty good today: her coloring was healthy, and she'd eaten all of her breakfast and lunch. Jules guiltily realized that she hadn't been keeping quite as close an eye on Vivian the past couple of days. But now her article was finished, and she could stop obsessing over it. As much, anyway.

"What is it?" Vivian said.

Huh? What was what? Vivian had been the one to call her in, hadn't she?

"What's your problem?" Vivian clarified. "You've been running around like a chicken with its head cut off for days, and you look like you haven't slept in a week." She scowled.

Should Jules tell her? Well, why not? It wasn't a secret. She certainly wasn't ashamed of it. Jules had only wanted to hold off until it was more of a sure thing, until she could say, "Actually, Vivian, I'm having an article published in *Salon*."

Then Jules would be on her way to becoming a person who deserved to talk to Vivian Carlisle. Someone much more interesting than a lowly assistant, someone who could bring more to the table than decaf and a schedule.

Someone who could show up at a fancy luncheon and not have everyone wonder why on earth she was there. Someone with a mind and heart to offer, not just an able pair of hands and feet.

But Vivian wanted to know now, and there was no use in lying or trying to cover it up, so she took a deep breath, clasped her hands together, and said, "Well, I-I've just been working on an article. I emailed it to *Salon* this morning."

Instead of looking impressed, Vivian frowned. "A *Salon* article? You?"

Like it was completely outlandish. Jules's temper flared. "What does *that* mean?"

"Not what you're thinking." She shook her head. "You're unknown. Someone like you can't just expect to get published on a popular site via the slush pile. You have to know someone."

Mollified that Vivian hadn't been slighting her, just her lack of exposure, Jules perked up. "Oh, I know! Simon helped me."

Vivian blinked. "He did?"

"Yep. He knows an editor there, and he said he'd put me on her radar. But I had to write the article first." She took a deep breath and exhaled it. "I sent it today. That's what I've been doing the past few days. Not while I was supposed to be working, though," she added quickly. "Just before work or afterward or whatever."

This time, Vivian didn't blink. In fact, she stared at her without blinking. Jules had heard somewhere that serial killers often did that. "I see."

She was starting to get a bad feeling about this. But why? "Uh, nothing's guaranteed, of course. I just have to wait and see."

"'Wait and see.'" Vivian's voice was clipped. "All right, then. Get my coat."

Tonight she didn't wait for Jules to assist her but just snatched her things out of Jules's hands and headed for the elevator without another word, without even looking at her.

Jules sat down at her desk, trembling a little. That hadn't gone well, but she didn't know why. Vivian didn't have any mortal enemies at *Salon*, and there was decent crossover between both audiences. It didn't make sense. All she knew was that her glow of anticipation was gone now because she was worried she'd upset Vivian.

It was just that, in some tiny, pathetic part of her head, she had wanted Vivian to be proud of her. She hadn't expected praise but had at least expected Vivian to see, for her to *recognize*…

So much for that. It hadn't happened, and Jules had pissed off Vivian instead of pleasing her.

That night, while she sat at home in her apartment, Jules thought about how she'd felt so excited and how Vivian had ruined it. And for the first time in a long time, she let herself hate Vivian Carlisle just a teeny little bit.

---

"So tell me," Simon said the next morning, "why is Vivian treating me like I have bubonic plague?"

Jules winced as she looked up at him from her desk. At least Vivian was out. "It's not your fault. She's mad at me. I mean, I think that's it. Unless you did something else."

"Something else? Other than what?"

"Other than talking to Casey Dukakis for me."

He glared at her. "You told her?"

"I didn't know I shouldn't," she protested.

He rolled his eyes.

"What? I didn't! She asked me what I'd been so worked up about for the last few days, and I didn't see any point in lying."

"Great."

"I still don't know what was so wrong about it. Not everything I do has to be related to *Du Jour*." Or Vivian. That had been half the joy of the thing, after all: to do a tiny something that belonged to Jules alone.

"Yes, it does," Simon said, confirming her worst fears. "Vivian relies on you, Jules, to an extent I've never seen before."

"But—"

"Now she thinks you're on the hunt for something better. She's afraid you'll quit. Which, by the way, if the opportunity arises—do it."

"Quit?" She glared at him. "I'm not going to quit!"

"More fool you."

"Oh, come on, Simon. Casey might not even like it. Even if she does, it's just one article. I'm not going to quit for that."

"I don't know for sure it'll get published," Simon said, "but I read it. I think you're in with a chance."

"You do?"

"Sure. It makes the fashion industry seem out of touch, which *Salon* readers will eat up."

Oh shit. Simon and Vivian *were* the fashion industry. Her article had pointed out that queer rep in fashion primarily came from the nightclub scene and streetwear, not the runway. Had it seemed like she was biting the hand that fed her?

"I didn't mean that," she said quickly. "I wrote about how new queer designers are incorporating more elements of street style and hiring models with different looks and body types. Vivian's been encouraging that all along, and so have you."

"I know. I've been present for every idea I've ever encouraged. Relax. It's fine that you're spreading the word. It's a decent article."

Jules brightened. "Really? You really think so?"

He pointed at her. "There it is. There's that glow. I bet you anything Vivian saw it too. And didn't like it."

"That's not fair," she said weakly. And it wasn't. It was monstrously unfair, in fact. Did Vivian still not know, did she not understand what Jules would do—had done—for her? Didn't she even trust her not to quit her job?

"Since when is Vivian fair?" He had a point.

Jules looked down at her desk. "I didn't know she'd be like that." Then she smiled bitterly. "I guess I should have."

"You should have," he agreed, "especially since you got me in trouble too."

"Simon, I really am sorry."

He waved his hand, his enormous ring catching the fluorescent lights. "Not your fault. You can't change her."

He was right. She couldn't change Vivian. Nobody could. Leopards didn't change their spots.

She glanced at the closed door to Vivian's empty office. Leopards might not change their spots, but they were pretty good at eating people alive. Why should Jules stick around to get devoured?

She immediately imagined being devoured by Vivian in a more pleasant way, throbbed between her legs, and wondered if it wouldn't be better just to jump out of the nearest window.

# CHAPTER 28

Simon wasn't the only one who got the cold shoulder. Vivian didn't talk to Jules all day either.

Talk about taking the wind out of someone's sails. She tried not to droop.

Vivian left the office at two to get a manicure, returned at four, and continued to ignore Jules. At four fifteen, Simon walked in, gave Vivian something, and walked out again. He paused by Jules's desk.

"So I heard back from Casey," he said.

Jules forgot about Vivian for two seconds and stood up, wringing her hands.

He grinned at her.

They were going to publish her article! Jules clapped her hands and jumped up and down with a little squeal. "It's going in *Salon*? She liked it?"

"She liked it." He kept smiling. "You should hear from her soon. Nice work."

"I couldn't have done it without you," she said honestly. "Thank you so much, Simon."

He opened his mouth to say something, but at that moment, Vivian growled from within her office, "Julia, get Ellen von Unwerth for me. *Now.*"

She sounded furious. Of course she'd overheard.

Simon left quickly while Jules scrolled through the fashion photographers group on her phone. Better take care of this one quicker than quick.

That was the most Vivian spoke to her until nine p.m. She'd stayed later than usual tonight for no clear reason. She had no parties or engagements scheduled. Jules hadn't been called upon to do anything in the meantime, and now it was just the two of them alone.

Then at nine, Vivian called out "Julia" in a cool tone.

It gave Jules a clue about how this conversation was going to go. Shit. Vivian was going to do it again. Jules was happy for the second time about her story, and Vivian was going to ruin her mood *again*.

But no. No, that wasn't going to happen. Forget it. Jules wouldn't let her do that. She was excited about her work, and she was going to stay excited. So she lifted her chin and marched into Vivian's office with her head held high.

Vivian was not sitting behind her desk or on the chic sofa by the corner windows. She appeared to be pacing the office, her brow furrowed, her lips pressed together. When she saw Jules, she straightened her shoulders and said, "Have a seat."

Oh boy. This couldn't be good. Jules sat on the sofa and tried not to think about how she'd had Christmas dinner with this woman, how Vivian's shoulders had looked in her New Year's Eve gown, or about anything else that would weaken her resolve not to let Vivian get to her.

"The article you mentioned," Vivian said. "*Salon* is publishing it?"

She braced herself. "Yes. Simon told me this afternoon. I don't know any more details yet."

"Mm." Vivian stuck her tongue in her cheek and looked out the window at the sea of city lights beyond. She'd turned off the fluorescent lighting in her office, gently illuminating the space with two white-shaded lamps. They made the city's hundreds of lit windows and rooftops easier to see. Vivian seemed to be floating in space, untouchable.

"Let's talk about this…article," she said.

What was going on? Would Vivian actually try to stop *Salon* from publishing Jules's work? She probably could with just one call.

"It's only one article." Jules hated the plea in her voice. "Vivian, I've been trying to get published forever. I'm really happy about it."

"I'm sure you are," Vivian said, still looking out the window. Her hands tensed behind her back.

"I thought—" Jules said, then stopped. What if she said, *I thought you'd be proud of me* or *I thought you'd be happy too*" and Vivian laughed at her? "I didn't think it would bother you," she said.

"Bother me?" Vivian asked, her voice neutral.

"You seem kind of upset." She tried hard to remember that night in London when Vivian had sort of, more or less, told Jules to be honest with her. That night seemed long ago now. She gulped. "Um…if it's about, I don't know, my job, or—"

"Your job?" Vivian finally looked at her, frowning. "Didn't you say you worked on it during your free time?"

"Well, yeah."

"Then what does this have to do with your job?"

Would she ever in any lifetime be able to keep up with Vivian Carlisle? "I-I don't know."

"You asked Simon to help?"

Did Vivian think Jules had been sneaky about this, trying to go behind her back? "I just told…"

"You didn't ask *me*."

Jules froze. She snapped her mouth shut and found herself re-evaluating every single event in the last twenty-four hours.

"You didn't ask me," Vivian repeated. "Why not?"

Jules needed another couple of seconds to pull herself together. "I told you earlier. Simon knows someone at *Salon*, and—"

"I do too. And I doubt you'd have had to 'wait and see' if they'd accept you."

Jules just looked at her, stunned. It had never occurred to her to ask Vivian for any such thing. She managed to smile. "Well, I didn't want to bother you either. You've got a lot going on."

Vivian did not smile back. "Yes. Yes, it would have been a huge bother for me to contact *Salon* and tell them to give your work special consideration."

"No," Jules said quickly, "I didn't want special consideration, Vivian. I just wanted her to look at my stuff. Just to give it a chance." Because, yikes. Simon showing Casey Dukakis Jules's work was one thing. Vivian telling *Salon* to promote it was something else entirely, and Jules didn't want that. She wanted to do something on her own merits, not with Vivian's help. That was the whole point.

"You didn't want to bother me," Vivian said.

"No."

Vivian looked her dead in the eye. "It never even crossed your mind, did it?"

Jules furrowed her brow.

"It never even *occurred* to you to come to me."

She opened her mouth to lie and deny it, then she wondered if she should. Then she realized she had no idea what on earth she should say, period. She was in the middle of a conversation from Bizarro World.

Vivian evidently took her silence as confirmation. "Why didn't it occur to you?" she bit out. She looked more upset by the second. "Why did you go to Simon?"

Jules opened her mouth, closed it, then said, "I have no idea what's going on here."

"Neither do I. I can't imagine what you were thinking. Or not thinking. Why in the world—" Vivian cut herself off and shook her head.

"I don't know what you want me to say," Jules said hesitantly.

"Tell me why you didn't ask me," Vivian barked.

Jules stepped back, startled.

"Tell me why you didn't ask me for something you wanted that I could give you. That's what I want you to say."

Jules, who'd been on an emotional roller coaster all day, said numbly, "Because I don't ask you for things."

Vivian sucked in her breath between her teeth.

"Nobody does. Nobody who works for you would ask for a favor like this. Don't you know that?"

"Are you serious?" Vivian smoothed down her hair in seeming agitation. "You're not *them*. I know you do a lot for me. Did you think I hadn't noticed? Do you think I'm totally ungrateful?"

*Think of something*, Jules ordered herself. *Say something*. But right now, right when she needed them the most, words failed her.

And that moment was all it took for Vivian to go a little bit red and say, "Oh. I see."

"No," Jules said, too quickly.

"Oh. Well." Vivian turned to look out the window again.

"That's not true!" Jules said, even though it absolutely was.

Vivian was right. It hadn't occurred to Jules to ask her for anything, not just because she didn't want special favors but because, even if she had, she never would have expected to get them.

"No, I'm pretty sure it is. It looks like I've been asking too much of you lately. I'll put the brakes on that."

"No!" Jules repeated, horrified. What did Vivian mean? No more doctor's visits or lawyer visits or pizzas or diet charts or FaceTime in the middle of the night? She didn't mean that, did she? "Vivian, you don't have to. I—"

"No, *you* don't have to." Vivian didn't turn around. "Not anymore."

"It's not because I have to," Jules pleaded. "It's not just my job. I-I like helping you."

"You do?" There was a trap waiting somewhere in Vivian's voice.

Jules was in too deep to find it, though. "Yes," she said in utter defeat.

Vivian was going to ask her to do something impossible just because Jules had been clumsy enough to sting her pride. And Jules was either going to do it just to prove she could or tell Vivian to go to hell and shoot herself in the foot for good.

"If it's not your job, why do you do it? Why do you like doing things for me?"

Because she hated it when Vivian looked sick and tired. Because Robert was an asshole who didn't deserve her. Because Jules wanted to have sex with Vivian like she'd never wanted anyone else in her life. And because together, all of those things coalesced into something that was terrifyingly like…

"Because I'm happy to do it," Jules whispered. "It makes me happy to do it."

Vivian finally looked at her. Her gaze nearly skewered Jules, it was so sharp and intent. "You don't say."

Jules opened her mouth to say "What?" but sat very still because she'd just been struck by lightning. Or it felt like that, anyway. Her eyes stretched open wide.

Vivian wanted to—she'd be *happy* to—?

"Oh," Jules gasped.

"Well, there goes the light bulb." Vivian looked out the window again.

"No," Jules said, though she was so breathless it was a wonder that the word made any sound at all. "I mean, yes. I'm sorry, Vivian." She licked her lips. "Next time I need something, I'll…I'll come to you."

"I certainly hope so." Vivian didn't turn around. "Now, call the car. Let's go home."

---

The ride to Vivian's place was just like it used to be before they'd stopped staying late at the office. Jules almost wondered if she'd hallucinated the entire conversation. There were the usual instructions, the usual periods of startlingly comfortable silence, which were then followed by more instructions. By the time Vivian left the car and climbed the steps to her house, Jules was fighting not to pinch her own wrist. Maybe this was all a weird dream.

Ben noticed something was off. He met her eyes in the rearview mirror. "Are you okay?"

Jules shook her head and blinked several times hard. "I think so."

"I'd offer to buy you a drink for whatever it is," he said dryly, "but she'd fire one of us, and I'm betting it wouldn't be you."

"Oh, my God," Jules moaned, and rubbed her hands over her eyes. "I don't get her."

He just laughed. If anyone could understand the feeling other than Simon, it'd be him.

No, she didn't get Vivian. She never would. But Vivian wanted her to ask for stuff. She wanted to give Jules something back for everything Jules had done for her.

It would make Vivian…happy…to do that.

Jules didn't know what that meant. She didn't care. But her glow had returned tenfold. Vivian appreciated her, *Salon* was publishing her article, and Jules would sleep very well tonight.

# CHAPTER 29

THE NEXT DAY, JULES PRACTICALLY floated into work with a La Colombe coffee tray in her hand. Nothing unusual had happened on the drive that morning: Vivian hadn't made any reference to the conversation they'd had the night before. But she'd looked especially beautiful in a brightly patterned blouse and gray-checked pants. Jules had enjoyed the drive very much indeed, although she'd had to be careful not to stare at Vivian or grin like an idiot.

Still, she was obviously in a good mood, and Simon saw it. "Kissed and made up, did you?" he asked when she stopped by his office to drop off some photos.

Jules fought her blush valiantly.

"Does this mean she forgives me too?"

"Sure, I guess. She doesn't seem mad about anything anymore."

"So you reassured her that you're still chained to your desk?"

What a weird way to put it. "Actually," she said, getting ready to tell Simon that Vivian hadn't been worried that she was going to quit, that her feelings had just been hurt.

Instead she said, "Yeah, I did." Something told her that telling Simon the truth was a bad idea. Vivian certainly wouldn't want anybody else to know that she gave a damn about Jules one way or the other.

Now that she thought about it, it was strange that Simon had misjudged Vivian. When he'd said that Vivian was worried about Jules quitting her job, she had taken it as the gospel truth because nobody knew Vivian like Simon did. If Vivian thought of anyone as a friend, surely it was him.

"I'm sure she found that reassuring." Simon sighed and gave her a folder in exchange for the photos. "I don't want to be all gloom and doom. I've just seen her burn too many people in my time."

Jules winced. Like Mallory, who'd made a mistake with yellow in the editorial spread. Or Lucia, who'd gone behind Vivian's back at Givenchy. Or heck, even Ben, who hadn't done anything wrong. Simon must have seen far worse than that over the years.

He continued. "Do me a favor and give this to her? I'd rather get a look at her from a distance before I come any closer today."

"Gotcha." She lowered her voice. "Thanks again, by the way."

He gave her a small smile as she left.

She brought the folder in to Vivian, returned to her desk, and started grinning again.

Then she tried to bring herself back down to earth. She hadn't told anyone about *Salon* except for Simon and Vivian. She hadn't even told her parents.

But even though Simon said she was in, there was always the chance the article wouldn't make the final cut. Vivian often rejected things from *Du Jour* at the last minute. Jules wasn't going to stop holding her breath until she actually saw the article on the *Salon* website.

In the meantime, she had a job to do. Several, in fact. It wasn't just drudgery anymore. And she wasn't going to quit anytime soon, no matter what Simon said.

---

Jules's happy glow persisted for forty-eight more hours. But then:

**Du Jour Editor In Chief Pregnant!**

As soon as Jules saw the headline on Page Six, she knew that today was going to be a very, very bad day. It was even worse because she saw the headline in Vivian's car. Vivian shoved her phone in Jules's face, her own white with fury.

"Look at this!" she spat.

Jules took the phone, hardly daring to breathe. Up in front, Ben's eyes were fixed firmly on the road. "Um," she said, "uh…"

"Read it," Vivian said.

Jules cleared her throat. "'Vivian Car—'"

"Not *out loud*," Vivian snapped as she turned to stare out her window.

Shit. Jules cringed and read the article.

*Vivian Carlisle, editor in chief of* Du Jour *and famously frigid fashionista, is expecting, according to inside sources. Is it her soon-to-be-ex-husband's? Will the pregnancy patch up her marriage to finance guru Robert Kirk? Not if the pictures of him with British hottie Lennie Jeff are any indication, although it might be easier to keep two women apart when they're on different sides of the pond. Maybe he can have it both ways?*

She took in a sharp breath.

"Charming, isn't it?" Vivian said through her teeth.

Jules wanted to suggest getting the *New York Post* reporter fired, but Vivian's influence didn't extend that far in the publishing world; if it did, Page Six would never say anything about her at all. It was weird to think that her power, which sometimes seemed all-encompassing, actually had limits. And that she'd reached them.

Jules heard a low, growling sound. It had just come out of her own throat, powered by a fury she had no right to feel.

Vivian turned at the sound.

Jules squeaked, but Vivian only looked bitterly amused.

"Was that therapeutic?" she asked.

"Yeah," Jules said. She bit her lip and returned the phone.

Vivian took it, pursed her lips in consideration, and growled too.

It startled a laugh out of Jules, who immediately followed it up with, "Oh, sorry."

Vivian shook her head in dismissal. "Not bad, but I'm going to need something a little more substantial."

"Like what?" Jules was already prepared to get it for her on a silver platter, no matter what it was. Anything to get that look out of her eyes.

But Vivian was way ahead of her. "Nothing you can help with," she said. "It's beyond your reach. No, you just leave this to me." Her expression turned into something much, much scarier. Her eyes gleamed with a light that could only be called diabolical.

Jules actually throbbed between her legs. If ever there was an inappropriate time…

"Ben," Vivian said, "stop by a bar. I'm going to buy an old fashioned."

Jules couldn't have heard that correctly. "You're what?"

"That's my favorite drink."

Her jaw dropped. "But… What? You can't—"

"I know that. That's why you're going to drink it for me."

After a long moment, Jules said, "You're kidding."

"No," Vivian replied, "I'm delegating."

Luckily, in New York, bars started serving at seven. So, sitting in a dive at eight thirty in the morning with Vivian Carlisle staring at her the whole time, Jules threw back an old fashioned. She'd never had one before.

"Huh," she said. "Not bad."

"Right? Someone once told me it wasn't a woman's drink. I ordered one right in front of him and never looked back."

Jules couldn't stop a grin. It wasn't returned, but the darkness had retreated from Vivian's eyes.

"I didn't have a big breakfast," she said. "You sure you want me to show up at the office after one of these?"

"Drink every drop," Vivian said firmly and watched with envious eyes as Jules gulped down the rest of it. Thankfully, she allowed her to chase it down with water and even eat a few pretzels so she wouldn't arrive too tipsy at the office.

Well, there were worse ways to start a day.

---

By ten thirty a.m., after another glass of water, some coffee, and two trips to the bathroom, Jules was sober again. She kind of missed the buzz, though, since you could cut the office tension with a knife. The news of Vivian's pregnancy had spread, and today *Du Jour*'s employees were more like groundhogs, hiding in their cubicles as much as they could.

Jules had no such luxury and was glad when the Audi whisked her and Vivian away from the office at the end of the day. The heated seats felt good as she watched New Yorkers hurrying down the sidewalks, their breath puffing clouds into the evening air. What a day it had been.

But it wasn't over yet. When Ben stopped in front of Vivian's house, she said, "Julia, come with me. Ben, she'll only be a moment."

Only months' worth of practice let Jules keep the shock off her face. She'd run plenty of personal errands for Vivian, but she'd never actually been in her home before.

Unlike many wealthy Upper West Siders, Vivian didn't live in a townhouse. She'd chosen a carriage house with a shorter, wider profile than its more traditional neighbors. The imposing entrance was gray stone topped with brown brick and two floors' worth of arched windows. Carriage houses in the heart of the city had formerly served as stables for Gilded Age magnates. There was nothing humble about them, though, and now they were some of the most desirable real estate in New York. Of course Vivian had been able to nab one.

Jules followed her up the stairs on shaky knees she could no longer blame on booze. *It doesn't have to be weird*, she told herself. *You practically lived with her in London for a while.* But this felt different. Vivian's London townhouse was basically her hotel. This was her home.

Jules shut the door behind herself as Vivian said, "Wait here."

She looked around after Vivian left the foyer. She knew from Simon that when Vivian had bought this place, she'd hired one of the most prestigious architectural firms to gut and redesign it.

The end result was *whoa*. The house featured an entryway with a fifteen-foot ceiling, a cast-iron winding staircase that led up to the private rooms, and exposed brick walls that might be original. The pale hardwood floors were polished to a gleam. Photos, prints, and paintings lined the walls. Jules was no expert, but she'd taken a contemporary art history class at Penn and recognized Shirin Neshat and Kandinsky. Holy shit, was that painting a real Lichtenstein? Pop art seemed a little unserious for Vivian.

Jules turned, then nearly jumped.

Vivian had returned with a glass of ice water and was standing at the entrance to the foyer, watching Jules silently.

"Mark Tavio called me this evening," she said. "About half an hour ago."

That didn't sound good. "What about?"

Vivian's chin jutted out. For a moment, she looked defiant. "He wanted to congratulate me on the pregnancy."

That sounded on the surface like a perfectly nice thing to do. So why did it make Jules's skin crawl? Judging by the look on Vivian's face, she felt similarly.

"He offered generous maternity leave." Vivian's voice hardened. "Said I could take as much time away from the office as I liked, especially *under the circumstances*, which I'm assuming refers to…" She gestured vaguely.

It felt rude to say it. "The divorce?"

"He made a point of mentioning that he sympathizes, although he can't *relate*, seeing as how he's been happily married to the same woman for over forty years. Isn't that sweet?"

"And he's trying to get you out of the office." Of course he was. If Mr. Tavio wanted to get rid of Vivian, it'd be much easier to plop a new editor down in Vivian's vacant office chair.

The thought made her chest clench. No way would she work for anyone who replaced Vivian like that. As if anyone could replace Vivian at all.

Vivian's eyes were hard. "He can try all he wants. I'll protect what's mine."

*Jesus.* Jules tried not to swoon.

"As always, this information remains private," Vivian added.

"Absolutely," she replied with all the conviction a pathetically infatuated assistant could muster. That was a lot.

Vivian regarded her in silence.

Jules regarded her right back as her heart started racing again. She had to be imagining the softened gaze in Vivian's eyes.

And…was her body tilting toward Jules ever so slightly? Her right heel left the ground; was she about to step forward? To do what?

Definitely not what Jules wanted her to do—definitely not an embrace followed by the kind of kiss you only saw in the movies. She'd never… Would she?

The moment broke. Vivian seemed to come back to herself with the slightest shake of her head. She cleared her throat. "Ah, I also wanted to tell you that we'll be hiring a new intern, and I want you to take care of it."

Jules crashed back down to earth. Well, this was new. She'd never been involved in the hiring process for anyone before, but out of all the new duties she'd taken up lately, this was hardly the weirdest. "Right. Where will they be working? Marcus says copywriting is understaffed."

Vivian glared. "Does he?"

Oh no. Jules hadn't mean to snitch. "Not in, like, a bad way! Just that it, uh, gives them a new challenge to rise to."

Vivian rolled her eyes. "Brilliant save."

Jules sighed. "So you didn't mean copywriting?"

"No. I meant our office. It's time you had some help."

She looked blankly at Vivian. "Wait. *I'm* getting an intern?"

"A double major in English and communication and you still don't get basic sentences?"

"Well—hey now." Jules scowled, which only appeared to delight Vivian, judging by how her lips twitched again. "I didn't know assistants got their own interns. Are you saying I need one?"

"Are you saying I don't keep you busy *enough*?"

"I-I thought I was handling everything." Did Vivian think Jules was slipping up somehow? If so, where? She'd been trying so hard. "Have there been problems?"

"Let's just say your time could be better allocated. Any college senior can be trained to answer phones and scan PDFs. I have a larger project coming up, and I'll need your help."

"What is it?"

Vivian folded her arms. "I'll tell you when it's time to get started."

This was starting to sound pretty exciting. Jules was getting her own personal intern so she could help Vivian with something important? Her heart leapt. "Understood. I'll contact HR in the morning about posting an ad."

Vivian lifted one shoulder to indicate she had zero interest in the details. "You do that. And clear my afternoon tomorrow from eleven to one. I'll be eating lunch outside of the office."

"Right," Jules said, hoping for clarification. Last-minute changes always threw everybody into a panic—especially the people Vivian was canceling on. But no clarification was forthcoming.

Instead, Vivian gave her another long, considering stare. She finally said, "I'll see you tomorrow."

Tomorrow, when Jules would look for an intern. Which was so cool. She couldn't help beaming at Vivian.

Vivian's cheeks seemed to go a little pink. Must have been a trick of the low lighting.

"Yeah," Jules said. "You will."

# CHAPTER 30

Four days later, Jules was buried under more résumés than she knew what to do with. Human Resources' software had supposedly weeded out the weakest ones and given Jules the cream of the crop. She wasn't sure how creamy they were, but some pretty big names had made it to the top of the slush pile: the sons and daughters of society people, kids with big trust funds and bigger expectations in life. They were pursuing degrees in fashion design, art, philosophy—very rarely anything to do with publishing.

However, getting the right degree still didn't mean you could do the job. The most important thing initially was to be the fastest draw in town in answering a phone and to possess self-esteem that could survive *Du Jour* dropping boulders on it every five minutes. That sort of experience didn't show up on a résumé.

In the car one morning, watching Jules frantically scrolling through the applications, Vivian said, "Have you found any likely candidates?"

"Three so far."

Vivian held out her hand. "Let me see."

Jules handed over her tablet showing the résumé PDFs. Vivian took ten seconds to look at all three of them and tossed the device back into Jules's lap. "No. Keep looking."

The dismay was nearly impossible to hide. These had been her top picks. "Okay. Can you tell me what was wrong with these so I know what to avoid next time?"

Vivian leaned over and tapped on one image. "I hate her mother." She tapped on the second. "Her mother hates me." She tapped on the third. "A 3.87 grade point average."

"She's at Columbia," Jules protested.

"Oh, that's right." Vivian's voice turned syrupy. "I'd forgotten that Columbia is the only school in the country that doesn't practice grade inflation. That 3.87 GPA is really a 3.5, and you know it."

Jules scowled. "So what was my 4.0?"

"Don't take this personally. By the time I hired you, you had qualifications that actually mattered."

"Oh. Thanks?"

"They don't have professional experience yet. All we've got to go on are academic records and extracurriculars. Don't settle for less than the best. We can afford to be picky."

At least that gave Jules one starting point: a pristine college transcript. But how the heck was she supposed to know about the other stuff? Vivian's feuds and squabbles with the New York elite were notorious and ever changing.

Well, so were everyone else's. Everybody who traveled in those circles swapped and dropped friends often, and they were all drama queens.

"Don't let me down, Julia."

Jules held back a sigh. No matter what, she dreaded disappointing Vivian more than almost anything. Making Vivian happy made her happy too.

She remembered more often than she cared to the sight of Vivian laughing on New Year's Eve, relaxed and amused. She would give her right arm to see it again.

And maybe she would. Vivian had a little more spring in her step these days, more of a sparkle in her eye. She'd had time to absorb the shock of her pregnancy, time to—well, not *get over* Robert's infidelity, but she didn't seem to be dwelling on it.

Reporters weren't bugging her as much now as they had in the forty-eight hours after the news about her pregnancy had broken. Vivian's position was still difficult, still something Jules wouldn't wish on her worst enemy (okay, maybe her worst), but she seemed to be dealing with it better than Jules would have expected.

It was totally nothing to do with her, of course. Just because Jules was there to make things easier, just because Vivian relied on her more than she'd ever relied on another assistant, that didn't matter. So what if she knew that Jules worked her ass off to make her happy? Why should that give her so much…bounce?

*Not the time to let silly fantasies go to your head.* If Jules really wanted to make Vivian happy and comfortable, she could start by doing her job and finding a halfway-decent intern.

Two days later, she finally preinterviewed a tall, willowy blonde who'd made it past the initial HR screening. She was majoring in art history at Columbia and had an impressive list of extracurriculars. She also had a permanent curl of her upper lip.

Nevertheless, Jules gave her a friendly smile. "Hi." She extended her hand.

The blonde took it limply before dropping it again.

"I'm Julia Moretti, but you can call me Jules."

"Huh," the blonde—whose name was Victoria—said. "That's cute."

"Er, I guess. So, Victoria…it is Victoria, right? Or do you go by Vicky or something?"

Victoria looked revolted, but she only said "no."

"Right." Jules felt her smile becoming strained. Victoria had better say something impressive in the next few minutes if she wanted to have a prayer of landing this position. "Have a seat."

They were in a small meeting room near Simon's office. Victoria seated herself elegantly and folded her hands on the glass tabletop.

"So, Victoria…" Jules glanced down at the list of questions she'd prepared. "To start, why don't you tell me about yourself?"

"What about me?" Victoria looked around, appearing impatient. "Listen, I'm sorry, but my time is kind of at a premium today."

She couldn't have heard that correctly. "What?"

"I came here for an interview," Victoria said. "Is Ms. Carlisle busy or something?"

"Ms. Carlisle?"

Victoria glared at her. "You're her assistant, right?"

"Yes," Jules replied, astonished.

"So you're in charge of her schedule. When is she going to be free? How long do I have to wait?"

"Well"—Jules looked at her watch—"no longer, actually. Come on."

She headed for the door, Victoria following her eagerly. Then, as it became clear that they were heading for the exit, Victoria stopped and frowned. "Wait a minute."

"Oh, sorry," Jules said sweetly, pointing ahead. "You probably know your way out already."

"Huh? What about my interview?"

"We just had it," Jules said. "Good luck with the job hunt."

Victoria's eyes bugged out. "*You* were interviewing me? An assistant?"

"Yep. I sure was."

"Do you know who my father is?"

Screw that. Jules gave Victoria her best glare, one modeled on Vivian herself. It must have been good because the young woman took a step back.

Jules slowly raised her arm and pointed at the exit. "Bye. We won't call you. We won't keep your résumé on file. And if you play your cards right, we won't send it to other people as a warning either. Or a joke."

Victoria opened her mouth.

"Goodbye."

Victoria turned beet red and actually looked about to cry. She turned and headed for the exit. When she was out of sight, Jules exhaled heavily.

She couldn't believe how terrifyingly good that had felt.

---

"What about that internship candidate you met with this morning?" Vivian asked in the car later that day.

"Totally disappointing." Jules sighed.

"I'd get used to that feeling, if I were you." Then Vivian tilted her head toward Jules, a smile playing around her lips as if they were sharing a joke.

Something in Jules's chest became so warm and light that she forgot about being disappointed at all.

---

Two days later, the world had mercy on her. A short, slight redhead stood in front of her. She was young, pretty, and fashionable enough to work at *Du Jour*. She seemed awed by the offices, awed by Jules, awed by even the idea of Vivian Carlisle.

She was also sweet natured, hardworking, and—as Jules's grandfather would have said—a few tomatoes short of a good marinara.

"The question is," Jules said carefully, "can you pretty much just do as you're told?"

"Oh yes," the girl—whose name was Allie—replied. She smiled brilliantly. "Everyone's always told me that's my natural area of expertise!"

"Sit right here." Jules then hurried into Vivian's office.

Vivian was on her cell phone, though it sounded like she was wrapping up the conversation. As Jules approached, she quickly said into the phone, "Why, that sounds marvelous, darling. Yes. I'll see you then." Then she disconnected and looked back at Jules.

*God, her eyes are blue.* "Sorry to interrupt. I just wanted to say there's an internship candidate I just interviewed."

Vivian glanced toward where Allie was sitting. "Well?"

"I think we've got a live one," Jules said, hoping against hope that she was right.

"Call her in."

Jules crooked her finger at Allie, who had been watching them both anxiously from the outer office.

She trotted in, smiling brightly, a copy of her résumé in hand. She was nervous and excited and offering her throat to Vivian like the zeta female to the alpha.

Vivian's eyes gleamed, and Jules knew she'd chosen well. "So," Vivian said neutrally, "who are you?"

"Alexandra Lake." Allie then added, "Allie, please."

Vivian's lip curled. "And what brings you here, *Allie*?"

Allie blanched. "Um."

"I'll just go mind the phones," Jules said.

Vivian nodded, a satisfied look on her face.

Jules sat down at her desk. She was listening in, but she couldn't help thinking, *She called her Allie. She calls me Julia.*

*Maybe she thinks I'm special.*

No. Time to pay attention. Jules focused back on the interview. She heard Vivian say, "think you can bring to the table?"

"Oh, I *love* fashion," Allie replied earnestly. "My mom got *Du Jour* in the mail every month when I was growing up, and I always read it cover to cover."

"Really," Vivian purred. "Well."

Jules could just picture the look on her face. She rather thought she could pat herself on the back. Score one brand-spanking-new minion. She tried not to preen. *Finally.*

# CHAPTER 31

THE NEXT DAY, SIMON TOOK one look at Allie, pulled Jules aside, and said, "You're kidding."

"Nope. I think she'll be just right."

Together they watched Allie, who'd been given a small table and rickety chair from storage. It was conveniently placed near Jules's desk but out of Vivian's sight as well as that of anyone else who might judge *Du Jour* for having furniture that wasn't straight out of a showroom. Allie still looked thrilled to be there—at least Jules was pretty sure she was thrilled. Her stare was a little vacant.

"Can she rub two thoughts together to create a spark?" Simon asked in a low voice.

"Time will tell." She patted Simon's arm. "Look at it this way. While she's making copies and bringing Vivian coffee, I'll have more time to bug you in your office."

He gave her a wry smile. "It's sad if you think that's true."

Over the next few days, his prediction bore out. Jules didn't have time to do anything other than train Allie. For the most part, Allie shadowed her, watching with wide eyes as Jules attended on Vivian, answered the phone, sent endless texts and emails, and ran errands.

Three days after Allie's hire, as Ben was ferrying her and Jules to Hermès, Vivian called Allie's cell phone.

"Hello?" she squeaked, then went pale. She stammered, "O-okay, Vivian," hung up, turned to Jules, and said, "She said to get her that footstool that she liked at that store. Do you know which footstool? And which store?"

Jules thought hard. Then she said, "Roche Bobois on Madison Avenue. We drove past it yesterday, and she glanced at the window. And then she had the catalog on her desk this morning."

Allie's jaw dropped. "Wow. But which stool?"

Jules shrugged. "We'll just have to see what they have in the window display." She gave Allie a serious look. "You've got to pay attention, Allie. Mostly this is going to be my job, but you'll probably have to step in once in a while. Vivian expects you to read her mind. Notice as much as you can. If she shows any particular interest in something, remember it."

"I don't think I can do this job," Allie whimpered.

Uh-oh. "Yes, you can," Jules told her sharply. "We had a ton of applicants. You made it to the top. Right?"

She nodded, looking a little perkier.

"So you can do this," Jules finished, not at all sure of that but desperate to keep Allie around until they got back from London Fashion Week at least. "Just pay attention and keep trying. Roll with the punches."

They arrived at Roche Bobois. There were two footstools in the window, but Jules immediately zeroed in on the one on the left. "That one. The blue one with the modern lines. That's the kind of thing she likes. Now, go in, order it, and have it sent to her home tonight. Not tomorrow or the day after—*tonight*. Rush delivery."

Allie hurried inside. Ten minutes later, she emerged, looking flushed with victory. "It'll be there by five thirty," she proclaimed.

"Great!" Jules patted her shoulder.

Allie became radiant.

"You've made a good start."

"I really want to do well." Allie beamed. "I won't let you down, Jules."

She could practically be on a fifties sitcom. Jules managed a smile. "I know you won't."

That evening, after Allie had left, Jules overheard Vivian speaking on the phone in her office. She couldn't hear the words, but Vivian's tone was light and breezy, and she even chuckled once.

Then she said clearly enough, "Ciao, darling," and in the same breath called, "Julia!"

Jules hurried in.

"Did the new girl do a good job picking out that footstool?" Vivian asked, looking at her phone. Her voice was mild, and she looked remarkably relaxed. Talk about being in a good mood.

Jules kept a straight face. "She sure did."

Vivian glanced up at her.

She returned the glance with her most innocent look.

Vivian's lips quirked.

For a second, Jules's stomach fluttered, but then Vivian's expression relapsed into its usual sangfroid.

She rose. "I'll be having lunch away from the office tomorrow." Just like last time, Vivian didn't say where or with whom. "I'll return by two. Make sure to update the schedule accordingly."

"Okay." Jules dared to add, "Good night."

"Mm. Where's my coat?"

Jules kept her hands steady as she slipped the Agnona cashmere around Vivian's slender shoulders. She kept her hands firmly on the coat. Never touched Vivian, no matter how much she wanted to.

That night, she went to bed thinking of the sound of her chuckle, the way her lips had quirked, and the faint but undeniable shine in her eyes.

---

Vivian's glow persisted through the next day. When she returned from her mysterious lunch, she gave Jules something that was almost an entire smile. Her eyes were sparkling.

Jules barely contained the grin she longed to give in return. It was hard. Vivian was happy, she was happy, and right now, right at this minute, things were pretty rosy. She was looking forward to London too. She'd had a blast at every other fashion week she'd ever attended, especially Paris, where Monique Leung had noticed her because Jules excelled at her job.

*Life,* Jules thought that night, *is good.*

Then the next day, she got a phone call.

It wasn't a number she immediately recognized. "Vivian Carlisle's office," she said as she picked up.

"Hello," a man's deep voice said. "Is this Julia Moretti?"

"Yes, that's me."

"Oh good." He sounded relieved. "Vivian said for me to talk to you if I ever couldn't reach her."

This was odd. "Uh, sure. What can I do for you?"

"Just tell her, when you catch her alone, that Stan Oppenheimer called. Tell her I have to cancel tomorrow evening. Something unavoidable's come up. She ought to understand about that." He chuckled.

"Unavoidable," Jules repeated. "Oh. Okay."

"Thanks. Tell her I'll try to call her again later on her private number. We'll get together soon."

"Right." She blinked. "Of course."

"Bye." The man ended the call.

She sat with her phone pressed hard against her cheek for a few moments before she snapped out of it. Then she realized that her free hand had been digging hard into the desk.

Stan Oppenheimer was one of the senior vice-presidents of Koening. He was also wealthy, divorced, and devilishly handsome. Great smile. Confident bearing. Wore bespoke suits. Rumor had it that he'd been interested in Vivian before her marriage to Robert, as a matter of fact.

She stood and walked into Vivian's office. She was in the middle of sending Charlotte from accessories away. As Charlotte left, Jules cleared her throat.

"What?" Vivian asked.

*When you catch her alone*, Mr. Oppenheimer had said.

So Jules kept her voice low as she said, "Stan Oppenheimer just called."

Before her eyes, Vivian's gaze became sharp and interested. And bright. She leaned forward eagerly. She…glowed.

"He, um, has to cancel tomorrow evening. Something came up."

Vivian's eyes narrowed in obvious displeasure. She sat back, drumming her nails on the mahogany surface of her desk. The glow was gone.

"He said he'd call you later," Jules said, "on your private phone."

"Thank you." Vivian's tone implied anything but gratitude.

Jules left the office and sat down so hard in her chair that it probably bruised her tailbone. Thank God Allie was making copies somewhere so she couldn't see her bird-smacked-into-the-window impression.

Those phone calls when Vivian had been laughing but hadn't wanted anybody else to hear. Those lunches. And they'd been planning to get together tomorrow evening.

Jules knew what it meant when a straight man and a straight woman got together in the evening. And Vivian had lit up like a Roman candle just at the mention of it.

She inhaled sharply. No—this couldn't be the special project Vivian had mentioned, could it? Getting Jules to coordinate an affair because she could be trusted?

*No,* Jules told herself, even though all her instincts told her it must be true.

*Vivian said to talk to you if I ever couldn't reach her.*

Stupid. Stupid. Vivian's glow—because of a man. An absurdly handsome and available man. Well, of course it'd have to be something like that instead of some lowly assistant who brought her coffee and scheduled her doctor's appointments. What the hell about Jules could possibly make her glow?

Jules was, yet again, an idiot.

# CHAPTER 32

It was February 17, there was dirty, slushy snow all over the ground, and London Fashion Week was less than one week away. Like everyone else, Jules was thrown into frantic preparations while also trying to train Allie to hold the fort while they were gone.

Vivian wasn't slowing down either. Their morning rides had no more silences; Vivian talked from the moment she got in the car to the moment she sat at her desk.

The good news was that now Allie was the one responsible for getting Vivian's morning coffee to her. The bad news was that now Jules arrived at the office with Vivian every single morning, and people had started to notice.

Jules felt the sting of raised eyebrows and muttered comments. Now she understood what Vivian had meant at Christmas about disliking passive-aggressiveness. What was the big deal? So Jules showed up to work with her boss. Who cared?

It wasn't as if anything inappropriate was going on. At all.

It was actually refreshing when a wide-eyed Allie asked her right up front, "Why do you always arrive at work with Vivian? Do you have it timed that well?"

Typical. Allie had come to be in awe of the way Jules kept up with Vivian.

"Er, no," Jules admitted. "Ben picks me up every morning before he gets her. It's so she can start giving me instructions right away."

"Wow," Allie breathed.

Right then, Vivian breezed in. Like everyone else, she had to be exhausted from the frenetic pace. More exhausted, considering her pregnancy, but she never showed it. "Bring me the latest prints from Creative," she said, and Allie scurried away.

"Confirm lunch with Stan," Vivian added to Jules in a low voice.

Jules couldn't quite speak, so she nodded and smiled brightly at Vivian as if nothing were wrong at all.

Without another word or look of acknowledgment, Vivian headed into her office.

Jules tried not to gag on her latest hot, miserable surge of jealousy. She'd never felt anything like it before. It was worse than the time she'd had acid reflux in middle school.

*Love my new special project. Just love it to pieces.*

How was it possible that Vivian already had a new guy just a few months after Robert had left her, in the middle of a divorce while pregnant? Was she that desperate to have someone else on her arm at parties? Apparently so. Shit.

There might be less to it than that. The bastard really was attractive. And Jules could tell from the way Vivian looked when she got in the car in the morning that she'd stopped throwing up and felt a lot better.

In fact, her research told her that after the first trimester, women often got their libidos back. Sometimes they got more than their fair share. Maybe Vivian didn't want someone at her side in public—maybe she wanted something a lot less complicated.

It was so unfair. Stan Oppenheimer didn't, couldn't know, Vivian. He didn't spend all day in her back pocket. But he got to have this?

And what was Vivian thinking? This was how she got in trouble every time: getting together with men who didn't understand her and who became threatened by her success. Didn't she know by now that it wouldn't work?

*So who would work?* she asked herself with gritted teeth. *You? Get real.*

Jules wasn't entitled to anything, and it didn't matter who Vivian got her rocks off with. It would never be Jules, and that was fine. It was *good*. And it would be ridiculous to think things could ever be different.

Somehow telling herself that a hundred times in a row didn't help.

That afternoon, as usual, Vivian returned from her little lunch date looking extremely pleased with herself. Probably nobody but Jules could see it, but Vivian was definitely…satisfied by something. Sated, even. She hadn't looked this happy since the pizza.

Because she was a glutton for punishment, Jules waited until they were alone and stammered, "D-do you want me to make another reservation? Appointment? With him?" She might as well beat Vivian to the punch and start trying to numb herself right away.

Vivian frowned. "Did I ask you to?"

"No," Jules croaked, wishing Stan Oppenheimer into the hottest part of hell.

"What I want you to do," Vivian said acidly, "is check on the London hotel reservations."

"I did that while you were at lunch," she said, trying hard not to think about her room—no, Robert's room—no, the *second bedroom*—at Vivian's London townhouse. "We've all got rooms lined up."

"'We'?"

"Well," Jules said with a forced laugh, "not you, obviously. You'll be in the townhouse. I meant…"

Vivian gave her a flat look. "So will you."

After a moment, Jules said, "Oh."

"Make sure there's enough room for Charlotte in the front row at the Ashish show."

Vivian strode away, and Jules took a deep breath before calling the Ashish organizers and then the hotel to cancel her room. Because she wouldn't be there anymore.

Then she found herself staring into space. So she was going back to the townhouse after all. It was stupid to feel happy. It would be stupid to feel anything at all. It wasn't a reason to be happy—it wasn't good, it wasn't *fair* of Vivian to get Jules's hopes up like that, whether she meant to or not.

Because she didn't think she could take it—living in Vivian's house again, talking to her at four in the morning again, making her breakfast and seeing her bare toes again, and knowing that none of it was for her. That even if Stan Oppenheimer wasn't in the picture, it still wouldn't be for her. That she couldn't afford to get used to it, no matter how much she wanted to.

"Hey, Jules?" Allie said.

She jumped. She hadn't heard her return from her errands.

But now Allie nibbled at her lower lip, which made her look like a worried, redheaded rabbit.

"Are you okay?"

"Fine," Jules snapped, and when Allie's face crumpled, she felt like a monster. "Fine," she repeated more gently. "I just, um, have a headache."

"Oh gosh!" Allie dug into her tan Chloé bucket bag, which Jules had envied for days. "Here. I have some ibuprofen."

With no reason not to, Jules took the pills. Might as well, since she really did have a nasty headache coming on. "Thanks."

Maybe a headache was better than heartache. Too bad she had a mortal case of that too.

# CHAPTER 33

Two days later, Jules realized exactly how far she'd fallen when her column appeared in *Salon* and she could only get mildly excited about it.

There it was in black-and-white on her screen: "From Clubbing to Couture: How a New Generation of Designers is Queering the Fashion Industry." Beneath it sat a photo from the Sophie Cochevelou show last fall, in which a male model strode down the runway in a checkerboard-print dress with fuchsia tights.

Jules skimmed through her own words. It looked like a copy editor had trimmed her language a little, but no paragraphs had been excised. All of the hyperlinks worked.

Anyone who felt like it could read her thoughts on new designers who openly embraced queer audiences and clients, bringing that indefinable *something* to the runway that Jules had seen in the two women in Domino Park. The clothes were still prohibitively expensive, but the shows always featured models of color, of different body types, often outside the gender binary. She hadn't included the phrase "as a bisexual woman," but the article made it pretty clear she had skin in the game.

At the end of the article, she saw her name: *Julia Moretti is a guest writer for Salon.*

Jules clicked on the article's "share" button and quote tweeted it with a perky message about how thrilled she was. Then she flopped back against her couch, crossed her arms, and sighed. Maybe she should give a damn about reaching a huge goal.

*Get yourself together*, she thought. *Enjoy it!* Not long ago, she'd have been over the moon about this. It was what she'd been working toward and hoping for. It was pointless to let a stupid infatuation get in the way of savoring her victory.

It would help to share the good news, wouldn't it?

Of course it would. Other people could amp her up. She texted Simon, who responded with the thumbs-up emoji and *Congrats*.

Allie was more enthusiastic, saying *omg soooo exciting!!!!* followed by a long string of pink hearts.

But then who was left? Moments like this reminded Jules how few friends she actually had. It seemed weird to reach out to people from high school or college. They rarely spoke and weren't in the same industries, which made it just felt like bragging.

And she couldn't text Vivian. Not now. She'd wanted to impress her, for Vivian to be proud of her, and now that memory was just depressing as hell.

Besides, Jules would hate to interrupt her if she was having a romantic evening with Stan Fucking Oppenheimer. God forbid.

There was one option left. Jules called her parents.

Five minutes later, she was on the end of congratulations so enthusiastic, even she found them excessive. It was sweet, though—nice to have parents who were always in her corner.

"Seriously," she finally broke in, "it's not like I won a Pulitzer. But thank you. I'm pretty excited."

"We're proud of you, honey," her dad said. "Text me the link. I can't wait to read it."

*Wait and see*, Jules thought. She could picture her parents reading about queer fashion shows and trying not to be taken aback.

"Honey, do you think you could get a raise?" her mom asked.

Jules closed her eyes. "How would this help me get a raise?"

"Well, it sounds like a big deal to me. Maybe you could tell that woman you'll take another job if she doesn't pay you more."

Time to choke back a hysterical laugh. "Mom, I've published two articles. I'm not getting a raise at *Du Jour*."

"Your mother's got a point, though. You never know what's going to lead to a new opportunity," her dad said.

"Exactly." Her mom sounded satisfied. "Keep your eyes open, and maybe you'll get out from under her thumb sooner than you think."

Jules's breath caught as she tried not to think about Vivian's thumb and a certain spot on Jules's body where it could apply just the right pressure.

"Maybe," she croaked.

"You sound stuffed up. Coming down with something?"

*A mild to moderate case of insanity, yes.* "I'm fine, Mom. I just wanted to tell you about all this."

"You don't sound that excited," her dad pointed out. "Are you sure you're feeling okay?"

Dammit, she was slipping. "Oh yeah, totally! I really am excited. Super excited!" Jules forced a laugh, but it came out weak. "It's just been a long week, that's all. And London's coming up soon, so I'll be busy every day."

"Like I said," her mom replied grimly, "keep your eyes out for something better."

"Yeah." Jules took the opportunity to turn around and lie flat on the couch so she could stare at the ceiling. Nothing better seemed to be up there, so she closed her eyes again. "Of course I will."

# CHAPTER 34

London Fashion Week was on. This time, there was no relaxing downtime in Vivian's townhouse, no chance to take a nap before the next big social engagement. The *Du Jour* group went to the hotel, except for Jules and Vivian, who headed for the townhouse.

They didn't stop for longer than it took to freshen up and change. Jules got out of her wrinkled clothes and threw on a new outfit, washed her face and reapplied her makeup, and combed her hair. There. She almost looked human again. Then she clattered downstairs toward the kitchen. Hopefully, the temporary staff had stocked it exactly as she'd told them to.

Vivian strode into the kitchen just as Jules stuck her head inside the fridge. "What are you doing? It's time to leave."

"I know." She pulled out a bottled smoothie. "But it's four hours until dinner, and I thought you might want one of these." She offered the bottle to Vivian, who already looked as fresh as if she'd never set foot on an airplane. "It's a protein and soymilk something. Mango flavored."

Vivian looked skeptical, but she took a sip and then nodded. Which meant she loved it and Jules should make sure she got more of them.

When she lowered the bottle from her mouth, Jules realized the smoothie had left a peach-colored milky ring around Vivian's lips. It momentarily hypnotized her, and her heart thumped pleasantly at the sight of it—it was cute and sexy, but nobody except Jules would think so.

"Ahem," she said.

Vivian frowned at her.

Jules started making circling motions over her own mouth with her index finger, then tapped her lips. "You've got, you know."

Vivian went pink. "I've got…to what?"

"You've got stuff on your mouth from the smoothie." She winced. It seemed rude when you had to say it.

Vivian's eyes opened even wider in understanding. Her cheeks went pinker too.

Jules quickly offered her a paper towel.

Snatching it, Vivian then dabbed at her mouth, peering at her reflection in a nearby glass cabinet and scowling all the while. "Let's go." She tossed the nearly full smoothie in the trash.

"Oh," Jules said, inexplicably crestfallen. "You don't want—?"

"I want"—Vivian cleared her throat—"to go. It's not complicated."

"I'll get your coat." Jules tried not to sigh audibly.

"This is an extremely important week, Julia," Vivian said, like that wasn't a massive understatement and like Jules didn't already know. "Don't let yourself get distracted."

"Distract—" Jules began, then cut herself off, going rigid when she figured out what she meant. Being distracted meant fussing over the pregnancy, which Vivian did not want and would not appreciate.

Not this week, anyway. Maybe not anymore, ever. Okay. Fair enough. Totally fine. Right?

"Right," she mumbled. She headed to get the coats, thinking hard about not thinking at all.

---

That afternoon, disaster struck. First of all, the front row at the Ashish show did not have a seat reserved for Charlotte, *Du Jour*'s top photography editor, a detail Vivian had told Jules to take care of personally. Fortunately, Jules noticed the mistake before Vivian (or Charlotte) arrived and pounced on the staging director immediately.

"Listen, I don't know what to tell you," he said.

"Tell me you're going to boot one of these people so Charlotte Cooke can get a seat," Jules said. "I spoke to Elyssa, and she said—"

"Oh, that explains it. Elyssa quit three days ago."

"Well, I'm sorry to hear that," Jules said, trying not to sound panicked because Vivian was due to arrive any second. "But Charlotte is in Vivian Carlisle's entourage."

"Oh-h-h." The staging director's eyes went wide as Vivian's name worked its usual magic. "Shit. Okay. Let me fix that…"

Thank God. He went to talk to the woman who'd had the temerity to take Charlotte's seat. Jules, bouncing on the balls of her feet and hoping the woman would vacate her place before the rest of the *Du Jour* crew arrived, checked out the other side of the room.

Stan Oppenheimer was sitting in the third row.

What? What the hell? He wasn't supposed to be here. At least Jules hadn't heard that he would be. Not that Mr. Oppenheimer's schedule was even remotely in her purview. But surely Vivian had known he was coming and hadn't mentioned it.

Why should she? Vivian wasn't accountable to Jules for her movements. If she didn't need her to schedule something, then Jules had nothing to do with any of it. They had gotten together in the evenings, after all, and Jules had never heard a word about it until Mr. Oppenheimer himself had called.

There was a flurry of attention by the door, and Jules knew Vivian had arrived. She always made an entrance: people got out of her way, cleared a path for her, watched her with equal parts envy and admiration, murmured to each other as they watched her pass.

Stan Oppenheimer was watching too. He looked approving.

Jules wondered how many punches it would take before his face actually caved in.

*Deep breath. Deep breath.* Charlotte's seat was free now, and Jules thanked the staging director as she took her seat in the second row behind Vivian, who didn't seem to notice the momentary glitch.

Then she tried to pay attention to the models on the catwalk and the clothes they wore instead of on the ridiculously rich, handsome, and available man across the way.

Thankfully, Mr. Oppenheimer didn't attempt to speak to Vivian after the show. And there were two more shows before a late dinner, so Jules was able to keep busy and try not to think about him. Then there was the dinner itself, and Jules definitely wasn't sitting at Vivian's table this time. Even Simon wasn't.

The editor in chief of *Du Jour UK* was, though. Vivian also sat with a Booker Prize winning novelist, the star of the latest West End hit, a publishing magnate or two, and Monique Leung.

Every time Jules managed a peek, Vivian and Monique were either not talking to each other or were exchanging frosty looks. Awkward.

It got even more awkward after dinner when Jules returned to Vivian's side. Monique stood only a few feet away and in front of Vivian. She smiled and waved at Jules. "I thought I'd see you around this week."

She managed a smile in return. "Wouldn't miss it. Did you have a good trip here?" That had to be a conversational gambit even Vivian couldn't get annoyed at.

"Well—" Monique began.

"*So* sorry to cut this important conversation short, but we need to get moving," Vivian said curtly. "It was good to see you, Monique. Julia, call the car. We're going home."

Did Monique seem curious at "We're going home"? Or maybe it was well-deserved annoyance at Vivian being a jerk for no reason at all. Again.

Jules couldn't even be mad about it. Vivian looked exhausted, nearly faint on her feet. She also didn't want Jules to get distracted, so there was no point in asking if she was okay. Better just to call the car and ride in silence to the townhouse.

The silence was oddly tense tonight. She wasn't sure why. She and Vivian hadn't had a disagreement; Jules had done everything right all day long. But the air in the back seat felt suffocating with all kinds of things unsaid.

Jules was probably imagining it. What was wrong with her? She was tired too, had endured a long couple of weeks, and she was still wrung out with inappropriate jealousy over an interest Vivian might not even have in some guy. And even if she did, it wasn't Jules's business to be jealous in the first place, as she'd told herself a *million times* already.

All of this tension was just in Jules's head. She was projecting it onto everything. So what if they weren't talking to each other in the car? Vivian didn't have anything to say. That was all. She had to be far more tired than Jules was.

Jimmy stopped the car at the curb, and Jules and Vivian headed into the townhouse.

Vivian's shoulders were as straight and proudly set as ever, but she was moving more slowly.

They both stepped into the darkened hallway. Jules turned on the hall light and helped Vivian out of her coat. Vivian didn't say anything, but she did give Jules a long look. Her own face was expressionless.

Jules normally would have fumbled for something to say. Not now. Now, for some reason, after that quiet car ride and in this quiet house, no words would come to her. She just looked right back at Vivian and thought about that peachy ring around her mouth, then her brain shut down in self-defense.

"You look tired," Vivian said quietly. "Get some sleep. I...need you rested."

That would be an easy need to fill. Jules had no idea how much longer she could stand upright. "Of course."

For a moment, something flickered in Vivian's eyes. Jules couldn't identify it, but whatever it was, it seemed to make Vivian open her mouth again.

Then Vivian snapped her mouth shut, turned around, and headed for the stairway without another word.

Jules removed her own coat and hung it in the hall closet, deliberately taking her time. When she reached the foot of the stairs, Vivian had already ascended them. By the time Jules got to the second floor, Vivian had shut her bedroom door.

Well...good. Jules needed rest too. Her shoulders alone seemed to weigh two hundred pounds.

She dragged herself into her bedroom, shut the door, and got ready for bed. Her alarm was set to go off at six, and it was ten thirty now. Her body's clock was completely screwed up again.

Just like her sense of self-preservation.

# CHAPTER 35

For the next four nights, Jules dreamed about work.

She dreamed about shows and clothes and people in fancy dress. In her dreams, she was always scrambling to make the next appointment, always running late, always trying to catch up. Always letting everybody down.

Daytime wasn't as bad. In spite of trying to train Allie at the same time, Jules had done her London legwork well, and except for the snafu at Ashish, everything she'd scheduled had gone off without a hitch. So far. She'd had practice at a couple other fashion weeks by now, which made this a little easier.

The whole *Du Jour* delegation seemed grateful for Jules's attention to detail. Keisha, Lucia's replacement, told Jules up front, "Hey, thanks for working so hard. You're making it easier for us."

"Thanks," Jules said and meant it. But Vivian had no such kind words. She hardly had any words at all. The most she did was ask every day about how Allie was handling things back at *Du Jour*, always in a faintly accusatory tone, as if it were Jules's fault that she'd had little time to train her before they'd left.

Jules called Allie every night and made sure her intern told her about every single message, every little detail, no matter how insignificant Allie might think it. The girl might not be bright, but she was good at doing what she was told. Besides, with Vivian and half the staff out of the office, there wasn't much to do.

Every evening, Jules was able to say, "Sounds like everything's going okay, Vivian." Then she'd pass along anything important that Allie had told her, which usually wasn't much. Sometimes Vivian would have her call Allie back with additional instructions; most often, she gave her a curt nod and sent her off on some other errand. Then, at the end of the day, they'd return to the townhouse and continue not to talk.

It was awful. And weird. They were staying in the same house, and Vivian was speaking to Jules less than ever. No more talk about the doctors, no more growling about the media, and certainly no more inquiries about Jules's parents or life or anything insignificant like that. Just silence.

Vivian was busy. She had a lot going on, and she wasn't being mean or anything. She was just doing her job, same as Jules. They weren't friends.

It was all wrong, though. It felt totally wrong in a way she couldn't put her finger on, and Vivian had to know it too. But if she did, she wasn't doing anything about it.

If anything, this just reminded Jules of what she'd known all along: it was ridiculous to have the crush of the century on someone who could never reciprocate, someone who could run hot and cold like a faucet. It was time to get over this infatuation and accept that she would never make out with Vivian Carlisle or fulfill any number of other fantasies.

She would get started on that any day now.

At least Vivian hadn't been in contact with Stan Oppenheimer, as far as Jules could tell. It was easier to keep track of her during Fashion Week, especially given that she was staying in Vivian's own house.

That didn't necessarily mean anything. Vivian was clever—she always had been—and if she wanted something, she'd find a way to get it. It wasn't as if Jules could keep watch over her every minute of every day, no matter how often they were together. Vivian and Mr. Oppenheimer had probably found one or two opportunities. They'd been able to get together and laugh and do things that made Vivian glow, like, like…

Yes, all in all, it was good that Jules kept so incredibly busy. Best not to dwell.

On Thursday afternoon, at yet another reception, Jules finally caught Vivian talking to him.

It didn't look particularly intimate (well, it wouldn't do to look intimate in front of other people, now would it?), and it certainly wouldn't appear unusual to anyone else. Why shouldn't Vivian chat with one of the higher-ups at Koening? In fact, when you looked at it that way, Stan Oppenheimer was practically Vivian's boss. Which was so gross and wrong and totally different from Jules's own situation in ways she was still trying to figure out.

Looking around desperately for a friendly face, or at least some kind of distraction, Jules came up dry. Simon was in a corner talking to Georg Schumann. Oh God, Jules hoped that didn't mean Mrs. Schumann was around here somewhere. Whenever she thought of Helga Schumann, she heard Vivian's voice calling her the "heinous hausfrau." It raised the urge either to laugh or to drown even more in self-pity, neither of which would be appropriate at this reception.

The rest of the *Du Jour* delegation seemed to be occupied as well, and as a lowly assistant, Jules couldn't barge into any old conversation with the fashion elite.

Just as she'd decided to fade into a corner and try to forget Vivian Carlisle existed at least until the reception was over, she heard: "You're Julia Moretti, right?"

She turned and found herself face-to-face with a man about her age and of Asian descent. Like Jules, he was dressed mostly in black and had a harried expression. A fellow assistant, then. She'd seen him around at the various shows but hadn't been introduced.

"Jules, yeah," she said. "Hi."

"Cool." He had an accent, but she couldn't place it. "I'm Randall, Monique Leung's PA."

"Good to meet you." She smiled, her instincts already on alert. "Did Monique want to schedule something with Vivian? I'm afraid she's…"

"Prabal Gurung's holding a private party tomorrow evening at eight." Randall kept looking back and forth between his phone and Jules, with the phone getting the lion's share of his attention. "The Blind Spot Bar in St. Martins Lane Hotel. You're invited. See you then."

"Wait!" She put a light hand on his elbow as he turned to leave. "Vivian's booked tomorrow night."

"This invitation is for you, not Vivian." Randall looked around after he spoke with a familiar rabbit-like expression of alarm, as if making sure Vivian wasn't within hearing distance. "Like I said: tomorrow, eight, Blind Spot, St. Martins Lane. She'll be expecting you. Bye."

"But—" Her objection came too late. Randall was already making a beeline through the crowd.

Jules looked around in confusion, but Monique Leung herself was nowhere in sight. At least Vivian's back was turned and she probably hadn't noticed anything—not that Vivian would have recognized Randall. Lowly assistant and all.

"Cute guy. Think he's available?"

Jules whirled to see Simon a few feet behind her holding a cocktail and sharply dressed. He had an amused half smile on his face.

"I think he's a few rungs down the ladder for you," she said.

"Oh, come on. He's not in my chain of command. But"—Simon held up his drink to forestall Jules's objections—"I concede your point. It's just as well." He sighed dramatically. "He's one of those men who would send my heart down like the *Hindenburg*. I can tell."

Simon had certainly picked up more about Randall from a distance than Jules had up close. "You've had a few, huh?"

"A few drinks or a few *Hindenburg* men?"

"Either."

"Both." Simon looked morose. "Every fashion week I wonder if I'll find my Prince Charming, and at the end of every fashion week I wonder if I should download Grindr again."

"I don't want to know," Jules said instantly.

"Sorry. Yeah, I've had enough." He gave Jules a look that seemed pretty shrewd for a tipsy person. "I've seen that guy around, by the way. Works for *Du Jour China*, right?"

"He's off-limits," Jules reminded him.

"Not where I was headed with that, although I appreciate how damn gay that publication's staff is. I can't believe Monique is still single. She broke up with her last girlfriend four months ago."

"That's not such a long time. Maybe Monique was really in love with her."

"Monique was the one who left, as I understand it." Simon gave her a sardonic look. "Vivian's the *Du Jour* editor who got dumped. Don't mix them up."

"Believe me, I'm not." Who could ever confuse Vivian Carlisle for someone else?

"Good. Keep your ear to the ground, Jules. You're not one to miss the chance when opportunity knocks."

He couldn't know about Jules's encounter with Monique on New Year's Eve, could he? Surely Vivian wouldn't have told him. "What's that supposed to mean?"

"Sorry?" Simon looked innocently over Jules's shoulder. "Oh, look. Our mistress calls."

Jules followed his gaze. Vivian was giving her an impatient look from across the room. "Whoops. I have to go. You coming?"

He waved his hand in dismissal. "I want to sober up before the Azzarello show at four. Just remember what I said."

*Remember what?* She hurried after Vivian. Simon could be cryptic at the best of times, and it was even worse when he'd had a drink or two.

Still, something interesting had happened. Jules couldn't deny she was intrigued, and she'd be able to make the Prabal Gurung party, since Vivian was otherwise engaged. What had Randall said? *Eight o'clock, St. Martins Lane, The Blind Spot.*

It was enough to put her in a good mood for a few seconds. Then Vivian said as they were approaching the car, "I've scheduled lunch with Stan tomorrow in the window between the Carolina Herrera and the Burberry shows. Keep it quiet."

Prabal Gurung's party might as well not even have existed then. So this was how Vivian and Mr. Oppenheimer were going to manage some alone time.

"Of course," she said, trying not to let her voice shake. Vivian hardly seemed to notice her as she got in the car.

*Don't dwell*, Jules had to remind herself yet again.

They got back to the townhouse almost at midnight. For only the second time all week, as Jules helped her with her coat, Vivian spoke. "I'll want to rest before the dinner tomorrow night. We'll return here at five."

*They* would? "Okay," she said carefully. "I'm not supposed to go to the dinner too, am I?" It wasn't on the schedule, but with Vivian's caprices…

"Of course not." Vivian clearly couldn't believe Jules had asked such a dumb question. She walked away.

That night, Jules lay awake thinking about Monique Leung, Simon's cryptic words about new opportunities, and Stan Oppenheimer. She also remembered, for some reason, the way Vivian had looked in her pajamas on New Year's Day. That seemed like years ago now.

When Jules fell asleep, she dreamed about Vivian's mouth and body. Her mind was a little fuzzy on the actual details; all she knew was that Vivian's skin was soft beneath Jules's mouth and hands, and that, for once, she welcomed Jules with open arms.

And in her dream, for the first time in a long time, Jules felt joyful. Like she'd come home, like this was the rightest thing ever, like everything was okay at long last. Vivian shuddered and whispered that Jules was wonderful, that what Jules was doing to her felt so good.

So of course Jules had to go and wake up in the middle of it.

Her skin was tingling, and she had a wet ache between her legs, even though the dream hadn't been super explicit. Still half asleep, refusing to let herself think, she reached between her legs and rubbed. She remembered only the noises Vivian had made in her dreams—soft, pleased little murmurs and moans—and the way Vivian had felt beneath her, so warm and welcoming. She remembered this and only this until she came with a moan of her own.

Then she lay still and waited for her heartbeat to slow down, still keeping her mind as blank as possible so she wouldn't start thinking yet again about how pathetic she was. She reached for a Kleenex from the box on the nightstand and wiped off her fingers.

Her last thought before she drifted back to sleep was that she should take a leaf from Simon's book and start looking for a Prince or Princess Charming at Fashion Week. It might be the only way off the *Hindenburg* at this point.

# CHAPTER 36

As they were driving away the next morning, Vivian told Jules, "I'll be leaving for dinner from the townhouse at seven thirty. And don't forget my lunch appointment with Stan."

"Right." Jules's tone came out too sharp.

It provoked a frown.

Jules cleared her throat. "Sorry. Right."

The lunch appointment was pretty short. Vivian and Stan Oppenheimer only had thirty minutes to spend together before the Burberry show. Jules spent the whole time thinking in agony about all the different ways a person could spend a half hour. She and a couple of her exes had tried several of them.

At least she had her own thing to do tonight. Her own puzzle to solve. Monique Leung obviously wanted something from her. Only time would tell what that might be, and ordinarily the thought would have made Jules nervous. Was going to the party an act of disloyalty?

*No,* she told herself. *It's a party, you're just going to see what's up, and nobody can make you do anything. And it's something just for you.*

That helped.

At least temporarily. Vivian arrived at the Burberry show three minutes before it was due to start. After her lunch with Mr. Oppenheimer, she was flushed as if with excitement. Her eyes glowed with satisfaction. With pleasure.

Jules wanted to vomit. She found it almost impossible to pay attention to the show, and only with a huge surge of willpower did she keep things running smoothly until five in the afternoon, when she and Vivian returned to the townhouse.

As usual, Vivian retired immediately to her room without a word.

Jules tried to catch some badly needed shut-eye. But she only managed twenty minutes of fitful dozing, then gave up and decided to get ready for the party well ahead of time.

She wouldn't wear fade-into-the-background black. She wasn't going as Vivian's shadow. For this, Jules was going to break out the deep green Vejas minidress she'd snagged a few weeks ago. Her credit card was still howling, but at least her legs looked incredible, especially when she slipped on nude vintage stilettos. Add a deep berry lip gloss, a fashionable tousle to her hair, *et voilà*.

Time to head downstairs and go over the schedule for the millionth time. Vivian would be ready soon.

Sure enough, as she stood in the kitchen looking at the schedule, she heard footsteps descending the stairs. Vivian had emerged from her room. Just as she had on New Year's Eve, Jules turned to behold her as she came into view.

Vivian was dressed for dinner in a satin-trimmed ankle-length Simone Rocha, so current that a version had appeared on the runway this week. She'd had it customized so that it draped flatteringly over her midriff, and the bateau neckline showed off the elegant line of her throat. She looked absurdly beautiful.

Jules had expected no less, of course, and felt an ache in her heart just at the sight. *It's not fair. And you're an idiot.*

When Vivian saw her, her eyes widened in surprise. Jules wondered why until she remembered that she was in evening clothes too. Showing a lot of leg, no less, and on her night off.

"Why are you so dressed up?" Vivian asked. "I said you weren't going to the dinner."

"I know," Jules said in surprise. Did Vivian think she'd forgotten? "I'm going somewhere else."

"What? Where?"

The jig was up. Vivian didn't like Monique Leung for some reason, and now Jules had to confess. It just hadn't occurred to her that Vivian would give a shit where she was going, not after the cool she'd been showing all week.

"I was invited to a party," she said. Maybe she could avoid mentioning Monique entirely. "Prabal Gurung's throwing it."

Vivian's eyes narrowed.

*Oh shit.*

Maybe she could still save this. "Since you're busy tonight, I thought—"

"Still thinking about moving to Beijing?"

The words fell between them like an ax, the meaning unmistakable, and the two of them stared at each other in silence.

Finally, Jules broke it. "No, Vivian, I am not."

In her head, Simon's voice told her that she really should, that escaping halfway across the world would get her out of this emotional clusterfuck. She shushed it.

"I never was," she continued.

"Then who invited you? Prabal Gurung himself, was it?"

Jules took in a deep breath to confess the truth.

"Don't bother lying to me," Vivian said. "I guessed right away." She crossed her arms. Her pale cheeks were starting to flush. It had been quite a while since Jules had seen her this pissed.

In fact, the last time had been when Page Six broke the news of her pregnancy to the whole world. But this couldn't compare. Vivian wouldn't get that mad about her personal assistant going to somebody's party. Right?

Either way, that had been a shitty thing to say. "I wasn't going to lie," she snapped. "There's no reason to accuse me of that. Yes, Monique's assistant invited me. That's the whole story."

"That's never the whole story, Julia." Vivian's eyes flashed. "You think you were invited because Prabal Gurung couldn't find enough people to attend? Of course there's an agenda."

"Oh? What is it?" She threw back her shoulders. "I'm all ears."

Vivian inhaled sharply. "You can't be serious. You're going to a party with this woman after she all but sedu—tried to hire you right in front of me, and you expect me not to believe we're in for act two? Why did her assistant wait to invite you until I was away?"

"Was he supposed to invite me when you were in the middle of telling me to do something?" After all, Vivian didn't tell Jules anything else these days. "Vivian, there's no way the editor in chief of *Du Jour China* would go to all this effort just to *maybe* hire someone as far down the food chain as me."

"Finally you're getting it." Vivian's eyes had gone from flashing to ice-cold.

Jules hadn't gotten that kind of look from her in a while. She shivered accordingly. *Get it together, Moretti. Don't let her win this one. It's ridiculous.* "So what are you so worried about?"

"I'm not *worried*." The frost in Vivian's voice could have killed all the houseplants. "I'm reminding you of your job, which I can't believe I have to do. You're forgetting yourself."

Wow. That was a *really* shitty thing to say. Judging by the way Vivian kept steady eye contact with her, she didn't give a damn.

Then again, when did Vivian give a damn about Jules, period?

"Forgetting myself," she said. "You mean forgetting my place, I guess. As a lowly assistant."

"Watch yourself," Vivian said quietly. "Watch yourself carefully, Julia."

"Watch *what*?" Jules's ears were getting so hot that maybe steam was actually going to start coming out of them. "What am I doing that's so awful? You're going to a dinner, and I'm going to a party because you don't need me."

That had come out all wrong. The words weren't so bad, but it was the little crack in her voice that gave her away. Fuck.

"Tonight," Jules added hoarsely. "You don't need me tonight, so why shouldn't I go?"

"You seem awfully sure that I'd ever need you at all."

Had Vivian been taking judo lessons? That had certainly been a blow to the gut. Jules's breath caught.

"Besides," Vivian continued, "what if there was an emergency? You're my assistant on duty at all times. You'd rush from your little tryst to help?"

"Of course I…" Jules trailed off and her stomach flipped over. "Did you say 'tryst'?"

A moment of silence followed. Silence that said absolutely everything. Vivian crossed her arms, her fingertips pressing into her biceps as if she were cold. She didn't take back the accusation she'd all but thrown into Jules's face.

"You're kidding," Jules said.

"I don't *kid*." Vivian sneered. "That's something else you should know by now."

Wrong answer. The worst answer. "*Seriously*? That's what you think of me? She isn't—and I'd never—that's not what I want!"

"You're the one person in the world who doesn't want advancement? Monique's going to be surprised. Is that what you're going to tell her when she tries to lure you away"—She raised a disdainful eyebrow—"or lure you into bed?"

"That's *ridiculous*."

Vivian's breath caught. Made sense. No assistant could have ever spoken to her like that before.

Might as well go for broke. This was absolutely unbelievable. "What? You want me to tell you when I'm mad, right? You just accused me of sleeping my way to the top!"

Vivian just looked at her.

"You don't mean it," Jules said. "You can't mean it."

But those eyes grew even colder, if such a thing was possible.

"You *can't*," Jules repeated. Her heart was slamming so hard in her chest, she was shaking with it. "I-I don't believe this."

"I might say the same thing." Vivian was plainly unaware that she'd just broken what was left of Jules's heart into a thousand pieces.

"I don't believe this," Jules repeated as if Vivian hadn't spoken. "You think I'd do that? You don't trust me? After everything I've—I've done everything you asked me to do!"

"Yes, after everything." Vivian's face was hard and unyielding. What the hell was wrong with her? She couldn't really think…

Then Jules realized the truth. This was it.

This was when she'd finally crossed the line, made the same kind of mistake that Mallory and Lucia had and all those other nameless employees Simon had mentioned. Jules had messed up in a way considered unforgivable—or Vivian *thought* she had—and nothing Jules had ever done mattered compared to that.

"Now, let's go." Vivian looked at her black evening gloves and adjusted the right one.

Jules asked numbly, "Now, what?"

"You're coming with me to the dinner. If you're only going to Prabal's party because you're desperate for entertainment, that shouldn't bother you, should it?"

"Coming with you," Jules repeated. "To the *dinner*."

"Evidently I need to keep my eye on you tonight. I'd thought I could rely on you, I admit it." Vivian's voice was as calm and cool as when she'd fired Mallory and threatened Ben. "Apparently not. How disappointing. We'll have to reevaluate your role, Julia."

*Reevaluate your role.* Vague words, but the cold look on Vivian's face said it all. Jules had seen it before, and it always meant the same thing, no exceptions. Specifically, it meant that Jules was finally, officially, yesterday's trash.

"Oh," she said.

"'Oh,'" Vivian mimicked. "Is that all you have to say for yourself? I'm surprised."

"I'm not," Jules said. Her own voice seemed to come from a long way away.

Vivian frowned. "What?"

"I'm not surprised by any of this at all."

The glare grew sharper. "If you do have something to say—"

"Oh, I do," Jules said. "Believe me."

By now, even her scalp was prickling with rage. Vivian had ignored her all week. Now, out of nowhere, she was accusing both Jules and Monique of something totally inappropriate. All Vivian's talk about wanting to help Jules, about being grateful for her devotion: bullshit.

Vivian scowled and continued, "Then I suggest you say it now."

"Why, because I won't get another chance?" Well. If that's what Vivian wanted, then here it came. Here came all the words, everything Jules had never meant to say, everything she'd kept stoppered up in her throat because it would do no good to say it.

She laughed. It sounded awful and horrible and felt worse. "I knew this would happen. I did everything right. But you don't care. It doesn't matter to you."

"Excuse me?" She tilted her head back. Her cheeks began to redden.

"You think I'd just throw it all away and go to Monique. Because... Oh shit. I get it." The revelations just kept coming, each new one worse than the last. "Because you think I'm like you. That everyone is. That explains it."

And it did. It explained everything. Jules couldn't believe she'd been so stupid, hadn't seen it until now.

Vivian's eyes widened. "What?"

"You think I'd turn on you, you think I'd throw you away, because that's the sort of thing you do to people. Right?"

"What?" she repeated, her eyes going impossibly wider.

"No, no, I've got it now," Jules said, still unable to stop talking. Everything was boiling up to the surface now, out of her mouth, and it was too late to put the lid back on it. Why bother? She was as good as garbage anyway, right?

"I just forgot for a little while," she continued, "what you're really like."

"What I'm *like*?" Vivian sounded disbelieving, even breathless. As if all this was some big surprise to her, like she didn't even know…

"Yeah," Jules said, not about to stop now, because what would be the point? "You treat people like things. As soon as they screw up once—just once—you toss them. And you think I could do something like that to *you*."

Vivian's face wasn't red anymore. Now it was chalk white, almost like what Jules said upset her, but that couldn't be true because *even after everything they'd been through,* Vivian didn't think of Jules as anybody worth keeping around. She could have screwed Stan Oppenheimer on the kitchen table while forcing Jules to take notes, and it would have hurt less than this.

And the worst of it was that Jules had been so stupid, so deluded, as to allow herself to hope. Vivian had said to be honest with her, had implied she'd like to help Jules, had said a lot of things that had gotten Jules's hopes up for no reason, except that it hurt that much more to have them crushed now.

The kitchen clock chimed the half hour.

The sound snapped her back to reality, and Vivian appeared to wake up too. But she was still pale and trembling, still had an unidentifiable… something in her eyes. Rage. That had to be it. Fury. She was going to kill Jules. Tear her limb from limb because Jules had finally dared to open her mouth and tell her something real.

Jules wasn't going to listen. Not anymore. She grabbed her clutch from the kitchen counter. "I never thought I'd say this, but Beijing's looking pretty good right now."

She bolted for the front door over the sound of Vivian's gasp. At least she had speed on her side so she could make her escape. Not that it mattered; Vivian didn't call after her.

Outside, Jimmy was just pulling in to pick Vivian up for dinner. Jules didn't even look at him as she ran for the nearest Tube station in high heels.

She had no idea how she was supposed to enjoy the party now, much less try to network. But she had to try. She needed to be somebody else for an evening, not the current wreck of herself, before she returned to learn she'd been fired and would never come within sight of Vivian Carlisle again.

Simon had said that she was good at recognizing opportunities. He didn't know she was even better at fucking them up. Well. He'd find out the truth soon enough.

# CHAPTER 37

The Blind Spot Bar was perfect for the intimate yet glitzy bash that Prabal Gurung was throwing. The lighting was low, the furnishings were elegant, and the bar at the end of the room glowed golden with the promise of alcohol. Small tables were grouped throughout the room so that guests could sit and chat cozily with each other, but there was still plenty of space to maneuver back and forth.

Yeah, it was nice. Maybe Jules could camp out here until morning, when she'd have to call her parents and beg them to buy her a coach-class ticket home.

Until then, she had to get it together. There were important people here, more important people than she'd ever met before without Vivian's help. And since she would never have her help again—

Because she'd just hurled herself right out of Vivian's life—

She might as well make the most of it.

Monique Leung's assistant was nowhere in sight, but the crowd was still building. It was pretty unfashionable of her to have arrived right on time. She should have stopped somewhere else for a drink first.

Time to remedy that, then. She headed straight for the bar and started to open her clutch. "Hi. Just keep a tab running."

He held up his hand. "Open bar tonight, miss."

Finally, something nice. Jules rested her elbows on the polished wood bar with an exaggerated sigh of relief. "Open bar?" she said. "They ought to call this the Bright Spot."

"Never heard that one before," he said with a straight face. "Long week?"

"The longest."

"Seems like. What can I get for you?"

Jules shouldn't order an old fashioned, which was suddenly the only thing she wanted to drink. "I'll just have a gin and tonic, please."

"One G&T, coming right up." He picked up a bottle of Tanqueray, and Jules watched him mix the drink as if it were the most interesting thing she'd ever seen. Then she took it like it was the holy grail. Delicious.

When she finished the drink, she said, "I mouthed off to my boss tonight."

"Did you?"

"Oh yeah." In a big way. *Mouthing off* didn't even come close. The ride on the Tube had calmed her down. And now that she was feeling saner, she realized she'd said things that would be beyond the pale for a lowly assistant giving sass to her boss.

Vivian had deserved every word, but still.

"What did you say to your boss?" the bartender asked, sounding hopeful for good drama.

*A whole lot.* "Um, I don't want to go into it. She said some bad stuff, and I got upset, so I said some stuff back, and then I walked out on her."

"Sounds more like a lovers' spat to me." The bartender set out two bowls of water crackers.

Jules couldn't even rise to the bait. Too depressing. She took a cracker and let it sit on her tongue for a second, flat and tasting of nothing. Then she started chewing and said around her mouthful, "Not exactly."

"Well, you'll find something else." The bartender looked over Jules's shoulder and smiled. "What can I get for you, sir?"

Jules took the hint and edged out of the way for the guy behind her to order the cocktail of the night. It was something called a Lavender Haze, made with vodka, soda, fruit liqueur, and actual lavender. It sounded good, honestly, and Jules ordered one.

As the bartender moved on to other customers, Jules reached for her clutch to get out her phone. Along with a drink, she could drown her sorrows by scrolling social media.

*Or I could see how many times Vivian's texted and called to rip me a new one.*

Jules yanked her hand back as if her clutch had caught fire. Hell no. Not now. She could have a couple more hours of blissful ignorance before facing the music.

She knocked back her second drink. Then she put the brakes on and tried the hors d'oeuvres so she wouldn't be completely sloshed. Not that she couldn't use the buzz, but on the off chance that she hadn't just torpedoed her career in the industry, she wanted to be able to look these people in the eye later.

*You'll find something else.* The bartender had said it with such confidence. She fought the urge to go back and beg him to say it again.

The problem, of course, was that she didn't want something else. She wanted what she had, only more of it. She wanted to be at Vivian's side, bowled over and besotted. She wanted all of that, and she wanted more. She wanted to see her own desire reflected in Vivian's face. Wanted those hard eyes to soften, those stern lips to curve in a slow smile for Jules and Jules alone.

*Dummy! She's not worth it. Remember everything she said. You want more of that? What's wrong with you? Grow a spine!*

Fury tightened her stomach again. She could let it give her strength. It had worked an hour ago. She could get over Vivian for real this time. She could…

"So you made it."

Jules snapped out of her reverie to see Monique Leung standing before her, clad in stunning fuchsia, her hair in an elegant twist.

"Yes." Jules fought the urge to look down at her drink to see how much was left. She was definitely a little buzzed. She should have had another hors d'oeuvre. "Thanks for inviting me. It's a beautiful bar. Um…how's the week going?"

Monique smiled. "It's going okay. I'm sure you've been plastered to Vivian's side, as per usual."

Jules's spine stiffened at the mention of Vivian's name.

Monique seemed to see this. "You caught hell for coming here, didn't you?"

"Yes," Jules sighed.

Her smile grew wry. She looked almost knowing—but what was there to know? "That speaks volumes. I'm glad you came in spite of that."

"Of course. Monique…" She had to ask. After the previous week, and her confrontation with Vivian, Jules's tolerance for artifice had officially run out. "Why did you invite me?"

Far from being offended, Monique seemed pleased by Jules's forthrightness. She smiled again. "You're right—let's skip the bullshit."

Jules flushed.

Monique shrugged. "I think your time could be better employed. You're up to your neck in industry contacts, you're a decent writer, you know how the sausage is made, and—to be honest—Vivian Carlisle's pissing me off."

Jules started in surprise. *Decent writer.* "You've read my work?"

"Of course that's the part you heard." Monique chuckled. "I keep up with *Salon,* yes. Your article wasn't a work of genius—I think you know that—but it's good enough, and it shows you have hustle."

Damning with faint praise. Jules's industry contacts would obviously be more useful than her talents as a writer. Plus the other thing.

"And Vivian's pissing you off," she said wearily.

"It's not a secret, is it? I wouldn't poach you just for that, but it's not a disincentive."

So Vivian had been right about at least one thing. Jules seemed to have found the one person at Fashion Week who'd find it a plus that she'd alienated Vivian Carlisle.

"Poaching me for what?" she asked. "You already seem to have a good assistant. And I don't speak any form of Chinese."

She couldn't help thinking about what else Vivian had said. Jules wasn't the only one she'd accused. Vivian thought Monique was trying to seduce her.

Even if Jules wasn't buzzed, she had a hunch that it wouldn't hold water. Monique showed not the slightest hint of desire. Jules just must not be an editor in chief's type.

"I'm not proposing you be my assistant," Monique said. "I'm proposing you get out of our incestuous *Du Jour* family and broaden your horizons."

Jules's eyes widened.

Monique gave her a level look.

Thoughts raced through her mind. Mark Tavio might be conspiring against Vivian, trying to replace her during her pregnancy. Now, Monique was trying to get Vivian's notoriously loyal assistant out of *Du Jour* entirely.

Was this a cog in some kind of plot? No matter how pissed Jules was at Vivian, she couldn't be a part of that.

"What do you mean?" she asked.

"I've started my own fashion label. I'm not surprised you haven't heard—it's China-based, and the Western fashion market's still learning to give a shit about that." Her expression went sour before clearing again. "But it's doing well and I'm branching out. We'll be in Paris, New York, and London this fall." She paused. "Especially London."

Whoa. This was a big deal. Also not a Mark Tavio plot *or* an indecent proposal. Looked like Vivian wasn't always right after all.

"Do you have a distributor in stores?"

Monique smiled at Jules's enthusiasm. "In Asia, I have my own boutiques. Here in London, I'm in Dover Street Market and Harrod's, and I'm planning to expand into my own store. In the States, we're still mainly an online presence on sites like Net-a-Porter. But Chinese street fashion is trending everywhere, and I've been careful to get my pieces out there, so I'm confident in my buzz."

Jules's head spun. "That's really cool. But …what can I do?"

Monique tilted her elegant head to the side. "How do you feel about being a Jacqueline of all trades to start? I need someone on the ground in our London office."

Oh. Another assistant-type job. She tried not to flag. At least it was something on a night when she'd probably lost everything.

Vivian thought she was going to jump ship. How depressingly on-point. But what choice did she have? Other than Monique, who in the fashion industry would give her a paycheck after Vivian put out the burn notice?

Monique appeared to see Jules's lack of enthusiasm for the job title. "In a new enterprise, there's more opportunity for promotion. Prove yourself, and you can move up the ladder pretty fast. I won't pretend it's not a risk, but I wanted to float it past you, whenever it comes to pass."

Jules pressed her lips together. "When might "whenever" be?"

Monique grinned. She had amazing teeth. "Stay tuned. My London group will be in touch when it's time to launch. Besides, you've got a steady job right now. What's the rush?"

Thank God the low lighting would hide Jules's blush. "Right, yeah. No rush, for sure."

"Figure out if you're interested and get in touch with Randall before you leave. He's hovering somewhere. Now, if you'll excuse me…" She smiled at someone standing behind Jules.

"Of course." She took a hasty step out of her way. "Thank you so much."

But Monique had already moved on, leaving Jules to find Randall on her own. After a few minutes, she located him in a corner, looking down at the glowing screen of his phone while his thumbs tapped furiously.

He looked up at her approach. "Hi. You joining Monique Leung?"

It took Jules a second to realize he was referring to Monique's new label rather than being weirdly formal about his boss. He'd asked a good question. Was she joining Monique Leung?

The opportunity would get her away from heartbreak while also exposing her to new facets of the fashion industry. She'd see more of the world too. On the other hand, it meant dealing with a host of logistical nightmares, to say nothing of moving far away from Vivian.

Vivian, who'd just said she didn't need Jules anyway, along with a lot of other awful stuff. Vivian, who would never care about Jules half as much as Jules cared about her.

The answer should be obvious, and yet all Jules said was "I'm not sure yet."

He sighed. "Me either."

"Really?"

"Really. I always thought publishing was where it's at."

So had Jules. She'd clawed her way past hundreds of applicants for her internship at *Du Jour*, and as maddening as it could be, she loved working there. Loved the energy, the industry, and the way everyone came to her if they needed to know something. In a magazine that was a revolving door, she'd somehow found her still center. Until now.

Randall continued, "But Monique's amazing, so I don't know. You should think about it. Share your contact card with me."

"Of course." She could just ignore her lock screen full of angry texts for a couple of seconds, right? But when Jules reached into her clutch for her phone, she touched only empty air.

Panic raced through her. Where had she left it? Oh…

On the kitchen counter back at the townhouse.

"Shit," she whispered, her blood going cold. "I left my phone at Viv… at my hotel."

Randall looked appropriately horrified. A phone was an assistant's lifeblood. "Then give me your number. I'll text you and you'll have it when you get back."

Sure. Yeah. That'd be fine. Jules breathed deeply. Vivian had left for dinner. If Randall texted with *Don't forget your amazing new job opportunity with Monique Leung,* Vivian wouldn't see it.

Not that she'd care at this point.

Jules gave Randall her number and thanked him. Then she escaped into the chilly night air of London in mid-February with too many things to think about for comfort.

Comfort would be a long time coming. She couldn't face going back to the empty townhouse, just waiting for Vivian to come home and ruin her life. And it seemed cowardly to go, grab her stuff, and bail to a hotel. She'd return after Vivian was home for the night, and what would be would be.

It just probably wouldn't be very good, that was all.

---

By the time she reached Vivian's townhouse, Jules's body was clenched with tension from head to toe.

*You were right,* she reminded herself, *and she was wrong. She should never have said what she said to you. You've got a way out. Don't forget that.*

During the past few hours, Vivian hadn't seen fit to cordon off the place with a chain-link fence, dig a moat, station a guard, or do anything else to signal Jules wasn't welcome. She took a deep breath, went up the stairs, and turned the key in the lock. Vivian hadn't thrown the latch. That was something.

Jules crept into the house, taking off her shoes as soon as she gained the hallway, and grabbed her phone from the kitchen counter. The display showed that Vivian had called her once. No voicemail.

She sighed and tiptoed up the stairs. There was no light shining from behind Vivian's bedroom door, but her coat had been hanging in the hall closet. So she was definitely home, even if she wasn't emerging from her lair to breathe flames in Jules's face before putting her onto the first flight out of London.

There was no sticky note on Jules's bedroom door reading *You're fired.* Nor a message written in blood-red lipstick on the bathroom mirror.

That just made it worse somehow. Vivian was just stringing Jules along, making her wait in agony for the final blow. Vivian was good at that kind of thing.

Sleep seemed impossible. Jules was ping-ponging between righteous fury and sheer grief at the probability of exile.

But the bed was soft and the covers warm, and even Jules's chattering psyche was no match for her weariness tonight. Too much. She'd been through too much today, too much all week, to keep her eyes open for another second. So she closed them and dropped into a deep, though unquiet, slumber.

Unfortunately, although Jules had dodged her earlier, Vivian was waiting for her in her dreams.

"I told you I couldn't trust you," she said. "Now I have to fire you."

She had Jules's phone in her hand. Jules reached for it, but Vivian pulled it away.

"Don't fire me," Jules whispered. "Don't make me go."

"I have to," Vivian said. "Everybody knows that. You knew this couldn't last. You know you should go."

"But you can't send me away! It's not fair. I didn't do anything wrong!"

Then Vivian pushed her shoulder.

"Hey!" Jules grabbed her arm. "What was that for?"

"Wake up." Vivian shoved her arm again. "Julia, I said, *wake up*."

She opened her eyes to find that someone had grabbed hold of her shoulder and was shaking her back and forth.

"Wake up," Vivian's voice repeated. She sounded pissed off.

Jules blinked and squinted. Someone had turned on the lamp by the door. It must have been Vivian, in fact, who was now sitting on the side of Jules's bed and shaking her awake. She dropped her hand when Jules opened her eyes and pulled it back into her lap. She was wearing pajamas.

The clock on the nightstand read 5:32 in big red numbers. Jules propped herself up on her elbows, ready to fly out of bed. It had to be an emergency. Something to do with the baby. "What's the matter? Are you okay?"

"No," Vivian said coolly. "And neither are you."

Her eyes were hard. Jules's sleepiness packed its bags and fled, never to return.

"Right," she said quietly.

"Is it? I wouldn't say this is 'right' at all. Sit up and pay attention. This is important."

Jules licked her dry lips. Her mouth felt like cotton and tasted awful. "Vivian, I know…"

"You don't know half as much as you think." Her voice seemed to shake on the final word.

Jules's eyes widened. She must have imagined that. Slowly pushing herself up from her elbows into a sitting position, Jules whispered, "Vivian?"

Vivian lifted her chin and crossed her arms over her chest. "Okay, Julia," she said. "Let's talk."

# CHAPTER 38

Her reprieve was over. Vivian hadn't even waited until sunrise.

Jules rubbed her hands over her face with a low sigh. "I'm sorry about what I said earlier. But when you said—"

"You're not sorry," Vivian said flatly.

"Yes, I am!" Jules snapped. What, did Vivian suddenly know Jules's feelings better than she did? "I was mad, but I shouldn't have lashed out like I did."

"But you meant every word of it. Me throwing people away and so on."

What could she say to that? It wasn't wrong. She might as well cop to it since she was about to get canned. "Yes, I did."

Vivian looked away, staring at the wall. For the first time, Jules noticed how straight her posture was—rigid, almost—and how tightly she was clasping her hands in her lap.

"I'll do whatever's necessary to keep *Du Jour* the top fashion platform," she said, still not looking at Jules. "To that end, I will hire and fire anyone I please. No one who works for me is irreplaceable, Julia. Not Mallory, not Lucia—not even Simon. I'll do what I have to do, and I'll never apologize for it. Do you understand?"

"Yes," Jules whispered, wondering if she would get any severance pay at all and how many therapy sessions she'd be able to afford with it.

"However..." Vivian kept her gaze firmly focused on the wall. She stopped, took a deep breath, and started again. "However, this *professional* tendency of mine does not extend to my private life. As I had assumed you were aware, but obviously you're not."

At the last part, her voice grew sharp, like it always did when she was pointing out someone's utter stupidity.

Jules's elbows were aching from the way she'd put her entire body weight on them. She dragged herself to a sitting position. It would have put her at eye level with Vivian, if Vivian had deigned to look at her. "Uh, okay?"

"People who are part of my personal life," Vivian said, her cheeks going a little red, "people like that—these people aren't replaceable. And I don't 'throw them away.'"

She had shocked Jules before. Heck, she'd shocked Jules more often than anybody else of Jules's acquaintance. But she'd never made Jules wonder if she was hallucinating or on drugs.

"Oh," she said.

"Oh," Vivian mimicked as she had earlier in the evening. It lacked bite this time.

"I'm…personal?"

"Yes." Vivian's voice was as clipped as if she'd just told Jules to get her coffee.

Vivian wasn't firing her? She didn't hate her? Vivian thought of her as somebody personal?

She pulled her knees to her chest and wrapped her arms around them. Her heart was pounding, but she had to focus. Some things had to be said, no matter what. "If we're getting personal, you said earlier you thought I'd go to bed with Monique. Which was not an okay thing to say. And then you said you didn't even need me. Is that how you feel?"

Vivian looked away. "Try not to take it too seriously when I say things in the heat of anger that I might not actually mean."

After a pause, during which Jules processed Vivian's words, she rubbed a hand over her forehead. She'd better not be getting a headache from this. Something was up with Vivian's inappropriate accusation about Monique, and Jules needed more time to figure out what it was.

"So are you saying I'm your"—she took her courage in both hands—"friend?"

It seemed impossible. Incredible. Vivian didn't have friends. Simon himself had said as much. But Jules might be her friend? She might occupy a role in Vivian's life that nobody else did?

Vivian did not reply, and Jules wondered if she'd gone too far.

Then Vivian said, "I've noticed the way you look at me."

*Huh?* Jules opened her mouth to say something when she realized what Vivian meant. What she had to mean.

Vivian snorted—not looking at Jules—and continued. "I'm observant, Julia. And you weren't exactly subtle on, oh, let's say, New Year's Eve."

She had never been so mortified in her entire life. Every muscle in her body seemed to lock up at once. What was the point of denial? "I'm—" she choked and finished with, "Vivian, I'm so sorry. I didn't know I was—"

What, *obvious?* Vivian had seen through her immediately. What if everybody had? What if Jules was the laughingstock of the office—of everywhere—the lowly assistant with a hopeless crush on her boss?

"I'm sorry," Jules repeated, sincerely wanting to die.

"Are you?" Vivian said.

There wasn't enough air. Jules fought for some anyway. "I never meant for you to know."

"Well, I know," Vivian said. "And for my part, I've never been attracted to another woman in my life."

Jules wondered if leaping from the window would actually kill her or if she'd just break a few bones. She should aim for the iron railings. "Vivian, of course I never hoped for—I know you'd never—"

"*That said,*" Vivian interrupted, using the shut-up tone Jules knew so well, "I have never understood why physical attraction has to be necessary for a relationship."

Whatever Jules had been about to stammer next died in her mouth.

Forget about before. She really and truly had never been so shocked as she was right now.

"What?" she said numbly.

Vivian looked at her at last. Then she stood up from the bed and began to pace the room. "You and I have both had relationships before. Several, I'm guessing," she said. "Considering where we are right now, obviously those have never worked out well." She glared at Jules fiercely. "Right?"

"I-I guess," Jules managed.

"Right. We've been with people who didn't appreciate or understand our goals. Our motivations. What drives us. Accurate, yes?"

"Well…yeah, but—"

"Yes. But." She took a deep breath. "I understand you. Better than you think. And you understand me."

"Um. No. I-I don't think so." *I've never understood anything less in my life.*

"Let me put it this way. You understand me better than anyone I've ever met. You anticipate everything. You know what I'll say before I say it."

"I didn't know you were going to say this." Jules was pretty sure her eyes couldn't get any wider. "Um…what are we talking about here?"

"You care about me," Vivian said flatly. "It isn't just sexual. You care *for me*. I know that."

Jules nodded, trembling in spite of herself. She lacked the power to confirm or deny anything at all. Or to speak, period.

Vivian looked out the window into the darkness beyond. Jules could see her only in profile now. No bump yet, but she knew what was there.

"I care for you," Vivian said abruptly.

An eon passed, an era, and when it was over, Jules was clutching her knees so tightly her arms hurt.

Vivian still wasn't looking at her.

Maybe Jules had dreamed that. She must have. Vivian couldn't have just said she cared for Jules. She must have meant something else, something that didn't so precisely match up with Jules's daydreams like teeth on a zipper closing.

"What does that mean?" she whispered.

"What do you think it means? I invited you to stay with me. Twice, for God's sake. I told you I'd do anything for you—"

"Wha—anything?" Jules sure as hell couldn't remember Vivian ever saying that.

"Anything within reasonable limits." Vivian waved her hand impatiently. She was still looking out of the window. "I even let you go toddling off to meet Monique—"

"Let me—"

She rounded on Jules with eyes full of fire. "*Never* do that again."

A wheezing sound came out of Jules's mouth. It was the best she could do.

"My point is, I care for you, *obviously*." Her voice growled with disbelief at Jules's thickness, and her glare got much worse. "But tonight's little display ruined my entire evening. I had to talk to important people about important things, and I had to do all that in an extremely bad mood."

Saying *you started it* seemed childish. "Um…"

"Which is when I realized that we had to talk," Vivian finished. "Now. What do you think?"

Then she waited. She actually folded her arms and tapped one bare foot on the carpet.

"Think?" Jules shook her head hard. She couldn't think. She might never be able to think again. This had just killed her brain.

Vivian rolled her eyes.

"Okay," Jules said. "I know you hate explaining things, but you're going to have to spell this one out for me. I do not understand."

"We do not have to have sex," Vivian said through her teeth, "to have a satisfying relationship. Is that clear enough for you, Julia?" Her face was bright red now.

Jules fell back against the headboard, utterly thunderstruck. Vivian wanted…Vivian was suggesting…proposing…

"Like a platonic thing?" she managed.

"Precisely." Her tone said, *you finally get it*.

"You and me, we'd be…*together*?"

Vivian paused, then nodded, looking relieved that Jules was finally catching on.

Jules sat in the ensuing stunned pause. Then she said, "I'm going to need coffee for this, aren't I?"

Ten minutes later, they perched on the kitchen counter stools while Jules clutched her mug of coffee and Vivian regarded her from across the island.

Jules took a long sip, grateful that her hands remained steady. "All right," she said carefully. "You…care for me."

Vivian nodded.

"But," she continued, trying her best to piece it together, "not like a friend exactly?"

Vivian shrugged in an apparent effort to look cool. Then she ruined it by swallowing visibly. "Not exactly."

Jules gulped too. She'd never had a relationship talk like this before, where both parties were braced for impact. She still couldn't believe she was having a relationship talk at all.

"But you said—" She cleared her throat, started again. "You said you were straight."

"I am." There was a slight edge in Vivian's voice. Annoyance or anxiety? "Are you expecting me to explain this logically? I can't. If I asked you for friendship and nothing else, I'd be selling us both short. I wouldn't care if…" She trailed off.

Jules leaned forward, clutching her coffee mug so hard it hurt. "If what?"

Vivian exhaled. "I wouldn't care if a friend did what you did tonight with Monique."

"I didn't do anything with Monique!" Jules threw her hands in the air. Well, at least now she knew why Vivian had been so irrational about the whole thing. "All that happened was she offered me a job, and—"

Vivian's hand slammed down on the countertop, and Jules nearly spilled her coffee.

"I knew it," she snarled.

"Come on. I didn't say yes, and it's nothing like what you were apparently thinking!"

"What is it, then? Something to do with her new fashion label?"

Of course Vivian knew all about that. "Yeah, she just—"

"She just offered you a job in *Beijing*, that's all?"

"In London, actually, and—"

Vivian inhaled as if she were about to breathe out fire.

"And I don't want it!" Jules exclaimed. "All I want to do is figure out what's going on here!"

Her voice cracked on the last word as she reached a high, almost hysterical pitch. A quick sip of coffee did nothing to restore her cool.

Miraculously, her outburst seemed to have knocked some sense back into Vivian. She even shook her head a little, as if trying to wake up. If she were anyone else, Jules would have said she looked embarrassed.

"As I was saying," Vivian continued, her voice lower, "you feel more than friendship. So do I. I don't see the point in pretending otherwise."

Jules set down her coffee cup and placed a hand on the countertop, hoping it looked casual and not like she was trying to keep herself from falling off the stool.

"You're saying you care about me in a"—Jules swallowed and went for it—"romantic way?"

Vivian tilted her head to the side, an almost nod.

Then a definite nod. A yes.

Jules got a little dizzy. She hunted for words and came up with "uh, wow."

Vivian's lips finally crooked in a wry smile. "'Wow' indeed."

"For how long?" Jules's eyes widened. "You said when I stayed with you the first time?"

"No. Not then. I don't know, Julia. I didn't check the time or mark it on a calendar."

"I sure didn't see it on the schedule." Jules managed a weak laugh.

Vivian did not look amused. The jokes still needed work, then.

Then Jules remembered something and decided she needed to clear it up fast.

"What about Stan Oppenheimer?" She swallowed around the bitter taste in her mouth that had nothing to do with coffee.

Vivian looked at her as if she'd shown up to work wearing a blouse from the Gap. "Stan? What about him?"

If Jules tried hard enough, maybe she could dissolve into individual blushing atoms. This would be pure torture. She was supposed to talk about Vivian's side piece? Worse, confess her own jealousy?

Might as well go for bravado. "There's that whole thing where you've been dating him, for a start."

"You think I'm *dating* him?"

She spoke as if it were the most ridiculous thing she'd ever heard. For the second time in their acquaintance, Vivian looked as if she were about to laugh in Jules's face.

"Don't act like it's impossible," Jules said, stung. "Why wouldn't I think that? All those lunches, and you met in the evenings, and you—"

"And I what?" Vivian pressed.

She had to say it. "You always came back looking happy," she mumbled. "Really happy."

"I did? How happy?"

"Just-had-sex happy," Jules admitted, flushing.

Vivian blinked. Then her lips curved into the hint of a smile. "How interesting."

Jules eyed her in confusion.

She waved her hand. "I am not sexually or romantically interested in Stan Oppenheimer."

The part of Jules's brain that was tuned in to office politics piped up: *She can still be interested in other ways.*

"You're up to something," she said.

Vivian didn't pretend otherwise. "Better for you not to know. You will in time. I'm asking you to trust me, Julia."

Jules's coffee mug was empty now. A brown ring surrounded the inside of the white porcelain. She focused on it steadily and said, "Okay. Just a second. I want another cup. You?"

Vivian shook her head, and Jules took the opportunity to get her head together while she went to the counter. Turning her back on Vivian helped. Vivian's eyes could probably make her agree to anything, but this proposition needed careful reflection.

*Careful reflection?* Jules almost laughed at herself. Understatement of the year.

She poured the coffee. "So you're not interested in Stan Oppenheimer? What are you interested in?"

There was a pause so long that Jules couldn't bring herself to turn around again, even after filling her cup.

Then Vivian said, "I won't stand in your way. But London—really, Julia. There are jobs in New York too. I could help you get any of them, if you—"

Jules whirled around in horror. "Are you *firing* me?"

"No!" Vivian's hands clenched on the countertop. She relaxed them and said calmly, "I'm offering you options with no strings attached. Options that mean you'll stay in New York."

Jules returned to the island with her coffee, miraculously managing not to spill a drop, even though her hands trembled again. "And that's important?"

"Very important." Vivian looked a trifle paler than usual. She said nothing else.

After a moment, Jules said quietly, "This is the 'caring for me' part, isn't it?"

Vivian swallowed hard. She kept Jules's gaze, but it seemed difficult. "I said earlier I didn't need you." She paused and with visible effort said, "I lied."

Jules let out a huge breath and looked down at the quartz countertop to steady herself. She could only manage, "Okay."

"And that—look. I'm your boss. I know that. Coming up through the ranks, I saw so many men— it's disgusting. The exploitation and coercion."

Jules looked up again, her heart hammering. "Did that ever happen to you?"

Vivian hesitated. "I knew how to play the game. I knew how to pit them against each other until I could climb another rung up the ladder and escape. I knew to find connections who could protect me. And I knew how to play dirty until they were afraid of me more than they wanted me. That was lucky."

Jules nodded, realizing only now how lucky she'd been too, to work for mentors like Simon and Vivian. Whatever their other demands, they'd never demanded *that*.

"Anyway, back to the subject," Vivian added with a bitter laugh. "My whole point is, I refuse to be like them, so I'm offering you the chance to spread your wings and fly, if…"

Jules's hands were too hot from clenching onto her coffee cup. She still couldn't relax them. "I can find my own chances. And I'm not worried you'll exploit me, Vivian."

Vivian bit her bottom lip. She flushed.

Jules's heart stopped. It probably wasn't good to think *but maybe you could prey on me just a little bit*. That wouldn't be nearly as sexy in reality as it was in fantasy.

Jules would just tell herself that over and over until she believed it.

Then she realized Vivian was still red-faced and staring at her with a look that Jules recognized. She saw it in her own mirror after spending a whole shower thinking about fucking Vivian. And it made Jules's nipples get so hard they ached in the space of one second.

"Right," Vivian said hoarsely. "I don't want from you what they wanted from me."

Jules fought to get her brain out from between her thighs. *Focus. Focus.* "Then what do you want?"

"I mean—" Vivian met Jules's gaze again. "I do want more out of you than an employee could reasonably be expected to give. Not sexually. I already told you. I'm not attracted to women."

*Except me*, Jules thought, her heart racing. Vivian seemed to believe what she was saying. She probably did. She'd married three men, and she hated being wrong. "Then what do you want from me that you're not already getting?"

Vivian sighed. The incredible intensity had vanished from her eyes, and now she appeared resigned. "Your companionship."

Companionship, which was apparently not the same thing as friendship. Jules had been an English major who'd also taken a queer studies class, and she had an idea of the distinction Vivian was drawing.

She cleared her throat. "Let me understand this: you're suggesting I find another job so you and I can be…uh…romantic companions?"

It wasn't like Jules had never heard of such arrangements before. People got together in all sorts of combinations. This just wasn't a combination she had ever imagined for herself.

Vivian folded her hands. "Well put, Julia. Better than I was putting it, anyway. I know it sounds unusual."

*That's one word for it.* "Yeah, that's what it sounds like, but what does it look like? What do you imagine us as, if we're not, you know…" She gestured back and forth between their bodies as if that was supposed to imitate passionate sex.

Vivian leaned against the back of her stool and crossed her arms. "Did you enjoy Christmas dinner?"

It took Jules a second to figure out that Vivian wasn't asking about the quality of the turkey. "I did," she said slowly. "I really did."

"And sitting in a bar with me?"

"That was pretty awesome," she admitted.

"And accompanying me to places where you, as my assistant, weren't expected to be? Lunches and dinners?"

"You made me do that, and it was stressful." Hey, Vivian wanted honesty. "But under other circumstances, it would've been nice. I think I'd like that a lot."

"I think you would too. And I—" Vivian took a deep breath and met Jules's eyes. "I might as well just say it. You're good company. You're a good writer. You're intelligent. I like having you around. I…eventually realized that I want to have you around all the time." She scowled. "You want to talk about being embarrassed? Going home early all those days so I could rest and wishing you were coming with me? *That* was embarrassing."

Really? The whole time Jules had hated watching her leave, Vivian hadn't wanted to go? It seemed impossible, incredible. "I wanted to go with you too."

"There!" Vivian slapped her palms against the counter, looking triumphant. "That's what I'm talking about. I wouldn't want that from a friend, much less an assistant. And if you want the same thing—"

"I don't know," Jules blurted out. "I want to be with you, I know that much. You're right. But I didn't expect any of this." Something Vivian had just said struck her. "Wait—did you say I'm a good writer? You've read my work?"

"You've only amassed a couple of bylines, so it didn't take long. The *Working Girl* article seemed a bit on the nose."

The sudden amusement in Vivian's eyes made Jules's cheeks heat. "It wasn't about us! It's about a boss and her employee, but I didn't mean—"

"I'm sure." Vivian's bland tone disguised whether she believed her or not. "The *Salon* piece had a little more meat to it. I agreed with most of it, although you missed the mark in a couple of places."

"I did? Where?"

Vivian gave her a challenging look. "Give this a chance and find out."

That was one of the most tempting things Vivian had offered so far: the chance to pick her brain. It was a prodigious brain. "I have to think about it," she forced herself to say.

For real. She had to consider whether she wanted to change jobs and have dinner with Vivian Carlisle instead of scheduling her appointments, whether she wanted more than this platonic…whatever she was being offered here.

For a second, the light in Vivian's eyes dimmed. Had she expected an instant answer? Probably. Vivian didn't like indecisiveness or dithering.

Too bad.

"Give me the day," she said firmly. "There's a lot to think through, and you've already had a chance to do that. I need one too."

"Fair," Vivian conceded, although she still didn't look happy about it. "I don't want you to make a decision you'll regret."

"I won't." Jules squared her shoulders and met Vivian's gaze head-on. "I'll think about it, and I assume you'll cut me a little slack if I'm not laser focused on everything today."

"Take the day off."

There was a moment of utter silence during which Jules decided that, yes, someone at the party definitely *had* slipped her an acid tab.

Vivian, however, looked completely serious.

"Take the day off," Jules repeated. "On the last day of Fashion Week."

"I'll survive somehow. Even assistants get food poisoning. That's your cover story. Stay here and text whomever you text to make things happen."

This was Vivian proving she could have Jules in her life as something other than an assistant. That was clear, but she was already cringing at the idea of Vivian trying to make it through the busiest day of the week without Jules at her side. It wouldn't be that much more restful to stay in the townhouse texting and calling people all day.

But at least Jules wouldn't have to worry about having a dopey expression on her face in front of others or tripping over objects or being so distracted by Vivian's presence that she couldn't make an informed decision.

"Okay," she said. "If you're sure."

"Oh yes. I'm sure." Vivian gave Jules a look full of purpose. "And I'll do whatever it takes for you to be sure too. If something's worth having, it's worth working for." The purpose in her eyes became a flame. "You're worth it, Julia."

The flame worked. Jules melted right on schedule. It took the effort of a lifetime not to agree to Vivian's idea then and there.

"Don't worry," she said hoarsely. "I'll make up my mind."

"That's what I'm counting on." Vivian slid off her barstool with a little grunt and looked toward the stairs. "It's time for me to get dressed. At least you get to figure out your life in your pajamas. Don't say I never did anything for you," she added sardonically.

"I wouldn't say that, Vivian," Jules said softly. "I wouldn't say that at all."

# CHAPTER 39

### Where would I go?

Jules looked carefully at the first question on her list of considerations, which was six items long and already made her want to tear out her hair.

Even worse, she kept getting interrupted. It was nine thirty in the morning and Vivian had left the townhouse an hour ago to attend a star-studded breakfast. Jules was already being bombarded with texted questions and requests from all corners. Most of them started off with a cursory apology for disturbing her, then launched into something complicated. All of which left Jules with little time to figure out something important enough to turn her life upside down.

For example, where she'd go and what she'd do if she left *Du Jour*.

She could find something. Monique Leung's offer proved it. If someone wanted to hire Jules all the way from London, she could get a job in New York. Once people established that she wasn't leaving because of any bad blood with Vivian Carlisle, they'd be interested in her. That wasn't the issue.

She chewed on her lower lip. The issue was that, even aside from her feelings for Vivian, she loved *Du Jour*. It was the holy grail of fashion. She got to be where things happened, doing what she was good at.

Hell, she didn't even like having the day off, as much as she appreciated the gesture. Yes, she needed time to think, but she loved being in the thick of things.

She and Vivian were alike in that.

Jules sighed and rested her hand on her cheek. She was ensconced in the living room armchair in her pajamas because, if she had to sit out a whole day of Fashion Week, she was going to be comfy doing it. Vivian had said so.

*I should be with her*, Jules thought. *At her side. They're probably screwing things up without me.*

As if it were a sign, she got another text, this time from Keisha.

*do u know where Charlotte is*

Jules sighed, opened her schedule app, found Charlotte's calendar, and texted back:

*Phoebe English show*

Keisha replied:

*Thanks, hope u feel better soon!!*

Right. Back to figuring out her life. Jules returned to her list.

**V's pregnancy**

Yeah. That was a big one. Vivian hadn't even mentioned it earlier, and Jules's head had been spinning too much to give it serious thought. But Vivian was having a baby. She was due in mid-July, and it was now the end of February. Although Jules had always seen children in her future and she loved kids, she'd never planned on being a mom in her midtwenties.

*Would* she be a mom? Was that even something Vivian wanted from her? She'd said she wanted to spend time with Jules, but once the baby was born, any extra time would go out the window. If Jules left *Du Jour* and wasn't involved in the child's life, she'd never see Vivian. So what would even be the point?

Making things even more complicated, when Jules thought about the baby she felt a sweet ache in her heart. She'd been there since the beginning, after all. She'd arranged the doctors' appointments, managed Vivian's menus, seen to her comfort, and she knew—knew for a *fact*—that if she stayed at *Du Jour*, pretty soon she'd be ordering furniture for a nursery. Plus finding a list of nanny candidates. Getting baby clothes and toys. And she'd love every second of it. It was the easy part, the part without midnight feedings and temper tantrums, but it was there nevertheless.

She imagined holding the baby while it smiled up at her. Her cheeks warmed, and a little squeal left her mouth before she could stop it.

Then she got herself together. She couldn't afford to be silly or sentimental about something this big. It was definitely a talk-more-to-Vivian moment. Time for the next item on the list.

### Discretion

Not as big as pregnancy, but still pretty big. Even if Vivian was divorced, even if Jules wasn't working for her anymore, discovery would raise a stink. People would call Vivian a cradle robber. And they'd accuse Jules of trying to sleep her way to the top, which was pretty rich after Vivian's accusations about Monique. Ironic too, considering:

### No sex?

Jules looked at the two words as if they weren't English. When it came to her feelings for Vivian, "no" and "sex" didn't belong next to each other. Everything Vivian had described to Jules sounded wonderful: companionship, care, prioritizing each other. It called to her as nothing ever had in any other relationship.

However, all of this had been kick-started by Jules's lust for Vivian on New Year's Eve. She couldn't just will that away, and why should she? Jules liked sex. It had been the best part of her relationship with Chelsea, the only reason they'd stayed together for four months. She liked the physical closeness, the sense of connection, and she wanted that in her life. Just because she was wild about Vivian in other ways didn't mean she was okay with being celibate at nearly twenty-six.

Her phone pinged with another text. She groaned.

It was Simon. He'd sent her a text that was just four green-faced nausea emojis. Then he followed it up.

*Sorry you're sick. Got everything you need?*

Aw. Jules smiled. No, she didn't have everything she needed, and she wasn't sure she'd be able to get it, but it was nice of him to ask. She replied:

*I'm good, thanks* ♥

*OK. Feel better soon.*

Jules sent the thumbs-up emoji, propped her chin on her hand, and regarded her phone. Simon was kind to reach out, but every time her phone had alerted her this morning, she'd hoped it was Vivian. She knew it wouldn't be—Vivian was giving her space—but it was weird not to communicate with her. Even during the weekends, texts would fly back and forth between them.

Jules missed her.

"Ugh, get it together," she muttered. "It's been, like, two hours."

**What about my family?**

What, indeed? Jules's parents were already afraid Vivian was up to no good with Jules. It wouldn't matter that Vivian was proposing a relationship entirely devoid of sex, much less sexual predation. They'd still say Vivian was exploiting her, and they'd think Jules was nuts even for considering it.

They might be right. She looked at the last item. On a list of questions that seemed impossible to answer, this one was the hardest.

**What do I want?**

She was young. Free. She had ambition. That last part had killed her previous relationship. How would a relationship survive when both parties were workaholics, to say nothing of having a child in the mix? Something would have to give, and what would that be? It might be something Jules wasn't willing to surrender.

Everyone always said to go with your gut instead of your head or heart. The gut, they said, never lies. But what if Jules's gut was just as confused as the rest of her?

After all, it was begging her not to let Vivian get away, which was the least sensible solution possible.

What did Jules want?

And when she figured it out, what if it was something she didn't need? Something that could wreck her in the end? People didn't always want what was best for them. So far, Jules's desires and goals had played well together. She'd always known what she wanted, and it had worked beautifully for her until now. And now…

Jules dropped her phone on the side table, rested her head back against the armchair, and stared up at the ceiling. It was a nice ceiling. Crown molding and everything.

List making only went so far. So did listening to her gut. This decision couldn't be a one-woman show. She needed more information. *I've got to talk to her.*

Her phone pinged. Jules's breath caught. Was it Vivian?

Charlotte.

*do u know where Keisha is*

Jules groaned and covered her face with her hands. It was four thirty a.m. back home. In either time zone, it was too early to start drinking.

## CHAPTER 40

When Vivian returned home, as much as Jules wanted to, she didn't bombard her with questions right away. Instead, she silently helped her out of her coat and led her back to the living room, where two hot cups of chamomile tea awaited them.

Good thing too. Vivian's face was drawn and her steps were slow. It was nearly eight o'clock at night, and she should now be changing for a brief appearance at a big Fashion Week after-party. Instead, she'd canceled, citing exhaustion.

"Everyone believed me," she told Jules as they headed into the living room. "I've gotten the whole range of responses on this pregnancy, from congratulations to people asking me if I'm out of my mind." She grimaced. "That second group's usually pretty plastered, of course."

"Of course."

Vivian sat down on the sofa with a grunt and looked up at her.

Jules automatically glanced at the armchair, took a deep breath, and sat next to her on the sofa without an invitation.

Vivian gave her a small smile in return.

"I'm glad they believed you," Jules said, "but that's not really why you returned home."

"With that acumen, why aren't you a detective?"

Jules refused to be offended. If Vivian wanted to retreat behind a shield of sarcasm, that was her prerogative. "I made chamomile tea."

Vivian looked at the steaming china cups with surprise. "Thanks. I see you got dressed up too."

"Don't knock leggings," Jules said evenly. "And the hoodie's Blanc Noir."

A pensive look crossed Vivian's face. "Too many people were surprised when women began wearing Lululemon outside the yoga studio. But I always thought—"

"Vivian, please. Can we talk?"

Vivian reached for her teacup and saucer. "Not much for civilized conversation tonight?"

"I was just getting to the point," Jules said incredulously. "Isn't that kind of your thing?"

"In the office, yes. Elsewhere, Julia, I enjoy talking to people I like about things we have in common. Is that a shock?"

It was, actually. Jules's face must have said as much because Vivian rolled her eyes. "Then let me be clear. I like talking to you about things other than my schedule. I like talking to you in general."

*I've never cared for yellow.*

For reasons she couldn't explain, Jules heard Vivian's voice in her memory. She was telling Jules about a color she didn't like, sharing a preference with her for no reason. The tiniest moment that was enormous for Vivian Carlisle, followed by a dozen other moments: observations, reflections, confidences.

Might as well admit it: "And I like talking to you more than I like talking to anybody else. More than I ever have with a friend." Jules had never spent night and day thinking about a friend, wondering what a friend would think about this or that, being reminded of that friend at every turn.

Vivian made a humming sound clearly meant to convey, *See? I told you I was right.*

Jules sat cross-legged on the sofa, propped her elbow on her knee, and put her chin in her hand. "You're having a kid."

For a second, Vivian went too still and her eyes shuttered. "Yes."

"We've got to talk about it. When you say you want to have me as a 'companion,' what does that mean? You're going to be a mom. It'll take up a fair bit of your time. How do I fit into that?"

Vivian nodded. She put a hand on her stomach, perhaps without realizing it. "I'm not asking you to co-parent, Julia. You have your whole career ahead of you, and it's not like any of this is your doing. You can be involved to the extent you want to be."

"I appreciate that, but I'll be involved one way or the other, won't I? The baby will be a full-time job on top of your other full-time job. If I'm not involved, when would we even see each other?"

"We'd manage," Vivian said with the stubbornness of someone who'd bent the universe to her will for years. "Julia, if you want something enough, you make it happen. I wouldn't be asking you for this—I wouldn't ask you for anything if I didn't take it seriously."

"I'm taking it seriously too. I made a list, actually."

"A list?"

"Yep." Jules reached for the tablet resting on the coffee table next to her saucer and opened the Notes app. "Want to see?"

Vivian didn't scoff. Instead, she took the tablet and looked over the screen.

Jules waited on pins and needles while she read.

However, Vivian's only reaction was the occasional nod and thoughtful "mm." Then she said, "Okay. Let's start. The pregnancy we've discussed—"

"Started to discuss," Jules pointed out.

Vivian raised a hand, still looking at the screen. "Discussions are ongoing. As for where you'll go, the answer is 'anywhere you want to.'"

"You're not getting me a new job," Jules said flatly. "I can find one myself, if I want."

"*If* you—" Vivian gave her a quick look but then shook her head. "Right. Well, 'discretion' lumps in with that. If you're not working for me, who cares?"

Vivian could be unreal sometimes. "You think it wouldn't be a scandal? People would say we were doing it while I worked for you. And speaking of doing it…" Jules nodded at the tablet and gave her a pointed look.

"Speaking of doing it, we wouldn't be doing it, so where's the scandal?" Vivian sounded exasperated, but her cheeks were pink again. "As for this"—she waved the tablet—"sexual attraction isn't the be-all, end-all for a relationship."

"I know that," Jules protested. "But I *like* sex. Don't you?" Surely Vivian had to. Jules knew lust when she saw it, and Vivian had looked at her lustfully this morning, even if she didn't know it.

"Sex is fine," Vivian said impatiently. "I've even had good sex, if that's what you're asking. Compared to the rest of your points, it's not that important."

"It's important *to me*." How could she make Vivian wrap her head around this? "Yes, I care about you beyond wanting to have sex with you. And I get what you're saying, but…it's not easy to shut that part of your brain off when you want somebody as much as I want you."

Vivian sipped her tea as if to hide any reaction, but the artery at the base of her throat visibly pulsed, a sight that made Jules ache.

"All right. Fine." Vivian's words strained through her clenched teeth. "It's not that important, but…maybe there are other possibilities for you."

Jules's mind raced. There didn't seem to be a lot of ways to interpret that. "Hold it. Do you mean an open relationship?"

Before she could add that she wasn't interested in that at all, Vivian snapped, "I do *not*. Of course I don't. You with some…some—"

"Some other female fashion editor," Jules said dryly, "not to be named here?"

"I'd be just as happy never to hear her name on your lips again, Julia. Or anyone else's name, for that matter."

"Then what are you talking about? If I'm not having sex with anybody else, how am I supposed to not go without?" Before Vivian could reply, she added, "Don't say I can take care of myself. I've been doing that. It doesn't cut it."

Even the tips of Vivian's ears went pink. Her mouth parted briefly, softly before she snapped it shut. Her voice sounded faintly strangled when she spoke next. Maybe it was the desire she was trying to choke out. "I'll think of something. That is, we will. There are no problems, Julia, only solutions."

There was something about Vivian that made anything seem possible, including an impossible compromise. "Um…right. But mostly you're just thinking about the 'companionship' thing."

"Yes. That part of you, the *important* part, would be—"

*Mine*, she didn't say, but they both heard it.

Jules bit her bottom lip to hold back the groan that wanted to escape. *You want me*, she longed to say. *Don't you see that? Don't you recognize it?*

Maybe she didn't. Vivian had said she'd never been attracted to another woman. Whether that was true or not, this had to be confusing as hell, especially to a woman used to putting her personal life last on her list of priorities. Vivian really might not realize what she wanted.

And Jules couldn't make her realize it, couldn't make Vivian sit on this couch until she did. If she said she didn't want to have sex, that had to be the end of it. The most Jules could do was wear strategically low-cut blouses and hope Vivian got a clue eventually.

Vivian looked back at her and sighed deeply. "You think this is ridiculous, don't you?" She shook her head before Jules could reply affirmatively. "So was the Iris van Herpen collection, and what did you think about that?"

"It's genius."

"And ridiculous."

"But genius," Jules conceded. "All right. I'm thinking about it. Keep going."

Vivian looked back down at the tablet. "I'll skip over your family," she said in a low voice. "The last question is all that matters. What *do* you want? Don't say it's me."

Jules, who had been about to say *you* yet again, closed her mouth.

"Tell me what you want out of life." She laid the tablet in her lap.

Jules straightened her shoulders. "I want to stand out. I have stuff I want to say, and I want people to listen, and I want it to matter and to—to change things, to—"

"So do PR for the Peace Corps." Vivian looked a little amused.

Jules took the bait. "Okay, so I don't know *exactly* what I want yet. I want to write and get published, and I also want to work in fashion because I love both of those things. So far, so good, right?"

"You've made a start," Vivian acknowledged. "Not much more."

Like Jules needed to be reminded that she was on the lower end of both ladders. "Come on, I'm working on it. I want to get *regularly* published, and I want to be at the forefront of whatever changes are happening in fashion. Who knows what the industry's going to look like in ten years?"

"It'll look like whatever I decide."

Vivian's face was serene, her voice confident at her assertion. It made Jules's heart flutter. She had to stop herself from blurting out *you're incredible.*

"I'm sure it will," she said instead. "You're at a place where you can do that. I'm not yet. I've still got to bust my ass to move up even a little, just like you did. How would we even have time for each other if I'm trying to get ahead? How could I give the baby what I want to?"

Then she stopped, nearly tripping over her own words. She'd meant to say, *How could I give the baby what they need?* She looked at Vivian, stricken.

"I'd understand," Vivian said. "More than anyone in the world, Julia, I would understand."

"But how would it work? Well, you've started going home early. I can stay a little later at the office and then join you. Have dinner or whatever, and then go back out, if I have to, or go home and write."

"You can write at my house, and what do you mean 'stay a little later'? You wouldn't be at the office."

Jules took a deep breath. "I don't want to leave *Du Jour*. I get why you think I have to, but I love it, and—"

"What? Julia, we couldn't—"

Jules gave her a flat, unblinking stare. "We can try."

Vivian appeared frozen in place. She shook her head. Then she managed, "You're my employee."

"Yeah. How'd it go without me today? Smooth as silk?"

Vivian stuck her tongue in her cheek.

"I thought so," Jules said. "I belong at your side. You said you needed me."

Vivian fisted her hands in her skirt. "I do need you, but not like that. I have ethical limits, believe it or not."

"If we're not having sex, why does it matter? We're having dinner, we're—doing whatever you imagine us doing, hanging out and talking. *I don't know. How is HR going to fire anybody for that?*"

"I don't care about HR!" Vivian rose to her feet, hands clenched at her sides. "I can stand anything except you feeling obligated or coerced."

"If it's not working out, then I'll quit. I know I won't work at *Du Jour* forever, but I don't want to deal with adjusting to a whole new job while we're figuring things out. Especially with this." She gestured at Vivian's abdomen.

"So there's something to figure out."

There was silence while Jules processed the tone of Vivian's voice: soft, questioning, and...hopeful.

It pulled Jules underwater like any siren song. "I think there is," she managed. "Yeah."

Vivian's eyes gleamed with triumph. She graciously kept it out of her voice as she moved to stand directly in front of Jules. Then to Jules's shock, she reached out and took both of her hands.

Skin on skin. Specifically, Vivian's skin on Jules's skin.

Heat swept through Jules's entire body, and she barely suppressed a whimper, already aching more from touching Vivian's hands than she had during entire naked nights with Aaron. How could it be possible that Vivian didn't feel this? That Jules was all alone in feeling this?

Easy. It wasn't possible.

"You'll leave *Du Jour* if it's too much?" Vivian pressed. There was another question beneath it that Jules heard loud and clear: *You'd choose me?*

"Yes," she said. "In a heartbeat."

Vivian's eyelashes fluttered only for a second but long enough to betray her relief.

Jules rejoiced in it.

"There's more than one way to be happy, Julia." Now Vivian's gaze was hypnotic, overwhelming, all-encompassing. "Let me show you. Let me make you happy."

"God," Jules whispered like a swooning teenager before she could stop herself. It was so embarrassing.

Vivian's chuckle somehow took the sting out. "Does this call for a drink?"

"You bet it does." She was still breathless. Vivian had promised to make her happy, like something out of an old movie. This was all nuts, but that had sounded so damn romantic, and Jules was only human.

A few minutes later, they sat at the kitchen island again, Vivian with a bottle of Perrier and Jules with a glass of the same brandy she'd destroyed her dessert with on Christmas. It wasn't half bad on its own.

"To new beginnings?" Vivian suggested.

"Sounds good to me." Jules couldn't keep the silly grin off her face as their glasses clinked. Well, this was going to be one hell of an adventure. "Oh, but just one more thing."

Vivian paused with her glass at her lips. She sounded rightly suspicious. "What?"

"I'll never pressure you. I promise." Jules rested on her elbow against the countertop. "But I reserve the right to look sexy."

Those elegant eyebrows raised. "Trying to get me to change my mind?"

"Nobody says you have to look."

Vivian focused on her water glass like it was the most fascinating thing in the whole world. "If it's office appropriate, how sexy can you be?"

Jules nearly chortled. *Challenge accepted.* "I'll figure something out."

There was no denying it: Vivian Carlisle was blushing again.

Jules smugly took another sip of her brandy, then said, "So what now?"

"What do you mean?"

"It's not even nine o'clock yet. What do you want to do?"

"Oh. You've spent all day cooped up here. I guess you're dying to go out." Vivian looked exhausted at the thought.

"No," Jules said. "I'm not."

They looked at each other. After a pause, Vivian said archly, "Then what are you suggesting?"

---

"Julia, are you into feet?"

"Yes, Vivian. I can finally tell someone. I have a foot fetish."

"You have a fetish for being a smartass. *Oh-h-h.*" Vivian ruined her snooty attitude with a groan of relief.

Jules smirked down at the feet in her lap, the feet attached to Vivian, who was stretched out on the sofa. She'd gone upstairs for a shower, then returned in her pajamas. And now she was getting a foot rub that, based on her reaction, was the sensory experience of a lifetime.

She rubbed cream into Vivian's skin reverently. Vivian got weekly pedicures that kept her heels soft and her toenail polish immaculate. Fetish worthy, if you were into that kind of thing.

"Tell me about today," Jules said, firmly rubbing her thumb against the instep, eliciting another groan. "I got a lot of panic texts from people, but that's not the same thing."

Vivian tapped her lips, clearly sorting through where she wanted to begin. Then her eyes lit up. "Remember what a disaster the Mary Katrantzou show was last year?"

Jules leaned forward eagerly. "Was it even worse?"

Her glee made Vivian chuckle. "The opposite. It was a truly clever collection. A combination of textures and colors that made you want to reach out and touch the pieces. So many designers today live in their heads—"

"But her clothes took up space," Jules concluded, impressed. "Made them a tactile experience."

"Exactly. There were several pieces that would have looked great on you."

She barely managed not to drop the foot in her lap. Vivian was looking at her with a fond little smile she'd never worn before. Jules heard the message loud and clear: *I was thinking about you.*

"Yeah? What were they?" she asked.

"A patterned linen dress with ostrich feathers at the hem and a pair of blue-striped knitted trousers were my top contenders. But the collection overall fit your aesthetic without reducing it to cliché. Christopher Kane, on the other hand—gorgeous, but not you at all. The color schemes…"

Jules let Vivian talk. She had spent hours imagining Jules in various outfits, thinking about how the cuts of the clothes would suit her body shape or coloring. At London *Fashion Week,* when she should have been paying attention to broader concerns.

But she wasn't attracted to Jules. No, sir.

Jules listened to Vivian talk about her day, enthralled as always. It wasn't the same as being there, but seeing Fashion Week through Vivian Carlisle's eyes was its own pleasure. She was the queen of the fashion world, and nobody got to hear her inner thoughts about it except for Jules. Moreover, Vivian didn't ask anyone else about *their* inner thoughts except for Jules.

*And we get to keep doing this.* The thought rocked Jules to her core. *We get to have this together.*

"Julia?"

Jules looked into Vivian's eyes, which now appeared a little worried. She must have a weird look on her face.

"Sorry," Jules said. She searched for an excuse, then realized she didn't need one. "I was just thinking about how nice this is."

Vivian smiled again.

The sight melted Jules's heart like butter. *I'm a goner, all right.*

"It is nice," Vivian agreed softly. "I knew it would be."

Her hands were draped over her abdomen.

An impulse seized Jules, unlooked for and irresistible. She took one of Vivian's hands and raised it to her mouth for a kiss.

Vivian gasped but did not snatch her hand back. Good thing too, because at the touch of skin to her mouth, Jules fell into a trance. She couldn't have let go if her life depended on it.

It was so warm, so soft, and Jules had been dying for this. Dying to touch and kiss her. She hadn't known how much until now.

The hand trembled. Jules snapped out of it and looked up.

Vivian's eyes were glazed and her cheeks were pink. She licked her lips and didn't appear to realize it.

Jules fought back an actual whimper while she throbbed between her legs.

"How chivalrous," Vivian said, her voice shaking.

"That's me," Jules rasped. She let go. Vivian's hand hovered in the air for a moment longer before resting back on her stomach. "Miss Chivalrous."

Vivian cleared her throat. "Well, don't…don't push it."

"Of course not. It was okay, though?"

"If that's what you need."

Vivian clearly meant it to sound like a favor, a concession she'd make for Jules. It came out instead like the thinnest of excuses.

"I need it," Jules whispered.

"Oh." Vivian swallowed hard.

"If I'm going to be your romantic companion," Jules said, "then I'm going to romance you. Just a little bit."

Red bloomed in Vivian's cheeks again. "All…all right."

Never breaking her gaze, Jules reached again for Vivian's hand, took it, and kissed it gently.

Vivian's eyelashes fluttered, but her breath remained steady this time, as if daring Jules to impress her.

The woman was a menace. But she was Jules's menace now.

# CHAPTER 41

Unfortunately, the next morning allowed no more leisure time. Jules was up at six thirty, directing porters as well as various minions who'd come at the last minute to drop off goodbye gifts from designers and friends.

Vivian—up, dressed, and perfect by seven—strode around the house with a wireless earbud, barking out constant instructions to poor saps all over the world. When they were within twenty minutes of leaving, she breezed through the living room where Jules was frantically packing up the gifts to be shipped back to New York.

"David Yurman said he'd sent me some carnelian earrings," Vivian said. "I'm sure you saw them in there. They'd go well with this outfit."

Jules couldn't refrain from looking said outfit up and down. She hadn't meant to do it suggestively, but Vivian's breath caught anyway.

Jules held back a smile. She kept her voice analytical. "Yeah, I can see that. They'd pick up the accents in your scarf."

"Excellent," Vivian replied before walking away quickly.

Jules grinned but then drooped as she looked back at the huge pile of gifts. Vivian might think Jules had perfect recall, but she had no clue where those earrings were. What a pain in the…

Vivian poked her head back into the living room. Her earbud was still in, but she said, "Don't forget to select something for yourself" before leaving again.

Jules blinked. *Select something for yourself?* She was used to scoring the occasional sample or castoff at *Du Jour*. It was different to be set loose in Vivian's personal stash of goodies. That was pretty freakin' cool.

She zeroed in on an unlabeled box and opened it to find no earrings but a medium-sized brooch—a gold-plated snake with malachite eyes. It wasn't Jules's usual thing, but it was gorgeous and she set it aside immediately.

Shortly after that, she found the carnelian earrings. Just in time too. At that moment, more porters came, and Jules told them with relief to haul the rest of the loot away. It was time to head to the airport.

Vivian returned with her handbag, earbud out and already wearing her coat. Jules told herself she was not disappointed that she didn't get to help Vivian into her coat today, that there would be many other opportunities.

"Here you go." She offered Vivian the earring box.

Vivian snapped it open and slipped the studs into her ears with Olympic-level speed. Predictably, they looked fantastic. "What did you choose?"

Jules showed her the snake brooch. "I loved this one."

Vivian raised an eyebrow.

"Unless it's too nice," Jules said quickly.

The other eyebrow went up.

"Oh. It's too nice, isn't it?" Jules started to panic. The damn snake was probably worth a thousand bucks or something. "I didn't know. Here—it'll look good with your shirt. You should—"

Vivian set down her purse, took the snake brooch, and affixed it to Jules's blouse near her collar.

Jules stopped breathing as she realized that this was as close to her breasts as Vivian's hands had ever been and that perhaps she should pay attention to how it felt because it might not happen again for a while.

Once the brooch was fixed, Vivian stepped back and gave her the stop-being-an-idiot look. Had it always been so affectionate?

"When I tell you that you can have something," she said, "then you can have it."

Jules blushed with pleasure. "Okay," she said, then added, "Same here." When she heard the words out loud, she realized they sounded like a total come-on.

Vivian obviously realized it too because she cleared her throat, glared, and said, "Let's go."

Jules followed her, still blushing and feeling the memory of Vivian's hands on her blouse a lot more than she felt the weight of the golden snake.

They arrived at Heathrow early, but the rest of the *Du Jour* crew was well used to Vivian's timing and had beaten them there.

Jules looked at her colleagues and wondered that they couldn't see her radiant secret. They'd be shocked breathless if they did. Disapproving too, and—she was pretty sure—jealous in a couple of cases.

Everything was different now, and none of the people she saw almost every day could know.

"Good morning."

She twitched at Simon's sudden appearance. His eyes were baggy and tired. He must have had a hell of a time last night.

*Simon definitely can't know.* What a weird thought. They'd shared so many stories of Vivian's caprices over the years. Now there was an invisible wall between them. She pressed her lips together and fought down a brief pang of regret.

"Feeling better?" he asked.

*Huh?* "Oh! Yes. All recovered, thanks."

"You sure seem to be. I haven't seen you this pumped since you told me about getting into *The Cut*. What's up?"

Jules was clearly not off to a good start when it came to acting casual. Maybe, just maybe, her happiness shouldn't radiate from her face. "I'm just glad I'm not puking my guts up anymore."

Simon wrinkled his nose. Then he saw her new brooch. His eyes widened. "Well, well. How'd you snatch that one from under her nose?"

"What?"

"The Stephen Webster." He pointed at the snake. "She's been coveting it ever since she saw it in the showroom a few days ago. Or is this merely a cunning and extremely quickly executed knockoff?"

"Would you believe me if I said knockoff?" Jules said weakly. Damn it. She'd fixated on a piece Vivian had actually wanted. Great, just great.

"I wouldn't believe you if I'd seen you knocking it off yourself."

"It was just in a pile of stuff," Jules protested. "She said I could take something from it. I just happened to pick this. She didn't say anything about it."

"I have to admit, it suits you," he mused.

A snake suited her? That didn't sound like a compliment. Jules glared at him; he merely returned his most benign smile.

"Careful," she said, "or I'll tell the flight attendants that you have a medical condition and can't be given alcohol on an airplane."

"Meow, darling." Simon patted her shoulder. "Just calm down, drink your coffee, and enjoy your eight-thousand-dollar token of Vivian's appreciation."

Jules *very* narrowly avoided spilling her coffee everywhere. Simon was a sneaky bastard. "E-eight—"

"That's what you get with eighteen karats and a big name. Oh, Paul," Simon called over his shoulder, "I need to bend your ear about June's accent feature."

Eighteen karats, not gold plating. Jules sat on the nearest available surface, trying not to hyperventilate. *It isn't a big deal.* In this business? Eight thousand was a drop in the bucket. Practically nothing. Holy crap, Vivian probably wore fifteen thousand dollars' worth of clothes, jewelry, shoes, accessories, and beauty products every day.

She self-consciously tugged at her jacket so that it covered the brooch. Wouldn't want other people to see it and get the wrong idea.

She glanced at Vivian, who was frowning at Charlotte garbling her way through some kind of explanation or plea. Fifteen thousand dollars had never looked so good.

Vivian tossed her head in irritation, Charlotte shrank back, and Jules's stomach flopped pleasantly before she remembered herself and looked away again.

She wondered how much better Vivian would look in zero dollars' worth of clothing. Wondered when—or if—she'd ever find out.

# CHAPTER 42

The Koening Building had not burned to the ground in their absence. Allie had made no unforgivable mistakes (although she'd managed several forgivable ones that Jules could conceal from Vivian). Within one day of the *Du Jour* group's return to New York, it was like they'd never left.

"Did you get lots of pretty clothes?" Allie asked wistfully as Jules went through a whole notebook of phone messages to see if anything had been screwed up too badly. "And did you meet all kinds of cool people?"

"Not as many as I wanted, and yes." Jules pointed at a name in the notebook. "There's no note for this one. Do you remember what Bernard said when he called yesterday afternoon?"

Allie pondered. "I think I remember him. He's the one who sounded like he had floppy hair."

"I, um—" Jules said, then, "Okay. Let's try this again…"

Luckily, she was the only one who had to lean on Allie today. Miracle of miracles, Vivian had taken the day off. Dr. Viswanathan had suggested heavily she do so. There were few galas or gatherings right after Fashion Week and the next print issue was put to bed, so Vivian reluctantly agreed to go to bed herself and rest. Jules was glad. She was wrestling with jet lag, and it was bound to be worse for Vivian.

It was also pretty bad for Simon, who asked Jules rather pitiably to bring him some lunch. "I beg where I once commanded," he said, rubbing a hand over his tired face.

She smiled, although there was still a tug inside her that urged caution. She wasn't quite over how Simon had pointed out the expense of the snake brooch, which was now in the back of her closet until she could rent a safety deposit box somewhere. "Your usual from the deli?"

"Please. I want food that isn't served in a tiny portion with an artistic zigzag of sauce over it. Get something for yourself too."

Mindful of her supposed food poisoning from a couple of days ago, she ordered Simon his usual pastrami on rye and only a cup of chicken soup for herself. It was comforting on a cold February day, even if she hadn't really gotten sick. They ate together in his office, portfolios and sketches pushed carefully out of reach.

Conversation was normal enough, mostly limited to the coming work week, until Simon crumpled up his sandwich paper and asked, "When's your birthday? Pretty soon, right?"

Jules blinked. "Yeah, in a couple of weeks. March 16."

"Better than the ides. Going to hit the big two-six?"

She would be twenty-six to Vivian's forty-two. She didn't like to think about that. "Yeah," she said slowly. "Why?"

"No reason," he said airily.

"What are you up to?" she pressed.

"I can't just be curious? I'm hurt. Maybe I'm planning to take you out for drinks and just want to make sure my schedule is open."

"Well, is it?"

"I'll have to ask my personal assistant. Wait. You're the closest thing I have to one now. Check my calendar for me."

Right after Vivian had whisked Jules away from Simon, the hiring freeze had struck, leaving him without a PA. Jules doubted he'd ever quite forgiven Vivian for that. "Sure thing."

She mulled over Simon's mysterious behavior for the next few hours. No matter what he said, he was plotting something. It would be nice to think it really was something as benign as taking her out for birthday drinks. Jules didn't have a lot of people around these days who could fill that role.

Which was just depressing.

Her curiosity was a nice distraction from wondering why Vivian hadn't called or texted. No way she was resting all day.

At three p.m., Jules gave in. She texted:

*How are you doing today?*

She didn't expect an instant response, but the ensuing fifteen minutes felt long until Vivian replied:

*Tired.*

She grimaced. Vivian's tired was an ordinary person's near-death exhaustion. She texted:

*What do you need?*

She expected an answer that would send her on an errand. Bring Vivian something, make a call, whatever. Instead, she got:

*Come to dinner.*

Her heart stopped. Then her lips stretched out in a wide grin as warmth spread through her body.

*What should I bring?*

*Nothing. Ellen will make extra.*

Vivian's cook. Jules had never sampled her food, but if Vivian employed someone for six years, it was a good bet they were on top of their game. She was already salivating.

*Sounds good. It's quiet today, I can leave around 6*

She could imagine Vivian's stern face as she replied:

*Don't hurry if you still have work to do.*

Jules laughed to herself.

*OK, I'll be good*

*I doubt it. See you tonight.*

Nobody was watching. Jules clutched her phone to her chest and allowed herself one quiet, delighted squeal.

---

In the end, Jules left Koening at six twenty, thanks to a last-minute email. When she texted Vivian to let her know she'd be late, Vivian responded:

*Good.*

Jules looked thoughtfully at the reply. Vivian had probably sent countless messages about being late to all three of her husbands. No wonder she'd said "good." Now she was with someone who understood.

She endured the cold walk to the subway and the ensuing crowded car with a grin on her face. *I'm having dinner with Vivian. At her house. Because she's super into me.*

Then she thought about Vivian really getting into her, blushed, and fought back the surge of arousal. *Down, girl.*

When she arrived, she rang the bell, anticipating Vivian letting her in, perhaps with a small but affectionate smile.

After a moment, the door automatically unlocked.

Ah. Right. This was a smart home. That took a bit of the fun out. Jules still smiled when she entered the foyer and smelled the rich scent of cooking garlic.

She kicked the slush from her boots on the doormat, placed her bag on the side table, unbuttoned her coat, and looked at the hall closet with some trepidation. She'd been invited to dinner, but it seemed invasive just to put her coat right there next to Vivian's things.

Jules opened the closet door, and to her relief saw a gray coat hanging there that was too big for Vivian. Ellen's, then. She hung her own green wool peacoat next to it. She'd known Vivian wouldn't be in the office and hadn't expected to be invited over, so she just wore a fuzzy black sweater, a striped skirt, and black tights and boots. Plainer than her usual.

"Hello, Julia."

Vivian stood in the hallway that led to the kitchen.

Jules hadn't heard her, probably because Vivian wasn't wearing shoes, just black hose. They were possibly the compression stockings Dr. Viswanathan had been after her to use. No wonder she was hiding them beneath a pair of gray slacks topped with a loose emerald green blouse. She hadn't graduated to maternity wear yet, but her clothes were more generously cut. And she was gorgeous.

Jules smoothed down her skirt self-consciously. "Hi. You look great."

"I wish I felt as great as I apparently look. Are you hungry?"

Her stomach growled in answer. "Guess so."

"Then let's eat. Ellen's just finished up, and I'm starving." She headed back toward the kitchen.

Jules followed. On the way, she glanced at the hallway mirror and winced at what she saw there. Hair frizzy and unkempt from her walk, cheeks flushed, and nose red. She was a mess. *Dammit.*

She made a futile effort at smoothing her unruly locks as she headed to the kitchen. It was a wonder Vivian hadn't looked at her in disgust, as she surely would have when Jules had started working for her.

She fought not to sigh as she entered the kitchen. Predictably, it was perfection, as the rest of Vivian's house must be. Acres of white Shaker cabinets and gray quartz countertops. Ellen stood before an island painted a lovely muted blue, turning off the gas on a six-burner range. The fridge was paneled with white wood so that it blended in, and all the other appliances were top-end brands in stainless steel. The room looked straight out of an interior design blog.

"Wow," she murmured. Then she remembered her manners. "Hi. You must be Ellen. I'm Jules."

The stocky brunette who looked to be in her fifties smiled at Jules as she wiped her hands on a towel. "Good evening. Have a seat. I'm going to plate everything."

"No need," Vivian said, plainly to Ellen's surprise. "Julia and I can help ourselves. Feel free to go home."

Ellen seemed to know not to question Vivian's whims. "Thank you, Ms. Carlisle. Good night."

Jules gave her a feeble wave and smile as she left. "Nice to meet you."

"Yes. Ms. Carlisle told me you'll be stopping by for dinner sometimes. Please leave a list of any allergies. Thank you."

"Uh—sure."

She could have sworn Vivian smiled, but it was gone quickly.

As the door closed behind Ellen, Vivian moved toward the stove, where two empty plates sat waiting.

Jules said, "Nuh-uh. Sit down. I've got this."

"I'm four-and-a-half-months pregnant, not bedridden."

"But you said you were tired. C'mon, sit down. Let me handle it."

Vivian appeared mulish, but she sat at the kitchen table and let Jules bring over two plates of pan-seared salmon, spinach salad, and risotto. It was simple, but it smelled amazing.

Jules fought not to wolf down her food.

It helped to slow down when Vivian said, "You don't need to assist me when we're not at work."

That sure was news to her. As an assistant, she was on call nearly 24/7, whether Vivian was in the office or not.

She knew what it meant, though. Things were supposed to be different now. So Jules said plainly, "I told you before, I like doing things for you. It makes me happy."

Vivian blinked.

"So don't worry about it. If you're tired, let me bring you a plate. I'm not being a servant or something, I'm being your…" She didn't even know the word. "Whatever. I'm being considerate."

"Being my 'whatever,'" Vivian mused. She sipped from a glass Jules had filled with peach-flavored seltzer water. "Julia, why do you like sex?"

Thank God Jules hadn't taken another mouthful of anything. Even if she was a "whatever" instead of an assistant, what a question to hear from Vivian Carlisle.

To gain time, she wiped her mouth with a linen napkin. Her face was hot, though, and she knew her blush was visible. "Why wouldn't I like it?"

Vivian shrugged. "You said it's important to you. Given our… circumstances, I think it's fair that I find out why."

"Well…" Jules pushed the salmon around on her plate as if it were a culinary Ouija board that would spell out the right answer. "It's nice to be close to someone you care about. It's intimate. I like that."

"So are foot rubs. You don't seem entirely content with those."

"Of course it's more than that. Good sex feels, well, *good*. You said you've had some, right?" She couldn't stop herself from leaning across the table a little as her curiosity got the better of her. "With who?"

Vivian actually chuckled before looking into the distance. "More than one man, but the one I remember most was during my senior year of college. Eliot. We met at a party. He wasn't the best-looking man there, but he had these eyes." Vivian's expression grew dreamy for a moment. "They were so intense. He looked at me as if he knew everything I wanted and was the only man alive who could give it to me."

Jules felt breathless. "And did he?"

"God, yes. Of course, I was twenty-two and my standards for a good lover were lower than they are now. But I was swept away. It was almost enough to…" She trailed off. The edge of her smile grew melancholy.

"To what?"

"To make me lose sight of things," she murmured. "To make me leave New York with him."

What could Jules say to that? It was a miracle Vivian couldn't hear how loud her heart was beating as she fought off multiple emotions at once: fascination, sympathy, rapacious envy. Somewhere out there was a guy who'd almost gotten Vivian Carlisle to throw it all away because he was so good in bed.

Vivian shook her head. "But I didn't, and that was a long time ago. My priorities are completely different."

That was all she was going to get? Jules swallowed around her disappointment. "Yeah, that makes sense."

Vivian glared down at her stomach. "I'm finally enjoying the delight of keeping breakfast down. That's what makes me happy these days. So you're bisexual?"

She was going to get whiplash from this conversation. It was always a titanic effort to keep up with Vivian's mind. "Yeah. I had a girlfriend for a few months in college."

Vivian looked unimpressed.

Jules knew what she was thinking: an experiment, no more, before she had settled down with a man. She growled, "It was the best sex I've ever had, and it only ended because we didn't work in any other way. I met

Aaron right after that, and we hit it off, but don't think for a second that I don't know what to do in bed with a woman."

Silence fell while they examined each other. Vivian didn't blush this time, but her eyes definitely glazed over a little.

Jules's heart was hammering in her chest again.

"I'm not saying you don't," Vivian said hoarsely. "I don't doubt your… competence. That's not why. I've just never been interested in women. I don't see the appeal."

*That's because you're around women who are scared of you,* Jules realized. *You're not around women who look at you like the college guy did. Like they know they've got what you need.*

*Except for me.*

She kept looking Vivian dead in the eyes. Thought about everything she wanted to do to her. Everything she thought Vivian wanted her to do too. "Some things can't be explained. You either don't want to touch somebody or you do."

Vivian's lips parted slightly.

Jules ached between her thighs. All of a sudden, she knew it didn't matter that her hair was messy or that her sweater wasn't sexy. None of that mattered at all.

"Dessert?" Vivian managed. "There's, ah, sorbet."

Jules smiled beatifically at her. "That sounds delicious."

---

Sorbet was followed by decaf in the den, and decaf was followed by slightly halting conversation, which ended when Vivian patted her mouth in a delicate yawn. "You'd better go. I'm wiped out."

Maybe she was. That might explain why she put up no protest when Jules leaned in close at the front door. And why she didn't back away when Jules gently pressed her lips against Vivian's cheek.

So soft. So smooth. It took everything Jules had not to move her lips just a few millimeters to the left and cover Vivian's mouth in the kiss she craved.

She was pretty sure, based on the way Vivian's breath broke into pieces, that Vivian would let her.

No. Not yet.

Jules pulled away to see that Vivian's blush was in full bloom and goosebumps were clearly visible on her throat. Her eyes were glazed again. Everything about her was begging to be fucked right there in the hallway.

"I'll see you tomorrow," Jules croaked and fled before Vivian could reply—before Jules could get ahead of herself and ruin everything.

*Not yet, not yet.*

But ten minutes later, as Jules stood on the subway platform with a tingling mouth, she dared to hope that *not yet* could also mean *soon*.

# CHAPTER 43

Jules kept up the teasing little kisses for the next week, an exercise she found both frustrating and fun. She would come over for dinner after work. The night would end with Vivian submitting reluctantly to a soft brief kiss on her hand or cheek that made her tremble.

Reluctant. Sure. Vivian was not a stupid woman. She had to know that even if she didn't go around kissing other women as a rule, she sure as hell liked being kissed by Jules. Maybe she just didn't like admitting she'd been wrong. It seemed all too likely. Why should romance be different from work?

But that was okay for now. There was nothing wrong with taking things slowly—not with important things like this. There was too much at stake, too much that could be ruined by careless mistakes.

If Vivian still needed a little convincing, Jules could happily do that. She could…woo. Yeah, that was it. Vivian would definitely be the sort of woman who felt she deserved a little wooing, that she was worth pursuing.

Vivian was open to being pursued. She could easily have let Jules depart her home without a kiss of any kind. She could have begged off dinner for a night or two because she was tired. She never did any of that.

On the seventh night, Jules felt secure enough to murmur as she leaned in, "You know, you absolutely don't have to let me kiss you."

"Don't I?" Vivian asked, her warm breath stirring the air by Jules's ear.

Jules opened her mouth to say, *of course not*, but Vivian turned her head. Ever so slightly. Just enough for her lips to touch Jules's own cheek.

She couldn't be—this had to be a dream—

Vivian kissed her cheek, light as a feather, soft as silk.

No. Not a dream at all. This was real because even Jules's feverish subconscious couldn't have come up with it. And she learned that if she'd been craving Vivian's touch, then she'd been fucking well dying for her mouth.

She realized she'd have to die a little bit longer as Vivian pulled away before Jules could collect herself enough to return the favor.

"Good night." Vivian turned and walked back into her house with just the faintest sway of her hips.

Jules opened her mouth to call after her, to order her to come back, but only a tiny croak came out.

Probably for the best.

She definitely made more noises after she got home. She pulled out her trusty vibrator and got off twice thinking about the softness of Vivian's mouth against her cheek, imagining what that soft mouth would feel like in other places.

When she was finished, she went to the shower on trembling legs, throbbing pleasantly between her thighs. Vivian sure had knocked her for a loop. Based on her sultry walk, she knew it.

Fine. Time to break out the big guns.

Jules turned her face into the shower's hot spray and smiled.

---

She headed into the office the next day with a more purposeful walk, her secret weapon concealed beneath a long puffy coat. In her gloved hands, she carried two hot cups of La Colombe. Her heart already raced with anticipation.

Allie beamed at her when she arrived. "Morning, Jules! Gosh, it's so cold today, isn't it?"

"Sure is." Jules set the cups of coffee down on her desk.

Vivian had a clear line of sight to Jules from here, and from the corner of her eye, Jules saw her raise her head.

"And it's March! Honestly, I think once it's March, it shouldn't be cold anymore, don't you?"

Jules began to unzip her coat. "Give it a couple of weeks."

"I was born in San Diego. I don't think I'll ever get used to… Oh, *Jules!*"

Jules let the coat slide down her body before laying it over her desk.

Allie's eyes had widened in amazement, but Jules was much more interested in how Vivian's shoulders had gone back.

*Office-appropriate clothing,* Jules had promised. She couldn't wear blouses cut down to her navel or skirts slit up to her hip. Besides, it was too cold. Plus there was the cardinal rule: show off your boobs or show off your legs. Never both at the same time.

There was no question that Jules's boobs were her greatest asset, but one should never underestimate the element of surprise. Today she wore a black-and-white houndstooth skirt that ended just under her ass, matched with fleece-lined burgundy tights, a form-fitting black turtleneck, and black ankle boots. She might not be five foot ten with legs that went on for days, but based on Allie's reaction, she was working it.

"You look amazing!" Allie said.

"Thanks." Jules tossed her hair back over her right shoulder. "Just felt like doing something a little different today."

"No wonder you were wearing a long coat. Wow."

"Yeah." Jules picked up the coffee cups. "This outfit is definitely not for street consumption."

Then she carried in the coffee to Vivian, who looked at Jules like she was water in the desert.

Jules's hands shook. With all her force of will, she steadied herself as she put one of the cups on Vivian's desk.

"Who's the other coffee for?" Vivian asked hoarsely.

Jules swallowed, meeting Vivian stare for stare. Why was it so hot in here? "Me, of course." She paused. "I need it too."

Vivian's eyes fluttered shut for a moment. Her voice was thick and low. "You'd better have it, then."

Her stomach flipped over.

Vivian opened her eyes. The blue of her irises, so often as cold as ice, seared through Jules like fire.

"I will," she heard herself say. "Every drop."

Vivian's jaw clenched, and her eyes burned brighter.

She wondered for a second if they might go for it then and there. Then Vivian silently gestured for her to leave.

For the rest of the day, Vivian seemed to keep that fire banked. She gave orders in her usual brisk tone, strode to and from meetings, and eyed the latest samples with a critical gaze. At no other point did she look at Jules with more than professional disinterest.

It was so convincing, in fact, that Jules's spirits began to flag. She'd spent the rest of the day being uber professional too, but she'd been fantasizing about exchanging hot glances with Vivian, building the smoldering tension between them in a way nobody else could see. It would have been such a thrill.

*Oh well,* Jules thought as she answered yet another phone call. *I guess she's just not that into it after all.*

She didn't learn differently until she arrived at Vivian's for dinner, tired and a bit irritated. She'd spent the whole day trying not to tug her miniskirt farther down, and wearing the long, puffy coat on the subway had just made her sweat. So much for seductive office wear.

But when she entered the house and headed for the kitchen, Vivian called out from the den, "In here, Julia."

*Huh. Cool.* Jules headed gamely toward the den. She hadn't gotten the grand tour yet, and it was neat to be let into another part of Vivian's sanctum.

The den, it turned out, was a snug haven tucked away off the main hallway, cozily furnished in shades of blue and green, the walls lined with books.

Vivian sat on a cream-colored love seat with a book in her lap. She'd changed into a soft green sweater and loose black pants and wore a pair of moccasin slippers. Jules's toes wriggled enviously inside her ankle boots.

Vivian didn't look up from her book. "No need to hover in the doorway."

Easy for her to say. Jules didn't know what her next step should be. There were two armchairs, and two love seats faced each other over a coffee table. Where did Vivian want her to—

Vivian patted the empty cushion next to her. "Here."

Jules's heart began to beat double-time. She did her best to keep a cool expression as she sat down next to her on the soft cushions.

Vivian was still looking at the damn book.

"What are you reading?"

Setting the book on the coffee table, Vivian faced her. "I have no idea."

Jules blinked.

"I've been reading it for the last half hour and couldn't tell you a single word," she continued.

"Are you feeling all right?"

"I don't think so."

Now Jules's heart skipped a beat from alarm, not desire. "What's wrong?"

As if in answer, Vivian let her gaze drop down to Jules's feet. Then it slowly rose, covering her body like a touch until Vivian was looking into her eyes.

Jules's heart was a firecracker in her chest.

"It must be pregnancy hormones," Vivian breathed. "Right?"

There were several inches too many between them on the love seat. Jules scooted in closer until their knees were nearly bumping. "I doubt it."

"And this—this *outfit*. What were you thinking?"

"What's wrong with it?" Jules reached out to take one of Vivian's hands in her own.

Vivian didn't seem to notice. She kept looking into Jules's eyes. The flame was returning, the one that made Jules dizzy. "Not for 'street consumption.' I heard you say that. Apparently it was fine for the whole office to see, though."

"Did that bother you?" she asked in true surprise. She'd wanted to tempt Vivian, but making her jealous hadn't been on the agenda.

Vivian continued as if she hadn't heard, "You were supposed to go to Dior for me today. I had to send Allie instead. Of course, she did everything wrong."

"That's why she went?"

"It's completely inappropriate." Vivian's eyes dropped back down to stare at Jules's legs in their burgundy tights. The miniskirt had slid up so high that it just barely managed to cover her nether regions. Any other time, Jules would have adjusted it modestly. Not tonight.

Tonight, she let her thighs part a little. Just a little. Enough to maintain deniability and also enough for Vivian's nostrils to flare.

"I've seen people at *Du Jour* wear more outrageous stuff than this," Jules murmured. "All the time."

Vivian's hands clenched on Jules's. "Yes. I *know* that. What I don't know is why I'm—I don't know how—"

Jules freed one hand and touched Vivian's cheek. Pregnancy had softened the lines of her face. *It suits her*, Jules thought as she rubbed her thumb over Vivian's cheekbone. "I don't know either." She'd never heard that deep, husky note in her own voice before. "I just know I want you"—she drew out the next two words—"so much."

Vivian's eyes closed. She exhaled so deeply it somehow sounded like a plea.

There was only one thing to do after that. Jules leaned in and pressed her lips to Vivian's softly, tenderly, a gesture that should have been sweet.

Vivian's breath broke, and sweetness was off the table as she grabbed Jules by both shoulders and leaned in for more.

What was left of Jules's brain began to dissolve. Kissing Vivian. Kissing *Vivian.*

Jules had been born to do it, clearly. Nothing else explained why it was so easy to slide one hand into Vivian's hair and curl her fingers there. Or why it was so simple to put her other hand on Vivian's knee and squeeze it helplessly. What else was she supposed to do? She had to hold Vivian in place so they could keep kissing. They could never, ever stop.

Vivian's mouth was hot and so soft. Would the rest of her be just as soft or even softer? How soon could Jules find out? Considering how they were devouring each other, it seemed like it could happen at any moment.

Jules moaned softly.

Vivian's breath caught in response. A shiver ran through her. An honest-to-God whimper came out of her throat.

"*Jesus*, Vivian," she groaned against Vivian's lips.

Vivian gasped. Then her hands were at Jules's shoulders again, and this time she was pushing Jules away. "No. Oh, please. Enough, enough."

Jules pulled back at once, her blood pounding in her temples and her stomach twisting with nerves.

But Vivian didn't look mad. She had her eyes squeezed shut as if she were desperately trying to pull herself together.

Jules ate up the sight of her flushed skin, her trembling hands, her breasts rising and falling rapidly with her breath.

"How…" Vivian managed. "How do you…" She took a deep breath and shook her head. Then she chuckled mirthlessly. "How do you do whatever it is you're doing to me?"

"I dunno," Jules muttered, trying to get her own heart rate under control. If Vivian started talking about how turned on she was, the cease-fire wasn't going to last long. "I'll do as much as you let me. As much as you want."

Vivian gasped again. She smoothed down her hair with shaking hands. "Ah…you seem to have a gift for this."

"Well, yeah." She'd told Vivian right from the beginning that she liked kissing and sex and everything else. "Want to unwrap it?"

Vivian stared at her. It made Jules want to sink through the couch.

"That's the worst line I've ever heard in my life," Vivian said.

Jules squirmed. "It's the worst one I've ever given."

"Well, it did the trick." Vivian's lips curved into a tiny smile as she regained control of herself. "I feel much calmer now, thank you."

So much for Jules's amazing gift. "Great," she sighed.

Vivian snorted and put a hand on the small of her back. Then she looked down at her stomach. There was a slight curve that hadn't been there a couple of weeks ago. "Well, give me a few more months, and it won't be an issue anymore."

"What?" Jules said incredulously. "You think I can only approach from the front?"

Vivian's eyes widened as she clearly imagined the same scenario as Jules. They sat in silence for a moment while Jules fought down another throb between her legs.

"Be that as it may," Vivian began, strained.

"Right. Right." She wiped her sweating palms on her tights. She looked at Vivian's mouth. Then she shot up to her feet, knees trembling. "Well, I better get going!"

Vivian stared up at her. "What? You're not staying for dinner?"

Her lips were still reddened and swollen from Jules's kisses. Jules had to close her eyes at the realization. "If I stay, you're going to be dinner."

More silence.

Then Vivian said in a low voice, "You can't control yourself? I thought you had more self-discipline."

Jules looked her in the eyes again. Vivian didn't seem angry. Her eyes conveyed sheer hunger.

"Besides, I'm spoiling you," she added. "You're getting far more than originally agreed upon."

"Sorry. I misplaced the contract. And I think I'm the one spoiling you."

Vivian scoffed. "How so? I'm sitting here frustrated and—" She cleared her throat. "Never mind."

"I meant I'm spoiling you for anybody else," Jules said. "That's the plan, anyway."

At the low, purposeful note in Jules's voice, Vivian's eyes dilated until her pupils threatened to swallow the blue. "So go," she said hoarsely, "if you have to."

It was the last thing Jules wanted to do, but somehow she found herself back on the sidewalk anyway, wearing her long coat while the evening air grew even colder. Her stomach growled. She was starving, and there was nothing to eat in her apartment.

And yet instead of heading in search of food or shelter from the cold, Jules lingered on Vivian's sidewalk, touching her own lips. Even at the tail end of winter, they still seemed to glow with heat.

*Our first kiss.* She grinned so hard, her face hurt. She bounced up and down on her toes and looked upward. Clouds covered the stars, but it was still the most beautiful night sky she'd ever seen.

# CHAPTER 44

THERE WAS NO BUZZKILL LIKE talking to your parents.

Jules had enjoyed her kiss afterglow for all of two hours before they had called to say hi. Now she was flopped back down on her couch, trying to figure out what to tell them about her life, imagining the conversation as if it were a military letter with whole stretches of text blacked out for security reasons.

She wanted to talk about Vivian. She wanted to pick her parents' brains about parenting and what babies were like and what she should do about all that. She wanted to ask about the secret to long, happy relationships. She wanted them to be excited for her, to be glad that Jules had…something… with the most fascinating woman in the world.

But she had to keep her mouth shut because the exact opposite would happen, and no way was Jules equipped to deal with that right now. She was about to burst tonight after that kiss, after all the wonderment of starting down a new path with no idea where it would lead.

"What about your writing?" her dad asked. "Got any more irons in the fire?"

"Not yet," she admitted. "I know I should. Simon always told me that once I finished something, I should start something else right away."

"Sounds like a recipe for burnout to me." Her mom's voice was firm. "I know that nobody at *Du Jour* ever stops working, but take some time for yourself once in a while."

Her mom had been telling her that since high school. "I like keeping busy. And Simon's right—I need to build momentum."

"Well…" her mom began.

"I've been thinking about my career, in fact. Where I want to end up someday."

*Whoa, where had that come from?* Jules hadn't been thinking about anything of the sort. She'd been too busy.

"Yes?" her dad asked. "Changed your mind about fashion?" He sounded almost hopeful.

She scowled. "No. I still want to work in fashion, and I want to write."

After a pause, her mom said helpfully, "So you want to keep doing what you've been doing?"

"No! I mean yes! I don't mean I'm going to stop *here*." She sat up and bounced off the couch. Restlessness was building in her chest, in her legs, and she started to pace her apartment. "I'm going to keep my eye out for opportunities. I'm not going to be an assistant at *Du Jour* forever. It's just that I'm happy there for now, and there's nothing wrong with that."

"We never said there was." Her dad sounded surprised.

"No, I know, but…" But what?

"You've got plenty of time to decide," her mom said soothingly. "Lots of life to live. You'll figure out what will make you happy."

*Will I? You don't want to know what's making me happy right now.* Maybe they had a point, though. What would make her happy in the long run?

"Uh, Vivian's pregnancy is coming along," she blurted out without meaning to.

A second of silence, and then her dad let her change the subject. "Yeah?"

"The next ultrasound is in two days." She bit her lip.

"Oh? Is that where she finds out what sex it is?"

Her heart skipped a beat at the thought. "Yes. Pretty cool, huh?"

"I remember when we learned that you and your sister were girls," her mom chimed in. "It made everything feel real, especially with Robin."

*It made everything feel real.* In spite of how closely Jules had been tied to all of it, sometimes Vivian's pregnancy still felt like a dream, like a baby wasn't really coming. Would the ultrasound change that? "Yeah," Jules murmured. "That makes sense."

"Remember what I said at Christmas, though," her dad said.

For a second, all Jules could remember was how her parents had believed Vivian was sexually harassing her. Her eyes went wide. "What?"

"She's asking so much of you. Don't forget to set appropriate boundaries."

"Uh…"

"Your father's right. If you're ambitious, you can't be changing diapers for your boss's kid."

At least the sexual harassment concerns seemed to be off the table. Jules's face burned anyway. "I'm still kind of excited, though. There's nothing wrong with that."

"Boundaries," her dad repeated firmly. "Remember that."

*Boundaries.* After the call, the word went round and round in Jules's head as she looked out her window onto Clinton Street below. The smoke shop across the street was closed. The pizza place was still open, the sign lit up with its picture of a smiling slice. It was nearly nine o'clock, but the tables were still full of people who had their own lives, priorities, and secrets.

Secrets, boundaries, all of it. For the most part, Jules avoided thinking about how she lived a double life these days. She couldn't avoid it forever, though, not as things with Vivian were getting hot and heavy. One of the reasons Vivian had agreed that it was okay for her to work at *Du Jour* was because they weren't having sex.

She gnawed her lip. It wasn't that bad. People did it all the time. She could have Vivian and her job.

Couldn't she?

# CHAPTER 45

The evening before the ultrasound was more subdued than usual.

Vivian appeared focused not on the baby's sex but on the other things the ultrasound could uncover. Irregularities. Abnormalities. Health concerns. Anything that would indicate matters weren't proceeding in perfect order.

After a dinner neither of them finished, they retired to the den as usual. But when Jules opened her mouth to speak, Vivian waved her hand and stared off into space. She looked haunted.

Jules took a deep breath, folded her hands in her lap, and waited.

But Vivian said nothing, and nothing, then some more nothing.

Finally, after about two minutes (which felt very long when you were waiting for someone to speak), Jules said, "You okay?"

"Of cour…" she trailed off, then finished, "Not completely."

No matter the circumstances, it still took Jules's breath away to be trusted with Vivian's honesty. "The ultrasound?"

"No, Julia, the sloppy Photoshop on the Charleston mock-up. What do you think?" Vivian snapped.

"Hey now. The Charleston mock-up was going to be my next guess."

When Vivian scowled at her, she added, "I'm not kidding. It would have been."

"It looks so cheap, it could—" Vivian stopped and shook her head. "I take your point."

Jules gave her a small smile. "It'll all be okay."

"You can't say that for certain. Nobody can."

"This time tomorrow we can," Jules said stubbornly.

Vivian rolled her eyes. "I appreciate the optimism." She put a hand protectively on her stomach. "There are certain facts that come with pregnancies past thirty-five. You should know that from all the reading you've been doing. My body's…not at its best for this."

She drummed her fingertips on her stomach and gazed toward the window while Jules figured out what she wasn't saying.

The easy answer would be *Vivian, you're in great shape*. Or maybe *women your age have healthy babies all the time*.

"You can't help being forty-two," Jules said. "It just…happened when it happened."

Vivian was silent, her eyes hooded, but at least she looked back at her.

Jules tucked one foot beneath her other knee and rested her elbow on the back of the love seat. She took a deep breath. "Is it okay if I ask why you canceled the abortion?"

Vivian drummed her fingertips again, but she didn't look away from Jules's face. Now she felt like the one getting cross-examined as Vivian seemed to stare directly into her brain.

"I had an abortion when I was eighteen," she said.

Jules's breath caught.

Vivian smiled bitterly. "You're surprised."

"Well…" Jules tried to find the words. "A little. It's more that I never thought about it at all."

"Well, I did. Knocked up at eighteen outside of Toledo, Ohio." Vivian snorted derisively. "Like so many other girls I knew."

Jules swallowed. "Oh. So you—"

"So I got out. I'd always known I had to get out. That as soon as I graduated high school…" She took a deep breath and let it out again. "I felt like I'd been running for the gate at a prison camp, and someone was trying to stop me right before I could cross. I couldn't let that happen."

"Oh. Would your family have—"

"I wasn't a minor. I was lucky." Vivian gave a short laugh. "And then I packed up and came to New York with a scholarship and six hundred dollars in the bank. Just like that. I've never looked back."

"Wow. So this is…?"

The word *atonement* hung unspoken in the air.

Vivian shook her head. "I've never regretted it. It was the right decision for me then."

Jules nodded. Then she dared, "And now?"

Vivian shrugged one shoulder. "I can afford a child now. And if I'm ever going to do it, this is the time."

"So you never wanted kids?" Jules guessed.

"I never felt strongly about kids one way or the other. I felt *very* strongly about having a career, and children weren't conducive to that." She snorted. "As I informed my first and second husbands, who both thought I'd change my mind for some reason."

Vivian sure had married some idiots. It didn't seem tactful to point this out. "And now you have."

"I wouldn't have put it exactly like that, but yes." Vivian smiled mirthlessly. "I got the job. The money. The fancy home. Everything I told myself I would." She studied Jules. "And some other things I didn't anticipate."

Jules grinned at that. "You got the girl, huh?"

"Looks like it." Vivian gazed at her thoughtfully, as if she were trying to decide whether or not to say something.

Jules held her breath, though she had no idea why. The moment felt weighted, significant, like Vivian was about to utter something momentous.

"I'm glad I hired you."

Jules's breath left her in a whoosh, and she bent forward, laughing helplessly. "Me too."

"What's so funny?"

"I didn't expect you to get sentimental on me." A lock of hair had fallen over Jules's face when she bent over. She pushed it out of the way, still chuckling, and grinned.

It was Vivian's turn to catch her breath. The by-now-familiar blush bloomed on her cheeks.

And just like that, the mood changed, crackled from reminiscence into electricity.

Jules's mouth softened and parted.

Vivian stared at it, biting her own bottom lip.

"Okay," Jules whispered, apropos of nothing, and leaned in.

She would never know if it was the stress, the worry, or the sight of Jules's mouth, but tonight Vivian leaned forward too and met her halfway. They lingered for a moment, brushing their lips together, little puffs of breath between them.

And tonight, Jules waited.

Vivian didn't. She pressed her lips to Jules's; she cupped her chin; she caught her breath and sighed when Jules tilted her head and kissed her back. That sound, that sigh, slid through Jules's brain and buzzed around at the base of her skull. She parted her lips and felt the lightest accidental brush of Vivian's tongue against her mouth. It made her whimper.

Vivian gasped at the noise and cupped the back of Jules's neck.

God. They might not be having sex, but they were definitely fucking each other right now.

Jules kissed Vivian again and thought about long looks and accidental hand-brushings and countless tiny moments. She and Vivian had been fucking each other for a very, very long time. Before London. About time they figured it out.

She moved her mouth from Vivian's and trailed it down to her chin, then her jaw.

Vivian gasped again, shuddered, and did not push her away.

Jules's head spun. She kept kissing, kept nuzzling while Vivian trembled and tried to catch her breath. Her grip was like iron on the back of Jules's neck.

Could Jules—would it be okay to—she touched Vivian's neck with the back of her index finger, stroked it gently up and down.

Vivian hissed and arched into the touch.

Jules promptly lost her mind, whispered, "Let me," and leaned down so she could kiss where her finger had touched, could kiss Vivian's throat for the first time. She barely pressed her mouth to the skin, kissing Vivian almost as much with her breath as she did with her lips.

Vivian made a breathless noise. Then she turned her head, rubbed her nose in Jules's hair, and whispered—pleaded—"No. No. Not here."

*Where, then?* Jules didn't say. Instead she pulled back, her head whirling.

Vivian was flushed and panting. She pressed a hand to her throat, closed her eyes, and tried to collect herself.

Jules watched her in agony. "So," she croaked, "so…I'll, um, I'm going home?"

Vivian kept her eyes shut. "I think that's a good idea." When she opened her eyes again, they were glazed with desire. Her breathing was back under control, but her face was still red and she still quivered.

*God.* Jules stood up fast. "I'll see you tomorrow morning," she gasped.

Vivian swallowed and nodded.

Jules grabbed her bag and stumbled for the front door.

Well. At least she might have given Vivian something else to think about tonight.

# CHAPTER 46

Whether Vivian spent the rest of the night thinking about their make-out session, Jules had no idea. Right at the moment, in Dr. Viswanathan's waiting room, she wasn't thinking about it herself either.

She'd been prepared for another session of waiting in tense silence. But instead Vivian asked, "What transportation have you arranged for the team going to the Charleston shoot?"

They'd already discussed that a few nights ago, but Jules gamely launched into discussing plane tickets and rental cars and hotel shuttles.

Vivian nodded silently until a nurse came to lead her into the examining room.

"Nervous?" Mary, the receptionist, asked Jules when Vivian was gone.

Jules nodded with a tight smile.

"She seems to be in good shape. Seems like you're looking after her pretty well. Or somebody is, anyway."

"No, it's me," Jules said, trying to sound casual instead of possessive and worried. "I try to help her do what the doctor says."

"Well, I think she's lucky to have you." Mary lowered her voice to add, "Are she and her husband still getting divorced?"

*They better.* "I think that's still the plan."

"That's a shame. I'm glad she's got somebody to be there for her at least."

*At least.* Even if it was just a lowly assistant. Jules gritted her teeth. "Yeah."

The procedures took forever, and she felt like an old woman by the time it was all finished. The nurse emerged and gestured for Jules to follow her.

Vivian was sitting in front of Dr. Viswanathan's desk again, sipping a glass of water. Her hand didn't tremble, and her breathing was steady. The look on her face was perfectly calm.

Dr. Viswanathan greeted Jules with a smile. "Shall we begin?"

"Please," Vivian said.

"As Vivian already knows," Dr. Viswanathan said to Jules, "everything checks out okay today for both mother and baby. The ultrasound detected no problems. Of course, no test is completely foolproof, but so far everything seems perfectly in order. So I suggest we all relax for a while."

Jules nodded again and glanced at Vivian, who appeared to be concentrating on her water.

"It's a girl," Dr. Viswanathan added.

Jules gasped. "It is?"

"Yes, indeed." Dr. Viswanathan looked amused for the first time.

*Play it cool. Jeez.* "Well, that's…neat."

Vivian was still refusing to look up from her water. Jules felt another, different, pang of worry. Was Vivian unhappy? Had she wanted a boy?

"It *is* neat," Dr. Viswanathan agreed. "Would you like to see the picture?"

She picked up a large sheet of paper from her desk, which turned out to be a printout from the ultrasound. It wasn't much to look at—a white blob surrounded by black space—but the white blob in the photo was the baby *inside Vivian* right at that moment.

Her mom had been right. This was the moment it got real. "Wow," she said faintly.

Dr. Viswanathan chuckled. "'Wow,' indeed. Vivian, would you like to take the picture with you?"

"No, thank you," Vivian said to her water.

Jules looked at her, stricken. The first baby picture and Vivian was turning it down? She fought back the impulse to say that if Vivian didn't want it, Jules did. But that might look weird in front of the doctor.

Dr. Viswanathan nodded and put the picture back down. "We can send it to you later, if you change your mind. Do you have any other questions?"

"No," Vivian said.

Jules shook her head mutely when the doctor looked at her. Her only question was about why Vivian was so subdued, and medical science probably wouldn't be able to answer that.

"Very well." Dr. Viswanathan glanced at her notes. "I'll want to see you in another two weeks, Vivian."

"Fine." Vivian's voice was as even and cool as ever.

Jules worried some more. Then she worried while checking out of the clinic, worried during the car ride back to the office, and worried on the way into the revolving doors of the Koening Building because Vivian hadn't said anything. She hadn't even given her work instructions.

The elevator doors shut, leaving them alone together, and Vivian exhaled a long, shaking sigh.

Jules quickly turned to look at her. She was pale and trembling, and her hand was pressed to her heart.

"Are you okay?" Jules asked urgently.

Vivian nodded, waving her hand at Jules for silence while she took another deep breath. "I'm fine. I'm fine now."

Jules fidgeted, twitched her fingers, balled her hands up into fists. Then when they passed the fourth floor, she reached out and hesitantly touched Vivian's hand with her own, not daring to say anything.

Vivian didn't look at her, but she grabbed Jules's hand so hard, it hurt.

There was a lot of relief in that squeeze. No wonder Vivian had been acting so weirdly. She must have been even more worried than Jules had known and overwhelmed when she learned everything was okay.

So maybe there was hope for getting a copy of that picture after all.

Jules grinned. "A girl, huh?"

Vivian covered her mouth with her hand but not soon enough to stifle a half-hysterical laugh. Her cheeks finally got a little color in them.

Jules laughed too, breathlessly, as relief overwhelmed her. It was okay, the tests had been fine, Dr. Viswanathan had been hopeful, and Jules and Vivian were holding hands in the elevator.

Not a bad start to Friday morning, all in all.

Then Vivian looked at her, her eyes shining with relief and happiness.

Jules got a little dizzy, and she wondered if the day would come when Vivian's beauty didn't shut down her mind completely.

But then Vivian got herself under control and let go of Jules's hand, and just in time too because then the elevator dinged and the door opened and they were staring at Keisha and Charlotte.

Jules put on a straight face right away. So to speak.

Keisha and Charlotte got out of the way immediately, and Vivian brushed past like she hadn't even seen them. Jules followed, but Charlotte grabbed her elbow and mouthed, *Is it okay?*

She couldn't stop another grin as she nodded, and both Charlotte and Keisha relaxed. The whole office had no doubt been holding its breath in a prayer that Vivian's entire pregnancy would go as well as possible because the alternative—and Vivian's resulting mood—were too horrifying to consider.

But that day went as smooth as glass. Even when Allie mixed up a photo spread from Prada with one from Phillip Lim, even when Paul was late getting back from a meeting because of traffic, even when Simon had to leave the office early because of a crisis at Donna Karan, Vivian didn't flip out.

The good mood persisted throughout the rest of the day, and sometime after lunch, it took a turn toward something else. Jules had seen the terrible tightness inside her all morning; now that it had loosened, it was like Vivian was letting herself feel other things.

And whatever those things were, they made her radiate sex appeal like Jules had never seen before. It seemed that Vivian didn't so much walk as saunter.

Her movements, always purposeful, now seemed almost languid; she had a slow roll to her hips, a slight sway in her walk. Taking it easier today? Balancing a little extra weight? Jules didn't know what it was, but while Vivian was in the office whispering her orders and being as terrifying as usual, her body was telling everyone within a ten-yard radius, "You should want to have sex with me."

Worst of all, she didn't even seem to be aware of it.

At least Jules wasn't the only one who saw it. Even Joey stared when Vivian returned from an afternoon meeting, and he was gayer than Simon. This couldn't possibly be what people meant when they talked about the glow of pregnancy, could it? Wasn't that supposed to be more of a maternal thing? Not a throw-me-down-and-fuck-me-now kind of thing?

Whatever it was, Jules was horribly distracted all day long until a quarter to five. That was when Vivian summoned her for something that demanded every scrap of focus she could get.

As she entered Vivian's office, she ignored the twitch between her legs and tried hard not to stare at Vivian, who was wearing a dark blue blouse that brought out her eyes and made her skin look like cream.

Were her breasts bigger? Probably. That often happened during pregnancy.

*Get it under control,* Jules told herself, *at least until tonight.*

Vivian leaned back in her chair, closed her eyes briefly, and hummed. She was obviously tired, but it looked like…something else.

Jules tried not to whimper.

Vivian opened her eyes again, stunned Jules into immobility with their beauty, and said, "Find a suitable venue for a little party in mid-April."

She hauled her brain to its feet with an effort that nearly killed her and said, "Uh…how little?"

"Let's say fifty people, definitely no more than sixty." Vivian tapped her lips with her fingertip.

This time, Jules did whimper, but she covered it with a cough.

"It'll be a dinner party. Call Hélène Darroze and see if she'll do the honors."

Hélène Darroze was a Michelin-starred Parisian chef. Her mind boggled.

Vivian continued, "Wine…Mouton Rothschild and Puligny-Montrachet for the six guests at my table. Get Hélène's recommendation for the rest. And speak to Tomás when you call my florist; he always knows what I'll like. Nothing *too* fancy. I'm thinking minimalist arrangements of orchids."

"Okay." Her head was spinning in a different, less pleasant, way now. She returned to her desk and picked up the phone.

Secure the chef first: no easy task as Hélène Darroze was what you could call in demand, but if Vivian wanted her, Jules would get her. Then the venue. Having a guest list would help, but for starters Jules would just find a few places in Manhattan and then one or two farther afield. Nothing less than five-star, naturally. For sixty people.

*Nothing too fancy, my ass.* All this in one month? On what, a whim? Vivian hadn't even said what the party was for or who she wanted to invite. It had been a while since she'd made a demand this over-the-top.

At least it distracted her from thinking about the lazy slide of Vivian's walk and the purr in her voice. Some. A little. Maybe.

Damn.

But nothing said she had to take it lying down. Well, she'd love to take it lying down. Which was the whole problem. She needed to fight back.

"Jules? You okay?"

Allie was looking at her with a little moue of concern.

She scrambled to get her wits together. "Oh! Sure, I'm fine."

"You just look kinda spacey."

"I'm fine," Jules repeated firmly. "We've got a new assignment. A big one."

Allie perked up. "Is it about shoes and aromatherapy?"

After a pause, Jules rubbed her forehead and said, "No, it is not. Okay, listen up. I'm going to need you to call Vivian's event planner…"

# CHAPTER 47

To Jules's consternation, Vivian's house was dark and silent when she entered—no light shining from either the kitchen or the den, no sounds of movement. Had Vivian fallen asleep? Was she pissed off that Jules had sent a text saying she'd be late? It wasn't *that* late—only eight thirty—and Jules had promised she'd be bringing a surprise.

The light went on in the stairwell.

Jules froze.

"I'm up here," Vivian called.

Jules wondered if she was actually about to faint as she headed up the stairs. Her palms were sweaty, and her long coat didn't help the heat suffusing her whole body.

When she reached the top, she saw that the light was on in the study. She took a deep breath and walked in.

Vivian was sitting on the couch. She looked up at Jules with bright, glittering eyes as she took in the coat. "Is it too cold in here?"

"No," Jules said softly. The tone of her voice was enough to get Vivian sitting up straight.

Jules began slowly unzipping her coat.

Now Vivian's eyes widened.

"Told you I was going to be late," Jules said, "because I was bringing a surprise."

"Oh God," Vivian whispered.

"Mm-hmm." Jules had the zipper down halfway. As the coat opened, Vivian could clearly see what she'd changed into: the red jumpsuit from

New Year's Eve, shoulders repaired and neckline practically slit down to Jules's navel.

No boob tape tonight. Jules was definitely about to burst out of this thing. And tonight, Vivian didn't seem to think that was very funny.

She let the coat fall to the floor. It thumped against the Berber rug. "Thanks for letting me keep this."

Vivian pressed her lips together as she looked at the peaks of Jules's nipples, hard and clearly visible through the fabric.

"You like it?" Jules asked.

"Come here."

The note of command in Vivian's voice was wobblier than usual. She still should have said *please*.

Jules let the command draw her forward anyway until she was standing over Vivian, looking down at her, drowning in her eyes. Instead of sitting, she touched Vivian's face with her fingertips.

"*Julia.*"

Now Vivian's voice broke, and that was good enough. Jules exhaled and sat next to her, close enough that their thighs were touching from hip to knee. The contact—more than they'd ever had before, not nearly enough—made her ache.

"Come here," Vivian repeated, but she was the one who reached out, cupped Jules's face, and pulled her in.

Jules slid her arms around Vivian's waist and went for it.

She started off gentle, as usual. And as usual, Vivian's face and body heated up against her own. Jules felt a shiver chase up and down Vivian's spine. And when she'd finished the first kiss, she gave Vivian another one. And then another. And another. Then she lost track and just thought about Vivian's unbelievably soft mouth and the way it kissed her back so hungrily tonight.

Suddenly, Vivian pulled back, panting, her face bright red. Jules's heart fell, but Vivian didn't retreat or push her away. Instead she said, "Please."

*Please what?* Jules didn't know, but she didn't stop to think about it. She couldn't think at all as she bent and kissed the angles of Vivian's chin, nipping at the place where the jaw met her throat.

Vivian gasped in her ear.

With a sigh, Jules moved downward, mouthing and kissing at her throat.

Digging her nails into Jules's shoulders, Vivian stiffened and arched. "God," she whispered.

"Good?" Jules breathed deeply, her head spinning from Vivian's perfume and beneath it the smell of her skin.

"D-don't stop."

She didn't. Given permission to drown, she did, and nuzzled at Vivian's skin as if she were in a dream. Vivian's pulse beat fast and hard near her mouth. She slid her hands up and down, pressing Vivian even closer to her.

"Oh." Vivian moved one of her own hands up to dig into Jules's hair. She gave a sudden, rueful laugh. "Y-you win."

"I do?" Before Vivian could reply, she kissed her again, a long kiss now.

By the end of it, Vivian was practically squirming. "You're driving me crazy," she whimpered when Jules let up. "My hormones are—and you, you've been t-teasing me for—"

"I never teased you." Jules let indignation take over her arousal for a moment. "You're the one who—and I told you I'd do whatever you wanted."

At those words, Vivian's eyes glazed over.

Jules's irritation vanished without a trace. She kissed her again as lightly as she had that first night and whispered, "So what do you want?"

"I don't know," Vivian panted. "I can't think." Her eyes slid shut. "Please, just…"

The raw need in her voice went straight between Jules's legs. Jules couldn't get past the blush in Vivian's cheeks or the smell of her or the tremble in her mouth or how soft her hair was when Jules slid her fingers into it and pulled her closer for another kiss. And this time, she nibbled and kissed until Vivian parted her lips and let her in.

*Drowning.*

When they parted at last, Vivian moaned.

At the sound of it, Jules did too, then kissed her again, sliding her hand up and down Vivian's rib cage, feeling the heat of her through her soft knit shirt. It was a wrap blouse: comfortable, stretchy, and promising easy access if Jules just popped open the three big buttons right here on the side…

*Not yet. Take it slow. Savor this.* Jules wasn't a teenager, for crying out loud.

So instead of trying to tear Vivian's clothes off, Jules started in on her throat again, and this time she didn't hesitate to use her teeth. Nothing likely to leave a mark, just little nips in between softer kisses while Vivian trembled and whimpered some more.

When Jules pushed her blouse aside so she could get to more of her shoulder, Vivian said, "Julia," and rubbed her nose in Jules's hair. That was more than enough to bring Jules back to her mouth. By the end of the kiss, they were clutching each other and panting for air, and Jules had slid one hand under Vivian's blouse to touch her soft, warm skin.

"Ah." Vivian pulled her in for another kiss.

Jules rubbed her hand up and down, her fingertips tingling because she still wasn't used to touching Vivian, certainly not like this, and she wondered if she ever would be. "You feel good," she mumbled against Vivian's mouth. She kissed a shoulder again, felt the shudder it provoked. "You like this?"

"Ah," Vivian said again, and added, "Don't stop." She slid her own hand down, cupped Jules's hip, and kissed just by the ear.

The brush of Vivian's lips on her cheek made Jules think of their first evening together on a sofa in London, when she had sealed their deal with a chaste little kiss to Vivian's hand that had nearly blown the top of Jules's head off.

She thought of the dizzy, terrifying joy that had taken hold of her at that moment and still hadn't let go. It had just been the two of them on that glorious evening. Nobody watching them. Nobody but them, nothing to stop them from—

*"God,"* Vivian moaned, arching into her touch, which was a good thing because Jules had cupped her breast without even thinking about it.

And now she couldn't stop, couldn't stop stroking that soft weight in her palm, longing to feel it without all the layers in the way. Vivian probably wouldn't object. She'd tilted her head back and closed her eyes.

"You like this?" Jules whispered again, so hot that she wondered if all her clothes were going to burn right off. She could feel Vivian's nipple even through all the layers of clothes, and she rubbed gently at it with her thumb. "Is that good?"

"Yes," Vivian gasped and kissed Jules again, whimpering when Jules kept moving her thumb. Between kisses, she managed to say against Jules's mouth, "They're more s-sensitive."

That tore it. Being prudent could go to hell. Jules fumbled with the buttons on Vivian's top.

Vivian let her mouth wander over to Jules's cheek again, then to Jules's forehead, then to her temple, as if she never wanted to stop kissing her. Fair enough. It worked both ways.

After a few more endless seconds, Jules's fingers finished their work, and the top slipped open to reveal a soft white bra that hooked in front.

Now it was Jules's turn to say "please" as she rubbed Vivian's nipple again, already stunned at how much warmer Vivian was with one layer removed. She touched the clasp between those breasts, and Vivian's breathing got even faster.

"Let me," Jules begged.

"Ah," was all Vivian could say.

Close enough to permission. Jules popped the clasp open. Then she pulled back just enough to see.

*Oh…God.* The world's most famous models had nothing on these. Beneath her blouse, Vivian's skin was as smooth and perfect as the rest of her, and her nipples were as pink and tightly furled as rosebuds. Jules rubbed her thumb over one of them. That wasn't enough. She bent her head so she could have a taste.

Vivian melted against the couch, sagging back into the cushions as she cried out. Her nails dug into Jules's shoulders.

The texture of Vivian's nipple was perfect against Jules's tongue. Soft and rough all at once. She'd been dreaming of this. She couldn't miss a single detail or leave a single inch undiscovered.

She licked just at the tip over and over again before taking it between her teeth and tugging gently. The nipple became even harder in her mouth. Hell yeah, it was sensitive. She licked it again, realized that wasn't enough either, and began to suck on it, alternating the softness of her tongue with the edge of her teeth.

Vivian gave a sobbing moan, and Jules felt one of the hands that had been digging into her shoulders move up to rub through her hair.

Feeling like she'd just been jerked out of a trance, Jules raised her head.

Vivian was staring back at her with glassy, wild eyes. "What," she began, her voice hardly recognizable. "Don't stop—please—"

Stop? Jules was never going to stop. She was going to do this for the rest of her life. Instead of wasting her breath saying so, she pushed until Vivian's back was propped up against the arm of the sofa, until she was nearly lying down, so that Jules could get to her other breast and give it equal attention.

Beneath her, Vivian sobbed again, arched up, grabbed her shoulders, and held on for dear life as she said, "Oh God" and "Please, yes."

Jules lifted her head again, giving the wet, reddened nipple one final lick—

"More," Vivian gasped. "Please, more."

And switched back to the first, earning a grateful moan. And then back again.

Back and forth between Vivian's breasts, again and again, for what seemed like hours while Vivian writhed and begged like she couldn't get enough. Her head tossed against the arm of the couch, and she seemed utterly shocked by the strength of her reaction, as if she'd never been this aroused in her life.

That made two of them.

"Oh, my God," Vivian panted. "Oh, my God, Julia."

Jules started pinching and stroking her other nipple in time with her mouth, which rendered Vivian too breathless even to moan.

How could this not be enough? How could Jules still want more, still want to devour every single inch of—she said, "I want to do everything to you. Everything." She bent and sucked again, long and hard, which coaxed a mewling noise out of Vivian's throat. "I want to make you feel so good. I'll do anything, anything you want."

Vivian pressed Jules's head down again, shaking all over, shaking so hard that it was a wonder they were both still on the couch. "Please, please…"

Jules licked.

"Ah! Oh, that's…that's so…I didn't…I've never, I've…oh-h-h—"

Jules sucked.

"Oh, I-I'm—"

Jules bit.

"God, I'm, I'm—"

Jules licked again.

"*Stop!*"

She paused, sure that she must have misheard, but Vivian was, in fact, weakly pushing at her shoulders, pushing her away.

"I can't," Vivian whimpered. "I can't…no more…please stop…"

Her blood pounding in her ears, Jules raised her head.

Vivian remained splayed back against the couch, her eyes closed, her blouse and bra open, and her skirt hiked up from the way they'd been lying together. She was panting, her throat, chest, and belly blotched with red. Her breasts were wet from Jules's mouth.

She looked like she'd just been fucked six ways from Sunday and had loved every second of it.

"Oh," Vivian whispered, covering her eyes with her hand. "Oh, my God." She was still trembling but less violently now, and in fact seemed actually to be relaxing against the sofa like she'd…

Like she'd…

No. No *way*.

"Did," Jules managed, "um, did you just—?"

Vivian nodded, then lifted her hand, looking at Jules with shocked, dazed eyes. "Twice," she rasped.

Jules stared down at her.

Vivian reached up. Held out her arms. And Jules bent down, kissed her, and came so hard at the first touch of Vivian's tongue that she cried out against her mouth.

This time it was Vivian's turn to whisper, disbelievingly, "Did you?"

"Uh-huh." Jules hid her face against the side of Vivian's neck, nuzzling there and tasting the salt, glad that the couch was so enormous.

Vivian said nothing, but she slid one hand up and down Jules's thigh. They rested there together in mutual stunned silence for a moment as they both struggled to get their breath back.

"You okay?" Jules asked when that moment had passed.

"Mm." Vivian took one more deep breath and let it go.

"That was, um," Jules said, "that was pretty good?"

It wasn't really a question. If two people could make each other come without once venturing down below, then, yeah, it had been pretty good.

"Yes." Vivian still sounded breathless.

Jules rubbed her hip, and Vivian shivered. "Please tell me we can do that again." She half expected Vivian to say something smart-assed or maybe not even reply at all.

Instead, she just said faintly, "Okay." And she stroked Jules's silk-clad thigh.

Jules decided instantly that, when time allowed, she was having this jumpsuit preserved and put in a display box.

In the meantime, though, Vivian appeared to be returning to herself, and Jules's joy was starting to make her feel a little silly, to say nothing of smug.

"'We don't have to have sex,'" she said prissily into Vivian's ear.

"Oh, shut up."

"Let's be all platonic and *chaste*.'"

"You respected that suggestion for an entire day, didn't you?"

"Nowhere near that long." Jules laughed, feeling downright giddy.

"Again with the snickering."

"Oh, come on. It wasn't that bad." Understatement of the year. "I know I feel better, anyway." She caressed Vivian's side, enjoying the way it made Vivian shiver again. "Don't you feel better?"

Vivian had been the one begging for a little relief after all, which she'd apparently gotten in spades.

"Yes." She rubbed her nose against Jules's ear, then paused. "Actually, I'm starving."

Jules laughed again. "Worked up an appetite, huh?"

"Are you going to start giggling every time we do this?"

*Every time.* That thought wasn't going make Jules stop smiling, that was for sure. Still grinning, she sat up. "Maybe. You want me to bring you something from the kitchen?"

Then a thought occurred to her, and she froze. "Or should I just go home?"

Having her way with Vivian on the couch was one thing, but making herself at home without an invitation was something else entirely, even now.

Vivian regarded her much too thoughtfully for someone who'd been a whimpering mess just a few moments ago, just long enough for Jules to squirm and be sure she'd misread the situation completely.

But then Vivian said, "Ellen put grilled chicken salad in the fridge. Let's eat."

Jules beamed.

# CHAPTER 48

Jules hadn't brought a change of clothes, but she'd worry about that in the morning. Vivian lent her a pair of pajamas as if they were having a sleepover, which Jules guessed they were. The second bathroom, she discovered, was fully stocked. It must have been Robert's. Had Vivian simply left it alone, unwilling to touch it, or had she planned this?

Now didn't seem like the time to ask, not when Jules was looking down at Vivian Carlisle's bed with its plush mattress and zillion-thread-count sheets while Vivian gazed up at her. Jules still throbbed pleasantly between her thighs. She'd never had sex like that before, never been that turned on before. Not even close.

Vivian lay on her side, propped up on an elbow and with her hand beneath her cheek. If she'd been wearing a filmy wrap instead of silk pajamas, she could have been in a baroque painting. Judging by the little smile on her face, she knew it.

"Wow," Jules said, frankly admiring the view. "You're amazing."

Vivian, as always, took praise as her due. "Thank you. Are you getting in? It's cold."

"Are you a cold sleeper?" Maybe talking would help Jules feel less out of place as she slid between Vivian's sheets in Vivian's bed in Vivian's house. "I can't sleep when I'm too warm."

The little smile turned sour. "Tell me about it."

Oh, right. Your body temperature was supposed to raise slightly during pregnancy. Jules turned on her side so she and Vivian were facing each other. "Your bed is nice."

"I agree."

"Sex with you is nice too."

Vivian pursed her lips, and a troubled look appeared. "We'll have to talk about this."

Jules sighed. Vivian was right, but the boss/subordinate-having-sex issue was the last thing she wanted to unpack right now. "Yeah, but can we do it in the morning?"

"That's why I used future tense. I thought you were an English major." She rolled onto her back with a grunt.

"You majored in journalism," Jules pointed out. "I've read some of your old articles in fashion magazines. They're really good."

"Editors thought so too. What's your point?"

"I dunno." Jules scooted closer until they were touching. Vivian's body was indeed warm, and her silk pajamas felt great against Jules's skin, even if the button-up top was tight over her breasts. "That's why I majored in communications along with English. I'm just saying we have things in common." Plenty of things.

"But you…" Vivian looked pensive. "You're different too."

"I am? How?"

She yawned. "That seems like a larger conversation than I want to have right now. I'll just say it's not a bad thing and leave it at that. Good night."

"I want to be the big spoon," Jules said, suddenly inspired.

Vivian merely glared at her before closing her eyes.

But halfway through the night, Jules woke to find herself wrapped around Vivian, holding her tight. The extra heat apparently didn't bother her, since she slept on peacefully in Jules's arms.

She was already looking forward to the morning. Vivian had told her to book no engagements for Saturday—which seemed premeditated, now that Jules thought about it—so that they'd have a chill first morning together. They could even sleep in. That seemed more luxurious than a thousand Hermès scarves.

At the thought, Jules drifted back to sleep with the comforting warmth of Vivian against her breasts and thighs.

---

However, Vivian had different ideas when it came to sleeping in.

Jules realized this when she woke up to the mattress shifting. She opened her eyes to see Vivian looking over her with disheveled hair and a fierce look of expectation on her face.

Jules turned and squinted at the clock on the nightstand: seven thirty a.m.

"I've been waiting," Vivian said and then, without further ado, bent down and kissed Jules hard on the mouth.

"Y-you have?" Jules gasped, winding her arms around Vivian's neck and tugging at her until they lay side by side again.

"I woke up an hour ago. I lay here and let you sleep." Vivian kissed her again. "But apparently you were going to laze the whole Saturday away."

"That was the plan," Jules said against her mouth. "We have the whole—"

"Cancel the plan," Vivian growled between kisses. Through the thin silk of her pajamas, Jules could feel how hot her skin already was. "You wanted this, you did this to me, and you'd better be ready to deal with it."

Well, there were worse ways to wake up. Jules grunted and sat up until she was leaning over Vivian, not lying on top of her exactly but at a better angle to *deal with* her. "I've created a monster, huh?"

"I fully expect to be catered to." Vivian began to spread her legs.

Then she paused as if the intimacy of the movement had occurred to her at the same moment it occurred to Jules.

*Vivian Carlisle's spreading her legs for me.* She fought down an incredulous laugh. "Makes a nice change." Then she stopped Vivian's impending growl by kissing her again. "So have you decided what you want?"

"A little more finesse than last night, please." Vivian obviously meant for it to come out sounding haughty, but she'd already started breathing faster from the kisses. She cleared her throat. "That is, not that I didn't enjoy it—"

"I noticed." Jules wasn't sure whether to grumble or be smug. She settled for getting a little nervous.

Finesse, huh? Okay, fair enough. It had been incredible sex, but she hadn't exactly demonstrated the most sophisticated moves, and Vivian clearly had as high expectations for lovemaking as she did everything else. Nothing less than five stars.

Only…that wasn't exactly fair, was it? Jules might not have deployed any amazing moves, but Vivian had done even less. And at least Jules had *some* sexual experience with women. It didn't seem possible, but maybe Vivian was nervous too, trying to compensate with hauteur.

Suddenly brimming with sympathy, Jules said gently, "Hey. I know you haven't done this before, but…"

Vivian rolled her eyes. "Rachel Maddow does it, doesn't she? And she can't figure out how to expand her closet past Jil Sander suits. It can't be rocket science." She tugged at Jules's pajama top. "Let's start here. I want to see you this time."

Okay, maybe Vivian wasn't nervous. Jules's face heated. "You already have."

Vivian snorted. "I saw you popping out of your jumpsuit after a party. I wasn't looking at them then. I want to now."

Fair enough. Jules unbuttoned her top and shrugged it off, letting the silk slither down to the bed. Then she didn't quite know where to look and found herself closing her eyes.

Having Vivian look at her was different than having anyone else look at her. Vivian looked at beautiful women's bodies all day. Those women were taller and thinner than Jules, and none of them had a roll of flesh beneath their belly buttons.

"Oh," Vivian said.

Jules opened her eyes.

Vivian was blushing too as she looked at Jules's breasts. She cleared her throat again. "Well, they're…" She reached up and cupped the left one.

Her palm was soft, and the heat from it raced through Jules's body like an electric shock. She gasped. Her nipples hardened instantly.

Vivian's eyes went wide. She actually looked alarmed for a second. Then she smirked. "Hmm." She rubbed her thumb over Jules's nipple and made her gasp again. "I see why you like mine."

"I really do." Jules was already having a hard time breathing. With Vivian lying beneath her, glowing with desire and anticipation, touching her—Jules was going to be lucky if she didn't come four seconds into it again.

But, God, this was what she'd been wanting for months, and it was *better* than what she'd wanted. "You turn me on more than anybody I've ever met," she blurted out.

Vivian looked up at her, startled.

She shrugged. "I mean, you do."

"Well." Vivian looked embarrassed for the first time.

Jules could see her wondering if she was expected to return the compliment. Her face burned again but for a different reason. She shouldn't have said that. God forbid Vivian should compare her to anyone else, like that guy from college who had rocked her world. How did you compete with a memory like that?

"I admit I didn't expect last night." Vivian coughed. "It was… Are we going to talk about this all morning?"

Jules grinned, her confidence back and waving little victory flags. "You don't like talking about it?" She lowered herself until she was tucked up against Vivian, rubbing her own bare breasts against Vivian's silk top. She sighed at how good it felt and watched Vivian's eyelids flutter. "I like talking about it sometimes." Their nipples brushed.

Vivian gasped and dug her fingers into Jules's hair again, tugging her in for another kiss. She was shivering when they pulled apart. "I don't like talking about—" she began, then gave up and kissed Jules again.

Jules slid her hands between them and began unbuttoning Vivian's top as she kissed her throat, already eager to see again what she'd seen last night.

Vivian arched her head back accommodatingly.

"Maybe you could just give me feedback as I go, then," Jules said. "The constructive kind."

As it turned out, Vivian had simple tastes for once. She loved being kissed anywhere: mouth, throat, shoulders, breasts. And she liked being treated and pampered, which surprised Jules not at all.

So Jules pampered her with lots of long, slow kisses, trying to do things all in a rhythm that would please her. Vivian smelled good, felt better, and tasted best of all, and eventually Jules forgot about nerves and just lost herself in doing to Vivian what she'd wanted to do for ages.

She got feedback, all right. Little moans and whimpers that gave Jules goosebumps, pleas that came out like commands ("do that again"), excited squirming and wriggling. She tried to touch Jules too, but then Jules would lick the side of her neck and she'd lose her concentration, or touch her breasts and she would forget how to breathe, let alone kiss.

Finally, when Vivian was starting to tremble and pant, Jules got her courage together and tugged at the waistband of Vivian's pajama bottoms. *Into the breach.*

Vivian went still.

Jules froze. "Do you want—?"

"Yes." Vivian might have needed a second to decide, but now she lifted her hips eagerly enough and helped Jules shimmy the pants down her legs.

Jules touched the inside of her thigh, and she shivered.

Vivian was wearing plain black cotton panties, bikini cut, that clung to her hips. They might not have been expensive lingerie, chosen more for comfort than style, but Jules fought not to drool nevertheless.

It seemed rude to yank them down, though. Vivian wanted finesse. Jules cleared her throat, placed her hands on Vivian's waist, and said, "Tell me what you like."

She hadn't meant to say it like that, to *command*, and as soon as the words were out of her mouth, she winced. Talk about lack of finesse.

But Vivian's breath caught and her hips arched slightly.

Huh. How about that.

"You're talented." Vivian's voice was a throaty murmur. "Figure it out. Or do you need a demonstration?"

Jules looked at her, stunned. "You'd…show me?"

She imagined Vivian touching herself, which, okay, she'd imagined several times before. The thought that she might see it in real life was almost unbearably hot, and she opened her mouth to say so.

But Vivian cut her off and went red. "Of course not! I meant I'd"—she touched Jules's hip—"to *you*."

"Oh." Jules tried not to feel disappointed. That was a heck of an offer, after all. "I'd like to watch you sometime all the same."

"I wouldn't like that," Vivian said, but she sounded uncertain. Well, by now she probably knew Jules was good at introducing her to new delights. "What's the point?"

"You could show me how you like it," Jules suggested, getting hot again just at the thought. Then she moved her hand to touch the cotton.

And got a shuddering breath in response.

Jules kept looking her right in the eye. "Show me," she whispered, slid her hand higher, and cupped.

Gasping, Vivian arched again.

Jules slid her thumb around over the cotton, which made Vivian bite her bottom lip and squeeze her eyes shut. Then it hit one particular spot, and Vivian's hips jumped as she squeaked. Her eyes opened wide again.

Jules held back a groan. *Focus.* This was about Vivian. "Here's good, huh?" She rubbed again.

"A little to the, um"—Vivian shook her head—"left."

Jules moved her thumb.

"No, my left!"

She obligingly moved it again and pressed down hard because, just this once, she could punish Vivian for giving lousy instructions.

But Vivian obviously liked it way too much for it to be a punishment, and Jules decided to forgive her instead. She rubbed until she found a pace that actually made Vivian cry out, then bent down and lapped at a nipple, sucking it in time with her strokes.

Vivian's body undulated like a wave. She didn't make any noise, but her sudden, frantic movement against Jules's thumb was unmistakable. And this time, Jules raised her head so she could watch Vivian's face, could see the way her head arched back and her eyes shut and her mouth fell open in a silent cry. One of her hands curled into a fist, and she struck the mattress.

Then she writhed her hips, managing, "Move—hand—down—"

Too sensitive now? Jules moved her thumb away from the clit and rubbed gently where she could feel Vivian's labia through the cloth. She could feel moisture there too.

Vivian sobbed in appreciation and relaxed, shivering gently. She even smiled.

Jules could not have imagined anyone less like the cool woman who cut everyone down to size with one flash of her blue eyes.

But it was the same woman, and she bent and kissed that woman before she could even get her breath back.

Vivian hummed and lazily slid her fingers into Jules's hair. Then she sighed in satisfaction. "You might have been on to something," she conceded.

"I'm full of bright ideas."

"Mm." Vivian said. "Now, let's see." She sat up, pressing Jules back down against the pillows. "Unless you did it again while we were kissing?" Vivian added, sounding hopeful.

"Not quite. You don't have a lot of work to do, though." It was true. She'd felt like she was going to explode, watching Vivian come. Now she couldn't stop squeezing her thighs together, chasing just a little pressure.

Vivian's brow furrowed as she studied Jules as if she were checking over an unsatisfactory layout. "It looks more complicated."

"Look," Jules said, trying desperately to sound calm, "it's not like I have a lever you can grab, but I promise—"

"Oh well." Vivian bent down to kiss her throat just as if she were someone who'd never advocated a chaste romance in her life.

She trailed her mouth down Jules's chest eagerly. Then Jules's nipple was in Vivian's mouth, and it wasn't like nobody had ever kissed her breasts before, but this was *Vivian*, and her lips were soft and her mouth was hot—

It was Vivian's blonde hair tickling Jules's chin, it—

She wasn't as quiet as Vivian when she came, and she was pretty sure she'd left nail marks in Vivian's shoulders. But she didn't seem to mind as she gave Jules's nipple one final, affectionate lick and murmured, "Hello, lever."

"Like you can talk," Jules wheezed, falling back against the pillows again. She closed her eyes, basking in it. "Oh wow."

"Maybe next time we'll get all our clothes off," Vivian said thoughtfully. "Unless—I'm assuming we're finished?"

Jules managed to pry her eyelids open. "Huh?"

"We're done, aren't we? That is, we both…" Vivian frowned as she gestured between them. "It really isn't like men, is it?"

"Well…no," Jules said, bewildered and trying to catch her breath. "We don't have to be done, I guess. What are you talking about?"

Vivian propped herself up on her elbow. "I mean, it's not like with men. What if neither partner comes? How are you supposed to know when to stop?"

"I guess we could set a timer."

That got her a scowl.

"Sorry. I just mean it's not about reaching a goal. You do what you like, and stop when you're ready to stop." How the hell else did she think it was supposed to go?

Now Vivian looked suspicious. "What if one of you is ready to stop and the other one isn't?"

"Vivian, I'm not sure this is going to be a huge problem," she said helplessly. She'd never pictured afterglow going like this. "Why don't we just play it by ear?"

Vivian still didn't look appeased. Which was weird. Why was she making this so complicated? Why had she been dead set on making it complicated from the beginning?

Jules considered that. Vivian had been married three times. For a woman so devoted to her career, she'd invested a lot of time and energy in relationships that had never worked out. If Jules wasn't used to relationships being this complicated, Vivian probably couldn't imagine they could ever be easy.

Time to finally answer one question. "Vivian? Why were you so sure that you didn't want to have sex with me?"

With a frown, Vivian admitted, "I didn't know that I wanted to." Then she blushed and looked even madder about that. "Until you kissed my hand. That was… I didn't expect it."

Jules remembered how Vivian's look of surprise had kept her warm during a few lonely nights. "I'm sure you didn't."

"Are you sorry I didn't jump into bed with you right away?"

It was Jules's turn to blush. "No! I didn't want to rush you or push you." *Much.* "I didn't want to screw anything up. I wanted it to be okay."

"Then we agreed on that," Vivian said lightly. "Or do you think you've 'screwed it up' now?"

"Not if I did it right," Jules dared, and Vivian finally smiled. *Awesome.* "Want breakfast?"

"You were breakfast." Vivian stretched and smiled again, relaxing visibly.

"Well, seconds are available," Jules said, "whenever you want them."

"Why do you say things like that?"

"I don't know." Jules laughed.

Vivian rolled her eyes but scooted in closer on the mattress.

She wasn't sure how it happened, but they both fell back asleep. So much for Vivian's idea that they shouldn't laze around.

When she woke up again at ten o'clock, Vivian had plastered herself to Jules's side and was sleeping like a baby. Her head was on Jules's chest, and she'd thrown an arm across Jules's stomach.

Watching Vivian sleep, she remembered the first time she'd ever seen Vivian at rest—that night in the car just after she'd learned she was pregnant. It seemed like years ago, or at least like more than four months.

Jules petted her hair, careful not to do anything that would tug at her scalp or otherwise wake her up.

The room, the whole house, was peacefully still. Sunlight was shining through the blinds now, falling across the bed, painting Vivian in stripes of light and shadow. There weren't even many sounds of traffic outside on Vivian's quiet street. Jules wondered how many people were doing what they were doing now: lying in, sleeping late on a Saturday. She wondered, in fact, if Vivian ever had done this before. Surely at least once.

Well, Jules wasn't going to wake her up to ask. She lay still, felt Vivian Carlisle's weight against her, and enjoyed her happiness.

# CHAPTER 49

Jules stayed at Vivian's house all day Saturday and had more fun than she could ever remember having. It was a specific kind of fun. While Vivian made a game attempt at getting dressed every now and then, it didn't last long.

Vivian also had a vague idea about preparing food of some kind, but Jules wasn't particularly interested in that either.

"You had me for breakfast, I'm having you for lunch," she said and slid her hand up under Vivian's skirt. "Fair's fair."

Vivian leaned her head back against the kitchen wall. "It's not fair… You're the one who's always after me to eat—*ah*."

Jules was already addicted to watching her lose her cool, forget how to talk. "You're the one who said 'deal with it.'" Then she leaned in and smiled against Vivian's mouth so she could feel it—Vivian trembled—and whispered, "So deal."

She slid both hands beneath Vivian's skirt, hiking it up around her thighs and then plucking at the waistband of her panties.

Vivian's breath caught, and she looked into Jules's eyes, her own eyes wide and shocked. "You're going to try this for the first time up against the kitchen wall?"

Jules, who remembered Vivian coming just from being rubbed through her underwear, said, "Try what?"

Vivian narrowed her eyes. "You're going to touch—touch *me*. Directly. Up against the wall?"

"Oh. Gosh. Did you want me to peel you some grapes first?"

Vivian glared.

Jules slid the fingers of her right hand gently up the inside of Vivian's thigh, and the glare wobbled.

"Rub your feet?" Jules whispered. "Fan you?" She tickled a little.

Vivian twitched and gasped.

"Or I could kneel," Jules said hoarsely, her temples starting to pound with her heartbeat, her blood rushing in her ears. She slid her fingertips farther up until she was cupping Vivian through her underwear. "I could kneel right here and…"

Vivian's head fell back and thudded gently against the wall as her eyes closed.

Jules realized she was thinking about it—they both were—about Jules sliding her tongue against those little folds and tucks and creases until all of Vivian's bones turned to water and her voice was rough with her cries.

"Maybe…" Jules swallowed hard. "Maybe later." She bent and began to nuzzle at the sensitive spot beneath Vivian's ear and tugged at her panties again. "Let's get these off."

Seconds later, the underwear was tossed onto the kitchen counter while Jules kissed Vivian to distraction. Then she reached for her courage once more and carefully—very carefully—slid her hand under and up until her fingertips brushed against soft, fine hair and heat and slickness.

She moved her hand carefully so that her fingertips were rubbing against the soaking lips.

Vivian practically climbed her wrist, and Jules's fingers slid farther back until they were…

"Please," Vivian moaned. "Oh, *please.*"

Jules wished she could see what she was doing. Vivian had a point about doing it up against a wall. But heck if Jules was going to admit it, so she just kissed her neck again and whispered in her ear, "Show me."

With a hiss, Vivian gave in, reaching down between her legs, taking hold of Jules's hand. She groaned, "There, right there." She shuddered and patted Jules's knuckles. "Use your whole h-hand against me."

Jules cupped her again, and her palm got slippery. She squeezed gently, then rubbed, and Vivian rocked her hips. Jules angled her hand so that the heel of her palm could grind against the clit.

Vivian's head tossed back against the wall again. She cried out softly.

Jules took a deep breath, trying not to faint, and began flexing her hand back and forth. On the rise, she rubbed Vivian's clit with her palm, and on the fall, she pressed Vivian's perineum with her fingertips.

"God!" Vivian's eyes squeezed shut, her face going red as she lifted up on her toes, writhing against Jules's hand.

"Beautiful," Jules choked. She rubbed her face against the curve of that throat, nuzzling her again while Vivian grabbed at her back. "Beautiful. You're so—"

"Inside," Vivian gasped, rubbing her own nose in Jules's hair. "Please… inside me—"

Jules moaned. Before she made another move, she kissed Vivian, slow and deep. And then she hunted ungracefully with her fingertips for a couple of crucial seconds until she found her target, soft and slick and giving beneath the pressure of her hand. She slid one finger in, shocked by how hot Vivian was down here. "Is that…"

"Be gentle," Vivian pleaded, cupping Jules's face in her hands and kissing her, not gently at all.

Jules pulled back a little, being so gentle with her mouth and her hand that Vivian nearly hyperventilated. "Nice and slow," she breathed, and sucked on Vivian's bottom lip. "Is this how you like it?"

Vivian made an incoherent noise.

Jules didn't wait for a better answer but instead pressed a second finger inquisitively at the entrance.

Vivian sobbed and bucked her hips, which Jules took for permission as she slid the second finger in. Very gently.

"Amazing," she whispered.

"Gentle," Vivian said again, but the word was without meaning—she was chanting more than talking now. "Gentle."

"Yes." Jules kissed the side of her neck. "Is it good? Can you show me how to make it good?"

"Ah." Vivian reached between their bodies again, between her legs. But she didn't guide Jules's hand this time. She just hiked her skirt up higher and rubbed frantically at her clit, then was clenching all around Jules's fingers, fast and rhythmic.

Jules lost her breath as she tried to watch it all at once: Vivian's hand, Vivian's face, and everything in between as Vivian stroked herself to climax, biting her lip and whimpering through her nose.

When Vivian was done, when her convulsions had slowed, Jules leaned in to kiss her. They were both gasping.

After they parted, Vivian managed to say, disbelievingly, "I couldn't wait. I had to…"

"*God*, Vivian." Jules pressed her nose into Vivian's throat. She slid her fingers out carefully and patted the inside of Vivian's sticky thigh. "You're incredible."

Vivian was panting too hard to reply. But she kissed Jules's temple, then her cheek, and slid her arms around her waist.

Jules was trembling and wondering if this was the pattern they were going to follow from now on: making Vivian come hard and fast and getting so turned on by it that she went off like a firecracker at the slightest provocation.

*Nothing wrong with that*, she thought dizzily as Vivian slid one hand up and down her back. And down to her hip. And then between—

Jules gasped, "Oh Jesus!" as Vivian cupped her through the silk of her pajama bottoms and the underwear beneath.

Vivian's raspy breathing had slowed, regulated itself, dropped down into something like a purr. "Is this nice?" she murmured into Jules's ear. "Do you want my hand now?" She squeezed. "Do you like my touch, Julia?"

Jules shut her eyes and tried to think of sad stuff or gross stuff, anything but Vivian's hand between her legs. It didn't work, so she tore at the buttons of Vivian's blouse until it fell open, shoved up her bra, and hungrily bent back down to her breasts.

Vivian groaned. Her hand began to follow the rhythm of Jules's mouth until they were rocking together, and Jules wasn't able to take more than a few seconds of that before she came.

As she rested her head against Vivian's shoulder, Vivian rested hers against the wall. They both struggled for air. Then Jules lifted her sticky fingers, sniffed them, and licked them. Delicious. She'd forgotten. She couldn't wait to drink it right from the source, so to speak.

She wondered if Vivian would be able to return the favor. Mm. That would be—

"Lunch now," Vivian said breathlessly against her forehead. "We could order something."

She sure recovered fast.

Jules still felt dizzy. That might not have been the sex, though. That might just be Vivian, Jules's own personal hurricane, who picked her up, whirled her around, then dropped her casually on her ass.

What else was new? Jules laughed a little. "Anything. You name it. Anything at all."

---

"Why don't you ever wear that brooch?"

"Huh?" Jules asked around a mouthful of broccoli melt from Daily Provisions. "Uh, what brooch?"

Vivian stuck her fork into her chicken Caesar salad. "The snake brooch I gave you in London. I haven't seen you wear it since then, and I know you liked it."

Her face turned hot. "I do," she said. "It's nice. Really nice."

Vivian tilted her head to the side.

"Too nice," Jules admitted. "I have it in a safe deposit box."

A look of displeasure crossed Vivian's face.

"I just don't want anything to happen to it!" Jules added quickly. "I keep it in a safe place because it's special."

Very special. It was the first thing Vivian had given her after they'd begun their…courtship or whatever it was. It was irreplaceable. Jules wasn't about to risk that brooch being lost or stolen.

"Jewelry is meant to be worn," Vivian pointed out.

"I will. It's just too nice for every day."

"Hmm," Vivian said. "Wear it to the party next month." Her eyes gleamed with secret pleasure.

"Okay," Jules said slowly. "What are you up to with that, anyway?"

She shrugged. "Just a little soirée. Why do I have to be up to something?" Before Jules could reply, she added, "I haven't seen you check your email yet today."

"Of course not!" Jules spluttered. "When was I supposed to do that, with my fingers in your—"

Vivian pinked. "Don't be crude. Anyway, why don't you look?"

Talk about being up to something. Jules grabbed her phone and opened her email.

Her eyes widened. At the top of her inbox was an email from someone named Carter Mathson.

The email read:

*Dear Ms. Moretti,*

*I hope this email finds you well. I'm reaching out to you in the hopes that you'd be willing to write a short feature for* Modernity's *June issue. We would be looking for a piece of about 1,000 words on the topic of your choice. We are particularly interested in pieces on fashion for this issue, which in your current position I believe you can readily supply. If you would like to submit a feature to* Modernity, *please reply ASAP with a brief proposal for the piece.*

*I look forward to hearing from you within the next two days.*

*Sincerely,*
*Carter Mathson*
*Features Editor*
Modernity *Magazine*

Jules read the email three times in dumb astonishment. *Modernity* was about popular culture, style, and politics that published celebrity interviews right alongside articles about world affairs. Her parents had had a subscription when she was growing up. It was, as her dad would say, the real deal. And they were reaching out to her…*her*…to write something?

It seemed unlikely that Carter Mathson had read her article in *Salon* and been swept away. Or in *The Cut*, unless he was really into *Working Girl*. Very unlikely indeed.

She looked up at Vivian, who regarded her with a smug smile.

"I overheard Allie mentioning your upcoming birthday to Simon," she said. "I have no idea why *you* didn't mention it to *me*. I know it's early, but I assumed you wouldn't object."

Jules looked back down at her phone. "You set this up? An article in *Modernity* for my birthday?"

"Well, I couldn't exactly send my assistant out to buy something for you. Besides, what do you get for the woman who already owns every boho necklace in New York?"

"This, I guess," Jules said slowly. Time to puzzle through her own reaction, which wasn't as thrilled as Vivian was no doubt expecting.

To say this was an incredible opportunity was an understatement. Magazines like *Modernity* solicited articles from well-known writers, people who won awards and gave guest lectures. People like Jules submitted to the slush pile and never heard back again.

Instead of that, Vivian had all but guaranteed her a spot. Jules hadn't gotten there on her own merits.

That wasn't the worst thing in the world; Jules wasn't naïve. Most writers would never make it big, no matter how hard they worked or how good they were. It was all about who you knew. That was and always had been the deal. And hadn't Jules wanted to work at *Du Jour* so she could make those valuable connections? What connection was more valuable than the editor in chief? Jules should be thrilled about this.

She was quiet for a few seconds too long. "Wow, Vivian! Thank you. This was so sweet."

Vivian was frowning. "What's wrong?"

"Nothing!" Now Jules's reaction was too fast. "I appreciate that you did this."

"It didn't take much," Vivian said dryly. "Out with it. What's the matter?"

Nothing should be the matter. It didn't make sense that Jules felt weird about this, especially since she couldn't pin down *why* it was weird. No matter what she said, Vivian had gone to some effort for this. She was a busy woman and didn't have a lot of spare time to contact magazine features editors.

Plus it showed that Vivian had been paying attention to what Jules cared about—given a lot of thought to what would please her. It was just like watching a fashion show and thinking about Jules in the clothes. Wasn't it?

Of course it was. She was being ridiculous. Besides, it called back to how offended Vivian had been when Jules had asked Simon for assistance with *Salon* and not her. Vivian only wanted to help.

"No, this is great," Jules said with more conviction. "Sorry, I just wasn't expecting it. It's awesome, I swear." She smiled. "Thank you."

"Remember what I said at Christmas," Vivian told her sharply. "If something's wrong, tell me instead of stewing."

Jules's stomach tightened, but that was weird too. Also Vivian was strangely insistent about this. "I will. Don't I always? At least since we started this?" Then the penny dropped. "Oh-h-h."

"What's oh-h-h'?" Vivian demanded.

"They stewed, didn't they?" Jules closed her email app and looked her dead in the eye. "The husbands."

Vivian scowled. "'The husbands?' You make them sound like a fifties rock band."

"But am I right?" Jules folded her elbows and leaned in on them.

"Couples shouldn't expect each other to be mind readers. I can't stand it when people bottle problems up instead of dealing with them."

Jules felt a pang of unease. Vivian wasn't wrong; Jules had been trying to hide her reaction. "I know. I'll speak my mind. As long as you do too."

Vivian gave her a disbelieving look.

"Which you do," Jules sighed.

"Frequently," Vivian agreed.

It was time to change the subject. Vivian was starting to look annoyed, which was not how Jules wanted to spend the afternoon.

"This is the best birthday ever," Jules said as she gave Vivian a winning smile.

"Humph." But Vivian's glare wobbled.

It made Jules's stomach flip pleasantly.

"Trying to charm me?"

A low, steady throb began down below as Jules thought of what was about to happen. Yeah, this was much better. "No, I'm just being greedy."

Vivian leaned forward on her elbows. "Oh?"

"I want another present."

"Explain."

About ten minutes later, back on the bed, Jules proved to a gasping Vivian that actions were better than explanations and definitely spoke louder than words.

Especially since Jules still wasn't quite sure which words she wanted to say.

# CHAPTER 50

"Think anybody'll notice if I slip out of here wearing the same clothes I was wearing twenty-four hours ago?" Jules asked.

Vivian shook her head as Jules refilled her water glass. They were just finishing up dinner at the kitchen table. Outside, the sky was dark.

The rest of the day had passed in a strange mélange of the ordinary and extraordinary. On the ordinary side, following their afternoon delight, they both had gotten to work: Vivian went through the mock-up of the next print issue while Jules took notes on her commentary. There was a lot of commentary.

On the extraordinary side, they broke up work shortly afterward to fool around. It started when Vivian said, "Ugh. Tell Joey we have to get rid of this photo in the big band spread. Joan Smalls looks completely ridiculous with that sexophone."

Jules had stopped writing and stared at her. Vivian obviously had no idea what she'd just said, but she kept on talking and said the word "sexophone" two more times before Jules gave up and doubled over with helpless laughter.

Vivian scowled, Jules explained, Vivian got snippy, and Jules had to take emergency measures. As it happened, she'd learned a couple of surefire ways to distract her by now.

Yeah. It had been a good day.

Dragging Jules back to the present, Vivian said, "Most people in this neighborhood don't actually spy on each other through the blinds. I doubt anybody saw you arrive last night, much less cared what you were wearing.

As long as the paparazzi are away, there's nothing to worry about. And I'm old news by now."

"Right." Jules finished her water. "That's good. I just figured I should leave after we eat."

Otherwise Vivian would never get any work done at all, and Jules couldn't stay the night again unless she wanted to creep out when it was still dark, which she didn't. Vivian's personal trainer was due at six thirty in the morning.

"Probably for the best," Vivian agreed, her expression not betraying any particular emotion. Then she added, "We didn't talk about it."

"About what?"

"About the ethical problems of me sleeping with my assistant and then sending her out to get my coffee."

Dammit. And it had been such a nice day too. "I don't mind getting you coffee or anything else. I told you—"

"You like looking after me." It was clearly not enough to appease her. "I heard you. Multiple times."

"C'mon," Jules protested. "Maybe you think it's sappy, but it's true."

"I didn't say it was sappy. If I couldn't see the appeal of caring for someone, I wouldn't be pregnant *or* here with you. I'm saying it's naïve. You think those feelings aren't going to change over time?"

Jules crossed her arms. A small part of her was whispering that Vivian might have a point. She shushed it for now. "So what are you saying? Am I looking for a new job?"

"No," Vivian frowned. "You know if you want to leave, you have my full support. But I won't dictate your comings and goings. Just think about it. Don't pull a Scarlett O'Hara and keep putting it off until tomorrow."

"Yeah," Jules sighed. "I'll think about it. I promise."

"Thank you." Vivian sounded resigned to the idea of Jules eventually running for the doors of *Du Jour* and never looking back.

Jules reached out and took her hand. "Hey."

"Hey, what?"

"I've got to be out of here in a few minutes. Want to get started on the goodbye kiss?"

Vivian rolled her eyes. But she kissed Jules anyway.

Jules hadn't really meant to honor Vivian's request. She'd intended to go home, listen to lovey-dovey music, have a glass of wine, and revel in her memories of the weekend. There would be plenty of time for solemn reflection later.

Solemn reflection showed up anyway when she sat on her couch and reread Carter Mathson's email.

The feeling returned, the one she couldn't name, the feeling that said, *This is kinda sketchy.*

Sure, on the outside, Jules could see how it might *look* bad. Her lover, who just happened to be her boss, was connecting her to influential people in a way Jules couldn't manage on her own. An ancient story.

But when Jules thought of other people who did that—the gross men Vivian was so determined not to become—it seemed different. With them it looked like the more powerful partner took sex as the price of entry for the other person who wanted favors. Tit for tat.

Vivian wasn't doing that. She was giving Jules a gift, and she didn't expect anything in return.

Jules began to pace her apartment in front of the mosaic-painted wall, the overstuffed ottoman, the poster from a special exhibit at the Pitti Palace. Nothing in here was Vivian's style, although it was well put together. This was Jules's space, where she was in control and had room to think.

Simon had done her a favor by putting her in touch with *Salon*. That had obviously been okay. Of course she owed him now and he'd be sure to collect, but that was also okay.

She remembered Vivian's troubled expression. Her worries about crossing personal boundaries with professional ones. Jules was starting, finally, to put a name to the feeling that had been plaguing her since she'd seen Carter's email: *Vivian is right.*

Ugh. That was always the worst feeling ever, no matter who was right when you were wrong. The question was, what was Jules going to do about it?

Deep down, she was afraid she already knew the answer.

# CHAPTER 51

In spite of her anxieties, by the time Monday rolled around, Jules was quivering with anticipation. She'd texted Vivian a couple of times on Sunday, trying to walk the fine line between checking in and not being clingy. That wasn't as good as being in Vivian's home, talking and eating and having sex.

The replies had been perfectly normal, as far as that went—which was to say, brisk and to the point. The texts of a woman with a lot to do.

Jules wondered how Vivian's Sunday had gone, if she really had kept so busy that she hadn't thought about Jules too much.

She found out on Monday morning when Vivian got into the car and refused to look her in the eye.

What the hell? It was too early for Jules to have screwed anything up at work. There could be a thousand reasons, but only one kept running around in Jules's head: was Vivian having second thoughts about making their relationship physical?

Her palms began to sweat. This was no good. The cold shoulder sucked. Wasn't Vivian the one who wanted to be forthright about things?

Maybe she would be as soon as they were alone—more forthright than Jules wanted her to be. *It was a mistake, Julia. It can't happen again.*

She gave the usual stream of instructions and commands, her voice calm and unwavering as ever. Jules scrambled to keep up, but she couldn't help noticing that Vivian didn't look at her for the whole car ride.

By the time they got to Koening, Jules's glow of anticipation had turned entirely into apprehension, and she was almost dreading the elevator ride to the office. What would she say if Vivian dropped the bomb?

But once the elevator doors closed, Vivian didn't round on her with apologies or accusations. She didn't look at Jules either. Instead she said in a faintly strained voice, "How was your Sunday?"

"Fine," Jules said, surprised. Even now, Vivian hardly ever made small talk. "I, uh, brainstormed for the *Modernity* article."

Then she wished she hadn't said that. It felt like the first step on a road Jules didn't want to travel right now.

"Mm," Vivian replied. At least she didn't want to follow up.

"What about you?" Jules prodded. "Anything go wrong with work? I'm assuming so—uh, I mean, you'd have called me if everything wasn't okay with work."

"Of course I'd have called you." Vivian's voice was hoarse and too loud for the subject matter. She seemed to realize this, and her cheeks went red.

Jules's eyes went wide.

Vivian's cheeks went redder.

*Oh.*

"I thought about you a lot yesterday," Jules said, feeling the beginnings of a smile.

"That's enough," Vivian replied at once, standing ramrod straight. Not straight enough to disguise her shiver, though.

Jules pressed her lips together to hide her grin. So that was why Vivian couldn't look her in the eye. She wasn't regretting anything. She wanted more. "Sorry. Sort of."

"Be appropriate today, Julia." Vivian's voice was razor-sharp. "The last thing I need is some insinuating, giggling…"

That got rid of Jules's grin right away. She stared in disbelief.

Thankfully, Vivian trailed off.

"Of course," Jules said pointedly. Like she'd ever be that dumb. Wearing sexy clothes to work was one thing. Looking all moon-eyed at the boss was something else, and Jules knew it. And Vivian knew that Jules knew it.

In fact, Vivian might need reminding more than Jules did. She hadn't been kidding about Jules's opening up a floodgate. As the day wore on, she grew more and more distracted. Her cheeks were constantly flushed and her voice was rough.

"Is she coming down with something?" Simon asked Jules after lunch with genuine concern in his voice.

*A bad case of lust.* "Uh…not sure."

Vivian had a meeting at four, followed by a thirty-minute facial. Jules hurried into her office at three forty-five to give her a folder for the meeting. Once again, Vivian refused to look at her, although Jules was pretty sure she didn't see the layouts right beneath her nose either. Her ankles were crossed tightly together, as if she were trying to restrain herself from wriggling in her seat.

"God," Jules breathed before she could stop herself as a sudden rush of heat hit her.

Vivian looked up at once into her face and read what was in Jules's eyes. Her own eyes glazed.

Jules thought for one wild second that there just might be some merit to closing the office doors and— "Here you go," she mumbled, shoved the folder into Vivian's hand, and hightailed it out of there at once.

Five minutes later, Vivian left her office without a passing glance, and Jules didn't exhale until she'd vanished from sight.

"She's been in a strange mood today, hasn't she?" Allie said after Vivian had exited.

Jules managed a smile. "When isn't she?"

An hour later, Simon arrived in reception. "Well," he said, "that was a fun meeting. I don't think she heard a word anybody said. It's a good thing she doesn't actually have to talk to her facialist."

Jules gave him a look of noncommittal sympathy.

Then he said, "Changing the subject, Jules, keep Wednesday night clear. Wednesday is your birthday, right? The sixteenth?"

She nodded.

"I'm taking you out for cocktails."

"Simon," she said, genuinely touched, "you don't have to."

"No, I do. I need something to look forward to. The Charleston shoot is going to hell."

"The shoots are always going to hell," she pointed out. "Then they always turn out okay."

"Well, yes. But that doesn't make them less of a pain in the ass in the interim." He sighed. "The shots along the Battery shouldn't be a problem. It's posing a bunch of stick-thin models on schooners and sailboats in the harbor that's giving me nightmares. Sun glare. Flapping sails. Wind." He shuddered. "And divas. My God, the divas."

"Aren't the models used to that kind of thing, though?"

"I meant the photographers."

"Oh."

"And of course you want it to be dramatic. Nothing all furled up and stationary, so the sails have to be out. Last time in the Keys, the shoot director didn't hire enough people who knew what to *do* with sailboats. So when the booms were swinging around like baseball bats and models and photographers were ducking and covering left and right…"

"Oh no." Jules laughed.

"Well, that's just a question of torque," Allie said casually.

Simon and Jules blinked at each other, then Simon turned to Allie. "Excuse me?"

"Oh, you know," Allie said, smiling at him. "Torque. It's just a vector that measures the tendency of a force to rotate an object around its axis. It's one of the rotational analogs of force, mass, and acceleration. The closer you are to the axis, you know, the sail pole, the more force you need to move your object, like the boom, around it. But the farther out the object is, like the end of the boom, the less force you need to move it."

"Um," Jules said.

"Exactly! It's like when you push open a door. You don't press at it close to the hinge because that's harder; you push it by the knob or the edge because that's where it's easier. You need less force. That's sort of like when the wind moves the end of the boom around. It doesn't take a lot of force, and next thing you know"—Allie swung her arm around in a wide arc—"whammo! So that's torque. Force is the push, and torque is the twist."

Simon and Jules stared at Allie with their jaws slowly sagging open.

"It's simple," Allie added. "I mean, that's just the basics. You don't really need to know all the formulae. Although it gets interesting once you start working out the scalar product of two vectors."

"Oh," Jules said.

"Anyway, just make sure the booms are stable where they connect to the poles," Allie added, beaming at them, "so the wind would have to exert a lot more force if it wants to move the ends. Maybe some kind of buttress, just for the photoshoot. I can draw you a diagram"—she blushed—"if you think it would help."

"I…" Simon said. "Uh…"

"Allie," Jules said, and blinked rapidly. "How do you know all that?"

"Oh!" Allie's face brightened. "I'm double-majoring in physics and media at NYU. I didn't put the physics major on my résumé, though. I didn't think it would look very stylish."

"Um—"

"My advisor said I should think about grad school and a career in astrophysics, but I told him that fashion was my passion." She suddenly smiled again. "Hey, that rhymed."

"Rhymed," Simon said. "Yes."

"I just couldn't see myself working in a NASA lab." Allie shook her head. "Talk about boring. I'm so glad I picked this internship instead of that one. It's a lot harder, though." She smiled ruefully. "Physics is so easy. But, you know, I wanted the challenge."

"Oh," Jules said. "Challenge. Right."

"Yeah. Hey," Allie added, "is it okay if I run to the ladies' room?"

"S-sure," Jules said.

She and Simon stared after Allie as she hurried away.

After a moment, he said, "Did I just dream that?"

"I have no idea," Jules replied, "but I think you better get her to draw you that diagram."

———

"Physics?" Vivian asked in disbelief.

"Astrophysics," Jules clarified as she put their plates in the dishwasher. "She told me about the senior research project she's planning for next semester. I think I understood every fifth word."

"And yet she mixed up Shiseido and Shu Uemura this morning." Vivian shook her head. "It's been a strange week."

"It's only Monday."

"Don't depress me. Speaking of surreal things…" Vivian hesitated. "Something came in the mail." She nodded at a small cardboard tube sitting open on the kitchen island. "I decided to have it shipped. Have a look."

Curiouser and curiouser. Whatever that was, it was something Vivian hadn't wanted Jules to ship on her behalf. Another birthday present?

But when Jules reached into the tube and felt a thin roll of paper beneath her fingertips, she knew.

Sure enough, she unrolled the paper to reveal the ultrasound photo. "Oh wow!"

Vivian shrugged. "I thought about it and realized, What else am I ever going to have that's like that?"

"Makes sense." Jules nodded down toward Vivian's abdomen, currently concealed by the table but also still barely showing a bump. "Is it starting to feel real?"

"It's felt real since I saw that pregnancy test result. But I haven't really thought of it as a *child* until now. I don't know if that sounds logical. I've been busy," Vivian added, sounding defensive.

"Oh, I know." Jules looked back at the ultrasound photo and couldn't help tracing her fingertip over the white outline of the tiny fetus. "How do you feel about it being a girl?"

"I feel the odds were fifty-fifty." Vivian pursed her lips. "But I feel more confident about raising a daughter without a man around than I would a son. Maybe you're not supposed to admit that kind of thing anymore."

"Makes sense to me, especially if you've never done this before." She returned to the table and sat down beside Vivian, taking her hand. "Have you been thinking about names?"

Vivian sounded oddly reluctant when she said, "Occasionally. I haven't spent much time on it yet."

That also made sense. Vivian didn't waste time, and she probably saw thinking about baby names before she knew the baby's sex as a waste of time. But now they knew.

Jules's heart beat faster as a smile stretched her mouth again. "Well, maybe now's the time! Want to look some up?" She reached for her phone. "Or do you have any family names you want to use?"

Silence. Jules, phone in hand, looked back at Vivian to see that her lips were pinched and her eyes hooded.

Oh crap. Vivian never talked about her family. "Uh…"

"No family names," Vivian said coolly. "But feel free to pull up a list, if you want."

That wasn't exactly resounding enthusiasm. Jules tried for a casual tone. "It can wait, if you don't feel like it tonight. There's plenty of time." She tried another smile. "She'll get a name eventually, right?"

Vivian blinked. Whatever darkness had appeared in her eyes vanished in a quick moment of wonder. "Yes. She will."

Jules rubbed her thumb against the softness of Vivian's palm. She meant it to be comforting. Judging by the sudden hitch in Vivian's breath, it had a different effect entirely.

Her breath hitched too, and they looked into each other's eyes for a long moment that lasted until Vivian leaned forward when Jules did.

The day's desire that Vivian had banked all evening clearly came roaring back. She dug her hands into Jules's hair and kissed her fiercely as if making sure she wasn't going anywhere.

She wasn't. She couldn't imagine it. She kissed Vivian back until it seemed like at least one of them would fall out of her chair. Then she stood up, reaching for both of Vivian's hands. "Bedroom?" she said, gasping.

Vivian looked up at her and licked her lips. "Bedroom."

"You got it. It's about time I show you what else my mouth is good for."

Vivian's own mouth said nothing. The sudden, hot plea in her eyes was all Jules needed to see.

---

*Just like riding a bike*, she thought as she kissed her way down Vivian's belly. It had been a while since she'd gone down on a woman, but some things were hard to forget.

Vivian had already begun to babble softly under her breath, and by the time Jules had slid to her knees between Vivian's thighs by the side of the bed, she'd started to pant. She struggled to sit up; Jules leaned in and pressed a tender, careful kiss; she fell back down.

And then Jules pushed Vivian's thighs wider apart so she could see everything, It wasn't as embarrassing as she'd thought it might be, and *wow* was Vivian ever soaking wet, all because of her. She leaned forward and licked. The taste down here was sharp, fresh, and it did pleasant things to Jules's brain.

Vivian said, "*Nnngh*!" and rubbed Jules's back with her left foot. Jules tried to remember stuff she liked herself. But she liked it rough, which Vivian obviously didn't.

She might as well learn by trial and error. Vivian had liked it when Jules had rubbed her here, just to the left (*her* left) of the clit, so she licked there too, very gently.

Vivian arched and hissed.

"Tell me what to do," Jules said. "Tell me what you like." How strange that she actually had to prompt Vivian to give her orders.

She licked again. A hand suddenly dug into her hair, and Jules asked, "What do you like?"

"I don't know—everything." Vivian panted. "Just keep, just…no fingers, though," she added suddenly. "I'm a little sore."

"Are you okay?" Jules pulled away as her libido instantly withered.

With a tiny cry, Vivian yanked at her hair.

"Ow!"

"I'm fine. Now, for God's sake, will you please—!"

Relieved and now sore herself, Jules quickly bent back down.

"Oh-h-h," Vivian finished, arching her back blissfully.

Jules thought fast. No fingers, she'd said, but she loved it when Jules went inside, so…

When she slid her tongue in just a little, Vivian stiffened and squeaked, and when Jules twitched her tongue up and down gently, Vivian sobbed. Then she moved up higher and lazily rolled her tongue over the clitoris again and again until Vivian's breathing went hysterical and she let go of Jules's hair to claw at the bedsheets.

She gasped. "Don't—stop—*please*—"

Jules carefully pushed back the hood, teased the little pearl directly with just the tip of her tongue—

"*Oh, my God!*"

Vivian's thighs clenched, and Jules suddenly found her mouth and chin soaked in come. *Delicious*. She licked again, and Vivian actually shrieked, pressing her hips up against Jules's mouth before jerking away again as she sank back down on the mattress trembling all over.

"Stop," she whimpered. "Enough…"

Jules had already figured that out, and she kissed the inside of one quivering thigh before wiping her mouth and face with her hand. Then she rose to her feet and crawled back onto the bed next to Vivian, who was staring blankly up at the ceiling while she got her breath back.

"Were you," Vivian began, then stopped, licked her lips, and started again. "Were you born with. Sex hardwired into. Your brain. Or something?"

Jules had never felt so brilliant in her life and probably never would again. She laughed. "I think I was hardwired for you, that's all."

She ran her fingertips over Vivian's softly rounded belly, which twitched beneath her touch. "Huh. Maybe you're wired for me too. What do you think?"

"I'm not capable of thinking." Vivian covered her eyes with a hand, a characteristic gesture that Jules was coming to recognize. Like Vivian just needed to shut out the world for a moment after sex while she got herself back together. "My God, I've never…"

This time, Jules didn't think her blush was due to arousal.

"Never what?"

Vivian peeped at her through two fingers. Glared, really. "Never… that," she said.

Jules's eyes went wide. "Nobody ever went down on you before?" Surely that couldn't be right. Three marriages, other lovers, and Vivian had *never*?

"Of course they did," she snapped, and Jules came back down to earth. Vivian grunted and sat up. "It just never worked before."

How should she respond to something like that with someone like Vivian? "Um…I'm sorry."

Vivian rolled her eyes, obviously finished with her little moment of full disclosure. "Lie down," she ordered.

Jules obeyed without even thinking about it. She blushed as Vivian looked her naked body over with gleaming eyes, then blushed harder as Vivian caressed her hip and side with one warm hand.

"Well now," she said softly, "it's your turn, isn't it?"

Just the tone of her voice made Jules's toes curl.

"You're so bold," Vivian murmured, "so insistent that I tell you what to do. What I like. That I should just come right out and say it."

"I mean—seems sort of in character for you—"

"Turnabout is fair play," she continued as if Jules hadn't spoken and kept moving her hand, stroking upward to play with Jules's nipple. "You've been thinking about this for a long time. Wanting this for a long time. Haven't you?"

"Yes," Jules whispered.

"I felt your eyes all over me on New Year's Eve. I was…surprised."

Jules wasn't sure if she should be elated, intrigued, humiliated, or what. She settled for saying, "Me too."

Vivian lifted an incredulous eyebrow.

"No, really. I saw you in that dress. And you were so… That's when it started."

"Yes?" Vivian plucked her nipple again. "When what started? What were you thinking about? What did you want, exactly?"

She smoothed her hand over Jules's belly, down into the hollow of Jules's hip, which Jules hardly noticed because Vivian's gaze was swallowing her whole.

"What did you want to do to me, Julia?"

"Jesus," she gasped, curling her toes again. She'd never been with anybody who could screw just with their voice, and it was—

"Slip off into a coat closet?" Vivian continued relentlessly. Her hand lay still on Jules's hip, no longer caressing her, no longer moving at all. "Or some quiet corner where you could have me up against a wall? Maybe get under my skirt in the back seat of the car?" She leaned in and inquired softly, "Did you like the dress? Would you have had me keep it on?"

"Oh God." Jules closed her eyes, unable to stop picturing it as she'd pictured it a thousand times before. Vivian in *that dress* with her head thrown back and her face flushed and her eyes closed, just as she'd been on this bed only a few moments ago.

"Or would you have brought me home? Taken me to my room and made me stay so quiet? On my back on the bed, covering my mouth with your hand, and me still in my gown because I couldn't wait?"

"Vivian," Jules sobbed, her hips twitching desperately, "Vivian, oh, my God…"

"My skirt up around my waist, legs spread, and my shoes still on, and me so ready for you, so wet and ready to come for you." Vivian's voice was as cool and as calm as it had been on the day Jules had met her, and Jules couldn't even open her eyes, her body was strung so tight. "Begging you to do whatever you wanted to me. Would you have fucked me in my dress, Julia?"

The word *fuck* on Vivian's lips here in bed made Jules arch her back and whine. Little lights were starting to go off behind her eyelids. "I-I—"

"Oh, Julia," Vivian breathed. "I would have let you."

"Vivian!" she shrieked and came without a single touch. She cried out more as she twitched and throbbed, knowing that Vivian was watching every second of it with avid, greedy eyes. That made her come all the harder, knowing she was on display for this woman she'd wanted so badly that she thought she'd die from it. Maybe she was dying right now; it felt like it, it felt—

She slumped back down on the bed panting, shaking so hard, she thought she was going to fly apart.

"Juh-juh-Jesus," she managed when she had her breath back. She opened her eyes.

Vivian looked unbearably smug. "That was lovely," she said, and stroked the inside of Jules's sticky thigh.

It made Jules moan again.

"So you were thinking about it. I can't wait to find out what else you've been thinking about. You obviously have a real imagination."

"M-me?" Jules croaked. "You're the one who came up with all that."

Vivian shrugged as if this was a minor detail, as if reading Jules's id was something she did whenever she felt like it. Oh God. Maybe it was.

"Would you really have let me?" Jules was hardly able to believe it. "On New Year's Eve?"

"Of course not," Vivian said, "but I thought you'd like the idea."

It figured. Jules took a deep breath and held out her arms. "Come here."

Vivian did. And as soon as her breasts were within striking distance, Jules leaned up and took a nipple in her mouth, sucking and biting. Vivian tossed her head back with a shocked cry.

"You love this," Jules said and tugged gently with her teeth.

Vivian made a sobbing sound.

"You think about this. You want me to do it."

Vivian didn't deny it. She couldn't deny it. "I can't, not again…"

Jules ignored her and suckled insistently while Vivian swayed and tried not to collapse on top of her.

"Yes, you can," Jules whispered, and switched breasts, feeling drunk, feeling like she was having a fever dream. She pushed, and Vivian lay down on her back, her eyes wild and glassy again. Jules bent down and kept at it, sucking and licking, while Vivian tossed her head back and forth against the mattress.

"You love this," Jules repeated.

"Yes," Vivian whimpered.

"So you tell me your fantasy," Jules said, already on fire with the desire for revenge as she slid her fingers back between Vivian's legs—not inside, just brushing lightly, gently. "Do you want this in the back seat of the car? Or in the copy room? Or do you want me to *fuck* you"—like it did to Jules, the word made Vivian moan—"on your desk with the doors closed until you get so wet it's all over your skirt and you have to bite your hand to keep from screaming?"

"I can't," Vivian said. "I can't," but she could and did. This time, Jules didn't let her cover her face with her hand.

Jules kissed her gently. "Are you okay?"

"I want to do this a lot," Vivian wheezed.

"Fantastic," Jules said, and didn't care that she was grinning like an idiot as she kissed Vivian once more.

# CHAPTER 52

Jules wasn't sure how she'd expected her birthday to begin, but it wasn't with a six thirty a.m. text from Ben telling her that Vivian's Audi was refusing to start. He'd have to take it to the shop.

Which meant Jules would have to arrange alternate transportation. She groaned to herself, sent Vivian a quick text apprising her of the situation, and got on the phone.

Just as she was in the middle of securing a Mercedes S-class from a car rental, Vivian texted:

*When will it get here?*

Jules asked customer service and answered Vivian:

*Around 8*

She could imagine Vivian's disgusted sigh and could picture her deciding she'd rather die before taking an Uber.

Vivian texted:

*Nothing else is available??*

*By the time I found something else, I might as well have ordered this one*

It was the sort of message she'd never have dared send to Vivian before, even though it was logical and true. But now things were different between them. Vivian wouldn't demand the impossible like she would have before.

Right?

Vivian replied:

*Fine. Let me know when it's on the way.*

Jules's chest lightened with instant, reflexive relief. Whew. Then she frowned. Reflexive relief, indeed. She'd gone back to being a lowly assistant in a flash, hadn't she? Freaking out about letting Vivian down. You probably weren't supposed to feel that way about interacting with your lover.

Especially when your lover was your boss.

"Ma'am? Are you there?" the voice on the phone prompted.

"Oh!" Jules shook herself out. "Sorry. Yes. That'll be fine. Thanks."

She finished the arrangements and looked at her phone. She texted Vivian again:

*I'll take the subway to work today*

Vivian replied:

*All right. See you soon.*

A few seconds later:

*Happy birthday.*

Something about the period after *birthday* made Jules snort with laughter. How festive. Maybe Vivian would show up carrying a bunch of black balloons too.

The amusement sustained her until she was on her way out the door. By the time she reached the subway, though, it had withered away. Instead, she kept going back to how it had felt to worry about disappointing Vivian professionally. Waiting for the hammer to fall the way it used to.

Vivian had told Jules in London that she wasn't like the other people who worked for her. That she wanted Jules to have faith in Vivian's feelings for her. At the time, Jules hadn't worried it would be a problem. But maybe Vivian had a point.

And that wasn't even counting the uncomfortable sensation Jules still felt in her gut whenever she thought about the *Modernity* article.

She rested her forehead against the subway pole she held. No, it wasn't hygienic, but sometimes you just needed a place to bang your head.

Happy birthday indeed.

Jules reached Koening at seven forty-five. Unfortunately, she just missed the elevator. She sighed, rocking back on her heels. At least she had some extra time, since Vivian would be late.

"Going up?"

Jules blinked and turned. Mark Tavio was standing behind her, smiling.

He was a tall, thin man with sharp cheekbones, a full head of white hair, and a love of bespoke charcoal suits. His gray eyes were known for lowering the temperature of any room by at least ten degrees. And he carried himself with the easy grace of a man who knew himself to be powerful.

Her heart jumped into her throat. The anxiety she'd felt about displeasing Vivian suddenly felt like nothing when she was faced with the chairman of Koening. Especially when that chairman had been gunning for Vivian for months.

Right now, though, Mr. Tavio's smile seemed benign as he looked down on her.

She summoned a bright smile of her own. "Good morning, Mr. Tavio."

"Good morning, Julia. It is Julia, isn't it?"

Mark Tavio knew her name? She nodded in surprise, but before either of them could speak again, the next elevator arrived. The door opened, and Mr. Tavio headed in. He saw Jules hovering and motioned her in with a chuckle. "Oh, come on. I'm not that scary."

Jules managed another smile and hurried in. The other people in the lobby didn't seem to share Mr. Tavio's assessment of himself, however, and hung back with anxious faces.

The doors closed. Mr. Tavio pressed the button for *Du Jour*'s floor, then his own. The elevator jolted into motion.

Her hands were getting sweaty on her purse strap.

"Things going well at *Du Jour*?" he asked, his gaze on the doors.

"Uh, yeah. I mean, yes." Jules kept smiling because he could at least see her reflection. "Busy as ever, but fine."

Mr. Tavio *hmm*'d. "And Vivian? What's she up to these days?"

Shit. She should have known. He was probing her for information. Who better to keep an eye on Vivian and then report back than her assistant?

"Just the usual." Her voice was shockingly steady, thank God. "You know, being fabulous and all that. The Charleston shoot looks like it's going to be great."

His chuckle was decidedly less friendly. "It better be, for what it's costing Koening."

Jules stared at the elevator buttons as they lit up floor by floor. Why was it taking so long?

"I've heard great things about you," Mr. Tavio said abruptly.

Her stomach flipped.

"Vivian puts her trust in you," Mr. Tavio continued. "Completely, from what I understand. That hasn't happened in all the time I've known her."

She said nothing.

He looked down at her, his white eyebrows drawing together as if he just didn't get the appeal. "Then again, these are unusual times for her. Times like this, you need all the friends you can get."

That gleam in his eye portended nothing good. Here it came. He was going to ask her to narc. Not that Jules would. Not that there was even anything to narc *on*. Vivian wasn't up to anything dastardly in the office. But Mark Tavio was paranoid and untrusting and undoubtedly thought a *lowly assistant* would jump at the chance to get in good with the chairman. Well, he was wrong. Never in a million years would Jules—

"I think Vivian could use one less friend," he said. "You're fired."

Silence, except for Jules's heartbeat in her ears.

He looked down at her with his subzero eyes.

"What?" she croaked.

"Don't worry," he said. "I'm sure you'll find something else soon, a smart girl like you. Get Vivian to help."

"Help?" Jules said. Her eyes widened. "Mr. Tavio, I don't understand."

"Not a lot to understand," he said. "I just fired you."

She stared at him. He stared right back.

"But," Jules whispered, "you can't just…"

"Oh yes, I can." Now his eyes were hard. "I think you'll find, Julia, that I can hire and fire anybody in this building, regardless of what Vivian Carlisle has to say about it. Make sure she understands that before you go. You can stay until the end of the business day. After that, you're done."

He looked back at the doors.

Jules couldn't respond. Surely none of this was real. Surely this wasn't actually happening.

They reached *Du Jour*'s floor. The doors slid open.

He glanced back at her, and this time his gaze was not without pity. "First-class flights to London cost a pretty penny, especially on the company card. Tell her to find a less expensive accessory next time."

Jules gaped at him.

He pressed the Door Open button and said, "I believe this is your stop. Goodbye."

Jules stood alone in the hallway that led to the *Du Jour* offices, dizzy and with a ringing in her ears. She might be about to pass out. Or maybe she was just having a terrible dream, imagining the whole thing.

But no. She hadn't imagined that: not the cold, hard purpose in Mark Tavio's eyes as he made Jules the first casualty in his war with Vivian Carlisle. Because that's what it was. After months of tension, he was taking aim at last. And Jules had been the first one caught in the crossfire.

What the hell was she going to do?

At some point, she made it to her desk—oh, but it wasn't hers anymore, was it?—and sat down, staring at nothing.

Suddenly, Allie's voice trilled out, "Oh, Jules! Happy birthday!"

Jules's head jerked around to see Allie hurrying forward, still in her coat and with her face flushed from the cold. She balanced a tray of La Colombe in one hand with a small bouquet of flowers in the other. A bouncy yellow balloon was tied to the slender green vase.

"Happy birthday," Allie repeated, setting the gift down on Jules's desk with an air of triumph. "I picked these up on the way. Do you like them? Whoops—let me just put Vivian's coffee out before I spill it—" She looked around, frowning. "Isn't she here yet?"

"Her car broke down," Jules heard herself say. "She won't be here until eight thirty or something."

Allie pouted. "I didn't have to rush this morning, then. I guess it was good to get the exercise."

"Yeah." Jules's entire body felt like it had been shot full of lidocaine: immobile and numb. She stared at the flowers. "Um. These are pretty."

Allie beamed. "Let me just find somewhere to put this coffee. Do you want Vivian's? I'll have to run out and get her another one anyway."

"No, thanks."

"Okay," Allie said, and added, "you look a little pale. You're not getting sick, are you?"

"Um."

Right then, Simon appeared. He grinned at Jules. "Good morning, birthday girl. How's the day treating you so far?"

Jules gasped, hid her face in her hands, and started to cry.

There was shocked silence for one moment, and then Allie asked, distraught, "Jules, what's wrong?"

"Nothing," Jules said, and then the sheer absurdity of saying that made her give a sharp, painful, hysterical little laugh. She hiccupped.

Simon offered her a tissue, grimacing.

She dashed it over her eyes and saw little mascara smudges coming away.

"Mark Tavio just fuh-fired me," she choked out. Jules had to be out of Koening forever by tonight, so what was the point in concealing the truth?

Allie gasped, "What?"

"H-he fired me—just now, in the elevator. I—"

And then Simon's hand, warm and firm, was on her shoulder. "Get up. We're going to my office. Allie, watch the phones and keep quiet."

"Okay," Allie whispered.

Jules obeyed the arm tugging her elbow. She covered her nose with another tissue and followed Simon down the hall, glad that not everybody had arrived at work yet.

He got them both into his office and shut the door, then eased Jules onto a high-legged stool. "Don't fall off. Now tell me what happened."

She related it all, every detail she could remember.

Simon's face went through a series of changes: first it was incredulous, then it darkened with anger, and finally it smoothed out in resignation. "It's been coming for a while. I didn't know it would come like this, though. And on your birthday. Christ, I'm sorry, Jules."

"Not your fault," she mumbled, staring down at her hands, limp and useless in her lap.

"No. But I think I can help." And now there was something else in his voice: the unidentifiable tone Jules had heard a few times before but never understood.

She looked back up at him, trying to blink her tears away.

Simon seated himself on another stool facing Jules. "I was going to tell you this over drinks this evening, but why don't we bump it up a few hours, hm?"

"Bump it up?" A cold weight sat in her chest, but Simon's familiar presence steadied her as if she'd put a hand on a solid surface before falling.

"Remember when I asked you about your birthday back in London?"

Jules sniffled as she nodded.

"And I said you should make the most of new opportunities?"

Another nod.

"Bet you thought it was a weird question, didn't you?"

She nodded for a third time. *Deep breaths, deep breaths.*

"Well, call me a sentimental fool, but I knew it was in March, and I figured the timing would work out. I didn't know it would work out *this* well, though."

"Simon…" Jules's voice wobbled.

He looked contrite. "Now's not the time for mysteries, is it? Let me make it simple: I'm offering you a new job."

She just stared at him.

He grinned and then stifled it as if realizing it wasn't quite appropriate. "That's what I was going to tell you tonight. A new job. Consider it a birthday gift to you from me, the newly liberated Simon Carvalho."

"Newly liberated?" Jules managed, shaking her head.

"I'm quitting," he said as casually as if this weren't the most shocking thing he'd ever said to her. "I'm leaving *Du Jour*. It's over, done, hey presto, *fini*. I'm gone. And I want you to come with me."

"*What?*" Jules rubbed her forehead. "What are you talking about?"

He sighed. "I wish we were at a bar. This sort of thing always goes over better when you have a drink in your hand. But here it is: for months, I've been in talks with Georg Schumann at Delton Wright."

Jules nodded. She'd met Georg at Christmas. And Helga. Couldn't forget Helga, his heinous hausfrau.

"As it happens, Georg has multiple interests beyond publishing. We got to talking at a party last year, and next thing you know we're swapping emails about my big idea."

"Your what? You have ideas?"

He glared.

"Sorry," Jules said quickly. "I didn't mean that the way it sounded. I meant…you've never mentioned any…"

"I couldn't. Not until everything was finalized. But it's happening, Jules. I'm starting a new venture that doesn't depend on Vivian Carlisle for its lifeblood, something that's going to let me call the shots and create something of my own."

"Create what?" Jules thought of Monique Leung, someone else who'd offered her a job recently. Maybe it was a new trend. "Are you starting your own fashion line?"

"Oh no. God knows there's enough of that out there. I don't want to make my own fashion, I want to *shape* fashion, change the landscape somehow. I want to…" Simon waved his hand vaguely. He began to pace the office. "Look, we all know about websites for discount designer stuff, right?"

"Sure," she said, more and more confused. "I use them."

"Everyone does. They're not good enough. That experience could be more." Simon looked at her, his hazel eyes sharp. "Vivian's trying to update the industry for the youth market. So am I. And they want the latest thing, but they're buried under student debt and grateful for entry-level jobs."

"I'm aware."

"It's not like *Sex and the City,* where everybody shoves all their stuff into an implausibly huge closet forever. They rotate and consign. Don't you?"

"Well, sure. There are online consignment shops too."

"Yeah, designer dumps where people buy and sell anything with a prestige label. You might as well be rifling through a clearance bin. And so many brick-and-mortar shops are just depressing. You might find what you want, but there's never this sense that you're having an *experience*, that you're being catered to or valued. You're embarrassed to tell people where you got that Salvatore Ferragamo bag."

That was fair enough. All of Jules's fellow assistants and other colleagues down the ladder did everything they could to save money on clothes and accessories. It was an open, dirty secret, where everyone swapped whispered tips on which secondhand store was having the biggest sale. Nobody liked to admit they couldn't afford new things.

"The youth market deserves better," he said, "and I'm going to give it to them."

Jules leaned forward. Simon's voice was rising with excitement, and he had a shine in his eyes she hadn't seen in a long time. "What are you going to do?"

"Start my own site. It's called Adrian & Jo."

"Adrian and…Jo?"

He shrugged. "Thank market research. Generation Z likes names—it makes a business sound like a person, somebody real they can trust. This tested well. The site's going to be a fully curated luxury experience where customers can buy designer goods at a discount, new or secondhand, and be able to tell their friends where they got it with a sense of pride, not shame."

"Curated? Like a museum?"

"Exactly. Would you be embarrassed to tell people that you got a Monet from the Louvre instead of right from his easel? Of course not."

"No, but Monet's been dead for—"

He glared.

"I get the metaphor," she conceded.

Simon held up his hands. "Picture a consumer saying this: 'Adrian & Jo is doing exhibits on Givenchy, Jason Wu, and Miu Miu this month. They're showcasing how each designer focused on autumnal influences last season, and when you log on you get to talk to a curator.'"

"A what?"

He grinned. "That's what we're calling chat support. You know when you go to a shopping site and you get those *want some help?* text boxes? That, but more upmarket. You create an account, log in, and you can get matched with a dedicated fashion professional who walks you through creating outfits you've never thought of before and that nobody else is going to have. Someone who curates your experience."

"'Dedicated fashion professional' means…"

"Interns, obviously. It won't be rocket science." He looked at Jules. "Where would you rather shop? That or the clearance bin?"

"Of course I'd rather—"

"I know. I can change the game, Jules. Do you know how many high-end designers burn excess inventory every year rather than let the 'wrong' clientele have it at a discount? They'll *want* to show up on this site—they won't take it for granted that people will buy whatever crap that shows up just because it has a label. They'll want to be on the front page, the top designers list, all that. We'll have a VIP mailing list for special clients who want early access to new items. And that's another thing: we don't call them customers. They're clients."

"I get the picture. How do I fit into it? I don't have a background in web design or business."

He pooh-poohed that with a shrug. "The whole point of entry-level is that you'd go up from there."

She took a deep breath and looked up at the ceiling. This was way too much to take in after the way her day had started. *Think*. "It's really exciting, Simon, but you're a creative director, not—"

He shook his head. "I've been Vivian's right-hand man for more years than I care to count. I've seen every aspect of this industry. Trust me on this one: I can pull off a start-up."

"But Vivian…" Jules whispered, imagining her face when she got the news. He'd been her go-to guy forever, and for him to waltz out the door on the same day Jules was fired…

"If I wait for Vivian to give me the go-ahead, I'll be stuck here forever. I'm ready to move on. She's not the only one with vision." He took a deep breath. "I won't lie to you. This is a huge undertaking, and it's risky. Bringing people together, mixing new blood with established talent, trying to figure out what sells as fast as possible. But Georg wants it. And he's making sure that Vincent Wright wants it too."

Vincent Wright. The CEO from the Boxing Day luncheon who was into Broadway musicals. This had to be a dream.

"We've got more venture capital from Delton Wright, full backing." He leaned forward. "I want you to be a part of it too. I've seen your work ethic; I've seen how fast you learn. As soon as I knew it was going to come together, I thought of you."

That sounded more polite than plausible, but he did appear sincere. "Thanks."

"I can't promise you the moon or stars. Not yet. But I need an assistant too. Someone who knows what she's doing, who knows the ropes beyond getting coffee and running menial errands—someone who can help me get this thing off the ground." His face was alight with enthusiasm. "I mean it. Inside a year or two, you can move up into anything you want, probably. Want to be in acquisitions? Head into management? Get into public relations? This is the time to do it."

*I want to write*, she wanted to say. Then her snide inner voice reminded her: *Don't quit your day job.* "I—"

"I know it's a lot to take in, especially after what Mark just pulled. But, Jules—now you've got no reason to say no. It's like destiny, if I believed in destiny. Fate. Karma. Kismet!"

"I guess so. Simon, I really should talk to Vivian first."

He sat back with a heavy sigh. "How did I know you'd say that?"

"I have to," she protested. "Mr. Tavio fired me. I have to talk to her about that at least."

"I know," he said. "And I know you feel like you owe her something too. You don't. She owes *you*. She owes you big time for everything you've done for her. And it's time for her to pay you back."

"It's not like that!" Why was her stomach cramping up?

"Of course it is," he said. "It always is. Besides"—he regarded Jules seriously—"this isn't the last move Mark will make, Jules. He's out for her blood, and he's the chairman of the company. He will beat her eventually."

"No," she whispered.

"Yes. Believe me, I don't like it either. I care about Vivian too."

It didn't sound like it. Jules gave him a dubious look.

"I do," he said firmly. "She's remarkable. An icon. But she's also taken everything I've had to give for years. It's finally time for me to look out for myself—you should do the same."

"I—"

"Mark firing you is like sending up a great big firecracker, and everybody will know what it means. Just picture rats fleeing a sinking ship. That's what it's going to be like around here."

"No," Jules repeated, wondering if she was going to cry again. All the denials in the world wouldn't change the fact that Simon was only speaking the truth.

Mark Tavio had somehow found a crack in Vivian's defenses. She was under fire, and nobody would want to weather it with her. Except for Jules, who'd already been thrown off the battlefield without being given the choice.

"Keisha's coming too." He interrupted Jules's train of thought.

"K-Keisha?"

"I sounded her out not too long after I lured her from *Elle*. I've always liked her. I'm getting together a good team, her and other people from all over the business. Come on, Jules. You owe me." He pointed his index finger at her nose. "For *Salon*. There's no reason not to pay me back now."

"I know. I-it's just a lot to, to—"

"To take in. Look. I don't want to kick you while you're down. This was supposed to be an exciting opportunity, not something you feel forced into because you don't have a job anymore." He grimaced.

"Simon, I appreciate it," she said at once. She had to make that clear. "I really do."

"Think about it and answer me soon. Within the next day or two. I need to know."

Jules relaxed. A day or two. That would give her time to talk to Vivian. Time to think. "I promise."

His eyes twinkled. "I hope you say yes. You and me, kid. Let's get the band back together and blow this popsicle stand."

She managed a weak smile. "Well—"

The door to Simon's office slammed open with such force that both of them jumped.

Jules, her nerves run ragged, cried out. And she felt no calmer when she saw Vivian Carlisle barreling into the room still wearing her coat and clutching her bag, her face tight and glowing with a fury Jules had never seen before.

Out of the corner of her eye, Jules saw Simon cringe.

Vivian didn't even seem to notice him. Her gaze was so fierce that Jules wondered if it might not actually bore all the way through her head and into the wall behind.

"You're, um, early," Jules said uselessly. "I guess the rental car—"

Breathing quickly, Vivian said, "Allie just told me, though I'm sure she's mistaken, that you said Mark Tavio fired you this morning. There was something about an elevator."

Jules swallowed, shivered, and nodded.

Vivian took a deep breath and held her shoulders up straight, quivering as though she might explode on the spot.

"Vivian," Jules whispered with no idea of what she'd say next. She wrung her hands.

"Don't worry." Her usually imperious voice sounded strangled.

Jules felt a tug deep in her gut, deep in her heart, and suddenly wanted more than anything to run to Vivian and wrap her arms around her, though who would be comforting whom?

"Don't worry," Vivian repeated. "I'll take care of it. He can't do this. You're not going anywhere."

"Don't be so sure," Simon said.

Jules whipped her head around. "Simon," she gasped because, oh no—

Vivian shook herself as if she'd just noticed Simon. "What are you talking about?"

"Simon!" Jules repeated, on the verge of panicking.

"It's okay," he said, never breaking eye contact with Vivian. "Jules, will you please leave? I need to talk to Vivian alone."

"Simon, wait. Let me talk to her first—"

"Vivian," Simon said, "I insist. Trust me."

"Vivian—" Jules began.

"Julia, please leave," Vivian said.

Jules froze.

Now Vivian was looking at Simon with that same deadly focus, as if she'd already figured out what he was going to say. Maybe she had.

"We'll talk in a few minutes," she finished.

And…that was that. There was no arguing with Vivian when she used that tone of voice. Jules slunk out of Simon's office, feeling as pathetic and inconsequential than she had on her first day as an intern. No, more pathetic. At least she'd had a job then.

"Jules?" Allie whispered when Jules returned to their desks. The phone rang, and she jumped to answer it. "Vivian Carlisle's office…"

Allie was going to be the only one doing this after today, Jules realized as she sat heavily in her chair. Allie Lake, holding down the fort as an intern. Would Mr. Tavio even let Vivian hire a real assistant again? Would he degrade Vivian as much as possible in the name of cutting costs before moving in for the kill?

She grabbed her purse and headed for the ladies' room, where she did her best to fix her ruined makeup. When she returned, she was just in time to hear the click of Allie's phone going back into the receiver.

"Jules?"

She sighed as she headed over to Allie's desk. Her shoes, fringed ankle boots today, pinched her toes. She usually didn't notice things like that anymore. "All right, Allie. Mr. Tavio says I have to be out of here by the end of the business day, and I can't come back."

Allie's eyes widened with horror. "But what about two weeks' notice?"

"That doesn't apply when you're firing people." Jules pushed her hair out of her face, which was when she realized that her hands were trembling. She tried to stop them—she couldn't quite.

"Oh no," Allie gasped. "Then…then—"

"So you have to do all this yourself," Jules confirmed. "I'm sorry. I don't even know if he'll let Vivian hire another assistant right away."

Allie went pale.

"Listen, I'll do my best." Jules swallowed. "If you can handle the phones, I'll throw together a couple of lists for you before I leave. Stuff you need to know, like phone numbers, the people you should always try to speak to, and Vivian's favorite restaurants and florists—"

"Jules…"

"Oh, and that big surprise thing she's planning, the one where we're hiring—where *she's* hiring Hélène Darroze. I still don't know what's up with that, but I guess that doesn't matter. I'll give you all that info too." No way would Allie be able to keep up with a big project like that on her own.

"Jules."

"And-and even when I'm gone, you can call me if you have questions, you can—"

"Jules!" To Jules's surprise, Allie slipped one arm around her shoulders in a half hug. She didn't look panicky, not right now: the opposite, in fact, like she was the one trying to calm Jules down. "It's okay. We'll work it out. We'll manage." She patted Jules's shoulder.

*No, you won't*, Jules wanted to say. *Nobody can do what I do. I'm indispensable.*

But she wasn't. Nobody was.

Perhaps even Allie figured out what she was thinking because she added quickly, "But I will call you, if you don't mind. I'm sure I'll need to. There's still so much I don't know yet."

"Right." Jules had to restrain herself from rubbing her eyes because she'd just reapplied all her mascara and she wasn't about to do it again.

Allie lowered her voice. "What'll you do now?"

"I don't know." She thought about Simon's job offer along with Vivian's furious insistence that Jules could stay on somehow, even when she had to know that wouldn't work. "Not yet."

"Julia."

Allie immediately jerked her hand from Jules's shoulders.

Vivian was heading toward them. Her face was pale but calm, and Jules couldn't read any particular emotion in her eyes anymore.

"Go home," she told Jules, her voice flat.

Jules stared at her. "What?"

"I said go home." Vivian slipped out of her coat and handed it to Allie, who scrambled over to the closet to put it away. Vivian took the opportunity to murmur, "It's for the best, before word spreads. I'll tell Allie to keep her mouth shut, and I'll call you as soon as I can. I have to speak with Simon some more anyway."

"Oh," Jules whispered. "Okay."

For just a moment, regret and anger flared in Vivian's eyes again. She looked as if she were about to speak. Then Allie clattered back to her desk, and the moment was lost.

Vivian jerked her head toward the door. "Go on."

Jules looked at all the stuff on her desk. "I have to pack this up first." Her shoulders slumped at the thought.

"I'll do it," Allie said quickly. "I'll make sure it gets to you. Don't worry."

That meant Jules would be lucky if her things didn't end up in Antarctica, but she couldn't even bring herself to care about that. She managed a smile for Allie as she headed to the closet to fetch her own coat and bag, maybe—probably—for the last time. "Thanks, Allie. I'll make that list from home. Feel free to give me a call."

Allie's chin wobbled. She needed not to start crying in front of Vivian, who looked about five seconds away from taking out her rage on the nearest available object.

Luckily, Allie managed a weak little wave, and Jules headed for the elevators, glad when she didn't run into anybody who seemed to know what had happened.

Home. She was heading straight home, eating something indulgent, and opening a bottle of wine. Why not? It was her birthday. Might as well celebrate.

## CHAPTER 53

First step: put on yoga pants and fuzzy socks. Second step: pour the wine. Third step: flop on the couch.

Jules accomplished all three in short order and turned on the TV, determined to revel in the freedom to be ratty and lazy. She couldn't remember the last time she'd done this. Vivian was surprisingly decent about letting her have the odd Saturday or Sunday to herself, but she'd broken that policy often enough that Jules was always mentally ready to jump at a moment's notice and complete the newest errand.

Not today. Nobody was going to ask her to do anything. Jules could lie here in her yoga pants, slightly buzzed and watching Hulu, because she had no job and nothing to do.

She was going to sit around and be miserable for a day. She'd earned that much. She watched TV until noon, got up, realized she had nothing in the fridge, and ordered Thai.

It was one o'clock by the time she finished lunch and decided that a nap was immediately in order because being unconscious was definitely preferable to the alternative right now. She conked out on the couch with a half-empty container of pad thai on the coffee table.

Jules woke to the insistent ringing of her phone, which she'd left in her bag, which she'd left on the kitchen counter. She banged her shin on the coffee table while trying to get to it but had managed to stop cursing by the time she answered.

*Vivian.*

Her heart began to pound. "Hello?"

"Are you at home?"

"Well, yeah." Where else would she be?

"Do you have plans tonight?"

Cocktails with Simon were probably off. "Nope."

"Fine. I'll stop by after work."

Jules's eyes bugged out. She looked at the wreck of her apartment. It had been ages since she'd cleaned. "You're coming *here*?"

"Isn't that what I said?" Vivian sounded irritable.

"How do you know my address?"

"You still have an HR file, don't you? It'll be easiest if I drop by after work. And we have a lot to discuss."

*We have a lot to discuss.* It was uncomfortably close to *We need to talk.* Ominous.

She shuddered. "I guess Simon told you about his new venture."

"Yes," Vivian said curtly. "We'll talk about it later. Look for me around seven thirty."

"Oh. Okay. Call me if—"

"I will." Vivian disconnected.

Jules looked around her apartment again, at the shelves that badly needed dusting, at the rugs begging for the touch of a vacuum.

Great. She'd always wanted to spend her birthday cleaning house. This was the worst day ever.

It was three thirty now, though, so she had a decent lead time. Jules sighed, rolled up her sweatshirt sleeves, and got to work.

Her parents called at five. Jules absolutely, positively couldn't handle that conversation, so she listened to their birthday greetings via voicemail and tried not to cry again.

Midway through scouring the bathtub, she thought, *This isn't too bad.* Cleaning kept her mind off other things like, say, the future. Or maybe that was just the bleach killing her brain cells. Either way, by the time seven p.m. rolled around, Jules's apartment was cleaner than it had been in months.

Then it was her turn. She scrubbed off her sweat in the shower. She'd spent a lot of time in this shower thinking about Vivian, first stewing over her standards and demands. Then it turned into sympathy, confusion, longing, and by their second time in London, it was impossible to figure out which feelings were which. Just lately it had been relentless fantasizing about Vivian being as naked as Jules was under the spray.

She loved those fantasies. She loved the reality even more. Whether it was Vivian naked or clothed, Vivian being infuriating or funny or haughty or sexy, Vivian giving Jules an arch look while Jules rubbed her feet. Pushing her leftover Christmas pudding toward Jules and acting like it was no big deal. Jules loved…

*I love…*

With a shriek, Jules threw her loofah sponge against the tile wall. It bounced off harmlessly.

She put her head against the wall, pressed her lips together. *Don't break down now. She'll be here soon.*

By the time she'd collected herself and put on clean leggings and a long-sleeved T-shirt, it was seven twenty. She settled in to wait.

Vivian didn't disappoint. At seven twenty-nine, Jules's doorbell buzzed, and at seven thirty on the dot, Vivian had climbed the stairs and was standing in the doorway.

"Uh, c'mon in." She stood to the side. "Hi."

"Mm," Vivian said as she entered, looking around the apartment.

Jules's insides tightened up. Vivian lived in a house right out of a showroom. Not to mention…

Oh God. She was looking at the accent wall with its geometric colored pattern—including lots of shapes painted a buttery yellow. Yellow, the color she hated most and which Jules had never thought Vivian would actually see here. Ever since they'd started up, there hadn't even been the slightest suggestion of Vivian coming to Jules's place.

No comment was forthcoming on the accent wall. She continued her silent survey of the apartment and then turned back to Jules herself.

She looked exhausted and unhappy. She'd probably had a worse day than Jules, who at least had been able to sit on her ass and watch TV for a few hours. They regarded each other for a long moment.

"Happy birthday to me," Jules said brightly.

A bitter smile twisted Vivian's mouth, and Jules wished she hadn't joked at a time like this.

"No kidding." Vivian inclined her head toward the couch. "Let's sit."

"Of course," Jules said, also regretting her poor manners. It had been a while since she'd had company. "You, um, want something to drink?"

"No." Vivian seated herself on one end of the sofa.

Jules took the other end, tucking one knee under herself so she could face her.

Vivian, however, kept both feet firmly on the floor and appeared fascinated by her lap.

Jules wanted a hug. Or a kiss. Or something comforting like that. That didn't seem to be what Vivian wanted right now. Jules waited.

"I can get your job back," Vivian said.

Jules's skin prickled all over. Of everything she'd been expecting, that offer hadn't been on the list. Only one thing made it possible, and it was unthinkable.

She leaned forward urgently. "I don't want you to ask Mark for anything."

No more calling him "Mr. Tavio" from now on, that was for sure.

Vivian shook her head. "You let me handle that."

"No, seriously—" Jules twisted her hands in her lap.

"Leave Mark Tavio to me." Vivian's voice brooked no opposition. "I know what it'll take."

So did Jules. It would mean Vivian asking Mark to let Jules return, humbling herself before him. What else would do it? Hell, he might have been anticipating that when he fired Jules.

And if he hadn't anticipated it, that would be even worse. Vivian would never do such a thing for an ordinary assistant. It would be enough to make him ask questions—along with everyone else.

"I can do it, Julia." She finally looked at Jules. "I'll make it happen. I'll give that to you." On the last sentence, her voice shook.

The hair on the back of Jules's neck stood up. *I'll give that to you.*

Vivian was offering to debase herself, show her underbelly to a foe to protect Jules. She'd give her something way more important and far more painful than a call to an editor at *Modernity*. And she knew it; the grim resolve in her eyes said so.

All day, Jules had been miserable that she'd lost her job. But now that she had it within reach again—even if the victory was tainted—it didn't seem half as desirable. The cost was far too high for them both.

Vivian lifted her chin, a lofty gesture that didn't hide the flash of pain in her eyes. "I'm not hearing an instant yes."

There was that awful stomach cramp again. "I-I need a second to think about it. Hey, um…why don't you have a look around my place while I think? I spent hours cleaning it up for you."

For a second, Vivian appeared mystified. Professional cleaners came to her house weekly. She'd probably forgotten a layperson could vacuum.

"It won't take you long," Jules said dryly.

"Well…" Vivian looked around. "I can't deny I've been curious."

Jules brightened at that. "Really?"

"Of course." Vivian stood. "I wanted to know if your décor is like your clothes."

Jules couldn't help glancing at the overstuffed ottoman that had belonged to her grandmother. It was covered in slightly worn pale green velvet with cream-colored tassels. She loved it, but she couldn't imagine anything less Vivian's style. "Boho?"

"Well, a *little* more interesting than that." Vivian began to wander the apartment, pausing at the IKEA bookshelves to scrutinize Jules's book collection before moving to the windows. Instead of taking in the view, though, she touched the rust-colored curtains, taking the edge of one between her fingers and her thumb.

"I made those," Jules blurted out.

Vivian looked back at her with wide eyes. Did she think Jules could afford to drop the money on overpriced curtains at Pottery Barn? She said, "They're…very nice. I like the, um"—she looked at the curtains again—"even stitching. Anyway, keep thinking while I look around your home." She left the room.

Jules held back a sigh. Vivian was right, though. That stitching was super even. Jules had spent hours on it.

She didn't like making mistakes. Better to get it right the first time, especially now.

Maybe Vivian thought she could handle Mark Tavio, but she wasn't thinking it through. She couldn't be. Otherwise she'd have come to the same conclusion Jules had. Vivian asking for Jules's job? It would be a huge red flag, begging him to look below the surface to see what was going on. Just what they didn't need.

It was a great excuse. Practical, logical. It wouldn't hurt Vivian's feelings. Jules could say it was why she wasn't coming back.

Because she wasn't coming back. The knowledge crackled up and down the back of her spine. In spite of everything that had happened today, she hadn't known that for sure until right now. Her time at *Du Jour* was done.

Her head spun. How to tell Vivian she was taking the job Simon had offered? That was a whole new conundrum. Vivian obviously hadn't seen Simon's departure coming either. Two knives in her back within minutes of each other. And now Jules was aiming a third.

No. It wasn't like that. Jules wrung her hands again. This professional move could be a great thing for her, yes. It could be great for their relationship too. They could make this work.

They had to. Because Jules loved…

She put a hand over her heart and clutched the thick material of her sweatshirt.

"Are you all right?"

She looked up to see that Vivian had returned and was frowning in concern. Before she could help herself, she reached out imploringly.

Looking no less concerned, Vivian came forward and took Jules's hands in her own. When Jules tugged, she sat back down on the couch and gasped when Jules cradled her face and kissed her forehead, hard. At that, she went very still.

When Jules pulled away, still holding her face, Vivian said, "You're not coming back."

The words hurt like a punch to the gut, but Jules's hands stayed where they were and she kept looking into Vivian's eyes.

Vivian's face was pale, but she held her lips in a steady line, her expression all too familiar: that of someone used to being disappointed and ready to soldier on anyway.

"You were right before," Jules sighed. "We can't keep doing both—our jobs and being together. I just didn't want to admit it."

"And now you have a backup," Vivian said bitterly. "How convenient."

Jules dropped her hands and stared at her. "Oh, come on."

"'Come on' what?"

Jules reached for her again, but Vivian waved her hands away. "If you're leaving, why won't you let me help you find something? There's nothing wrong with that."

*There's something wrong with that*, Jules's inner voice muttered, just like when she'd gotten the email from *Modernity*. Again, it made no sense, and if she didn't have a job offer on the hop already, she might have felt differently.

She had the offer, though. And it meant she wasn't beholden to her lover—however well Vivian meant—for her livelihood.

"It's a job," she said. "It seems like a good one. The sort of job you'd encourage me to take, I'd think. Uh, at least it's not in London. Ha, ha."

The joke *definitely* didn't land. Damn.

"No," Vivian said coldly. "It's right here in New York, courtesy of Simon Carvalho. Right after he…" She trailed off.

"After he bailed on you too," Jules said.

Vivian crossed her arms, but it was more like she was hugging herself than being standoffish.

"I'm sorry about that," Jules muttered. "About all of this happening."

Vivian glared. "You're sorry? Out of all the people who should be *sorry*—" She spat out the final word, then turned to gaze off into the distance.

Jules had no idea what to say. None. Even now.

"I should have seen it coming," Vivian said. "Simon. I should have seen it."

"You've been worrying about other stuff," Jules said feebly.

"It must have been going on in January, when we had lunch with Vincent and Georg and Helga. Simon told me Delton Wright had a hand in it. It would have been in the works." She clenched her hands. "And of course they didn't say anything. Why would they? Just because Simon was my—" She sounded like she was choking when she cut herself off.

*Right-hand man. Friend. Whatever you think about a guy who's been at your side for years.* Aloud, Jules asked, "Do you not want me to work for him? Do you want to cut your ties with him completely?"

She had no idea what she'd do if Vivian said yes. She didn't have any other non-London-based prospects lined up, and she didn't want Vivian to find her a job. But how could she work somewhere that would make Vivian resent her?

Luckily for them both, Vivian said, "No. Well, I *want* to, but it wouldn't be wise. I doubt he's outlived his usefulness just yet."

The words would have sent a chill down Jules's spine, except that Vivian seemed to be trying to convince herself, retreating behind a cold wall of practicality to hide the pain of betrayal.

Vivian kept talking. "He proved that today. At least he's got a place for you. He knows your worth. And he's right: it's time I did something for you."

Jules sat up and glared. "He said that?"

"He said a lot of things." Vivian looked more tired than ever. "Things he's apparently been waiting to say for a long time."

"Oh God, Vivian."

She waved her hand. "I can handle it, Julia. I'm still able to look at myself in the mirror, no matter what Simon Carvalho says."

Jules managed a smile.

"The irony might kill me, though. Telling me I ought to *do something* to help you when you won't let me. I wanted to wring his neck."

Jules stopped smiling. "Um…"

"Is this what I can do?" When Vivian looked into Jules's eyes, she appeared bewildered. Her eyebrows drew together. "Just turn you over to him and hope for the best?"

Part of Jules wanted to argue that she wasn't a volleyball for Simon and Vivian to knock back and forth. Most of her, though, heard what Vivian was really saying: *I'll give you up to make you happy.*

"Hey." Jules kept her voice firm when it wanted to shake with emotion. "I'm still going to be with you. I want that more than anything. I—"

*Love you.* The words stuck on her tongue. It wasn't the time. Vivian would say she was just being sentimental, that it was too early for that. Worst of all, she wouldn't say it in return.

Vivian took Jules's chin between two of her fingers. She leaned in and pressed her lips to Jules's.

Maybe it was meant to be comforting. It didn't work out that way. It ended with Vivian shoving her hands into Jules's hair while Jules put her hand on Vivian's thigh, fighting not to push up her skirt right away.

When they parted, Vivian whispered against Jules's mouth, "Will you do one last professional thing for me?"

"What?"

"Text Ben and tell him to stop circling your block. I'll find my own way home later."

Jules looked at Vivian, her mouth agape. "But won't he think that's weird? Like…he'll wonder…"

"I don't care." Vivian's voice was low and deadly now. "You're worried about me in the office? You're worried about Mark Tavio? Watch and learn."

Sure. Yeah. Okay. Jules's phone was on the coffee table. She reached for it and began to type with shaking thumbs while Vivian watched.

*Hi Ben, Vivian says not to wait for her*

After another moment's thought, she added a line.

*It's been great working with you btw* ☺

At the emoji, Vivian rolled her eyes but did not protest. Hey, it couldn't hurt to be diplomatic.

After a moment, the reply came.

*Sure thing. I'm sorry about what happened. Wishing you the best*

She looked at the last sentence in some confusion. That sounded pretty final. Now that she thought of it, Ben could easily have asked her out. He'd obviously been interested, they weren't working together anymore, and as far as she knew, he wasn't dating anyone.

Except, of course, he'd just realized exactly why Vivian was here and knew the claim was staked.

That same knowledge shimmered in Vivian's eyes, her expression possessive and satisfied. She put her hand on Jules's knee; it seemed to scorch through her leggings.

"You're still going to be here, hmm?" she asked.

Jules set her phone down and drew Vivian in closer. "That's what I said."

In answer, Vivian bent down and nuzzled against one of Jules's breasts through her sweatshirt.

"God!" Jules arched up as the ache, familiar now, began between her thighs.

"Let's move to your bedroom." She kissed Jules's throat. "I want to end this god-awful day on a high note."

"You and me both," she replied fervently.

Minutes later, they lay on Jules's lumpy mattress, moving together while the springs creaked.

"Oh, please," Jules moaned as they rocked on each other's fingers, dipping down, driving higher. "Yes, Vivian."

"Yes," Vivian muttered, low and ardent, into Jules's neck. "Yes. More."

More. Always more, for the both of them. Could *more* ever turn into *enough*?

*Doesn't seem likely.* Jules drew Vivian even more tightly into her arms.

# CHAPTER 54

By rights, the sex should have knocked them both out for hours. Jules's rest was uneasy, though, and when she woke at six, she saw that Vivian was awake too, thumbs flying over her phone.

"Who're you texting?" she mumbled.

"It's an email." Vivian put her phone down without further clarification.

"You can't sleep either?"

"What do you expect? This mattress feels older than both of us combined." She shifted and winced. "My back hurts."

Jules sat up with a grunt. She pushed a lock of hair out of her face and looked at Vivian, at her blue eyes and messy blonde hair right here in Jules's bed. And in spite of the complaints, Jules's face split into a grin.

"Since we're both up, I'll make us some coffee," she offered. "It's not as good as La Colombe, but I can bring you a cup in bed."

Vivian regarded her, and sudden hunger flashed in her eyes. She reached out, cupped Jules's face, and pulled her in for a kiss.

Her mouth was soft and warm, and Jules hummed softly when they parted. "Good morning to you too."

"Forget the coffee," Vivian said. "We can get some on the way."

"Huh?" Jules looked at the clock. Yep, it was 6:02 a.m., all right. "Where are we going?"

"I don't know. You choose. I want to go somewhere, I want to move. I can't keep still. I want to go somewhere with you."

The way Vivian's gaze kept darting around the bedroom told the story too. She didn't look scared exactly, more like someone who was champing at the bit. Strange for someone who so often sat in icy stillness, letting the world orbit around her.

But Vivian's mind never stopped moving, and today her body seemed to be following suit. If it weren't six in the morning, Jules would be able to relate.

Her sluggish mind came up with exactly one solution, inspiration like a bolt from the blue: "What do you think of Domino Park?"

---

Plumes of fog curled up behind Jules, and the first rays of sunrise limned their edges. In the background rose the outline of the massive syrup tanks that belonged to the old Domino Sugar factory.

This early in the morning, Jules and Vivian were alone except for the occasional runner who paid them no mind. It was just past seven. They'd taken an Uber here with a La Colombe stop on the way, and now steam curled from their coffee cups.

They meandered down the paths in silence for a while, Jules in comfy sweats, Vivian in yesterday's clothes. It was probably sloppier than either of them had looked in public for years, even if a lot was hidden beneath their coats.

The thought made Jules grin, and she drifted a smidgen closer to Vivian as they walked, almost enough to jostle her shoulder.

"Feeling better now?" she asked.

"Yes." Vivian looked around. "I went to a party here once, but I didn't pay much attention to the place."

"It's beautiful," Jules said. "I wish it wasn't so far away. I appreciate you agreeing to come out here."

The unintentional choice of words landed between them, and Jules couldn't help a grimace.

"Well, if we don't come out here, we'll have to do it somewhere else," Vivian said dryly.

"You know what I meant." Jules dared to link her arm through Vivian's, hoping to reassure her for what she said next. "I think we should wait a while for that."

Thankfully, Vivian didn't seem offended. In fact, she said, "Of course we should" in her familiar don't-state-the-obvious tone.

It would do no good to ask how long they should wait; even Vivian wouldn't know the answer. Wait until after the divorce was finalized, certainly. After Vivian's job was secure, probably. After the baby was born, possibly. Too many variables. It made Jules's head hurt.

And if today was the first day of the rest of their lives, she didn't want to spend it with aching temples, especially not when a familiar bench came into view.

"Want to sit down?" She nodded at the bench. "Right there."

Something in Jules's voice clearly caught Vivian's attention. As they sat on the bench, Vivian asked, "What's so special about 'right there'?"

*Right there* was where Jules had seen two women holding hands. She'd dreamed of doing the same thing with Vivian and told herself that was ridiculous, that it would never happen.

Jules looked toward the East River's smooth expanse, at the shining resoluteness of Manhattan's skyscrapers on the other side. They were pink and gold in the dawn. Her breath clouded the air as she exhaled.

She took out her phone. "Here."

Then she showed Vivian the photo she'd taken of Bomber Jacket and Pink Lipstick—it seemed like a lifetime ago. In spite of the cold, her face warmed as she looked at their smiles, the way they were unapologetically themselves.

"I was walking out here trying to figure out what I'd write for *Salon*," she said. "I saw them sitting here, and it started to click. They're..." She didn't have the words, so she waved the phone uselessly.

Vivian took the phone,, her lips pursed in thought. After a moment, she said, "Yes. I get it."

If Vivian said she got it, she *got* it, but Jules kept talking anyway. "They seemed so happy, just sitting there holding hands. They really got me thinking about my topic, about..."

Vivian looked at her, clearly waiting.

"About you," Jules admitted. Even now, confession was embarrassing. "I was thinking about what it would be like to be here with you. And here we are."

"Don't get sentimental on me, Julia."

But then she took Jules's hand. Her thumb rubbed over the knuckles. The morning light softened her eyes.

"I wouldn't dream of it," Jules whispered. The sudden warmth in her chest was enough to banish the cold, no matter what she wore. Together, their hands came to rest against the curve of Vivian's belly.

"Good." Vivian squeezed Jules's hand. "That's the last thing I need."

"I think we've already got what we need."

"Do we? This isn't going to be easy." Vivian's tone left no room for argument. "This is going to be the furthest thing from easy."

"I know," Jules said. "I'm ready if you are."

Though upon reflection, that might not be totally true. As she leaned forward, Jules wondered if she'd ever be ready for Vivian Carlisle.

*I sure hope not.* She pressed her lips gently to Vivian's in the full glow of sunrise.

**END BOOK ONE**
**The Story Continues In:**
**ABOVE ALL THINGS**

# OTHER BOOKS FROM YLVA PUBLISHING

www.ylva-publishing.com

## THE X INGREDIENT
**Roslyn Sinclair**

ISBN: 978-3-96324-271-7
Length: 285 pages (103,000 words)

Top Atlanta lawyer, icy Diana Parker, is driven and ruthless, and stuck in a failing marriage. Her new assistant, Laurie, seems all wrong for the job. Yet something seems to be pulling them into a secret, thrilling dance that's far too dangerous for a boss and employee.

How can they resist the irresistible?

*A smart, sexy lesbian romance about daring to face the truth about who you are.*

## THE BRUTAL TRUTH
**Lee Winter**

ISBN: 978-3-95533-898-5
Length: 339 pages (108,000 words)

Aussie crime reporter Maddie Grey is out of her depth in New York and secretly drawn to her twice-married, powerful media mogul boss, Elena Bartell, who eats failing newspapers for breakfast. As work takes them to Australia, Maddie is goaded into a brief bet—that they will say only the truth to each other. It backfires catastrophically. A lesbian romance about the lies we tell ourselves.

## WRONG NUMBER, RIGHT WOMAN
### Jae

ISBN: 978-3-96324-401-8
Length: 370 pages (116,000 words)

Shy Denny has a simple life as a cashier who helps raise her niece. Then she gets a wrong-number text from a stranger named Eliza, asking her for dating advice.

Eliza, the queen of disastrous first dates, finds an instant connection with Denny that makes her question everything…like just how straight she really is.

*A slow-burn lesbian romance with likable characters and low angst.*

## THE MUSIC AND THE MIRROR
### Lola Keeley

ISBN: 978-3-96324-014-0
Length: 311 pages (120,000 words)

Anna is the newest member of an elite ballet company. Her first class almost ruins her career before it begins. She must face down jealousy, sabotage, and injury to pour everything into opening night and prove she has what it takes. In the process, Anna discovers that she and the daring, beautiful Victoria have a lot more than ballet in common.

*This age-gap, workplace lesbian romance is a sizzling, award-winning page-turner, whether you're into ballet or not.*

# ABOUT ROSLYN SINCLAIR

Roslyn Sinclair was born in the southern USA, but she's now enjoying the Northeast and its beautiful fall weather—not so much the colder winters! She loves to travel and has gotten writing inspiration everywhere from Kansas City to Beijing. Roslyn lives with her wife and a cat who, while old and cantankerous, is nevertheless a very good boy.

### CONNECT WITH ROSLYN
Website: www.roslynsinclair.com
Facebook: www.facebook.com/roslyn.sinclair.338
Twitter: @writingroslyn
Instagram: www.instagram.com/roslyn_writes
E-Mail: roslynwrites@gmail.com

***Truth and Measure***
© 2022 by Roslyn Sinclair

ISBN: 978-3-96324-644-9

Available in e-book and paperback formats.

Published by Ylva Publishing, legal entity of Ylva Verlag, e.Kfr.

Ylva Verlag, e.Kfr.
Owner: Astrid Ohletz
Am Kirschgarten 2
65830 Kriftel
Germany

www.ylva-publishing.com

First edition: 2022

No part of this book may be reproduced, scanned, or distributed in any printed or electronic form without permission. Please do not participate in or encourage piracy of copyrighted materials in violation of the author's rights. Thank you for respecting the hard work of this author.

This is a work of fiction. Names, characters, places, and incidents either are a product of the author's imagination or are used fictitiously, and any resemblance to locales, events, business establishments, or actual persons—living or dead—is entirely coincidental.

Credits
Edited by Lee Winter and Julie Klein
Cover Design and Print Layout by Streetlight Graphics

Printed in Great Britain
by Amazon